SLEEPING *with the* DARK

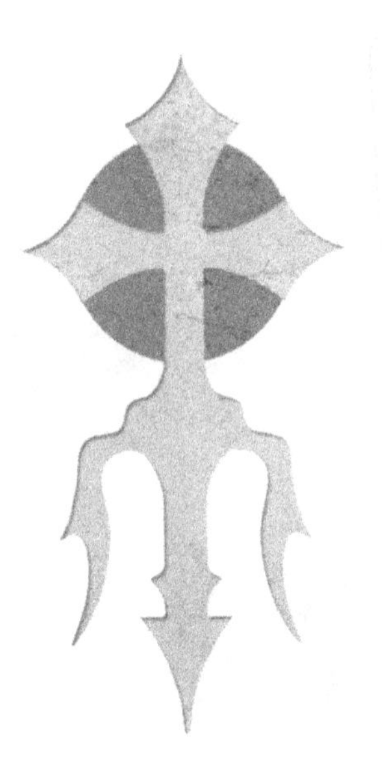

THE RIGHTEOUS SERIES BOOK 3

BROOKLYN CROSS

PEREZ
SCOOTER
MEL

FIRST EDITION.

Edited by: Arielle Stafford at Just Ask Her Productions

Cover Art: Books and Moods

Names: Cross, Brooklyn
Brooklyn Cross
Title: SLEEPING WITH THE DARK, a first printing.
Ebook ASIN: B09P5B1DZH
Paperback ASIN: B09NSCB6V6

Read at your own Risk

Warning to the reader:

This book contains sexually explicit material and adult language that may be offensive to some readers. This book is for sale to adults ONLY, as defined by the country's laws in which you made your purchase. This book is a dark romance and contains violence, profanity, references to child abuse both physical and sexual, non consensual and dubious consensual sexual scenes, sodomy, and alcohol, tobacco and drug use. If you are a reader sensitive to such material, this might not be the book for you.

With Appreciation

I would like to dedicate this instalment of The Righteous series to my Beta readers. You ladies know who you are.

Each one of you bring your honest opinions, even when it's hard to hear. Your dedication to notes and suggestions even though you all have full and busy lives. As well as an unbridled excitement, that on many occasions has kept me in stitches.

But you also bring something intangible to the process, something that I appreciate more than I can put into words and that is pure joy.

There are many times during the writing and editing journey that as an author I could easily loose my way in the weeds, feeling frustrated, and question my ability as a writer. But, your enthusiasm, encouragement, and humour are the fuel to my soul, that keeps my fingers on the keys and pushing for the next book.

Thank you, for being the kind individuals that you are, and for choosing to spend your time on my work.

Your unwavering support is the comfort in a sometimes very lonely room.

ALSO BY BROOKLYN CROSS

The Righteous Series

(Vigilante/Ex Military Romance - Dark 3-4 Spice 3-4)

Dark Side of the Cloth

Ravaged by the Dark

Sleeping with the Dark

Hiding in the Dark

Redemption in the Dark

Crucified by the Dark (Coming Soon)

Dark Reunion (Coming Soon)

The Consumed Trilogy

(Suspense/Thriller/Anti-Hero Romance - Dark 4-5 Spice 3-4)

Burn for Me

Burn with Me (Coming 2022)

Burn me Down (Coming 2023)

The Buchanan Brother Duet

(Serial Killer/Captive Romance - Dark 4-5 Spice 3-4)

Unhinged Cain by Brooklyn

Twisted Abel by T.L Hodel

The Battered Souls World

(Standalone Books Shared World Romance- Dark 2-3 Spice 2-3)

The Girl That Would Be Lost

The Boy That Learned To Swim (Coming Soon)

The Girl That Would Not Break (Coming Soon)

The Brothers of Shadow and Death Series

(Dystopian/Cult/Occult/MFM Romance - Dark 3-4 Spice 3-4)

Anywhere (Coming Soon)

Seven Sin Series

(Multi Author/PNR/Angel and Demons/Redemption - Dark 2-5 Spice 3-5)

Greed by Brooklyn Cross

Lust by Drethi Anis

Envy by Dylan Page

Gluttony by Marissa Honeycutt

Wrath by Billie Blue

Sloth by Talli Wyndham

Pride by T.L. Hodel

The Only Thing We Know - Bob Moses (Series Anthem)
Let's Get It On - Marvin Gaye
The Real Slim Shady - Eminem
Natural - Imagine Dragons
Against The Wind - Bad Seger & The Silver Bullet Band
SexyBack - Justin Timberlake
Hello - Adele
Do I Wanna Know - Arctic Monkeys
Let Somebody Go - Coldplay X Selena Gomez
Edamame - bbno$
Stressed Out - twenty one pilots
Take Me Home, Country Roads - John Denver
Human - Rag' n' Bone Man
Fall Into Me - Forest Blakk
Beethoven: Fur Elise - By Ludwig van Beethoven

Chapter 1

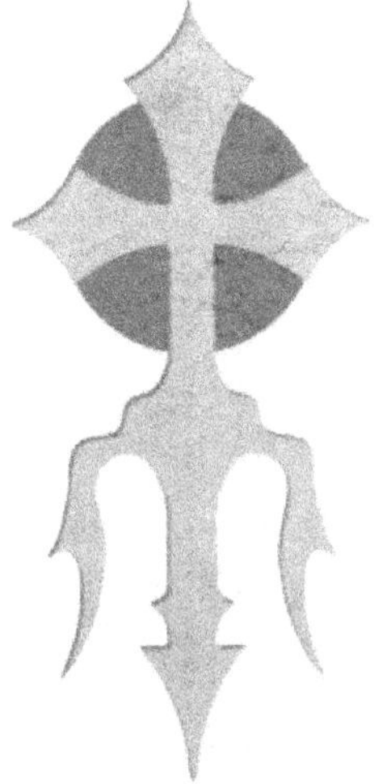

Taking on Renee's brother's case was risky. He was not one known for charity work, and to take Cody on had to seem like this was business as usual and not a favor. He'd been reluctant, but there wasn't anything he could deny Arek. It had been that way since childhood. There was also the fact Cody, the former Ice Man, had held true to his word and helped Arek. There was honor in that—Trev respected family ties and honor above all else.

In comparison to some of his trials, this one had moved along at light speed. He was happy a verdict was back, confident that he'd poked enough holes in the prosecution's case to get Cody off, but it was a little bittersweet. Surprisingly, he had found himself enjoying his time with Cody. So, questions that could have waited to be asked, he had been making a special trip to the jail to ask, just to have a few moments alone with him. From the sweet smiles that always made his dimples show to the tantalizing conversation, Trev couldn't get enough.

Trevor walked up the courtroom steps, briefcase in hand, and met Arek and Renee at the top.

"Are you ready for whatever happens in there today?" He laid a hand on Renee's shoulder. Her eyes stared down at her belly, still flat despite entering her second trimester. She laid her hand protectively over her stomach before she slowly met his eyes.

"I'd love for Cody to be an Uncle, to get back the life he gave up to protect me, but…." she lowered her voice to a whisper. "He also did a lot of bad things."

She sighed as Arek laid both his hands on her shoulders.

She continued, "Whatever happens, you did your best. You were brilliant in there. I know what Cody has done, and you nearly convinced me that I'd been mistaken."

Trevor smiled wide at the compliment.

"I was pretty incredible, but it's up to the jury now." He glanced at the Rolex on his wrist. "Better not be late." Trev led the way and held the door open for his soon-to-be-sister-in-law and brother. As his brother went to pass he stopped him and whispered in his ear. "You should wait out in the hall."

"We already discussed this."

"Fine." Trev shook his head, giving up. It was hard to imagine his brother tied down to one woman for the rest of his life, but he'd also never seen Arek happier.

With his usual air of confidence, he marched to the front of the courtroom, and the corner of his mouth pulled up as Cody stood to greet him. He looked particularly stylish with the steel grey suit and tie that matched his eyes. Trevor's cheeks warmed as he took in the broad shoulders that were the definition of as wide as a mountain. He could remember all too well the feel of that muscular chest from when he and Renee had rushed him to the hospital. A few inches to the left and the bullets he suffered at Tyson's hands would have left Cody dead.

"You nervous?" Trev gave him a small comforting smile.

Cody turned to stare out of the high windows, the light catching his masculine jaw and casting shadows across his face. The thin scar that traveled from his temple to the corner of his lip was more pronounced.

"I don't want to go to jail. I—It doesn't matter what I want. My choices were my choices. I would do them all over again if it meant keeping my sister safe." Those silver eyes locked with his, and he'd never wanted a verdict to go his way so badly in his life. He glanced over his shoulder to where Renee sat, she was putting on a good face but worry was etched in her features.

"All rise."

The meager group assembled stood for the judge, and the jury filed into the jury box.

"You may be seated," the judge said and immediately turned his attention to the jury. "Have you come to a verdict?"

"Yes, we have your honor." The foreperson rose and handed the verdict to the court officer, who handed it to the judge. Trevor watched the piece of paper like a cat as it went from one set of hands to the other and eventually back to the foreperson.

"The defendant may rise."

Trevor and Cody stood in unison, and he stopped himself from looking over at the man beside him. They needed this win. He stared at the foreperson as if the weight of his gaze alone could influence what was written on that piece of paper.

"In the case of the State vs. Mr. Walters in regards to the charge of five counts of opioid possession, we find the defendant guilty."

Trevor swore in his head as the foreperson continued, "In regards to the charge of drug trafficking, we find the defendant not guilty. In regards to the charge of two counts of assault with a deadly weapon, we find the defendant not guilty. In regards to the charge of obstruction of justice, we find the defendant not guilty." Trevor wanted to cheer as the foreperson sat down. Trev's attention turned to the judge.

"Based on the court's ruling, I find the punishment to be time served, but let me be clear young man, getting involved with drugs of any quantity is a dangerous and serious endeavor. I never want to see you in my court again. Court is adjourned."

Trevor smiled as the judge walked out. He had barely turned his head before Cody gripped him in a bear hug. His body shuddered with the sudden contact. He caught the scent of ocean and musk body wash, and Trev breathed the fresh, clean scent deep into his lungs. He immediately envisioned laying out on the sand by the lapping waves with this man and had to step away to stop the vivid images.

"Thank you. I don't know how to repay you for this." Cody smiled at him and then turned to Renee, who was smiling and crying as she opened her arms for her brother, who stepped right into the hug.

"You did good, brother," Arek whispered.

"Was there ever any doubt?." Trev raised an eyebrow at his twin and then looked around to make sure no one was paying them any attention.

"Stop worrying. I've stayed away until now, you know why I came in." Arek jutted his chin toward Renee as she chatted animatedly with Cody.

"Yes, I understand. At least this was a low-profile case, no cameras." Trevor straightened his suit, clicked his briefcase closed. "I will be on my way, see you at home."

With that he strode away from the small party and their celebration. As much as he wanted Cody to be set free, the ruling also meant that their time together had come to an abrupt end. He slipped out of the courthouse doors, his mind directed toward his next case. He was going to need something new to occupy his mind and distract him from Cody, and he had a couple of excellent prospects for that.

"Trevor, wait," Cody called out, and he turned to see the object of his desire jogging toward him. "Dinner. We're all going for dinner. Please join us. I wouldn't be free to start my life over if it weren't for you."

Trev was tempted to say no—this was a terrible idea in the grand scheme of things, but he didn't seem to have the heart to turn the smiling man down with his dimpled cheeks and happy eyes.

"Sure, I could eat." Cody's eyes lit up, and Trev had to look away from the enthusiastic stare. They settled on a posh Italian restaurant down the street from the court, and Trev's stomach rumbled as the rich aroma of pasta and garlic reached him. It had been a few days since he'd taken the time to have a decent meal.

"God, I'm so relieved. This barely feels real," Cody said as they sat down. "Although I could hold my own in lockup, I didn't want to go back. I mean, I would have done any time they gave me, but…." Cody shook his head back and forth.

Renee reached out and squeezed her brother's hand. "And you're free of Tyson. Nothing is holding you to that life anymore," Renee said, her voice clogging with emotion.

The glimmer in Renee's eyes and the smile on Arek's face made this victory all the sweeter for Trev.

The conversation was light, the wine delightful, and the food even more so, but it was the man beside him that kept drawing his attention. His mind drifted off into a sea of its own fanciful making—the simple act of Cody taking a sip of his wine made him lick his lips. The way he sucked in his bottom lip when he was finished drinking made him picture those lips doing something far less innocent. It didn't help that every time Cody moved he'd get another whiff of the delicious musk cologne scent. The people and sound becoming nothing more than background noise as his mind drifted from one image to another. Cody laughed, putting his hand on Trev's thigh. At the unexpected touch, Trev jerked and almost spat out his mouthful of wine. Heat seared through the thin material as he stared down at the large hand on his leg before daring a glance at Cody.

"Are you alright?" Cody said, his eyes filled with concern.

"Why wouldn't I be?"

"We asked you a few questions, but you were zoned out. You weren't responding at all." Cody removed his hand, and Trev immediately felt the loss.

"My apologies, I must be more tired than I thought. I should be going, but thank you for the invite." Trev pulled his wallet out, and Cody gripped his hand and shook his head no.

"Your money is no good tonight."

"Are you sure about that? You haven't received my bill yet," Trev smiled teasingly. He had no intentions of charging Cody, but he loved the blush he received in return for his efforts. Trev caught the look Arek was giving him from across the table, and he suddenly felt very self-conscious. Trev pulled his hand away and stuffed the wallet into his coat.

"No matter what you charge me, it was worth every cent. Just to be able to wake up tomorrow and know that I'm not spending the rest of my life in a six by six cell—I can never repay you for that."

Trev ignored the compliment. He needed to put space between himself and Cody before he said or did something unwise.

"Thank you all for the company, but I must get going." Trev glared at Arek, a knowing look in his twin's mischievous eyes.

Dammit. Sometimes he really hated how in tune they were with one another.

Chapter 2

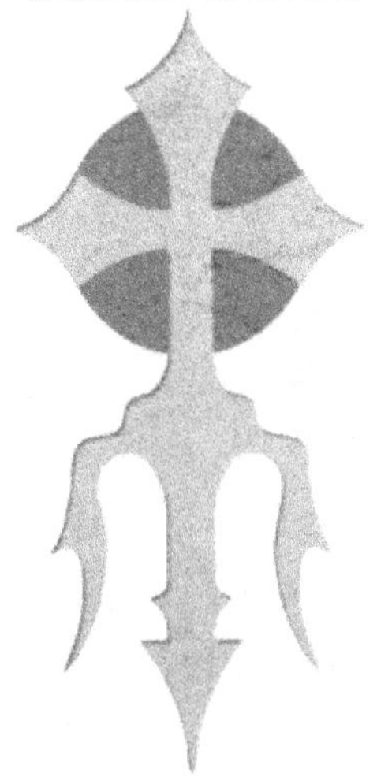

Trev bit into his toast and swore as his teeth nicked his tongue. That's what he deserved for not paying attention to what he was doing. Taking a sip of his juice, he winced a little at the sting. He sat the rest of his breakfast aside as he continued to read.

The opioid crisis is worsening, and the police are no closer to shutting down the operation, killing thousands a month. Our politicians seem more concerned with being re-elected and protecting large corporations than making laws that help our citizens. The turmoil between those wearing a badge and the ever-increasing gang numbers has reached a critical high, with more innocent lives lost in the streets every day. Don't expect pharmaceutical companies and doctors to back off on prescribing the dangerously addictive narcotics as they have never seen their ever fattening paychecks so high. Is there no one brave enough to stop the madness? Is there no one left that has not been paid off to sweep this epidemic under the rug?

Trev sighed as he continued to read. He and Arek were doing what they could, but even they felt like they were swimming upstream when it came to this issue.

Glancing up as the shadow of someone walked into the kitchen, his jaw hit the floor. Cody strolled in, looking all too scrumptious in nothing more than a pair of silk boxers. His mind drew a blank as his eyes openly roamed over the tight contours of Cody's abs, and the glint of a nipple bar he didn't know he had. Then as Cody passed, the heavily tattooed back and tapered waist greeted his eyes as Cody poured himself a coffee. Cody's ass flexed under the shimmering material, and Trev unconsciously licked his lips.

"Morno," Cody said. He turned to face Trev, and once more, Trev was greeted by the sight of a muscled chest and the red-eyed viper on Cody's right peck. Cody blew on his coffee before taking a sip, and Trev cleared his dry throat.

"I beg your pardon?" Trev asked. His brain finally caught up to the fact Cody had spoken. How was any respectable person supposed to concentrate with that roaming around your house?

"Morno, you know morning."

"Then why not just say morning or good morning or even how are you this morning?"

Cody's brow furrowed, his eyebrow raised a moment before he broke out in a deep rumbling laugh that rolled over Trev's skin. Little goosebumps rose the hairs on his arms, and he gripped his cappuccino to busy his hands. "If I spoke like that back at Ty's, I'd be beaten to an inch of my life. I'll take it you're not much for slang?"

"Why would I be? Words were created for a reason. I don't see the fascination in shortening everything down or making other words mean something else. They were fine for many generations just the way they were and then," Trev snapped his fingers. "Just like that, the words created by our ancestors are no longer good enough. Tea, for example. Is it something I drink, or do I want to gossip? What an utterly disrespectful way to misappropriate a word. It makes no sense to me, simply illogical." Trev averted his gaze and glared at the words on his tablet, no longer really seeing them. "What are you doing here anyway?"

His excellent peripheral vision tracked Cody's movements as the man grabbed a peach off the island and then wandered in his direction. Trev worked hard not to notice the distinct outline of a very large cock swinging behind the soft material of those damn boxers, nor the way Cody's arm flexed when he moved it to take a sip of his coffee. By sheer willpower alone, he managed not to fidget as his own cock stirred.

"Arek and Renee asked me if I wanted to move in and stay for a while after you left last night," Cody took the seat across from him.

"They what?" His voice came out harsh as his head snapped up to meet Cody's gaze. Trev couldn't live under the same roof as this man. He was already having thoughts that would distract him from his task for The Righteous or his law-abiding work, for that matter. The last thing he needed was for the actual object of his desire to be prancing around his house in practically no clothes.

"I'm sorry if you're upset. I thought they had cleared it with you already."

"They most certainly did not."

Cody's face fell, his icy silver-colored eyes dropped to stare into his cup. Trev pinched the bridge of his nose as his stomach clenched—he couldn't stare at that face and be angry. "It's fine."

"No, you're upset. I don't have anywhere to go at the moment, but I'll make it a priority. I'll be out by the end of the week." Cody's eyes met his, and Trev's heart hammered hard in his chest. His head yelled yes, get the fuck out, but the racing heart in his chest and the panic in his gut screamed no, don't go.

"No, it's fine. Seriously, stay as long as you like. I was just thrown off —I don't handle change very well. I'm sure you're shocked to learn that." He gave Cody a slight smirk. "I just seem to be collecting a lot more house guests than I ever thought I'd have," Trev said, his voice softer although he felt anything but relaxed.

"You're sure?" The enthusiastic waver in Cody's voice was not lost on Trev.

"Yes, of course. This is a huge house with more room than any one person could ever need." Trev picked up his plate and tablet.

"You were in the army like Arek, right?" Cody asked, and Trev froze.

"Navy, I was a S.E.A.L."

"That's sick. You were a real badass then. I can picture that—you have this aura about you." Trev's eyebrow cocked up. "What was it like? I mean, is it as rough overseas as everyone makes it out to be, or is that all movie bullshit?"

Trev could hear Arek, Renee, and J.J. coming down the hall. Straightening his shoulders, he locked eyes with Cody and said the only thing that he could, "It's worse." He left his plate in the sink and said good morning as he passed the new arrivals. He ruffled J.J.'s curls as the kid beamed up at him like a little ray of sunshine. He figured the kid was destined for politics—he was the best negotiator in the entire house.

"Trev, could you wait a moment? I'd like you here for this," Renee said, and he paused in his retreat. "Cody, we didn't tell you this earlier with the trial and all. We just thought it would upset you when your future was uncertain."

"Okay, this sounds serious." Cody joined them at the island, his eyes giving away his worry.

"No, it's not bad news. In fact, it's good news."

"Well, don't keep me in suspense. What is it?" Cody asked, leaning against the island. He reminded Trev of a large cat lounging as the sun streamed in the window and bathed him in light.

Renee cleared her throat and looked up to Arek. "We wanted to wait until the verdict came back to tell you that you're going to be an uncle."

Trev smiled as Cody's mouth fell open. "You're serious? You got knocked up?"

"Yes, it's true." Renee blushed as Cody yelled in celebration. He scooped Renee up and twirled her around as she squealed.

"My turn, my turn," J.J. jumped up and down.

Trev slowly backed out of the kitchen, letting the happy little family moment continue. He could feel Cody's eyes on him and made the mistake of looking into his eyes. Cody mouthed, *we'll talk later,* just before he slipped out of the room and down the hall. The last thing he wanted was to talk about that part of his past with Cody. As far as he was concerned, it was behind him. He'd never been the share your feelings type, and he certainly didn't need to start now.

Chapter 3

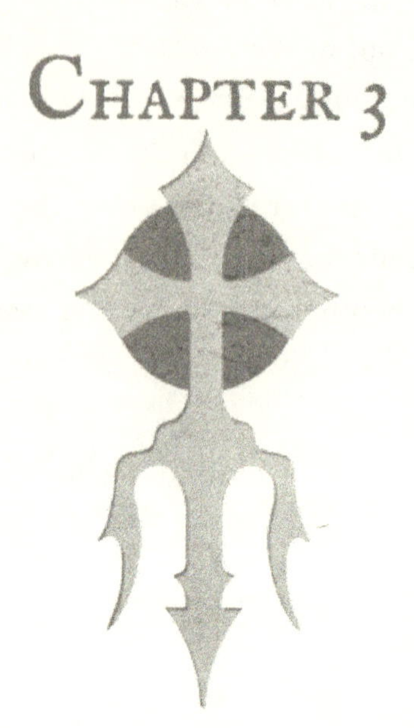

Cody stared up at the cloudless, clear blue sky, his fingers idly playing with the water as he floated around the pool on an inflatable martini glass. He'd bet his life that Trev picked this unusual floating contraption. On closer inspection, he'd bet that the man had picked everything around the pool, just like he probably picked everything in the house. Not only did Arek not seem like the type to select a martini glass over a beer can, but everywhere you looked was perfectly coordinated. Everything matched and was as well put together as the man himself.

He tilted his head to the left and let out a little laugh as his eyes fell on the towel rack with a label stating what it was. He smirked, his lip pulling up as he wondered what it would be like to pull back all those perfectly crafted layers surrounding Trev. What kind of animal lay beneath the calm exterior? He adjusted himself as the thought sent heat right to his groin.

He rubbed his face and then swore as sunscreen ended up in his eye. "Shit."

So much for coming out here to not think about Trev. He hadn't been able to get the incredibly sexy man out of his mind since he first laid eyes on him. Technically, he'd seen his face before on Arek, but other than being able to appreciate Arek's good looks, there hadn't been a spark. Trev, on the other hand, hello, Fourth of July. The man consumed his thoughts. How many nights had he laid alone in his cell and dreamt of holding Trev? Wondered what it would be like to taste his lips? For fucks sake he lost count of how many times he'd shamelessly jacked off to the image of the man kneeling between his legs.

"Shit." Here he was again, with only one thing on his mind even when he had much bigger problems to occupy his mind. Like should he finish school or just get a job? Should he stay here or move out? He had some money stashed away, but not near enough to last very long if he decided to go back to school to get his degree and move out.

He rolled off the floaty, the cool water refreshing against his heated skin. He opened his eyes underwater and regretted it, the ghost of an image he tried to forget floating in front of his eyes. Cody broke the surface with a gasp and leaned against the side of the pool—guilt flowing through his body like icy tendrils as he remembered all too clearly his first ordered kill. The girl was one of Tyson's playthings—a tweaker and desperate. What she'd been running or hiding from, he had no clue. Cody had arrived on the scene not long after she'd joined the gang, and he had to admit he liked her when she wasn't getting high. She was a straight-shooter and easy to talk to with a great sense of humor.

Then, the girl had to go and fuck shit up. She made the grave error of stealing from Tyson. The guy always caught on to someone ripping him off. Cody had come to find Tyson often placed his workers in positions with opportunities to steal, just to see if they would. He could still hear her screams as Tyson beat and raped her to within an inch of her life before he dragged her out of his office like a bag of garbage.

He'd prayed that Tyson wouldn't look his way, but just his shit luck—Tyson stared straight at him. "It's your turn to prove your loyalty. Take this bitch out and kill her." Cody had stared at the beaten and bloody face of the once cute girl and swallowed hard. He pulled his gun and walked forward, but Tyson grabbed his arm. "No, don't shoot her. That's too good for her. I want her to drown. I want her to feel her lungs burn as she chokes to death. Oh, and Cody, I want pictures of everything, make sure I can imagine being there.." His hand had been so large around her neck as he held her under the dirty water, her hands clawing at his arm as he cried. He kept saying sorry like that made up for what he was doing.

Just like a dog shaking off water, he tried to shake the memory away. It never worked long. The faces of those he murdered in the name of Tyson haunted him like a fucking bloodhound on his heels.

Cody ran his hand through his hair. He deserved jail. Even if he was happy to be free, even if he had never wanted to hurt anyone, he still deserved it. It was his choice to work for Tyson. His intentions might've been good, but what he did once he joined was burn-in-hell worthy. Cody thumbed the scar running down his cheek. Tyson had ensured that his soul was forever scarred and tainted in an evil that ate him alive. He couldn't even look in the mirror without seeing the product of his choices, his face was a warning, nothing good touch him.

"I see you found the pool." Cody started the water jostling as he looked up to the sudden voice. His gaze traveled up the tall figure until he stared at his own reflection in the black-out sunglasses Trev was wearing. He hadn't heard nor seen the man approach. "I recognize that look. Whatever it is that you are feeling guilty about, there is no need. What you did and who you were are in the past. If you want a shot at a new life, then learn from the shit mistakes and only look forward."

"Is that how you cope?"

"I don't need to cope. I accept that I became a lethal killing weapon for the government. I accept that I am still lethal in a different way, and even sharks need to eat. I also accept that it is not all that I am."

"I'm not sure how to do that," Cody said. He stared at a small ant running across the slate surface before him. Sometimes he felt that small.

"You just do, or what's the point in having a second chance to make different choices? Ghosts are just that. They can only hurt you if you let them."

Cody didn't feel like it was that easy, but he did love the air of confidence that blanketed everything Trev did. And holy hell, that suit made him look like he'd stepped right out of a mob movie. Fuck he was hot, there was no denying it, and he already knew that under all that tailored material, Trev was built like the elite specimen that he was.

"What happened to you, Trev?" Cody asked, and only the twitch in Trev's jaw told him he was uncomfortable with the change in topic. "In all our time talking at the prison, you never mentioned your past."

"Nothing happened, at least nothing that I ever want to relive, and in most cases, the past is better left where it is—in the past. Arek took Renee and J.J. out for the day. Will you be fine here alone, or would you like to come with me?"

His heart skipped a beat with the offer. "Go with you?"

"I have a meeting. It's nothing glamorous, but I can drop you off at the beach or something? If you'd like to get out of the house, that is."

His heart sank stupidly at the thought of being left like some teenager not invited to the party. "No, I'm good. Thanks for the offer, but I need some thinking time to figure out what I'm going to do with my life." He couldn't decipher the look that Trev gave him, but he fidgeted under the intense stare that penetrated through those black-out lenses.

"Very well. There is an abundance of food and beer in the fridge. Help yourself." Trev headed toward the gate, and Cody admired the view. "But don't touch anything in the wine cellar," Trev called out, just before the gate clicked closed behind him.

Cody pulled himself from the pool and stared at the place from which Trev disappeared.

For as cool as Trev could be there was so much warmth hiding under that suit. He smiled as he remembered the stern no nonsense expression Trev gave him the first time he called him Mr. Anderson.

"Call me Trev, that's what my friends and family call me."

"Is that what I am? Family?"

Trev gave him that cocky grin. "Is that what you want me to be?"

So like Trev, to answer a question that turns the tables, even that was a fucking turn on.

Great, of all the people he could be attracted to, this very unattainable man had to be the one his heart wanted, figures.

Chapter 4

Trev dabbed his mouth, savoring the last bite of ribeye before he reached for his glass of wine. He casually sized up the man across from him. To say he was surprised to get a call from the head of the Streetlores would have been a grave understatement. When he walked into the restaurant and laid eyes on Alejandro, who was not who he thought he would be meeting with, all sorts of red flags went off. His mind began pouring over everything he knew of the man.

He'd always heard Alejandro was the walking epitome of death itself. Tattoos adorned his entire body, his back riddled with small scars, each one representing a kill. His eyes were supposed to be dark brown or black, and the only hair on his entire head was a small goatee. Yet, the man who sat across from him looked better suited for an accountant than the leader of a gang. He wore a soft grey suit, no tattoos visible on his hands or neck, and his eyes were soft and caramel in color. This imposter no more screamed killer than he looked like a soft cuddly teddy bear. Now, the man sitting in the far corner trying too hard not to be noticed was another story.

Trev's eyes raked over the man across the table once more and decided he'd seen all he needed to know to call this man's bluff. Trev sat his wine down and folded his hands on the table. "So tell me, who are you really?"

The man pretending to be the infamous Alejandro huffed out an irritated noise, crossing his arms over his chest. "I don't know what you're talking about." Taking his time, Trev leaned back in his chair as he stared the scared rabbit down. "Why do you think I'm not Alejandro?"

"For the same reason that I know shit stinks no matter how you dress it up."

"Did you just call me, Alejandro, a piece of shit?"

Trev sighed, he'd enjoyed his lunch, but he was quickly losing patience. "Why did your boss call me, and more importantly, why didn't he show up himself? I'm a busy man, I have many clients, and I don't have all day to sit and make small talk with a cheap imitation."

The man burst from his seat, fists clenched, his face turning an unsightly shade of red. The man seated across the room rose and did a slow clap as he sauntered closer. He was quickly joined and flanked by two large men that Trev wouldn't want to be forced to mess with, but he easily picked out their weak spots just in case.

"Your reputation precedes you, Mr. Anderson. *Puedes irte ahora,*" Alejandro said, and the man who had been Alejandro's stand-in bowed his head before leaving. Alejandro slipped into the seat across from him. Now, this man was a killer. This man, you didn't turn your back on, and you certainly never crossed. Unfortunately for him, Trev had already planned on doing a lot more than killing a few lackeys. "When did you know it wasn't me?"

"The moment I laid eyes on him," Trev said, as a small smile lifted the corner of his mouth.

"And yet you sat through an entire meal?"

"The steak was free. You never turn down an expensive meal from a five-star restaurant. That is just stupid."

Alejandro burst out laughing. The table shook, and the silverware jingled as he smacked his hand on the top, drawing the attention of the other patrons. "I like you. You cut right through the bullshit."

"Well then, let me do so again. Why am I here?"

"All of you take note. This is how you conduct business." Alejandro pointed around the room, and Trev's eyes followed the action, taking in every face now focused on them. Until that exact moment, he thought the other patrons were simply enjoying a meal. Apparently, he was off his game, or he would have noticed the discreetly hidden weapons they were all sporting. He could only blame his lack of concentration on a certain man with silver eyes.

"What I want, Mr. Anderson, is to find out who is killing my men. My men mean money to me, but more than that, they are like a small family. When members of my family turn up dead, you can understand why I might be upset. I keep being told that the Golden Dragons are responsible, but you see, I find this hard to believe. I am their best client, after all. It wouldn't be wise for them to kill the men selling their product. This is lawyer-client confidential, of course," he smiled wickedly and pushed a hundred across the table.

Trev eyed the money and snorted at the insult. "Well, to start, you're not my client. So you can take that back." He cocked a brow at Alejandro and then spread his arms wide. "But, with that said, I wouldn't be stupid enough to say a word about this for far more important reasons than losing my license."

"You would have trouble sleeping if you did, that is for sure. That is if you were breathing at all, of course."

"Of course." Trev smirked and waved over the waitress. "More wine please."

"You are a bold man, Mr. Anderson."

The waitress half filled his glass and he took a sip before continuing. "As far as the Golden Dragons are concerned, it would certainly benefit them if they thought they could take over your area and cut out the middleman, so to speak. That is hypothetical, of course. I like to play devil's advocate."

Alejandro ran his hand over his short goatee a number of times before speaking. "I do see your point, but I still am not sold that it's them."

"Maybe, maybe not. I don't know them or have dealings with them to hypothesize any further."

"No, you have given me more to think on, but tell me who else do you think it could be?"

"I think you are mistaken on what it is I do for a living. I'm a lawyer, not a private investigator." Trev tipped his head and took another mouthful of wine before he stood and buttoned his suit jacket. "Now, if you're ever in need of a bloody good lawyer, I can certainly help you there."

"Please, Mr. Anderson, sit."

The two bodyguards moved to block his path to the door, and with a quick glance, he counted out how many seconds it would take to grab the steak knife and slit the first guard's throat before he stole the gun in his waistband and slammed the knife home in the second guard's throat. There were twenty-three bodies in the room, and he pictured just how many bullets he would take if he tried to run for it. The odds were difficult, but not impossible. Still, he had no intention of starting a showdown like that, it did him no good when he had Alejandro right where he wanted him.

Trev sighed and sat once more, the guards noticeably relaxing. "I'm confused. Please explain what it is you think I can do for you, Alejandro," he asked even though he had a pretty good idea where this was going.

Alejandro smiled wide and yelled to bring out dessert before he continued. "I know well what you do and who you do it for—I also know that you hear things, many things from many different individuals. I would pay very well to be kept in the loop on what you happen to hear about my men."

Trev stared at the man in what he hoped would seem like genuine surprise before his mouth curled up in a smirk followed by a laugh. Alejandro laughed along with him, but the sound was more murderous than joyous.

"So, let me understand this correctly. You'd like me to spy on my other clients and relay private yet, relevant information to you for a large sum of money? I'll assume that if I don't fall in line, then there will be some unpleasantness?"

"Well, Mr. Anderson, I certainly don't want things to go that far, but I need to protect my family. I also think that a hundred thousand per tip is reasonable." A waitress sat a tray of small one-bite desserts on the table.

Trev ignored the small pastries and other decadent pieces. "One million."

It was Alejandro that laughed this time. "Two hundred thousand."

"I don't roll out of bed for anything less than five hundred thousand. Not for my retainer and not for this, no exceptions. I am the best, and I know it."

"You drive a hard bargain. I do like your style." Alejandro drummed his fingers on the table. "Fine, if the information is accurate and leads me to the real murderers, then I will pay what you ask."

Trev stood, and the guard inched closer. He glared at the man and held back the smirk as the man took a step away from his hard stare.

"Alejandro, you have given me a lot to think about, but this is not a decision I can make at this moment. I have your number. I will give you a call and let you know my answer in a couple of days." Trev took a step, and the large man stepped into his path.

"Let him leave," Alejandro waved at his guard. "Mr. Anderson is our guest not our prisoner. We will speak again soon, Mr. Anderson."

"Call me Trevor, and by the way, the steak was excellent," Trev called out as he walked out the door.

Well, well, well, this day was looking up.

Chapter 5

"Thank you, Sally, and you may go for the night," Trev said.

"Don't forget Arek is waiting in the hall." Sally cleared her throat as she opened the door and waved in his brother.

"Oh, how could I ever forget," Trev mumbled under his breath.

"What the hell is up with keeping me out there like some client?" Arek slumped in the chair across from him, his face red with irritation.

"Let's just say it's a little payback for asking Cody to move in without clearing it with me. Didn't we already go through this with Renee and J.J.?"

"Yeah, but this is different." Arek was brimming with a mischievousness that Trev hated, it never led anywhere good. Arek's face was practically alight with the uncontained joy as he reached for the bottle of scotch on the desk. "You like him, and don't try to deny it."

"I can't deny it. I do like him. He seems like a nice person once you get to know him. You were right not to kill him." Trev shrugged. "He could prove to be useful."

"Fuck off with that shit, Trev. You know what I'm talking about—you want to bend him over your desk and see if you can make him scream." Arek jerked his hips in the air repeatedly as he made a stupid grunting noise.

Trev jumped up and marched to the door, and with the flick of his wrist, flung it closed with a bang. "You don't know what you're talking about," his voice heated as he spoke. Worse was the fact that the image Arek portrayed made him hot all over.

"You can't hide that shit from me, brother." Arek sipped the scotch, and all Trev could picture was messing up that pretty face as he wiped the smirk off of it. "Why are you fighting it? I've never known you to be scared of anything."

"Scared? Who the hell said I was scared?" Trev asked, heading back to his desk. He was going to need a drink.

Arek stood and casually leaned against the desk, his eyes searching Trev's face, and he didn't like it one bit. "Interesting. You like him more than a fuck buddy to get your rocks off, not that you tend to do that either." Arek shrugged.

"Don't be ridiculous, I barely know him, and we've never even been, as you say, fuck buddies. Can we get to why I needed to see you?" Trev didn't spare Arek a look as he rounded his desk and sat down once more.

"Nope, we are definitely talking about this first. You have all this pent-up sexual tension around you, and the way you look at him—like he is a fucking scotch dipped piece of art" Arek slowly turned to face him, and his whole face was lit-up like they were still kids who had just walked into the living room on Christmas morning. Correction, it was Arek's 'I have got a fucking brilliant idea that ends with Trev apologizing to someone' look. "And!" Arek held up a finger, making Trev roll his eyes at the dramatic display. "You haven't been able to think straight, like you are mentally or maybe emotionally pent-up?"

"You brother are unbelievable. I am not any of those things and I'm certainly not verklempt."

Arek laughed, his whole body shaking and almost spilling the high-end scotch. "The fact you used the word verklempt makes you verklempt."

"Don't be ridiculous." Trev tried for casual as he stared at his brother. "I don't want to talk about this." He grabbed the Streetlore file and slid it across the desk. "I got a call from Alejandro this morning to have lunch."

"Yeah, yeah, we will form a plan. Now tell me, what is it about him you like? I mean, Cody is a good-looking man. Wouldn't that be something if we married siblings? That is just a little fucked up, and yet, I'm so down. Holy shit, could you picture mum? She'd love it. A double wedding. Dad would shit his rubber boots full. Damn, I can picture it now."

Trev rubbed his face and grabbed the bottle on his desk, pouring himself two fingers, hesitated, and then added another two. He was going to need it, and he suddenly wished he'd never brought up the subject of Cody.

"Does dad even really understand what it means to be bi? I mean, he knows you dated in high school and were into guys as well, but do you think he understands or thinks you were experimenting? It seems like forever since that overly fun family dinner."

This entire conversation was entering dangerous territory that Trev refused to discuss. "I don't know, Arek. It's not like I've sat down and had a heart-to-heart with him about it. Now, if I admit that I like him, can we move on?"

"Nope, not good enough. You never go all girl or guy crush, not since...well you know." He held up his finger like what he was saying was important. "This is like a one-in-a-million opportunity for me. You know, you barely sleep with anyone. Are you sure your dick even remembers what it's supposed to do?" Arek laughed and ducked as a pen whizzed past his head.

"Don't drop any of that scotch, you fucker," Trev said and glared at his brother. "My cock, which is much larger than yours, I might add, works just fine, thank you very much."

"Pfft, don't you wish? Want me to get the ruler out?"

Trev shook his head. "The reason I don't sleep around, dear brother, is because one of us has to be the public role model. We can't all be super vigilante at night and then fuck everything that moves the rest of the time. I am the reason we live in this lavish lifestyle, or have you forgotten that part?"

Arek's face sobered. "Are you saying I don't pull my weight?"

"No, I'm... look, I simply don't want to talk about Cody anymore. I'm sorry I brought it up. You pushing my buttons is making me edgy. Can we just move on? You know that I'm not interested in settling down with anyone. At one point, we had that in common until Renee showed up." Trev rubbed his face. "And before you go getting all pissy, I don't mean I don't like her because I do."

Arek sighed and slouched back in the chair once more. "You're an ass when you're all tied up in knots." Trev raised a cocked eyebrow at Arek. "Fine, I'll leave it alone, but you're no fun. Speaking of vigilantism, with the baby coming, Renee is worried that one day, I won't come home."

Trev leaned back in the large chair, the leather squeaking in the otherwise silent room as he analyzed the bomb his brother had just dropped. "I knew this was coming. What would she do if you were still enlisted?"

Arek raised a shoulder and let it drop. "I don't know, but I don't want to do as much until she gets used to this lifestyle and understands that I'll be fine." Arek swirled the drink, not meeting his gaze.

"You do realize that is never going to happen?"

"Renee is a lot more accepting than you're giving her credit for."

"Would you like me to get her an award?" Trev bit out sarcastically.

"This is not a good time for you to be backing away. The Righteous is not going to like it, not when we are so close to taking down our assigned goal."

Arek sighed as he crossed his arms over his chest.

"Besides, if you'd ever let me speak, you'd know that the Streetlore's want to hire me to feed them information. I mean, we couldn't have asked for a better situation."

"Damn, that is good news. Look, I'm not saying that I won't do what I signed up for, but I'm going to be a dad, like a real father, and I'd like to see my kid born." He placed a hand over his heart, and the gesture touched Trev more than words could have. "I am the last person on this earth that deserved to have a second chance like this, but I want it. Renee makes me feel like I'm not a monster."

Trev sipped his drink as they lapsed into silence. His brother had not really asked for anything in a very long time. It was time he dusted off his boots anyway. He could play both sides for a few months. Arek was right, he'd earned the opportunity to see his son or daughter born, and Trev wanted nothing more than to see that smile on his brother's face when it happened. It was something he'd dreamt about for himself, but fate had other ideas.

"Alright, I'll cut you back to as little as possible for now."

"Thanks, Trev. I don't know what I'd do without you. Me, a fucking father, can you even picture that?"

"No, I can honestly say I never saw that one coming," He smiled as Arek laughed. Arek lit up as he talked about decorating the nursery in camo and buying little fatigues. Yes, he needed to protect this. He'd do what he had to, to keep his brother safe.

Chapter 6

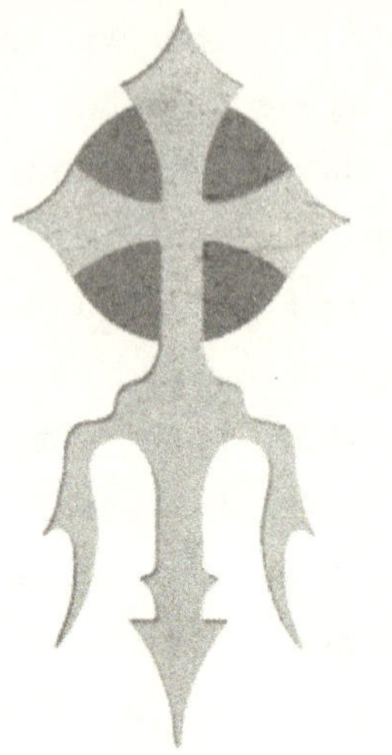

Was it possible to be a ghost and keep breathing? Cody couldn't answer the question, but it certainly felt like it. He shouldn't complain. He was a free man, had his sister back, and was building a relationship with J.J., which he'd always been too scared to do while he belonged to Tyson. So why was he feeling so dejected?

He kicked a little pebble along the sidewalk, not really paying attention to where he was headed. It was already hot out, but he loved it and turned his face up to the sun and sucked in a deep breath as he tried to calibrate his emotions in a more positive direction.

"What the fuck are you doing on this side of the tracks?"

Cody jerked out of his internal struggle, his fist clenching automatically. He spun toward the voice and relaxed, not able to keep the smile off his face. His eyes landed on Ray sitting on the front steps of his apartment building.

"Hey, man," he said as he met Ray and gave the guy a brief hug. He'd known Ray his entire life, they met in the playground one day and hit it off immediately and had been tight since. Ray had always been top-shelf, just dealt a crap hand. "Shit, I thought you were still inside the big house."

"I was just released the other day. My lawyer was pretty incredible. None of the charges stuck, got time served."

Ray let out a low whistle. He was one of the few that knew all the dirty details of what he'd done during his time with the Vipers, but Ray was no snitch. He had lips like a vault. "Damn, I need that guy on retainer," Ray joked. Ray was more of a dabbler. He worked a regular nine to five and tried to keep his nose clean, but his little sister required special meds so he would pick up the odd bit of work as a runner.

"Trust me. You can't afford this guy. I couldn't afford this guy, but I had a connection." Cody leaned against the rusted rod iron fence that surrounded the small front lawn of the building.

"You always got a connection, man. What is the famous Ice Man going to do now that you're free? Nasty bit of shit that went down with Ty." Ray visibly shivered. "Did you hear what happened to him?"

"Not all of it, but I got the run-down. I was kinda busy with the whole being shot and then arrested thing. Although, I'm sure everyone thinks I did it and that's fine if it keeps them from comin' lookin' for me." Cody looked down at his feet. He hated Tyson. He wanted to be the one to put a bullet between his eyes, but having your cock and balls cut off was next-level shit. He wouldn't be quick to admit it, but Arek fucking scared him a little. "As far as what I'm going to do now, I'm weighing my options."

"You gonna take the reins for the Crimson Vipers? Those left alive is looking for a new leader." Ray lit up a smoke and offered him a drag. He shook his head no as Ray leaned back on the steps like he was sitting on a fucking Lazy Boy.

"Naw, man. I'm thinking of staying out of the game. I have a chance to go back to school, maybe get out of this neighborhood for good."

"Too good for us now?" Ray teased.

"Fuck you. You know my heart will always be here no matter where I go. Besides, if I end up with a sexy ass job, maybe I can hook your stupid ass up. No one else would want your sorry ass."

"Watch your mouth with that shit. I'll hold you to it." Ray looked down the street, and Cody followed his stare. A black and white was slowly driving toward them, and Cody tensed, his body ready to run if they stopped even though he no longer had anything to hide. Old habits died hard, and he had never had a great relationship with the popo. "Man, to not have to worry about money, being shot at, arrested, or dead is almost too much to dream about." Ray's eyes followed the car as it continued on, the occupants only giving them a glance over.

"How's Little Spice?" Cody asked, and Ray laughed.

"She loves that stupid nickname, refuses to go by her own name now. So thanks for that." Ray smirked, his eyes speaking for him how much his sister meant to him. He finished the smoke, crushing the butt under his heel. "You know she fucking loves you, man. She is already planning your wedding, but if you ever touch my sister, I will fuck that pretty face up."

Cody laughed hard. "Dude, first, you know your sister is not my type, but even if she was, jailbait is not my thing. Anything still in pigtails is simply fucked up shit."

"Good to know. She's fine." Ray lifted a shoulder and then looked around. "The meds are going to break me, though. I had to do three runs last week to pay for two weeks' worth." Ray rubbed the back of his neck. "I can't get caught. If I did...." The sentence trailed off, but Cody knew Ray meant that his sister would die, and he couldn't live with that.

"If I can get my ass out of the fire, I'll take you with me, man." He held out his knuckles for Ray to hit. "That's a promise. I mean that."

"Is the Ice Man melting?" Ray stood and touched his knuckles.

"Maybe. See ya, man. I gotta go. Stay Lysol."

"Fuck off with your cheese, man," Ray laughed, shaking his head as he jogged up the steps.

By the time Cody got back to the house, it was late afternoon, and the piece of shit thing he called a heart skipped a beat when he caught the sight of Trev's Bentley parked in the driveway. That car alone could buy him his ticket out of town and a new life. The old him would have jacked that hot little bitch and run for the closest chop shop, but that was another life, another him.

He unlocked the door with the way too high-tech panel and let himself in—his heated skin both soothed and shivered as the air conditioning hit him. Cody stuck his head in every room but didn't see anyone until the sound of laughter from the kitchen drew his attention. He followed the sound until he spotted Renee and Arek sitting outside in the backyard.

"Am I interrupting?" he asked as he stuck his head out the door.

Renee and Arek shared a look before Arek stood and gave him a shoulder squeeze. "She's all yours. I have a few things I need to take care of."

"I didn't mean to chase you off."

"You didn't. Your timing is perfect." Arek disappeared inside the house, and Cody dropped into the way too comfortable chair on the patio. The view was out of this world. In all his time alive, he never thought he would get the opportunity to relax in a pad like this. Well, at least not in one that wasn't vacant while he was illegally crashing because that came with certain risks.

"It's pretty, isn't it?" Renee asked.

Cody looked over at his sister, and he'd never seen her more beautiful. They weren't joking when they said women glowed when pregnant. She was radiant. Her eyes were unguarded and happy. Whatever he had to endure to make sure this life was possible was well worth it.

"Yeah, it really is." He looked out over the picturesque green of the grass with the decorative shrubs and flowers. The pool sat not far off the clear water glittering in the sunlight begging for a swim, but he was happy to take a load off in the comfort of the covered porch. The shade gave a reprieve from the heat of the day.

"I've been wanting to talk to you," Renee said.

"Oh yeah, what about?" he asked and tensed for the worst.

"Dad."

"Dad? He ran off years ago. What about him?" Cody leaned over and opened the small bar fridge to grab a bottle of water before meeting his sister's serious expression.

"Dad didn't take off. That's the thing."

"I don't understand." Cody took a swig of the sparkling water with a hint of lime. He smacked his lips with the fizzy taste. Even the bloody water was expensive.

"It's a long story, and one that, well, um, Arek found Dad." Cody's jaw fell open, but no words came out. "Before you freak out, I was angry at first, but once I got the whole story and even looked over the proof of what he was telling me," Renee sighed. "Look, the point is, I'm rebuilding a relationship with him, and I think you should consider trying as well."

"Has this place made you soft in the head?" he bit out angrily.

Renee's eyes narrowed and gave him a steely glare that could rival any gang member he'd faced. "You talk to me like that again, and you're going to see just how not soft I am."

"Fine, but Renee, I'm not giving him a second chance to lie to me. He left us. No matter the reason, the result is the same. You can forgive him and go back to being daddy's little girl, you always were his favorite, but you can count me out on any family reunions."

"Why are men so fucking stubborn?" Renee huffed and crossed her arms over her chest.

"Sis, it has been an entire lifetime with a world of hurt and pain since his ass left. I had to become the man of the house. Do you even know what that was like for me? All that responsibility on my shoulders to keep my family safe? I was a fucking kid myself." He chugged the fruity water and met his sister's steady stare.

"First, I know almost as well as you what it was like to look after the family. I had to do it when you cut off all ties. Whatever *your reasons* were, you still did it. Isn't that the same thing he did?"

Cody made a disgusted noise and looked away from his sister, he couldn't even comprehend letting that man back into his world.

Renee sighed and slumped into her chair. "Cody, I'm telling you that you're mistaken about what happened, and all I'm asking is for you to look at all the facts before you write him off forever. He is your father."

"My father died the day he left. Forget it. I'm not playing this game." He stood and made for the back door.

"Don't do something you will regret, Cody."

"I regret a great many things, Sis, but wiping that worthless piece of shit from my mind is not one of them. I don't care what or why he did what he did—I'm out." He yanked open the door.

"Hypocrite."

Cody paused, his hand gripping the door frame, he glanced over at his sister, but she'd already turned away. He didn't like the fact she was calling him out on his own words. Grinding his teeth, he stormed into the kitchen.

He just got rid of one demon. The last thing he needed was to invite a second one into his life.

Chapter 7

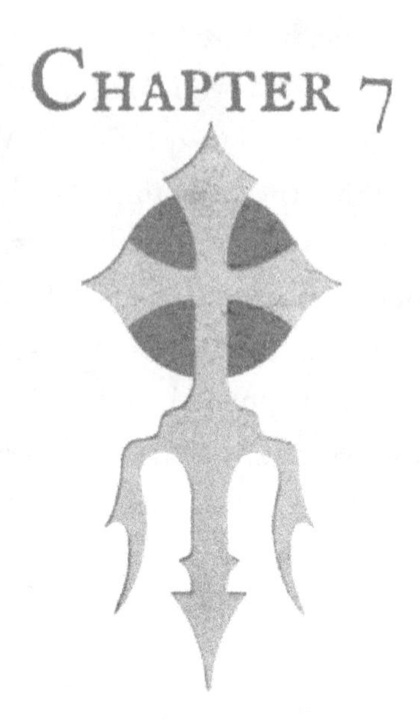

Trev slammed the pen down on his desk and swiveled his chair to stare out the large bay window. He couldn't focus properly. It didn't seem to matter what he came up with—he hadn't figured out a way to get good intel on any of the Golden Dragons. Their members were highly secretive. Other than the signature baggies of their drugs, he hadn't found any solid leads on a single dealer. Let alone on when, where, or how they were receiving their drug shipments.

He'd figured that with all the high-profile cases he'd done lately for the other gangs that they would seek him out for his services, but if they needed any, they didn't come to him. Without solid information, he couldn't bait Alejandro into believing the Golden Dragons were the ones killing his men. The Syphon Kings were too depleted in men after the warehouse attack on the Crimson Vipers to be of any use.

"Dammit." He couldn't hold Alejandro off any longer. He needed to accept the offer and worry about giving him a carrot later.

He groaned as his cell rang, and it was the devil himself. He answered and stood, going to lean against the window and stare at the view of the city in the distance.

"You have impeccable timing," he said. "I was about to call you."

"I hope you were calling to accept my very generous offer?"

"As a matter of fact, I was. I don't have anything substantial to offer as of yet, but I will notify you as soon as something interesting crosses my desk."

"I must tell you, Mr. Anderson. I'm not a patient man. When my family and my bottom line are affected, I tend to become ornery."

Trev smiled at the veiled threat. "Luckily for you, I tend to be somewhat of a workaholic. I do feel the need to mention that if you want reliable information, you cannot rush the process. If I start unnecessarily asking too many questions, people are going to become suspicious. I know you most certainly would. This wouldn't do anything to help the cause."

A deep sigh came through the line, and he could picture that arrogant face on the other end of the line. "Yes, I guess you have a valid point. I will be waiting to hear what you find out."

"Oh, and Alejandro, do not threaten me again. I do not take kindly to it, and you may find yourself on the wrong side of what I can do."

The rumble of a laugh came through the phone. "I do like you, Mr. Anderson. You are a real man, but don't forget who you're speaking to."

"I would never. Now, I have much to do before I am able to retire for the evening." Trev hung up before Alejandro could say anything further. He needed to remain in control of all their interactions, or Alejandro would pounce.

He closed his eyes and swore under his breath as his finger tapped on the glass. He needed an in. He needed a way to get into the game and get close to his mark. Not having Arek doing his thing was proving to be more of an issue than he'd originally thought, not that he would tell his already fat-headed brother that.

"Hey, Trev, I'm sorry to interrupt, but Sally asked if I could bring this in as she was leaving." Trev's body responded to the deep voice behind him, his suit jacket suddenly feeling very stuffy. Not wanting to appear too eager, his eyes traveled to the reflection of the man in the window. Trev's heart hammered as he took in that hesitant smile. He steadied himself before he turned to face his walking desire. Did the room just become smaller?

The white basketball jersey he wore showed off his chiselled arms and defined chest. Trev had to order himself to stop staring like a high school boy.

"It's Earl Grey. Sally said you like to have a cup at this time of night."

"Yes, of course. Thank you, Cody." Trev rose, meeting the man in the middle of the room, and with each step, his heart pounded a little harder. He couldn't explain the strong reaction to this man's nearness and it was equal portions of frustrating and exciting. Reaching for the teacup, he felt their fingers connect, his breath catching with the electric jolt. It was the barest of touches, but the shock to his system had his mind racing in ways it hadn't done in a very long time. The delicate china cup rattled slightly on the saucer as he wandered back to his desk.

"Sorry, I didn't mean to eavesdrop, but was that Alejandro of the Streetlores you were speaking to?"

"It was." Trev sipped his tea, black with a dash of sugar, and stared at the paperwork on his desk.

Cody didn't take the hint and instead came to stand in front of his desk. "He's not quite as certifiable as Tyson, but he's not much better. I hope you're not getting involved with him."

Trev looked up at Cody, and he could see the worry in those silver eyes, but there was also another emotion lurking there that he couldn't quite figure out. "What if I am?" he asked, and although he was talking about business, it felt like they were speaking about something of a more personal nature.

"I don't want to see you hurt. He will turn on you, no matter what deal you have struck. The man isn't to be trusted, Trev. He's big on talking up the family card, but when it comes down to it, he would sell his own mother if it suited his needs."

Trev leaned back in his chair. "And what makes you think I would trust him? Are you sure you're not more worried about losing your new place to stay?"

Cody's jaw stiffened, his eyes narrowing as he crossed those muscled arms over his chest. Trev liked that heated glare, his mind wondering what it would feel like to have those arms push him up against the office wall. He'd let Cody think he had the upper hand until he turned the tide and put him flat on his back as he ravaged those undeniably alluring lips. He was so unbelievably hot, he wanted to rip off his suit jacket and throw it across the room. It took a great deal of effort not to show his discomfort or his growing arousal.

"I told you I'd find a new place as soon as I could, but if you want me to move, just say so."

"Cody, sit, please." As Cody sat across from him, he formed his words carefully in his mind. "I told you that I don't want you to move. I meant what I said. My little joke was in poor taste. As far as Alejandro is concerned, you need not worry. I am far more aware, cunning and lethal than I appear."

Cody looked away from his eyes and stared at the large modern painting on the wall. "You're a strange contradiction, Trev."

Trev laughed and smiled at the words that were not meant to be a compliment yet were nonetheless. "Would you like a drink? I will even share my prized stash."

Those silver eyes met his, and his heart thumped as his cock stirred and stood at attention. Trev quickly pushed aside the memory of the last time he felt something even close to this. Memories were painful, and emotions led to mistakes. Mistakes led to people dying.

"I guess one glass wouldn't hurt, especially if you're breaking out the good stuff." Cody smiled, two deep dimples showing and softening his normally square jaw. Trev took a moment to admire Cody and his ability to look so sexy and sweet one moment and in the next breath he was reminded that the Ice Man lurked underneath the surface. That would terrify most, but to him it meant Cody wouldn't scare easily and that was a good thing in this world, in his world.

Trev reached into the bottom drawer, retrieving the new bottle of whiskey he'd purchased and two crystal glasses. "How do you like it?"

"Neat."

"A man after my own heart." Trev pushed the two fingers' worth toward Cody. "So tell me something about yourself."

Cody sipped the drink, his lips moist as the glass left his lips. Trev licked his own and visualized sucking the taste off Cody's.

Cody gave a little groan as he stared at the bold and full-flavored drink. "Now that is the good stuff, damn that is good." Trev shivered slightly with the deep timbre of his voice but managed to appear relaxed as he leaned back into his seat. "There really isn't that much to tell about me."

"You must have some interests. Something that you have a passion for or gets your juices flowing?"

Cody looked up from his drink, and there was no hiding the carnal look in the eyes staring back at him. "I think I should go."

Trev cocked his head to the side. "You don't need to go so quickly. I thought we were getting to know one another?"

"Trust me. I really have to go." Cody gulped the rest of this drink down and placed the now empty glass on the desk. He quickly stood, his long strides eating up the distance to the door. Cody paused, his hand on the door and stared across the space at him. "I know you're the badass and all, but be careful with Alejandro." Cody slipped out the door, hearing it click into place as it closed behind him.

Trev was confused by Cody's sudden departure. Had he asked something inappropriate? Maybe he'd been mistaken about the look in Cody's eyes.

His phone vibrated as a text came in, and he sighed as he picked it up. It was just as well. He had an objective, and he needed to focus on that.

Chapter 8

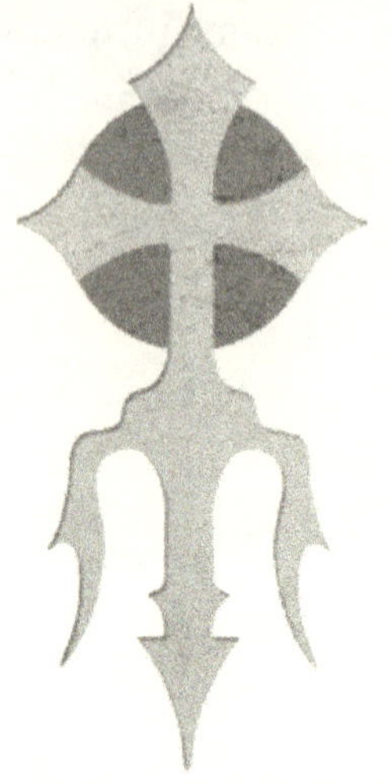

Cody couldn't sleep. Every time he closed his eyes, all he could see was Trev's way too sexy face and his tongue licking the whiskey off his lips. Those intelligent sky, blue eyes of his that could look right through your body—it was like Trev could see every scar and stain on his soul and didn't give a fuck. And then there was the suit. Trev and his perfectly manicured suits that never had a wrinkle, like he fucking walked around with an iron in his pocket all day. How was it humanly possible to look that perfect? And why did that turn him on so bad? He had no idea, but he'd tried to ease the tension multiple times in the shower, and yet his cock still ached to be touched by more than just his own hand.

"Shit, this is pointless." He swung his legs out of bed and dropped to the floor punching out fifty push-ups. Standing, he felt a little more at ease, maybe if he went for a run. He rummaged through his clothes and pulled on a pair of track pants and a t-shirt. The house was quiet when he stepped into the hall. Mind you, the house was so large it seemed empty all the time. He stuffed his feet in runners and earbuds in his ears before he slipped out the door. Cody paused to do a few stretches and leaned against the wall as he held his foot in his hand.

The sound of a garage door opening had him sneaking around the edge of the house just in time to see a blacked-out Hummer he'd never seen, pull out from a garage door he'd never seen open before. He jumped back around the side of the house and peaked around to watch the strange vehicle. It pulled out onto the street and headed for the city.

Not even sure why he marched for his car. "What the hell am I doing?" He mumbled as he pulled keys from his pocket and jumped in behind the wheel. He slammed the car into reverse and hit the gas hard. The wheels on the sporty little suped-up car squealed as it jumped into action. It was a good thing this area was fairly remote with the neighbors few and far between, he thought as the car reached the road, and he punched it, making it zip forward. He could just barely make out the Hummer's tail lights in the distance.

He loved his car. Trev had asked him what got his juices flowing, and other than the man who'd asked the question, this car was the answer. He loved to race his car, the feel of flying down the street, the world a blur as you passed it by, the thrill of winning, and of course running from the cops.

It had been months since he'd last visited the Underground and longer still since he'd actually raced. He was trying to make a new life for himself. Getting arrested for street racing seemed like a bad idea, yet he couldn't deny that the pull in his gut was there. He caught up to the Hummer on the freeway but stayed a good distance back. This had to be either Trev or Arek, and if so, they'd be used to spotting and shaking tails.

The shiny black vehicle traveled toward downtown and then continued on into the area of the city he'd grown up. The poorer areas of the city were dangerous to be roaming around at night, any time really, but worse at night. Ironically, he once was the dangerous thing to watch out for in this neighbourhood.

He continued his tailing and then darted toward the curb and pretended to park as the Hummer turned into the back parking area of a massage parlor strip. Once the Hummer was out of sight, he slowly pulled out of his spot, killed his lights, and crept closer until he could see into the parking area and pulled over again.

Cody opened his glove compartment and pulled out the small pair of binoculars—he'd had to spy on more than one person while working for Ty. It was dark, and the black vehicle blended into the shadows, but he was just able to pick out the glint of the driver's side door window. He held his breath as the door opened, and much to his dismay, it was Trev that emerged. The brothers may look alike, but they were very different once you got to know them. He'd stared at that ass enough to recognize that walk anywhere, and holy fuck Trev looked the hottest he'd ever seen him.

Dressed in all black that clung to his body like a second skin. His bare arms flexed as he slung a large gun over his shoulder and placed another into the strap on his leg. And this is why there was army calendars, he suddenly had a new fetish. Trev's face was lined with black paint, and a ball cap pulled low over his features. Those cool, calculating eyes took in everything. He scrunched down as low as he could in his seat when Trev began to turn in his direction.

"What are you up to?" Cody whispered and then swore as he spotted a cop car coming down the road. He was like a fucking magnet lately.

He grabbed the seat handle and pushed back until it was laid down flat. His heart hammered hard as the lights drew closer. *Just keep going.* The last thing he needed was to end up running from the cops tonight. The car's entire interior was illuminated, and he knew they were using some sort of a projection light to shine into the cars on the street. He closed his eyes tight and said a little prayer as he held his breath. The car began to dim, and he looked up and watched the light disappear further down the road.

He sat up and fixed the binoculars on the last spot he'd seen Trev, but the man had disappeared. Cody tapped his fingers on the top of the wheel as he debated what he should do.

"I'm gonna regret this." Cody took one last look around, and satisfied that no one was watching, he got out and jogged across the street. He'd only made it to the second door when gunfire erupted from somewhere inside. He ran as fast as his legs could carry him toward the sound grabbing for the gun he never left behind. Of course, his new life didn't need one, or so he thought, so his hand grabbed air. More gunfire, the sound muffled and further away.

"Fuck." Cody pulled open the door, and taking a deep breath to steady himself, he stuck his head inside. Whatever was happening was down the hall, but that didn't mean a stray bullet couldn't find him. Having been shot, he could say with certainty that he had no interest in trying that again.

He looked around at the closed doors lining the one side and clued in that all the businesses were attached with a long corridor that didn't go directly outside. The dim lights showed a number of bodies bleeding out in the hallway—each was dead. The sightless look and lack of breath were all he needed to know. He quickly knelt and picked up a discarded gun off the closest man with a bullet between his eyes.

Cody's eyes traveled to the next man and the next, and all of them were the same with a direct bullseye. He swallowed hard. He knew what kind of skill this took—he considered himself a good shot, but this was straight-up lethal. He stepped over the splayed limbs, and a tattoo caught his attention. Cody stared at the logo and swore under his breath.

"You're gonna get yourself killed," Cody mumbled.

He jogged to the end of the corridor and the now eerily silent T-intersection. The stench of gunpowder, blood, and piss was strong in the air making his nose curl. Cody peeked around the corner, and other than more dead bodies, the only thing to move was an exit sign—the plastic smashed and hanging by a cord flashed and sparked dangerously. He swallowed and stepped out into the hallway, not sure which direction to head.

Cody gingerly stepped over an arm and paused as he heard something dripping. This place was too damn dark. He couldn't figure out from where the sound was coming. He jerked and turned toward the sound of something dropping on the floor and froze as he came face to face with the barrel of a gun. He didn't recognize the guy holding it, but the way he was dressed and the tattoo lining the side of his neck told him he was one of Alejandro's guys.

"Take it easy. I didn't do this," he whispered.

"I know you. You're the Ice Man. Why shouldn't I fuck you up?"

"Because based on all the men on the floor, you need help. I was out for a jog when I

heard the shooting."

"So, you ran toward the sound and not away? That's fucked up shit." The guy narrowed his eyes. "How did you get out of lock-up so quick? Are you working with the cops?" The hammer clicked, and he didn't dare even blink. "Are you?" The guy repeated, pressing the cool barrel harder into his forehead. Most would probably shit themselves with a gun pressed to their forehead. Unfortunately, this was not the first time this had happened to him, but it might be his last.

Cody opened his mouth to answer when a muffled pop reached his ears a moment after a hole opened up in the man's head in front of him.

"What the fuck?" Cody stumbled backward as the body fell unceremoniously at him with a thump. He spun and looked into the shadowed corridor, his heart pounding hard in his chest as a figure slowly stepped out of the darkness.

"Are you following me?" Trev asked, keeping his voice low while very accusatory.

Trev's tone set Cody on edge. He crossed his arms over his chest and glared at the other man. "I thought you might need my help. I didn't set out to follow you. It just sort of happened."

Trev moved like a panther. One moment, he was calm and still. The next, he was diving to his left and opening fire, the bullets sailing past Cody and found the mark of two more men that had appeared from seemingly nowhere. Cody stared at the new arrivals for a moment, his eyes taking in once more how perfect of a shot Trev was. It was almost superhuman.

"Does it look like I need help? You put me at risk by being in here, and you're slowing me down." Trev walked past him, not sparing him a glance. "Wipe the gun off and anything else you touched on your way out, and run along home."

Cody reached out and grabbed Trev by the arm. The muscled bicep flexed in his grip as those normally calm, and calculating eyes bore holes into him. If looks could kill, he would've been dead. "I'm not a fucking damsel in distress, don't treat me like one."

The small green square that was covering Trev's left eye glowed softly upclose. He could only assume was some form of night vision, he'd never thought he'd see something like this in person. The illumination gave Cody just enough light that he could make out Trev's eyebrow rising slightly before his face turned into a neutral mask once more.

"Do you know what happened to the last man that grabbed my arm?" Trev's voice was no more than a whisper, but the dark edge sent a snaking of fear down Cody's spine. The corner of Trev's lip twitched ever so slightly with his apparent amusement. "Unless you want to find out the hard way, I'd suggest you let go of me." Cody released Trev's arm like a fucking hot potato. He had no doubt that Trev would and could follow through on his threat. The problem was, if it wasn't for the dead guys lying around like dominos, he'd welcome it. Then pull him down to roll around on the floor perhaps.

"Fine. Since you're already here, stay behind me and don't try to be a hero." Trev looked him up and down, those icy blue eyes practically glowing in the dark. Cody wished he knew what the guy was thinking. He was impossible to read.

"I wouldn't dream of being your hero," he spat out sarcastically.

Trev gave him the signature annoyed look he'd become accustomed to over their time together, but didn't say anything further. Cody made a face at the back of Trev's head as he followed a few feet behind.

"I saw that," Trev said. Cody froze as Trev shot him a look over his shoulder. "I see everything. You should remember that."

Cody swallowed hard and nodded. As Trev continued to move among the darkened hallway, two things struck Cody. The first was that he was silent. Not even a slight scuff from a boot sound could be heard. The second thing was Trev's attire up close. Black combat boots and cargo pants that fit the man's ass like it was a goddam glove. He found himself staring at the firm ass and wide shoulders. The guy didn't even try, and he was a walking fuck me stick—heat radiated off his body, and the soft minty fresh scent of Trev's body wash filled his nose. The logical part of his mind bitch slapped him for even thinking about him like that, especially now, but everything below the belt didn't care where they were or what they were doing. One-track mind that sucker. Didn't help he hadn't gotten any since before he went into the slammer.

Trev held up his fist, and he stopped moving. Cody never had anyone do that to him before, and he smirked. Despite the seriousness of the situation it felt very cool, all covert and shit. His eyes searched the darkness. He couldn't see any further than across the hall clearly, but nothing seemed to move, and the only thing he could hear was the sound of his own blood pumping through his veins.

"Sweet Delilah, how many more heat signatures do you read in the building?" Trev asked, and Cody turned to look around the hallway. He didn't know Trev had a partner or brought anyone with him.

"Who are you talking to?" he whispered.

"Shhh." Trev held a finger over his mouth and cocked his head. "Why is my sight not showing that?"

Cody took a better look at the side of Trev's head, and sure enough, there was a bud in his ear. He had no idea who Trev was talking to, but this was seriously the coolest shit he'd ever been a part of—it was like being plunked into the middle of one of his video games.

"Hold image, I can see now." Trev looked him in the eyes. "Two more men in the room at the end on the left, both are armed, and police have been dispatched. Approximate arrival time is ten minutes. You still want to stay?"

"More than ever." Cody rubbed his hands together with the building excitement.

Trev nodded, and they silently slipped down the hall to the aforementioned room. Trev once more held his finger up to his lips and then stared at the solid wall. He pulled what looked like a flat plastic square out of his pocket and placed it on the wall. Then, he went a little further, mimicking the action.

Marching back toward him, Trev grabbed Cody's arm and pulled him away from the room.

"Duck and cover your ears."

Cody did as he was told, and Trev immediately draped his body over Cody's. If his one-track minded cock hadn't already been stirring, it sure as shit did with the feel of Trev pressed up against him like a second skin. This man was addicting, and his close proximity was making Cody's head swim. Trev's cheek rubbed against his neck, and he bit his lip to not moan at the heat. His fresh, clean scent seeped under his skin and into his subconscious. That minty scent would haunt him forever. Even though the moment only lasted a few seconds, he knew he was done. He had to find a way to have Trev.

Cody tried to relish in the man's touch a little longer, but instead, a loud explosion went off. What felt like a gale whipped past them, billowing his track pants around his legs. Even with his ears covered, the sound left his ears ringing as he choked on drywall dust falling in the wake of it.

He coughed while Trev disappeared into the cloud of dust. He stared straight ahead into the hole that had just been created, but Trev was simply gone. The guy was like a fucking magician. He could hear a yell and then the distinct sound of Trev's silencer firing two shots. Cody knew without looking they would be perfect kills.

"Here, take this." Trev emerged from the hole, stepping over the rubble to hand him two large duffel bags. Trev disappeared back inside the room and came out with a third bag. "Okay, let's move out."

"Try not to step in the blood," Trev said and then sprinted down along the corridor. Easier said than done when you couldn't see where you were stepping and lugging massive bags. It was a bloody good thing he was in good shape, or he wouldn't have been able to keep up behind Trev.

The man was certainly faster than he would've placed money on. Cody's shoulders were burning with the strain of the bags that felt like they weighed a ton each. They burst out the door he'd snuck into the building by, and Trev led him to the Hummer.

"Sweet Delilah, open trunk." The hatch lifted, and once more, Cody wondered who Trev was talking to...the sky, and ivory tower somewhere? "Put the bags in."

He did as he was ordered and could just make out sirens in the distance. "What the hell was this for? You left a small massacre back there."

"Why is not your concern—did you drive?"

"Yeah." Cody ground his teeth together and crossed his arms over his chest.

"Okay, get going. Head west, and don't draw any attention to yourself. I'll meet you at home, and we will be having a discussion about your stalker behavior," Trev commanded, jogging toward the door.

"Where are you going?"

"I need to wipe your prints," Trev growled back.

"And, I wasn't stalking you," Cody called out after him before marching to his car.

At least I hadn't set out to stalk you. He thought but kept that to himself.

The thought of Trevor punishing him had a fresh wave of inappropriate thoughts racing to the surface. This was insane, he had literally been in the middle of a shootout with a gun to his head and all he could picture was unzipping Trev's pants and getting on his fucking knees to suck that cock and dead people be damned. He needed to find a new hobby if he had any chance of getting this guy and the lapse of mental judgment out of his head.

The mental image of Trev in that outfit was going to give him wood for weeks.

Chapter 9

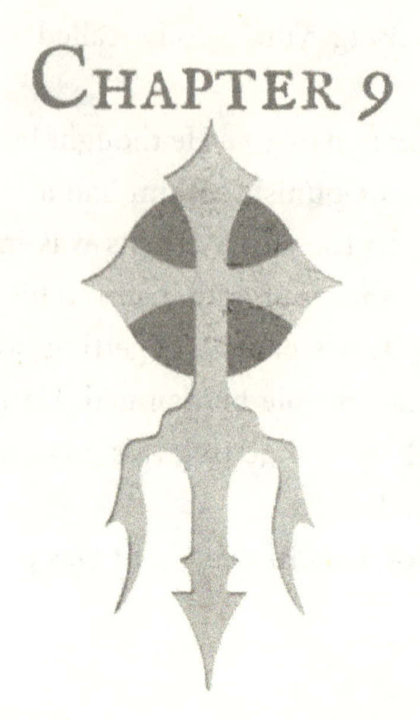

Arek jumped from the warm bed and pulled on boxers as he ran toward the sound of yelling. It was coming from Trev's office, and as he got closer to the door, he was easily able to make out Trev and Cody's voices.

"Whoa, what is going on in here? You two are going to wake up J.J.," Arek said as he walked in on the pair. He paused as he took in Trev's attire. It had been so long since he'd seen his brother dressed for battle, well, non-courtroom battle, that it seemed wrong, and yet he immediately had the urge to salute him.

"Cody here thought it was a bright idea to follow me tonight," Trev said by way of an explanation.

"I'm sorry I followed you. I didn't know if it was you or Arek when I saw the Hummer leaving. I just thought...."

"You thought what? That we would need help with our mission? That you wanted to play soldier? Or that you'd get dirt on one of us?"

"Yes, no...fuck. Yes to the help part, no to the get dirt on you part. I started out for a fucking run and curiosity got the best of me when I saw the strange vehicle leaving the garage. Then when I saw it was you at the mall and you were armed I thought you may want help, which turned into concern when I heard the gunfire," Cody rambled out in a single sentence before taking a breath "Why the hell would I want dirt on either of you? That guy," Cody stopped long enough to point his finger in Arek's direction. "Is with my sister. And you kept me out of prison for fucks sake—it wouldn't even make sense."

"Gunfire? What doesn't make sense?" Renee asked as she stepped into the room.

"Great, the entire family is here. Why don't I go and make some popcorn? We can make a real event of it," Trev practically growled as he stormed over and grabbed a bottle of tequila. That wasn't a good sign. He never broke open tequila unless it was a really bad day. Trev didn't even bother with the glass, which turned the not-good sign into an oh-shit moment. Arek had only seen him this level of pissed a couple of times in his life, and it was never pretty.

"Look, why don't we just all calm down and talk about this?" Arek tried for referee status.

"Fuck you," Trev yelled, and Arek took a step back. Those livid eyes found Cody once more. "I don't need help from anyone, least of all from a common thug with no training."

"A common thug? I am not a fucking thug." Cody balled his fists.

"You were second in command to the leader of a gang. What would you call it?"

Arek's eyes darted between the two men squaring off and didn't know how to diffuse this situation. It was normally him getting into fights and Trev talking him off the ledge. He really didn't like being on this side of the coin.

"You bloody well know I was trapped in that hell with Tyson. I can't even believe you'd say that to me after everything I shared with you."

Cody clenched his fists, the muscles around his neck flexing as he did. "I suffered abuse you can only imagine, but I had dreams, you know. I had aspirations to do something great with my life, and I tossed it all away to be that sadistic fucker's second in command for my sister's sake."

A soft sob sound came from Renee's mouth, tears shimmering in her eyes as she covered her mouth. "Shit, Sis, I didn't mean it like that." Renee took off out of the room, and Cody was hot on her heels, calling out her name.

Arek closed the door, making a soft thud as it closed into place. He slowly turned to face off with his fuming brother. "And here we thought I was the one bad with relationships. I'm no expert but, I'm pretty sure you're screwing this one up."

"How many times do I have to tell you I don't want a fucking relationship? Just because you've decided to play house does not mean I have to as well." Trev took another swig from the bottle, and Arek watched as he chugged, a dribble escaping the corner of his mouth.

"You know I'd almost believe you if you weren't so worked up. You'd only be this hot under the collar if he meant something to you, if you were worried." Trev turned away with an annoyed get lost whisper under his breath. "Fuck Trev, Cody is not Mel."

"Don't you mention her name," Trev spun and pointed the quickly emptying bottle at Arek. "Don't you ever say her name to me again."

"Or what? You gonna try and take me on? You know I'll beat your ass. You're out of shape."

Trev snorted a short, bitter sound, but his eyes softened. "Have I ever mentioned I do not like it when you're right?"

"Don't worry, it doesn't happen often." Arek smiled and held out his hand for the bottle. "Mel was always a go-getter. Even when we were kids, she was jumping out of trees and swimming in dangerous waters. What happened to her was not your fault, she knew what she was getting into. You must know that."

Trev sat down at his desk and took off the black ball cap—he ran his hand through his hair a number of times before his eyes lifted to meet Arek's.

"I never should've been assigned to that mission, and she never should've been under my command. She never should've been there, I shouldn't have chosen her for the team." Trev stopped and held his head in his hands as his elbows found the desk. "She was my responsibility. It was my job to make sure she was safe, and I failed. I allowed emotion to get involved, and it got her killed. Those are the facts."

Arek stood silently until his brother finally looked up at him. He took a deep breath and sat down. Neither of them needed to say anything to understand the ghosts that were laid bare in their eyes.

"Trev, you never said anything to me, and I didn't ask, but I think I need to know. Did you love her? I know you to were shacking up, you had been for years, but I always assumed it was like a fuck friends kind of thing. Was it more than that?" Arek asked, and a shadow crossed Trev's face.

Trev's shoulders sagged, and Arek had never seen his brother so defeated. "I did, or at least I thought I did. How am I supposed to know? How can someone claim to love another and then put them in harm's way?" Rubbing his eyes, Arek kept quiet, waiting for Trev to continue. "I miss her every fucking day. Is that how it is for you? I mean, how did you know you were in love with Renee?"

Arek sighed as he tried to put what he felt into words. "I craved her, needed to see her, touch her, taste her, but more than that, I could picture a future with her. She is to me as that painting you love so much is to you." Arek nodded toward the wall.

"She is your 'Woman with a Parasol.'" The look Trev gave him was a cross between disbelief and impressed. "Well then, Mr. Parasol, you better go speak to Renee."

"Nah, I will let them work that shit out, I have no interest in being in the middle of that convo. Besides, I have my own family drama to worry about. Sorry, you're not getting rid of me that easily."

Trev laughed, a short burst of amusement. "Too transparent, was I? Does this mean I'm the dramatic one now? How times have changed."

"Tell me about it. I'm like a domesticated house cat now." Arek smiled at his brother. "Well, as domesticated as I get anyway." The snort from his brother made him laugh. "So, what were you up to anyway?"

"Nothing for you to worry yourself about."

"You plan on shutting me out?" Arek grabbed the bottle off the desk and took a gulp. He smacked his lips and looked at the brand. Nope, this shit still tasted better with salt and lemon.

"No, I would never cut you out, but you were right. You do need to spend this time with Renee. Enjoy all the miracles you can because you never know when they will be gone." Trev swiped at the blackout on his face and then stared at his fingers as he rubbed them together. Arek watched his brother closely. There was something that just wasn't right. He couldn't put his finger on it, but his twin sense was telling him that Trev was off his game.

"Arek, at some point, I'm going to need you, but tonight was not that night. I will ask that you not worry about what I'm up to. You know I can take care of myself."

"Brother, it's not whether you can take care of yourself that worries me." Arek stared at his brother. He couldn't have asked for a better man to be by his side from the moment they came into this world. Trev had been taking punches for him, covering for him, and emotionally propping him up for his entire life, but at what personal cost? What had his selfish, needy behavior cost Trev?

"You need to apologize to Cody."

"Like hell I do." The leather chair squeaked as Trev leaned back. "What I need is a new damn chair." He wriggled back and forth, and as it continued to make noise, he jumped up and knelt down to take a look at it.

"You're avoiding." Arek hit his brother with a hard glare. "You're secluding yourself, locking yourself away in this room, and it's not healthy."

"I have many things to occupy my time." He pointed to the chair. "Case and point."

"Bullshit, the only thing you have is a seventy-year-old woman working for you and me." Trev stood and quickly rearranged the items on his desk, making sure nothing was out of place. Arek recognized the signs of his brother's unease. He was always the same, always had been, he needed to make something orderly, had to put something right.

"I don't need Cody in my life to fulfill me. I'm not like you Arek, I have never been the type that had to have a relationship, or as you put it, get my rocks off."

Arek slumped into the chair. He was at a loss as to how to get Trev to open up to him or listen to reason. "You can keep telling yourself you're fine, but you were never this stilted before. Life is not remembered in days, but moments."

"What are you a fucking greeting card now?" Trev shook his head, and Arek wanted to hit his stubborn brother's face. His hand twitched with the thought of connecting with that jaw.

"Fine, that might have been over the top, but you know I'm right, and Trev," he stopped to make sure Trev looked at him before continuing. "Cody may have been in the wrong to follow you, but he didn't deserve what you said."

"Didn't he?"

"No. The fact you didn't see him says one of two things—either he is good, or you are out of practice, maybe both. Besides, even if you don't want a relationship, would it hurt to have a friend?"

"All my friends are dead." Trev pushed his chair into the desk, signaling that he didn't want to speak anymore on the topic. "It's late, and I'm going to bed. I appreciate your concern, Arek, but Cody is a big boy. I'm sure he will be fine. I'm fine. Hell, we are all fucking fine." Arek watched as Trev left the office, the bottle of tequila swinging from his hand. Trev might insist he was alright, but Arek knew better.

There was something Trev was hiding, something that happened while they were deployed. The mission had been like running naked through hell while being shot at. They all lost so much, but this felt different, it felt too raw.

Arek stood and wandered around the desk to pick up the picture of their unit. He thought he knew everything there was to know about his brother. They were as close as any two siblings could be. So why would he hide what was bothering him? He'd always assumed that the compulsive behaviors and keeping to himself issues would sort themselves out on their own. There was something from the larger picture he was missing. It was hard to picture his orderly brother coming undone at the edges. Trev was always the incredibly strong one. Arek ran his thumb over the image of all the smiling faces from another life before setting the frame down in the exact place he'd removed it.

But now, he wasn't so sure.

Chapter 10

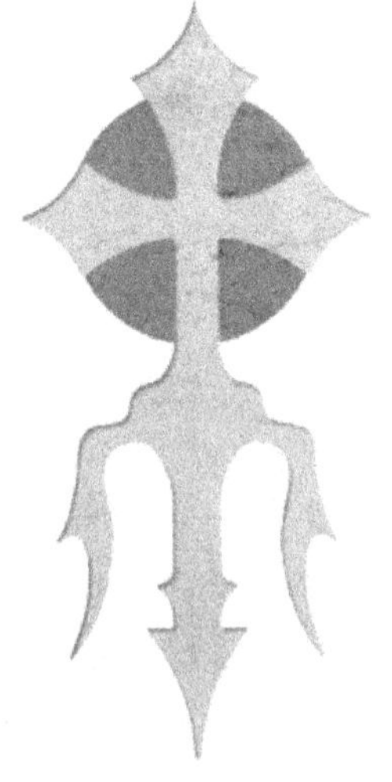

Trev would be happy to get back to the ship. This wall-to-wall hot ass, devil's sandbox was so not his thing. Give him a cool breeze, waves and sharks over endless stick to your dick granules and stubborn camels any day. It normally cooled off to a reasonable temp at night, but not tonight. Nope, he had what felt like rivers of sweat trickling down his back inside the command tent that did nothing to keep heat out or cool in. Other than shade, the thing was completely useless.

The fabric door to his tent flew open. If it were wood, the force with which it was ripped open would have smashed into a far wall.

Mel marched in and stopped in front of his desk. Boots tossed sand as she came to an abrupt halt. Her back was ramrod straight, hands behind her back and eyes glaring at the tent wall over his shoulder. She waited for him to invite her to speak, but her eyes were snapping mad. He'd become very accustomed to that look over the years. Her mother would say that her temperament was worse than any snapping turtle.

"You may speak, Mel," he said casually and then turned his eyes back to the map on his desk.

"We need to end things. The guys are all talking and saying the only reason I got promoted is because I'm fucking you. I'm not that girl, I've never been that girl, and you know that. Yet, here I am, labeled as the fuck myself up the chain-of-command type," Mel fumed.

"At ease, Mel," Trev said.

Mel, Arek, and himself had been friends for as long as he could remember. Their parents were neighbors, and she was born a week before himself and his brother. That was a fact she never let them forget—she was the older, wiser of the three. They'd been like Velcro. She'd always been more comfortable hanging with them than the girls at school. It had been her idea for the three of them to join the Navy together, and he'd found he couldn't say no to her. Since joining, the two of them had become more than best friends. Dare he say—he was sure he was in love with her. He suspected he always had been.

"Mel, you are over-thinking this for nothing. The guys would tease you no matter what. They always have. This is just the latest thing to bug you about." Trev folded the large map on his desk. "Do you really care this much about what they say?"

"I don't care what they say, but I do care what they believe, and so should you. There is teasing, and then there is pissed-off disguised as teasing. They are the latter. They want to know why I was promoted over guys that have been here twice as long."

"Mel, I had no say over your promotion. You're not even in my unit."

She made a strange grrr-ing noise and walked away to stare out the tent. The sun was beginning to set, and the extreme heat was easing only slightly with late-afternoon shadow.

"You don't understand," she finally said.

"No, I don't think you do. You were promoted because you are excellent at what you do. You have what it takes to lead your own team one day, and those that make the decisions have taken notice."

"Did they ask you about me?" She wheeled around and glared at him.

"Yes, of course, they did, and I told them the truth. Would you have preferred I lie and say you are terrible at your job? Sabotage your chances, maybe tank your entire career so that you could say that I didn't recommend you get your promotion?"

"No, of course not," Mel sighed, and he pointed to the chair across from the small desk. She mumbled but made her way over and sat in the simple wooden chair. She looked too beautiful for this place, for this tent, or even that fucking chair. But, he'd never hold her back from her dream, and this was what she wanted. The desire to help others had always run deep in her blood.

"I'm proud of my hard work, but it's not the same for me as it is for you, Trev. No one questions how many people you've slept with or if screwing them had anything to do with you making Master Chief. I bet you could fuck this entire encampment, and all the guys would do is cheer your dick on—ra, ra, get some more," she mocked.

Trev got up and rounded the desk. He leaned against it and held out his hand for Mel to place hers into his. She hesitated but accepted his offering. "You don't need to prove or explain yourself to anyone."

"But I do. I need to retain their respect. If they don't respect me, they won't listen to me, Trev. I'm already at a disadvantage because I have tits instead of a dick. This thing we have going on between us is only making it harder."

Trev stared out the slim tent opening and watched a jeep as it rumbled by. "Do you really want to end us?" His heart pounded hard as he waited to hear the verdict.

"No," she finally said. Mel looked down at her boots. "You know how I feel about you, how I've always felt."

"I don't want us to end either, but I will respect what you choose to do." Trev gave Mel a gentle tug to her feet and pulled her until she stood between his legs. He stared into her soft green eyes and tried to figure out when his feelings had shifted from best friend to lover and now in love. There was no wild rip your clothes off passion like the romance movies depict, but he could picture a quiet life with her once they both finished touring. He wanted to wake up beside her

every morning. She made him laugh. They had everything in common, right down to how they liked their coffee.

He'd fantasized about purchasing a small farm near his parents and having a large family. "You let me know what you decide, but know that I love you. I don't see what we have as simply friends with benefits." He caught her eye as she looked away. "You know that, right?"

"I have never wanted two things so badly in my life, and I'm scared that I'm going to have to give up one to have the other," she whispered, her voice hoarse with emotion. "I love you, Trev. So much it hurts." She captured his lips, and he savored the taste of her sweet mouth and strawberry lip balm.

Moaning, Mel gripped the front of his fatigues in her fists, and the kiss quickly deepened. Trev slid his hands down the sides of her body until he could grip her ass and pull her firmly between his legs.

"This is a mistake," Mel mumbled against his lips.

"We could never be a mistake." He softly ran his lips down the side of her neck and hated the collar blocking his access. "I can't wait to get you out of this uniform."

"You're my addiction, Trev. I told myself I would march in here and end things, no matter what you said. How do you always convince me to do what you want?"

He lifted his head from sucking on the small patch of skin on Mel's neck. "Me, convince you?" He laughed. "I think that's the other way around. But, maybe it's because it's what we both want." Trev cupped her face, kissing her forehead and then her nose. She closed her eyes and smiled. "Sometimes you are simply more stubborn coming around to the same conclusion." He laughed as her eyes snapped open to glare at him—her finger poking him in the side.

"Maybe, but I'll never admit it."

"Oh, I know you won't. It's part of your charm."

"Do we have time for me to push you on this desk and ride you?" Her soft green eyes glittered and his cock instantly stood at attention with the image.

Trev sighed and adjusted himself, only making her smile wider, the minx. "Unfortunately, I have a meeting to get to—we can pick this up later. But, I may drag you back here to follow through on that fantasy cause that's fucking hot." Mel laughed and gave his cock a rub through his pants. He groaned and pressed his lips to hers briefly. "Devilish woman."

Trev stood, forcing Mel to step back before he bailed on the meeting. He ran his thumb across her bottom lip. "You can have the world if you want it. There is no need to compromise on your dreams because you're a woman. Don't let them push you around Mel, you are a fucking good soldier, and I will fight beside you, always."

Grabbing the papers on his desk, he made his way toward the tent door when Mel called his name. Looking over his shoulder, he stared at the woman he planned on marrying. She didn't say anything but smiled wide. What she didn't say told him more than words could've.

"I love you too."

Trev took a swig of the tequila, the burn filling his belly and warming his limbs. He'd never regretted anything more in his life than what he said to Mel that afternoon. He squeezed his eyes closed and pushed down hard on the memories trying to surface. He should've listened to her and walked away. Arek was right. He was scared for Cody. When he recognized the man with a gun to his forehead, he had the same flash of fear as years ago—the same sinking in his gut that pulled on his soul and made his heart stop.

If what happened to Mel taught him anything, it was that emotions had no place in war. This new life with The Righteous was nothing but one big war. He looked at his reflection in the mirror over the fireplace. With a mighty heave and yell, he threw the bottle that smashed into the fireplace, sending little glass shards skittering in every direction.

His chest heaved as the emotion clogged his throat. He stumbled to the bed and flopped on the mattress.

"Never again."

Chapter 11

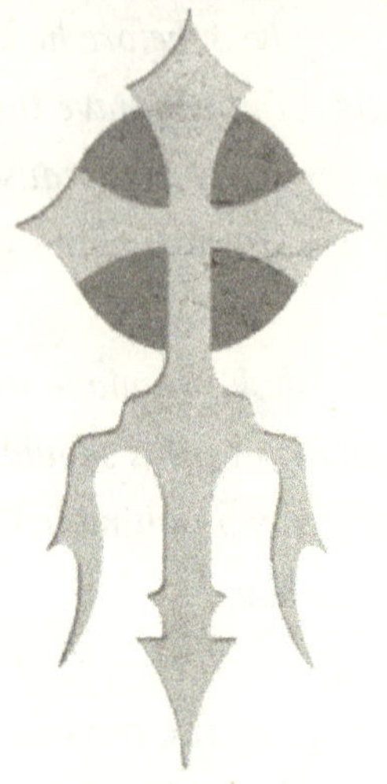

Cody groaned as he pushed the heavy bar over his head, the shiny silver bending slightly with the stress. His muscles strained under the intense weight. With a roar and a mighty heave, he stepped out from under the bar and let it drop to the floor with a bang. He had to give it to Trev—this workout room was stacked. He grabbed the towel off the floor, and when he stood, the man himself was in the room behind him.

This man was like a fucking cat. He never heard him coming, and suddenly, he wanted to strap a bell around Trev's neck. Maybe even attach a leash. The image had the corner of his mouth pulling up in amusement until he remembered what Trev had said to him last night and how much it cut to the core.

"Would you like me to leave so you can have the room?" he asked Trev's reflection in the wall of mirrors. He stared into those intense blue eyes, his stupid heart thumping hard in his chest as his body instantly responded to his presence.

"No, stay as long as you like." Trev broke the staring match first and made his way to the treadmill. Cody watched his every movement. He was fascinated and drawn to this cold man, and he was infuriated with himself and yet couldn't stop yearning for more. What gnawed at him was how different Trev was now than a few days ago. He'd gone from feeling like they were friends that wanted more, to feeling the cold air of a door being slammed in his face. How had he read the situation so wrong?

Apparently, he was more screwed up than he thought.

Trev paused with his hand on the machine, his back to Cody. "I'm sorry. I don't say that word often, so it doesn't come lightly, but I owe you an apology for the way I spoke to you last night."

Cody turned around and couldn't help noticing the slight droop in Trev's normally straight spine. His head was down, and his shoulders were curved forward—he was the image of apologetic. Without worrying about the consequences, he closed the short distance and laid his hand on Trev's shoulder. The muscles flexed under his touch a moment before Trev spun to face him. He thought he was going to end up on his ass from the dark glare in Trev's eyes, but Trev simply froze in place. The air sizzled around them, and Cody took a shuddering breath.

A flash from when he was taken to the hospital danced before his eyes. He'd be dead without this man and his brother. Trev had doctored him in the back of that Hummer—he calmed Renee and got her to apply pressure to the bleeding wounds. The touch of Trev's strong hands had plagued his mind every moment since. When the police arrived after his surgery, he could barely remember his own name because of the heavy sedative. However, he distinctly remembered Trev standing in the room, neatly pressed suit in place and a stern expression on his features. Trev had told the police he was Cody's lawyer, and they could get out until his client was well enough to give a statement.

The tension between them was palpable and as Trev's eyes flicked to his lips he was unable to contain himself any longer. Cody grabbed Trev's face and crashed his mouth to his slightly parted lips. A soft gasp met his contact and the electrical surge that flowed like a real thing between them. He braced himself to be shoved away, but Trev didn't pull away as he had expected. Instead, Trev deepened the kiss, their tongues fighting in a battle for dominance, which only served to heighten his runaway desire. He pushed Trev back until they came into contact with the wall, and he was able to get a better angle on his mouth. Trev's hands gripped Cody's ass, and he groaned into this gorgeous man's mouth, his cock throbbing inside the flimsy shorts. Cody had never wanted someone as bad as he wanted Trev.

The terrifying part was not the physical desire, it was the rapid beating of his heart and the pull in his gut screaming he wanted more than sex.

The heady scent of Trev's heated skin mixed with the new woodsy aftershave made him unsteady on his feet with need. His knees shook slightly as his hands explored the wide shoulders, his hands snaking out along those arms until he could grip Trev's hands and draw them above his head. They gripped one another tightly as if they were both trying to hang on for dear life to the flood of crashing sensations.

A raging hunger burned in Cody's blood, making him feel out of control. He broke the kiss and gently bit into the skin of Trev's neck.

"Oh fuck," Trev's voice was deep and rough.

The sound, a spur, and Cody's body reacted. He pressed himself up against Trev, needing more contact. He was rewarded with another groan as their cocks pressed together. Cody thrust his hips up and down, relishing in the sensation of their hardened lengths rubbing together. The man was no slouch in the size department, and his own throbbed and jerked with the images of being taken by Trev—used by this man. The tip of Cody's shorts was wet and not with sweat as his cock wept, desperate to feel skin on skin.

"I can't do this," Trev mumbled. Cody broke the seal of the hickey he'd been administering to the base of Trev's neck, and he could feel the man drawing away from him. Desperate to keep whatever this was going, he grabbed Trev's shaft and squeezed. Trev's eyes snapped open, and those normally calm eyes held a dark wildness that Cody craved.

"I think you can." Cody lowered himself to his knees, hooking his fingers into the waistband of Trev's shorts as he went. "In fact, I know you can. I know you want to." He gave the shorts a tug, and the swollen and angry-looking head of Trev's cock became visible. It was glistening with pre-cum, the whole head so shiny it looked like he'd just stepped out of a shower. Cody drew his tongue across the tip and moaned with the salty taste that filled his mouth and invaded his senses.

Trev's legs shook as Cody stared up at the body of the sexiest man he'd ever met. His eyes traveled upward until their eyes locked, and he knew he would do anything to have more of this. He'd sell his fucking soul to the devil himself to have this man, even for a single night. Cody tugged a little more on the shorts until they slid over Trev's ass and showed off the grand majority of the deliciously hard cock. More pre-cum slipped from the tip, like a miniature climax, the clear liquid landing on his face.

"Fuck, you're sexy," Cody said and then didn't waste another moment before slipping the cock into his mouth. Trev tensed and tried to back up, but he was already against the wall. He wasn't letting Trev escape that easy. Gripping Trev's hips hard to keep him from running, Cody quickly swirled his tongue around the sensitive tip of his cock, and Trev swore loudly before sliding his fingers through Cody's hair. Cody groaned as those hands held him in place, Trev's hips thrusting hard into his mouth.

"Oh fuck," Trev mumbled.

Cody glanced up at Trev as the heated flesh that was like steel, slipped between his lips. Cody's body was taut and ready for whatever Trev was willing to concede to as Trev pulled back and pressed into his mouth again. The subtle moans filling the room was the sweetest music to his ears.

Cody moaned and swallowed as he choked on the large dick invading his throat. Trev's fingers gripped his hair hard as he held his cock down Cody's throat longer than he'd ever managed before. His eyes watered, and lungs burned as Trev stared down at him and relaxed his hold. He gasped as the cock slipped from his mouth. Cody wiped the back of his hand across his chin as saliva dripped down his chin. There was a feral look in Trev's eyes, a mix of the same wild need Cody was feeling, but there was an aggression that warned of a darker side to his personality.

Not caring if he had tears running down his face he took that dick into his mouth again and internally smiled as Trev's legs shook. He grabbed his own throbbing dick and gave it a number of desperate tugs, the pain building between his legs, sweet agony. He drew his head back, to get a much needed breath, and Trev thrust his hips home until Cody's nose was touching skin once more. Every time he pulled away, Trev would pull him close and hold him til he strained.

Hollowing his cheeks, he sucked hard, and the grip on the back of his head loosened again, Trev's fingers quivering. Cody moaned as Trev's all-male scent filled his nose. His face was wet with saliva and sweat as he bobbed his head on the cock bucking in his mouth for more.

"Stop, please stop," Trev begged. Cody licked the hard silky-smooth skin from the tightened sac to the tip of the cock before gazing up at Trev.

Pulling his mouth off with a *pop*, Cody said, "Let me do this for you. I want to do this."

Trev bit his lip, his face an open book for once—the torn thoughts racing inside his brain were plainly written across his face.

"Please let me." Cody licked the tip of his cock again. "I need this." He kissed the head and circled the rim of the dick with his tongue. Like the man was his personal piece of candy Cody sucked that flared head into his mouth and savoured the feel before it fell from his lips. "I want this." Cody's hand twisted slightly as he fisted the heavy length. He kissed the tip as his hand met his lips. A guttural sound left Trev's lips. "Let me make you feel good."

Trev's eyes squeezed shut, his whole body trembling, and Cody instinctively knew Trev was trying to rein himself back in. He wanted none of that perfectly put-together man right now. No, he wanted the beast hiding under the sheep's clothing to come out and play. Before he could do anything further to convince Trev this was a good idea, Trev jerked away from his hold off to the side and yanked his shorts back into place. He backed away from Cody, who was still on his knees.

Trev's cheeks were flushed, his eyes still held the passion of a few moments ago, but his words were cold as ice water.

"I said I can't. I have my reasons. Maybe it would be best if you found a new place to live sooner rather than later." Trev marched out the door and didn't look back.

A wave of humiliation flooded Cody's body. His body trembled as he pulled himself upright. Cody rubbed at the pain in his chest, he couldn't understand why this man affected him so, but his heart hurt.

He wouldn't throw himself at Trev again. He deserved better than to be treated like last week's garbage. It was time Trev saw that.

Chapter 12

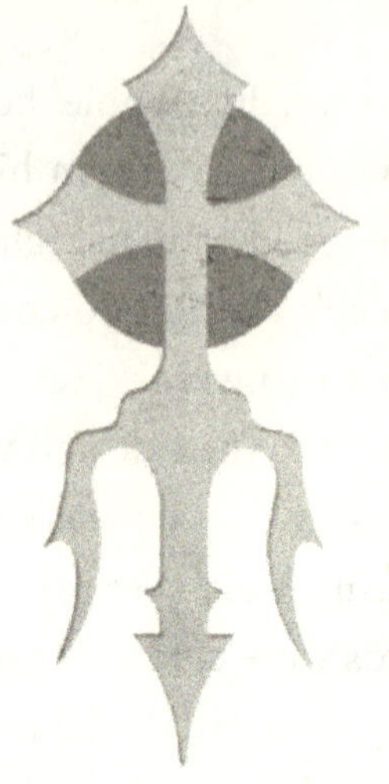

Trev ran like a coward from Cody, and the feelings he was dragging to the surface from the dark depths of his soul. He'd buried his emotions along with the hopes and dreams of a real future with someone deep down. That was where he wanted this shit to remain. Why couldn't Cody accept that? Why couldn't he have stayed away and left this ridiculous notion of something happening between them alone?

As he neared the kitchen, the distinct sounds of J.J.'s laughter and his brother's voice could be heard. He had no interest in running into the other members of his family and veered off his original destination to race up the stairs. His heart hammered in his chest faster than it had at any other time in his life. What the hell had Cody been thinking?

Trev didn't have to look to know that he still had a raging hard-on. The painful throbbing while it smacked him in the stomach with each step, that was enough. In his haste, he missed the handle to his room and turned, fully colliding hard with the door. He stumbled back and barely caught himself before he ended up on his ass.

"Shit." He rubbed at his nose, which took the brunt of the assault. He glared at the door like it was the door's fault for his own stupidity. Gripping the handle tightly, he twisted it again, and as soon as he stepped through, he slammed the door back in place.

Trev paced the floor, his rage not helping to ease the aching need that Cody had stirred. It wasn't just the unnerving passion that had come alive. Like a once snuffed-out wick in a lantern, hope for something real was burning—real feelings, real love, anything other than his dedication to work. He closed his eyes as he took a few deep breaths. He couldn't stop his pulse from pounding hard, making him feel lightheaded. The room began to swim like he'd been on a three-day binge, and he collapsed to his knees. Grabbing his head, he fought the images that wanted to break loose.

"No, no, no."

Boom.

Trev flew backward and landed hard, his helmet smacking against the hard ground. Dirt raining to the earth pelted him in the face, and he slowly rolled to his side. He coughed as he tried to piece together what had just happened, his mind feeling like a dish of his mother's scrambled eggs.

His ears rang, but he could make out yelling as he laid on his back dazed. Wiping his face, he stared between the two sets of truck tires on either side of him at the running booted feet. The dirt and smoke making it hard to see as he blinked it away. His mind raced as it pulled the pieces together like a puzzle. Flipping over on his stomach, he got on his hands and knees. He shook his head, trying to clear the last of the fog, but the fuzziness in his mind was stubborn. What happened? He patted down his body and didn't find any immediate signs of injury. All parts moved, and nothing seemed to be missing. A smile flashed before his eyes.

"No," Trev screamed as his brain showed him what it had been reluctantly holding back.

The rancid scent of burning flesh filled his nose until it was all he could smell. His eyes burned with the smoke as he jumped to his feet and ran.

He crashed into the side of the large truck, unsteady on his feet, but didn't care as he bounced off and continued running.

He didn't know who was yelling but wished that they would shut up, then realized as he began coughing uncontrollably that it was his own voice in his ears. Someone was pulling on his pack, but he dropped to his knees, his fingers digging into the course dirt as he crawled and fought off whoever had a hold of him. His mind did not want to register what he'd seen. There was a chance, there had to be a chance. The scorched earth and deep recess in the road told another story. Blood and bits of human flesh scattered across the beige-colored surface like a smattering of paint from hell.

"No, no, no."

"Trev, stop."

Trev continued to pull on whoever had him. "Let me go."

Arms wrapped around his shoulder, trapping his arms to his side as he turned to take a swing at his unknown assailant.

"Stop it. It's me. It's Arek. It's your brother, and you're in your bedroom, in California. You're safe, Trev. Listen to me, stop struggling," Arek's voice broke through the memory, pulling him back into the now. His body shook, sweat trickling down his back as the remnants of the memory began to fade and drift back into the sea of his subconscious

Arek let him go when he stopped fighting, but he turned in his brother's arms and let the emotions loose. Trev cried as he had that day. Tears slipped down his cheeks in streams as the pain of his past made an unexpected appearance. He gasped for air as he clung to his lifeline. The only thing keeping him from completely breaking was his brother's arms.

"It felt so real, like I was back there, like..." Trev couldn't complete the sentence

"It's okay. You're okay."

Glancing up, Renee and J.J. were in the doorway, and Trev couldn't stand the look of pity in their eyes. Even at such a young age, J.J. understood just how fucking messed up he was, oddly the kid probably understood him better than anyone else in the room.

Pulling away from Arek, he stood and marched for the bathroom door, locking himself inside. Stepping into the bathtub, he flopped down.

"Trev, don't lock me out. Trev, open up," Arek called out, but he couldn't look his brother in the eye.

He needed to pull himself together. He had a mission to complete.

"Trev."

"Go away, Arek. I need to be alone."

"I'm not leaving you. I won't leave you."

"I need you to go. I'm fine. I just need a moment alone." He could hear the heavy sigh and knew that Arek had to have his face pressed to the door.

"Fine."

He'd had small flashes and memories from his time before, but nothing like what just happened. Trev held up his hands, and they shook with the lasting effects. Closing his hands into fists, he clung to his anger. His mind turned to Alejandro. That was his mission. That was what he needed to focus on, and having an episode or whatever the hell that was just wouldn't do. Standing, he turned on the water, not caring his clothes were still on. He needed to get his head back into the game. He just had to.

Chapter 13

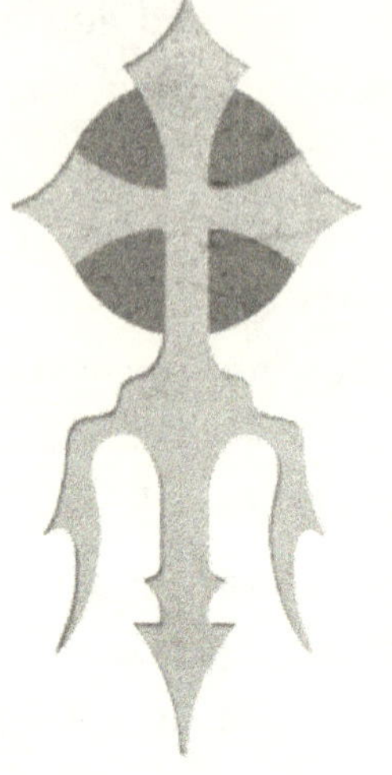

Trev stepped out of the massive courthouse front doors and smiled for the cameras that were already assembled. The large group of awaiting reporters looked like a pack of hyenas waiting to pounce.

He'd successfully gotten another one of his clients off the hook for a charge that should've sent him to prison for life. Not that he was surprised, there was a reason he was paid so handsomely. If there were even a sliver of doubt in the prosecutor's case, he'd find it, and he'd exploit it.

It had been over a week since the episodes with Cody and then with his brother. He'd made a point of avoiding the house and those in it by staying at the penthouse he owned in the city. He put every ounce of energy he had into this case and his quest to get dirt to lure in Alejandro. He wanted the man to trust him enough to give him information on the Golden Dragons. If Alejandro happened to kill off the Dragons, he wouldn't complain about that either. Either option was a win-win. It was completely infuriating that his efforts the night Cody had randomly shown up had seen no results. Millions in drugs and cash had been stolen, eight men dead, and they hadn't retaliated with any of the other gangs at all. In fact, it had been too quiet, eerily quiet.

"Good afternoon, everyone. Thank you for coming. As I stated at the beginning of this trial, my client is innocent," He paused for effect, the only sound that of the gentle breeze as those assembled hung on his every word. "The verdict today should set everyone's mind at ease that Mr. Oliden was wrongfully accused. Mr. Oliden would like to say a few words." Trev stepped aside, and as his client began to speak, he slipped away toward his car. He had no interest in a celebratory dinner with this piece of human garbage that had drugged and raped numerous teens. Their only mistake had been working for him and trusting him.

He looked over his shoulder at the man in question, and a small smile lifted the corner of his mouth into a smirk. Unfortunately for Mr. Oliden, his life was going to be cut short by a tragic accident, but not until he received his final payment. Rule number ten, don't kill off the client before you get your money. He really should move that one up in the order of rules.

"Mr. Anderson?" Trev turned at the sound of Sally's voice.

"Sally, what's wrong?" he asked. In all the time Sally had worked for him, she only ever came to the courthouse if he called her. She patted at her normally neat hair that was coming undone from the bun on her head. As he made the final step to the sidewalk, he could easily see that her eyes were puffy, like she'd been crying. She dabbed at her nose, and he grabbed her shoulders before pulling her into a hug.

"I'm so sorry," she mumbled between the sniffling. "I didn't do it, but I..." Sally took a small step back and removed her glasses to wipe at her eyes.

"What didn't you do?"

"I had this man come to my home a week ago and offer me money for information on you. I told him to go to hell, but when I tried to close the door, he pushed his way into my apartment. I wanted to talk to you all week, but you never came back to the house and—." Sally paused and looked around. He instinctively did as well, his eyes scanning over every pair of eyes that were standing, walking, or driving by. Even those drinking a hot beverage in the coffee shop across the road were not spared his scrutiny.

"Come on, let's get in my car." He wrapped his arm around her shoulders and led her to the Bentley. Once inside, he started the engine and got the air conditioning going before turning to look at her. "Okay, what did this person do, Sally?"

She covered her mouth and shook her head. Reaching into her purse, she pulled out a memory stick and held it out to him.

"I'm so sorry. I almost handed this over." He picked it up out of her hand, and Sally broke down again. The dark that had settled in his soul poked its head up.

There was one thing you didn't do, and that was to threaten those he loved. Sally was a good person who'd already lived through more than her fair share. He thought of her as family, and someone had made her cry, for that they would pay.

"He didn't hurt me, but he promised to do terrible things to me if I didn't do what he said. I didn't believe him at first, but then I found a dead cat on my doorstep yesterday morning." She covered her mouth. "The poor thing had its throat slit, and there was blood everywhere. Luckily, I found it before the kids next door would've been heading for school." Her voice hitched as she paused. "Then this morning, a man followed me from home to work. He followed me to your house. If I'd been smart, I would've had him follow me right to a police station, but I was scared and just wanted to get to you. He didn't say anything and didn't approach me, but..." She looked down at her hands as she played with the tissue in her hands. "I decided to meet you here. It's off my normal schedule, so I didn't see him when I snuck out of the house."

Arek held up the silver stick. "What's on this, Sally?"

Her lower lip trembled. "He wanted personal information. Financial records, who you are close to, what you used to do for a living." Sally turned and looked him in the eye. "I found a file on our shared drive. I'm sorry I shouldn't have looked. I've never snooped before."

She didn't have to say which one. He knew exactly which folder she was referring to—that file could ruin both Arek and himself. He thought he'd hidden it well among the hundreds of layers in that drive, but apparently, he should leave that sort of thing to Delilah from now on. He reached out his hand and laid his on hers. "It's okay, Sally. The fact you came to me and didn't hand this over tells me all I need to know about your loyalties. I'm a little surprised, though. I thought you might decide to take this to the authorities."

He thought she was going to give her head a concussion with how quickly she shook it back and forth. "Trevor, you are the only reason I have a home, that I could finish my treatments, that..." Tears flowed over her weathered cheeks. "You are the closest thing I have to a son."

Reaching out, he laid his hand on her much cooler one, the bones still too prominent under her skin, if you asked him. "Do you know who threatened you?"

"No," she shook her head again. "But, he had a tattoo on his hand. It was fancy letters with a skull, but I couldn't make out the letters."

"The Streetlores," Trev mumbled. Alejandro was playing games. He didn't think the man would be this impatient. It hadn't been that long since he agreed to his offer. He rubbed at his chin as he thought. Whatever the reason, this was a game that was going to get Alejandro killed sooner than Trev planned. "I'm going to drive you home, and you're going to pack and come stay with me."

"I can't do that, Trevor. You've already done so much for me. That is too generous, and you have so many already staying with you."

"Nonsense, you are part of my family, Sally, and I know how much everyone loves you. They will be happy to have you around." Releasing her hand, he started the Bentley. "I can count on one hand the number of people I would trust with the information on that stick, and you happen to be one of them. There is no more negotiating. You will pack what you need, and you will stay with me until the threat has been neutralized."

Sally placed her hand on his arm. "What do you plan on doing?"

He gave her what he hoped was a comforting smile. "Don't you worry about that."

Pulling away from the curb, he instantly began forming his plan. His foot pressed down on the gas, the sound of the car revving expressing exactly how he felt.

No one came after his own, no one.

Chapter 14

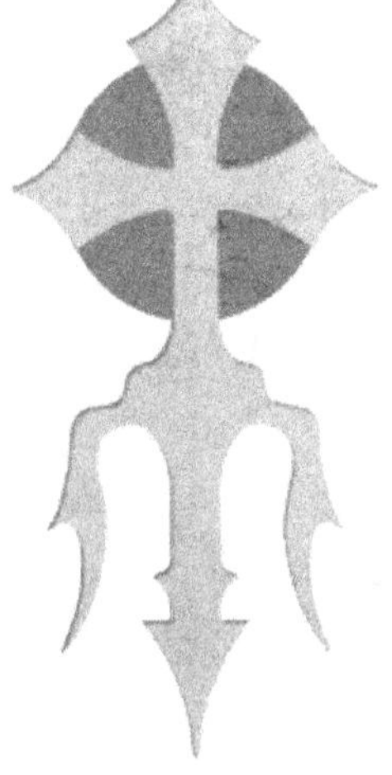

Cody stuffed the last of his items in the large duffels he'd brought with him. He looked around the room one last time, making sure he hadn't forgotten anything—not that he had much, to begin with. When he lived with Tyson, he was constantly on the move—he never put down roots. He figured he'd see about crashing on Ray's couch for now and then formulate a plan to get back on his feet.

"Where are you going?" Arek asked.

Cody started and jumped to glare at Arek. Both of these fucking brothers needed a damn bell. They were way too quiet, annoyingly so. Did they have a, *learn to be a fucking ninja day,* in S.E.A.L. camp? He envisioned them having to tiptoe across bubble wrap without making a sound.

"I'm moving out," he said, stating the obvious.

Arek's eyebrow cocked upwards as he leaned casually against the door frame. He wanted to wipe the look right off his face. It was too similar to the look Trev would give him. He zipped the duffel and then crossed his arms over his chest.

"I will assume this has something to do with Trev since I don't think Renee or I have offended you. Although those farts J.J. was sporting at lunch could offend anyone."

Cody smirked. He couldn't help but smile. "True dat. What the hell do you feed that kid?"

"Don't look at me. I'd let him eat junk, but he insists on eating like Trev and only wants healthy food. I keep telling Trev that shit is bad for you. Trev's just a bad influence, I mean, what kid wants to eat spinach omelets for breakfast anyway?" Arek pushed off the wall and came into the room. "Tell me, what did Trev do?"

Cody sucked in a breath. He didn't want to share the intimate moment that crashed and burned like a runaway train nor the fact that Trev had been avoiding him ever since. "It's just not going to work with me living here. Trev…I don't know how to describe it, and I don't really want to get into the specifics."

"Did you make a pass at him?" Arek was blunt, and he wasn't expecting the direct question.

Cody flushed, heat spread throughout his body as the image from that dreadful morning re-entered his mind. He didn't know what to say, so he kept his mouth clamped shut.

"It's okay. You don't have to tell me. Look, I know my brother can be cold and difficult at times."

"At times? Tell me that's a joke. The man is a stone-cold wall of zero fucking emotion. I've gotten a better reaction from a bag of ice cubes." Cody stomped away and stared out the window. "Maybe it's my fault. I thought I was getting the vibe. You know when someone is interested." He lifted his shoulder and let it drop. "But maybe I was only seeing what I wanted to see. He was my lawyer and we were spending a lot of time together, I could have simply read the situation wrong."

The pool looked stunning tonight. The aqua blue glittered as the light from the tiki lanterns danced on the surface. "The thing is, I coulda' sworn we had this connection, but I guess I was wrong. He's been straight up avoiding me after he ordered me to find a new place to live."

"First, Trev is not emotionless. In fact, he probably feels more than the rest of us in this house combined."

"Excuse me if I don't believe you."

"The thing is, Trev is complicated. He...look, the point is, the reason Trev is treating you like you mean nothing to him is because he likes you." Arek wandered over and mirrored his position.

"I don't understand."

"It's not really my story to tell, but I will say that Trev was not always like this. I mean, he was always protective and a little stuffy, and sometimes overly proper, but that's off topic. He always has been the better brother, but he wasn't always cold with everyone. He was..." Arek looked away, the muscle in his jaw twitching as he glared out the window. "He was the best. He still is, but this version of him is pain-induced. Do you understand? The man that lives under that cold shell is warm and loving. I know you've seen glimpses of it. Fuck, I love my brother. I would die for him." Arek swung those icy blues at Cody, and the expression said it all. "He is a good person Cody. A hurt one, but he is the best guy I've ever met."

"What happened to him?" Cody asked, a shimmer of hope blooming in his chest. It was stupid to hope, but he couldn't help himself.

"Like I said, it's not my story to tell. He will tell you when he's ready, but you're going to need to be patient. Don't push too hard, or he will back away faster, and definitely don't move out." Arek's eyes locked with his, and there was a pleading in them that he didn't understand.

"Trev told me to leave, and this is his house."

"Technically, it is both Trev's and my house, and I'm asking you to stay. Trust me, Trev doesn't mean it. He may have said it, he may even be avoiding you, but at the moment, he is also avoiding me." Arek took a deep breath and sighed, the sound coming out defeated. "What he said was a knee-jerk reaction, but he wants you here, and he does like you. I haven't seen my brother so tied up over someone in a very long time."

"This is him tied up over someone? I'd hate to see what he gets like when he hates someone then."

"No, actually, you really don't. It never ends well." Cody didn't know if Arek was joking, but since he didn't laugh, he had to assume he was serious. "All I'm asking is for you to give him a chance to come around. He needs someone willing to be patient with his demons."

"We all have demons, Arek. It doesn't give Trev the right to treat me like shit. He is not just icy—he's rude."

"You're right, and I can't excuse his actions. Just think about it." Arek gripped his shoulder before he made his way across the room.

"Arek?"

"Yeah?"

"Thanks."

"You're welcome." Arek gave him a smile, and it was the first time he felt a real connection to the guy.

"Did you want to come to the Underground with me?" Cody tossed out. He never took anyone to the Underground, but if he was going to bridge a gap, this just might help.

"What is the Underground?" Arek cocked his head.

"Fuck yeah, an Underground virgin. Now you have to come with me." Cody smiled as he marched toward Arek.

"By the look on your face, you're gonna get me divorced before I'm married, I can feel it." They both laughed.

"Renee may kill you if you get arrested, but don't worry, we won't." He smiled wide at the confused look on Arek's face.

He would stay for now, how much longer still needed to be seen, but Arek had said enough to make him swing one more time from the thin thread of hope.

Chapter 15

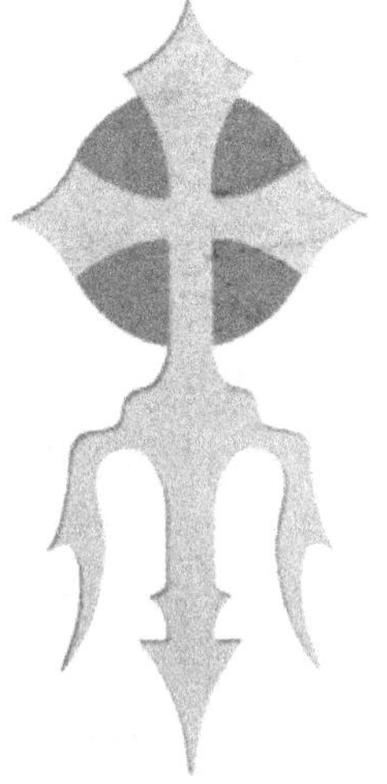

"Fuck," Arek hollered as he gripped the holy-shit handle and leaned into the door. Cody's car streaked around the final bend, the wheels screeching as they slid sideways. They came close enough to a telephone pole that he could read the small print on one of the labels but didn't give a shit. The mustang was hot on their ass. Arek looked behind at the guy and then at Cody. The guy was tough as nails, no flinch nor flicker of worry as they entered the final stretch. Cody smoothly shifted the car back up, and the small sporty car had him smacking his head back into the seat. He'd never guess this thing had this kind of speed. The mustang made a final move to pass, but it was too late as they flew across the finish line a car length ahead of their competitor.

"Hell, yeah," Cody yelled as he let off the gas. He drummed his hands on the top of his steering wheel excitedly. "Man, I missed this."

"How come I did not know about this place?" Arek smiled as Cody laughed and slowed to turn around and claim his prize.

"I don't know, man. Maybe you just weren't cool enough to get an invite," Cody teased.

"Dick."

Cars angled along the strip of road that was still within city limits but in a remote part of town. Men and women alike stood around talking or polishing their cars as they got ready to race or just admired the show. Arek couldn't get enough of the eye candy. Everywhere you looked, there was another sexy car. Everything, from new and sporty to muscle cars, was present. He'd even watched a pair of low-riding pick-up trucks go head-to-head. Each of these beautiful creatures was unique and glittered under the streetlights. They slid into an opening not far from the starting line, and Cody cut the engine.

"Could you see Trev's Bentley down here? It would be like the butler showed up for a rave party."

"Fuck, I'd pay money to see the look on all their faces. We shouldn't knock it. I bet that pretty little bitch would do well out here," Cody said.

"Are you still talking about the car or the man that drives it?"

"Shut up." Cody's body flushed with heat as he looked away from Arek's teasing face.

Arek pushed open the car door laughing and then leaned against the car to watch the countdown of the next pair of cars to line up. The air was filled with the strong scent of gasoline and burnt tires. He could sit and breathe that smell in all day.

"I shouldn't be here, man. You are officially a terrible influence. Renee is going to kill me if I get killed racing a car. Even dead, that woman would find a way to beat my ass."

"Ha, try us. She will string me up if I get caught out here. It's like swinging something red in front of a bull. She's never approved of me racing, said it was too dangerous and a waste of my time."

Arek laughed hard. He could picture his woman yelling at her older brother. She was not one to hold back her opinions, and he had to admit that her yelling got him hard.

They wandered over to the cherry red car they'd raced, and Arek cocked his eyebrow at the guy hugging it. "I'm so sorry, baby. I'm so sorry. I'll win you back, I promise." He screwed up his face as the guy kissed the roof of his car. He was pretty sure he saw a bit of tongue.

"Alright, that's enough molesting my car. Keys, man." Cody held out his hand for the decked-out Mustang. Arek had to admit it was a damn sweet ride. The only thing he'd change was the color. Black was more his taste.

"There is no way that little piece of shit beat my baby." The guy whined, his fist tightly clenching the keys in his hand. "What did you do to my car?"

"Yo, bro, don't be talking shit. I didn't touch your cherry virgin bitch before the race." Cody took a small step toward the smaller man. "But I sure as hell plan on touching her lots now. Keys now, or I tell Spike you played for pink and didn't hand it over. You'll never race in L.A. again, that is if you manage to walk away from the beat-down, I'll give you." Cody cracked his knuckles. "Don't forget who I am."

The guy looked like he was going to argue, but he gave Cody a once over before turning to look at the guy, Spike, that Cody mentioned. The man with the low cut mohawk in a soft blue was standing not too far off, and even though he wasn't staring, Arek knew the guy was watching. He got the feeling Spike didn't miss much with the way his eyes glanced around, his arms crossed over his chest as he directed the show. There was an aura around Spike that Arek recognized. It screamed he didn't take shit from anyone. This bi-weekly race was his show, and according to Cody, he ran a very tight ship. No bringing outside beef to the race, no physical fighting, no going back on bets, and absolutely no weapons allowed.

The guy Arek didn't know the name of, looked over his shoulder at his car and sighed. A strange gut retching noise of pain left his throat as he held out the keyring with the miniature version of the car dangling off the end.

"It's been a pleasure." Cody smiled wide and stuck his head in his new car. "What do you think, Arek?"

Arek could hear the guy grumbling as he walked away with a small group of friends. Looking away from the sad show of a grown-ass man crying over a car, he answered Cody, "I think it's fucking sweet."

He wandered over to the passenger side and leaned on the open window to stare inside. This wouldn't have been his first choice in car, but he could appreciate what this car had to offer.

"Honestly, I still can't believe you won. No offense, man, but you don't seem like the street racing type."

He made to open the passenger side of the car to get in, but Cody gave him a classic, what the fuck are you doing look.

"You do know you're driving this girl home, right? Second, there is a lot of shit you don't know about me yet."

Arek laughed as Cody tossed him the keys. "When did you start racing?"

Cody shrugged. "I don't really remember. I used to hang out wherever I could find races before I could even drive. It seemed like the next logical step once I could."

The cars and cheering got loud as the racers made their way toward them. Arek's hair blew around his eyes, and the mustang shook as the cars passed where they were parked. A rush of adrenaline filled him as he contemplated racing a round himself. He could do it. He was a fucking good driver.

Arek opened his mouth to ask another question when his phone began beeping wildly. He pulled the cell from his pocket, and his heart sank. His Sweet Delilah was sending out a distress call. Trev was in trouble.

"Shit, Trev's in trouble. I need to go." Arek slipped behind the wheel of the Mustang and revved her to life.

"I'm coming with you. Don't say no—I know how to handle myself."

"Fine, get your car and follow me." Arek hit the code on his phone and dialed into the AI.

"Sweet Delilah, status?"

The tech was designed only to send out a distress signal if life systems dropped significantly. That alarm was one he prayed he'd never hear.

Peeling away from the race area, Arek sped away, smoke rising as the wheels squealed on the muscle car.

"All communication with Crosshairs has been disconnected," came the response. Arek gripped the steering wheel tight as he continued to fly down the road.

Hang on, Trev. Hang on.

Chapter 16

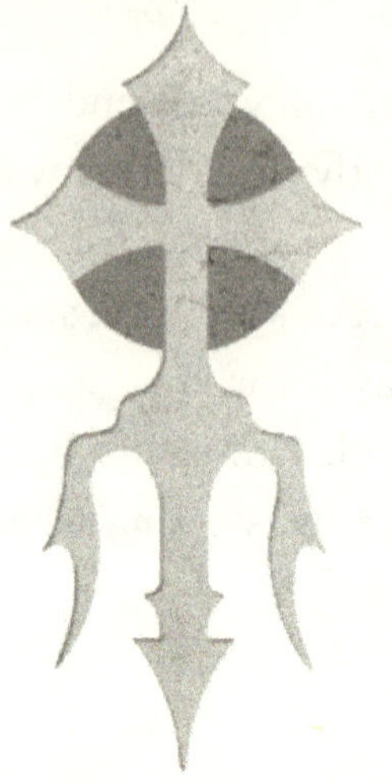

Trev coughed, his mouth filled with blood from the impact of the hit. His jaw had gone numb a few hits ago, and he was pretty sure his jaw was partially broken now, not that it mattered. He wasn't giving up any information.

He spat the blood onto the ground and groaned as the movement sent a sharp pain racing up the side of his head. His head was pounding, and his vision was constantly slipping in and out. He reasoned that he had a concussion, and by the way the room had suddenly become fuzzy around the edges, there was more than that to worry about. That last hit rattled the teeth in his head and rocked his head back enough to see stars. The grey roof literally sparkled. Relatively speaking, that was not the hardest hit he'd ever received, but this was definitely the most compromising position he'd ever found himself in.

Alejandro had large guards standing around in the shadows of the warehouse, each one glowering as they watched on, but the guy didn't need the muscle. Trev glanced up at the chains and shackles that were digging painfully into his wrists. Blood was trailing down his arms in thin rivers. It was all a very real reminder he wasn't getting out of this one alive. By the time Delilah signaled Arek, it would take him too long to arrive from the house. He wanted to kick his own ass—he had no one to blame but himself. He came in like Rambo without a good plan, a rookie mistake, and he was no rookie.

"I'll ask you again, who the hell are you?" Alejandro asked. The man had peeled off the dress shirt he'd been wearing long ago, and the scars lining Alejandro's back were a vivid visual of just how many people he'd dug graves for. "FBI, maybe? Or how about the CIA? You don't have an accent, but you could be MI-6. You have to be one of those fucking acronyms." He began swearing in Spanish and then switched to Portuguese.

Trev understood every word but simply stared at the floor like he was never the wiser.

"You know who I am," Trev repeated the same answer. "But, if I was one of those organizations, I'm not sure killing one of their agents is the best way to make friends. There are a few books I could recommend on making friends if you like?"

Alejandro spun around a long blade gripped tightly in his fist. "You think you're funny, do you? Tell me, Mr. Defence Attorney, is night vision standard attire these days for the courtroom?"

"Just doing some poaching." Trev fixed the man with as much of a smile as he could muster.

"In L.A.? In a warehouse? And where is this infamous buck that is not even native to this area?" Alejandro held his hands out and turned in a circle. All the while, a deadly-looking blade spun in his hand like a carnival toy.

"I chased the buck in here. What can I say? They are smart. The bugger ran back out before I could get him. Sorry about your men though, I'm apparently a terrible shot."

Alejandro laughed as he tapped the blade against the palm of his hand. “Yes, marksman shots between the eyes are how I would describe a terrible shot too. You know, I still like you, but you see that alone is a red flag for me, because other than my daughter, I don’t like anyone.”

Alejandro walked over to a table and came back with a tablet. A few taps later, he turned the image so he could see that there had been a camera in the drug room that Delilah had missed. Probably only had an internal feed, rookie mistake. He really was out of practice. He watched as he ran into the room, finished stuffing the mostly packed bags, and ran back out. The image was dark, and he had his hat pulled low, but this explained why there’d been no retaliation.

“You see, Mr. Anderson, I know that is you. You are probably going to say that a buck ran in there too or that you have a look alike.” He tapped the screen to stop the video from repeating.

Trev wanted to laugh, even the truth Alejandro wouldn’t believe at this point. “I actually do have a twin, but would denying it help my cause?”

The tablet thumped as it was set back down, the blade in Alejandro’s hand tapped against the metal of the table. Like a horror movie monster, he turned and faced Trev. A look of malice shining from his dark eyes.

“Even if I ignored everything else, including this video, that first meeting prickled in my mind. You were too calm back then, for being surrounded by my men armed to the teeth, and you are too calm now.” Alejandro stepped forward and shook his head from side to side. “The fact that you can look at me with humor in your eyes tells me you’re not who you say you are.”

“Oh yeah? Why is that?” Trev turned his head slightly to keep his eye on Alejandro as he stalked him. He shivered as the tip of the blade touched his skin, and the sound of skin scraping away was loud in his ears even though the touch was light. The dizziness was worsening from the number of times this man decided to walk around him.

Alejandro reminded him of the movie Predator, the fierce look in his eye, the intelligence shining through. He couldn't stop the Arnold Schwarzenegger lines racing through his head.

Maybe like the movie this man was planning on eating him. The hunger for the meal of pain told him he was going to endure a lot more of it before he got to die. He'd become the goat for the T-Rex. He always knew his luck would run out—he just didn't think it would be this soon.

Alejandro stopped in front of him, his eyes piercing as he got right up into his face.

"Because you're not afraid to die. You're a man that has been very close to death, has smelt it." He leaned forward and sniffed Trev's shirt. "You've tasted it." Alejandro ran the blade across his tongue, a thin line of red showing as he stuck his tongue out and then moaned as he swallowed the blood down.

"You have stared into the eyes of Nuestra Senora de la Santa Muerte and have lived to tell the tale." Alejandro used the tip of the knife once more to draw lines down Trev's chest with the blade. The sharp tip was drawing a tiny bit of blood as he drew a symbol that Trev couldn't make out. There was a sharp bit of pain, but he was delayed in feeling it, like his nerves were late to the party.

"We are kindred spirits. I see you, Mr. Anderson, and you may, in fact, be a lawyer, a great one even, but you're also guardian de la muerte."

"My Spanish is a little rusty. Did you just call me a guardian of the universe?" The now bright, red metal knuckles once more collided with his face and was followed through with a sharp pain to his side. He stiffened and bit his lip hard as Alejandro pushed the blade deeper into his body. Blood poured down his side, the heat a stark contrast to his chilled skin. Alejandro pulled the blade quickly from his side, and he slumped against the chains. He glanced down at the seemingly harmless narrow line but knew that wound was deep. Probably hit a kidney or worse.

"See, this is what I mean. You don't even scream. What fun is there in no screaming, right boys?" Alejandro rubbed at his goatee. "I guess I will have to try harder then."

The room narrowed in for a few seconds, the sounds seemingly far away. It was the loss of blood and he knew it was only going to get worse. He'd suffered a bullet wound in his leg that was still bleeding, and it added with the wound in his side. He was going to struggle to stay conscious. Then again, maybe it was better if he passed out for what was to come. The soldier in him screamed no that he had to fight, he had to find his opening and never give up. That voice had been a chant that saved his life once, but could that chant work again?

"You really need to work on your hospitality," Trev slurred.

Alejandro picked up two wires, and Trev swore in his head. He hated being electrocuted. He would have preferred just about anything else. Pull out his nails, break his bones, stab him again for all he cared. Fuck, shoot him in the head and get it over with, but electricity…that shit just sucked.

"Do you know what this is?"

"I don't know. You planning on boosting a car?"

Alejandro gave a small laugh. "I will give you one last chance to tell me who you are, who you work for, and where you put my missing product? If you speak now, I will kill you quickly. If you don't…I'm sure you can figure out the rest."

Trev stared into the eyes of the man that was going to take his life, and there were only two things he wanted—to tell his brother how proud he was of him and to see his niece or nephew born. Actually, three things, because if he could, he'd go back in time and he would take Cody to his bedroom and fuck him the way he wanted to.

"My name is Trevor Anderson. I'm a defense attorney and was out for a nightly hunt, but shhh, don't tell the cops," Trev managed, and then Alejandro's face became distorted as blood dripped into his eye.

"It's a shame you tried to screw me over. I could use men like you in my family. Your resilience is admirable, your skill impeccable, but it's also going to make this a lot more enjoyable." Alejandro stuck the patches to his skin.

His skin was almost completely numb now, but he still shivered as the patches were applied to his body. "My name is Inigo Montoya, and you are the six-fingered man. You killed my father, prepare to die," Trev mumbled.

Alejandro paused in what he was doing. "What the fuck does that mean?" Alejandro barked out. "Is it code?"

"I'm pretty sure that is from the movie Princess Bride, sir." Trev heard one of the guards say, and he smirked. If he was going to die, he might as well have a little fun.

"You're a comedian now. Let's see how funny you are after this. Hit him," Alejandro clapped his hands as Trev's body went rigid and shook violently against the restraints. He couldn't breathe, couldn't blink, and he was pretty sure he just shit his pants. The current stopped, and he slumped, panting hard.

"How did you like that, Mr. Anderson?"

"Death is a day worth living for," he said, his voice shaking, but he couldn't stop himself.

Alejandro narrowed his eyes into slits, his lips peeling back from his unnaturally white teeth.

"That one was from Pirates of the Caribbean," the guard yelled, and Alejandro shot him a glare.

"Your men may be crap shots, but they know their movies," he wheezed, his chest burning.

"Hit him again and up the level."

He sucked in a breath just before the power hit, and he jerked violently in the chains like a fish out of water. The bravado was erased as the excruciating white-hot pain ripped through his body. He could feel liquid dripping from his ears and nose, and it felt like his heart was going to burst. The power shut off only long enough for him to get a couple of breaths in, and then they hit him again. This time, as the electrical currents raced through his body, he did scream.

"I love that sound," Alejandro said as he once more slumped in the chains, trying to gasp for air.

"Yes, Satan? Oh, I'm sorry, Sir. You sounded like someone else," he panted out.

"That one was..."

"Shut the fuck up," Alejandro spun to yell at his guard, his voice echoing off the walls. "I fucking know that was Ace Venture."

As Alejandro turned to face him, he laughed hard even though his entire body hollered in agonizing pain as he did so. Lifting his head enough to stare into his death. He smiled wide like a mother-fucker. "Do your worst. I live for death's embrace."

Like an enraged bull, Alejandro closed the distance, and once more, that blade sank deep. Trev closed his eyes and bit back the whimper.

I'm sorry, Arek.

Chapter 17

Cody wheeled into the vacant area behind Arek and jumped out to meet him at the Hummer. On any other occasion, he wouldn't have left his baby anywhere near this area or alone in an alley, but this was an extenuating circumstance.

"Why are we here?" Cody looked around at the empty street of the old industrial section that was mostly boarded up.

"Our target is a couple of roads over. Trev parked here to keep from being seen driving in. Sweet Delilah, override lockdown, password Echo Charlie Romeo Alpha Kelo Foxtrot."

"Override disabled, good evening, Sandman."

"Holy fuck me sideways, is that the Hummer talking to you?"

"High tech AI, you never saw this." Arek glared at him.

Cody held up his hands and nodded yet couldn't help feeling like a kid in a toy store as he stared at the beautiful black vehicle with all new eyes. "I need to get me one of these."

"Here, put this on." Arek held out a bulletproof vest and helmet. "Sweet Delilah, I need schematics of the building, and get me a number of unfriendlies."

"Oh, this is sick. If Trev weren't in danger, I'd be all fanboy right now." Cody pulled the vest on over his head and fastened the Velcro straps. "Fuck that, I'm still fanboying. This shit is cool."

As soon as he put on the helmet, he gasped in awe. The little piece over his left eye was scrolling information. He was able to read a complete rundown of the entire op up to their arrival. There was even a short video of Trev killing off Alejandro's men. His heart sank as Trev was hit in the leg and collapsed to the floor before it all went dark.

"Twelve unfriendly heat signatures remain. Their locations are mapped," Delilah said.

"Only twelve?" Arek asked.

"The other fifteen Crosshairs already disposed of."

"Crosshairs?" Cody asked, his eyes going wide as Arek handed him a large blade.

"That's Trev's code name."

"Fuck, I want a code name." Arek glared at him, and he quickly shut his mouth.

"Sweet Delilah, are all electronic devices in a mile radius blocked?"

"Yes, Sandman."

"Good, then hack the power grid, and be on standby to shut the building down."

Cody's mouth fell open. This was not even possible, was it? To hack the city's power grid was sci-fi shit.

Arek stripped to replace his jeans with black fatigues and a matching t-shirt, complete with leather straps, fitting in knives and guns that he couldn't even name. Cody took the opportunity to look around. This was an area he'd only ever driven by once or twice.

"Here." Arek held out two guns and a handful of clips from the back seat. Strapping the first one into the leg strap, he checked the second and stuffed the extra clips into the pockets on the vest. No wonder the cops wanted to become S.W.A.T. He felt more badass than he ever had before as Ice Man.

Arek swung a large sniper rifle over his head to fit against his back before checking the chambers of the handguns.

"Resume lockdown. Codeword: Fuck me sideways," Arek closed the door and gave him a smile.

"Codeword established."

"Alight, let's go. You do as I say and don't go all cowboy on me. I don't need to make this a two-person rescue. Besides, your sister is definitely going to kill me if I get you killed."

"I make my own decisions but understood."

"You're not the one that has to go home to her and sleep in the same bed."

"You have me there."

Cody fell in step with Arek as he picked up a jog and weaved his way through the alleys. All he could hear was his own feet, and no matter how he altered his stride, he couldn't seem to be as stealthy as they slinked through the shadows.

The little red dots slowly moved in the sight, and Cody was once more amazed. This was deadly tech, like total video game come to life kind of crap. Arek held up a fist and signaled to get down, and he instantly obeyed.

Arek pulled the sniper off as he settled on the ground. He watched in fascination as Arek focused in on something Cody couldn't see with the naked eye. Arek began mumbling to himself and he quickly realized he was running through all the particulars he needed to make the shot. His eyes scanned the buildings in the distance, and two shots later, a couple of the dots disappeared. They'd been so bloody far away his mouth fell open in admiration for the sheer skill. Arek rose like a deadly panther from the ground, his face a mask of concentration. Cody swallowed hard. Even though he was aware of how deadly the brothers were, to see it in action was something else altogether.

"We need to keep this fast and quiet," Arek whispered. "There are three men between here and where the main hallway is."

"I see them."

"Good. Your target is the one in the room to the right."

Cody nodded and followed Arek the remaining distance to the building. There was music playing, a loud thumping that was so loud the door was vibrating. Arek pulled on the handle, and the door opened.

"Either the guards are idiots, or they're expecting more to show up, and this is a trap. I'm thinking it's the first, but keep your eyes peeled."

He'd been pushing it down, but now that they were inside the building, he was consumed with Trev's safety. Alejandro was not known for his kindness. He was the one person Tyson refused to fuck over or try to take territory from, which said all there needed to be known.

Arek picked up his pace and disappeared around a corner further down the hall. Cody peered around the partially closed door at the man that was inside. He was sound asleep, slumped over in a chair with a television playing in the corner. He had no idea how this guy was sleeping through the music that was being blasted through the intercom speakers.

Taking a deep breath, he mentally went to the place he had to go to when he killed. He had to become one with death. It was just something that happened. There was no emotion to the kills. Cody took aim and, without any further hesitation, pulled the trigger—he caught the guy in the throat. The man gasped awake, falling to the floor. He held his throat as his mouth opened and closed, but no sound came out. Cody stared into the wide eyes as the man stared back. Blood pooled on the floor like a red river. The shock and fear that had been evident in his eyes began to fade. In the breath of a heartbeat, the man was dead. The part of his soul that allowed him to give a shit learned to take a back seat a long time ago. Cody moved on and followed the green dot to Arek's location.

"What took you so long?" Arek asked harshly. "If you can't keep up, then leave. I can't slow down for you."

"Sorry, I'll be more efficient."

Arek paused a moment, then nodded. "You go that way. I'll go this way. If you need to communicate, press this and speak." Arek pointed to the small button attached to his vest. "The power will be cut on my command. Ready?"

"Ready." Arek jogged off, and even with the heavy boots, Cody never heard a single footfall. He turned to his task when a scream that ripped his heart from his chest pierced his ears and echoed off the walls. Cold fear spread through his body as another scream reached him. He'd know Trev's voice anywhere, and screaming in pain was one thing he never imagined to hear. His hand clutched the gun a little tighter.

"Trev, I'm coming," Cody whispered.

He took off in the direction of his targets. As Arek said, they were plummeted into darkness with a quiet command in his ear, but he was still able to see everyone and everything with the fancy tech.

"What the hell happened? Did we blow a breaker torturing that fucker?" A man said as he stumbled out a door and headed straight in Cody's direction. He was fumbling with his phone and finally managed to get the flashlight turned on. He held it up, and his step faltered as he came to an abrupt halt—the light bathed Cody in its cool white glow. Cody already had the gun pointed at the man's face, the click of the hammer loud in the sudden silence. The man's adam's apple moved visibly as he swallowed. The scent of fear and sweat hit Cody in the face, but it wouldn't affect him, not now, not anymore.

"Please don't…." Cody cut him off. It would only delay the inevitable. He squeezed the trigger, and the shot was true and hit the man between the eyes. He dropped like a stone as he crumpled to the ground. Cody wiped the back of his hand across his face, removing the blood splatter, and he didn't even want to know what else.

Cody barely made it to the door's opening when his next target came running out of the room. He braced himself and took the hit like two colliding bulls. Cody smacked hard into the wall, pushing all the air out of his lungs as the mountain of a man slammed into him. A fist connected with his gut, luckily the vest took most of the assault. Using his foot as leverage, he heaved with all his strength and pushed the much larger man back a few strides. Taking advantage of the man's unbalanced position, he raised the two guns. Pop, pop, the two guns fired at the same time. He looked down at his chest, his hands going to the open bleeding wounds. Hands shaking, he lifted them in front of his face, even though he wouldn't be able to see the blood. Fear-filled eyes lifted to Cody's face, his eyes blindly searching the darkness before dropping to his knees. He kicked away the man's fallen gun and left him to bleed out.

He could hear yelling in the distance, barking out orders echoing down the long corridor. He knew without seeing who it was that it was Alejandro's voice. He'd sat in on too many meetings with that voice to not recognize it.

The hallway he was jogging along was going to open up into a much larger space, which was where Trev was being held based on the little green dot. There was one more guard to take care of, and he stood at the mouth of the entrance. He couldn't see the top of the man's head. He was unbelievably tall, and his shoulders were almost as wide—it was like he was playing a game with Russian nesting dolls in reverse and was working his way from smallest to the biggest mother fucker.

Cody softly stepped closer. One foot in front of the other, he slunk toward the beast of a man. He weighed his options as he drew closer and decided to make this one as quiet as possible, so Trev didn't pay for his actions. He slipped the guns into the back of his jeans and had just started to pull the blade that was on the vest when Alejandro yelled.

"Find the fucking breaker," Alejandro's distinctive voice rang out. "I finally got him to scream, and I want more before he dies. Go now."

The man turned and sprinted straight at him. He had no time to maneuver out of the way or get the knife pulled when he was sent flying backward and landed hard on his ass with the freight train of a collision. The guard stumbled, sending his phone clattering to the floor. The light shone upward, casting a horror movie quality of shadows on the guard's fierce features. The tear tattoos running down his cheeks and thin scars that snaked his thick neck wrote a clear story.

Not wasting another second, Cody jumped up as the man, regaining his senses, pushed off the wall. They circled the cell phone and the small glowing light like two lions getting ready to fight. Their eyes roamed over one another's body, and an evil curl lifted at the corner of the guard's mouth.

"I know you, Ice Man. You're the backstabber that killed Tyson."

That wasn't accurate, it was Arek that had killed Tyson while he was strung up in the corner like a slab of meat, but he wasn't about to correct the guy.

"I have big aspirations," Cody smiled. "Maybe you'd prefer to join me then die?"

The guard rolled up his sleeves, and a large smile spread across his tattooed face. "I'm not the one dying today."

A fist flew at Cody's face forcing him to leap out of the way. The guy came again with a relentless flurry of fists. For such a large man, he sure as hell could move fast. Cody ducked and landed a hard blow to the kidneys and smiled as the man groaned and bowed away from the hit. The guard spun, darted forward a couple of strides, and grabbed Cody by the vest. With a massive force, he was slammed into the wall, his helmet going askew with the impact. Fighting this guy was like trying to wrestle a rhino.

The guard yanked him forward only to slam him against the wall again, all the air forced from his lungs on impact and the helmet clattering to the floor. Clenching his fist tight, he brought it up as hard as he could in an uppercut to catch the man in the jaw with the vicious strike. The guard paused in his attack but didn't release him as he'd hoped.

Another slam against the wall, and Cody was gasping for air. He needed to put distance between them. Cody reached out and slammed his hands against the side of the guard's head, boxing his ears. The man groaned and stumbled back, holding his head as he released the vest—Cody leaned against the wall a moment to catch his breath and clear the stars behind his eyes.

"What the hell was that noise?" Alejandro called out.

Cody couldn't let this man warn Alejandro. He freed the knife from the sheath on his vest and dove at the guard as he was straightening. The guard managed to move at the last moment, and the fatal blow ended up slicing his arm.

"Son of a bitch," the guy hissed and grabbed for the deep wound as blood flew from the wound and landed on the floor.

Cody allowed rage to consume his body as he attacked again, the guard opened his mouth to call out, and he flipped the blade in his hand to backhand it as hard as he could toward the man's throat. The blade was so sharp that even though Cody knew he'd hit his mark, he hadn't felt the impact. Forgetting his wounded arm, the guard grabbed at the gaping wound forming across his throat. Blood flowed freely through his fingers as his mouth opened and closed, but no sound came. The eerie light cast the dying man's shadow on the wall and then flickered as droplets of blood landed on the little light of the fallen phone.

Cody took a step back as the man dropped to his knees. "You should have joined me instead."

Cody grabbed the man's hair, forcing him to look him in the eyes. "No one comes after my family." With a violent and precise strike, the blade sank into the man's open mouth. His arms fell limp, and eyes blank as death took him. He pulled the blade free and kicked the man in the chest. His breathing was hard, his chest rising and falling with the burst of adrenaline. His hand shook as he bent and wiped the blade off on the man before returning it to its home and retrieving his helmet. The little lens had a wave behind the partial crack, but it was still working. He could see the red dot of Alejandro pacing a small line.

Straightening, he turned toward the entrance. Nothing and no one was stopping him from saving Trev.

Chapter 18

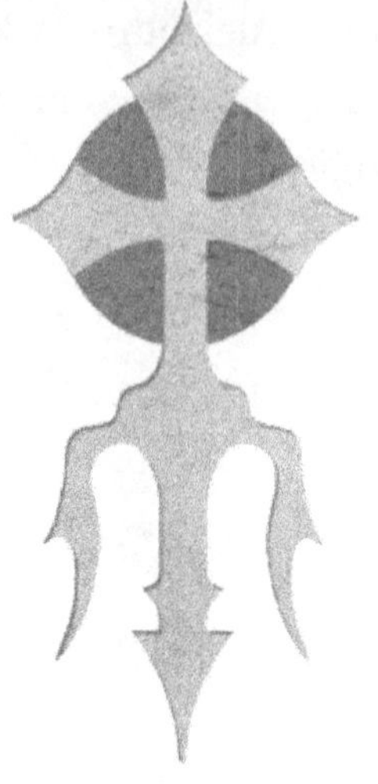

Cody palmed the handles of the guns as his long strides ate up the distance to the entrance, but he faltered as Arek's voice startled him.

"Hold your position." Arek's earpiece crackled, halting him mid-stride.

"What are we waiting for?" he whispered. The anger seeped into his voice as his mind screamed to keep going.

"I said hold your position." Cody ground his teeth together as Alejandro yelled for his guards. They were wasting time. What the hell was Arek doing? "Lights will come back on, on my command. Get Alejandro to face you, and if at all possible, to step around Trev."

Cody could hear Arek softly counting, and as soon as he said zero, the lights flashed then flicked back on. Doing as he was told, he flexed his shoulders as his Ice Man mask was pulled into place. He casually walked through the open doorway, and his heart fell through the floor.

Trev was covered in blood. What could only be whip lines stretched from his shoulders to the top of his pants. The little bit that he could see of his face was swollen and caked with blood. He clenched his fists and took a small step, ready to race across the space and kill the man that had done this.

"Know your job," Arek said.

Cody swore under his breath. The guy was getting on his nerves. Taking a steadying breath, he focused on his task. He stuffed the one gun back into his pants and rolled his shoulders. Showtime.

"It's about fucking time. Now get your asses back in here, or you're going to miss the show," Alejandro yelled.

"Hey, Alejandro," Cody leaned against the wall, and he tapped the gun casually against his leg. Alejandro spun in his direction, and the man's eyes narrowed as they stared at one another. He made sure to keep the gun down. It allowed him to portray the illusion of being less threatening. "It seems your men are a bit indisposed. I do hope they weren't your favorites," he smirked.

"You're working with him?" Alejandro pointed to Trev. Cody lifted his shoulders in a non-committal way. "The rumors are true then. You took out Tyson? Did you really cut his balls off? That is hardcore, brother, even for you, Ice Man. I wouldn't have pegged you for the sort that could do that." Alejandro waved a hand in the air as he tried to find the right words. "You don't have the right je ne sais quoi."

Cody pushed off from the wall and took a step toward Alejandro. "What can I say? Tyson had it coming."

"Maybe, maybe not. So is it you that is attacking and killing my men?" Again, Cody lifted a shoulder but smiled at his opponent. "Why are you attacking me? We never had any beef?"

"Keep him talking, and get him to move forward. I don't have a clear shot," Arek said in his ear.

Cody took a couple of steps to the side, looking around like he was interested in the warehouse and what it had in the large brown crates.

"I have my own aspirations. We don't have beef, per say, Alejandro, but you do control the west side of the city. That is a big area to have all to yourself. I thought it was about time you learned to share. Tyson was too weak to go after what he wanted." Cody paused in his slow stroll and looked Alejandro in the eyes. "But, I'm not."

Alejandro laughed, the sound grating and making Cody's teeth grind together. "You think you're the one to teach me the lesson?"

"You don't think I can?" Cody took a few more steps to the side, and Alejandro was forced to move or lose sight of him around Trev's hanging body. Cody could now see the front of Trev's body, and every instinct was telling him that he didn't have long. He was clearly out cold, his muscles hadn't twitched, and his fair skin was turning an unnatural shade.

"I think you're too attached."

"To what? To him?" Cody nodded toward Trev. "Not really. He just found my offer more beneficial to him than yours was." Cody had no idea what deal Trev and Alejandro had struck, but he was hoping that he could bullshit his way through this.

"See, I think you are lying." Alejandro took a step toward Trev and didn't even look away from Cody's eyes as he hauled off and punched Trev in the side. A soft groan left his lips, but he didn't move or blink otherwise. Cody took a step forward and stopped as Alejandro pushed the tip of a blade into Trev's side.

"Aw, see, there it is, that flicker in your eyes that says this man means more to you than you let on. Do you call him friend?" Alejandro waved the knife around slowly. "Or maybe you call him an associate? He may indeed work for you, but there is more to it than that Ice Man, I see it in your eyes. Do you call this man a lover? Does he get your cock hard?" He flicked his tongue out and waved it in the air. Alejandro held up something black in his hand that looked like a remote control. He had no time to figure out what it meant when his thumb hit a button, and Trev's body shook in the chains. His eyes snapped open, and a sound that would follow him to his grave ripped from Trev's throat.

Fear raced through his system as he frantically tried to figure out what to do.

"Oh, that sound," Alejandro said as his finger released and Trev slumped against the rattling chains.

Every muscle shook as his hand gripped the gun tighter. He stared at the mocking expression and so badly wanted to wipe that look off Alejandro's face.

"Just a little further," Arek whispered. Cody could hear the desperation in the man's voice.

It took all of his control but, Cody pretended to ignore Alejandro and the obvious pain he had to be causing. Cody knew what the bite of cold steel felt like. He turned toward the small table off to the side of the torture area. He took a couple of strides in that direction. "Don't move, or I'll gut him." Cody stopped moving and held up his hands.

Alejandro stepped around Trev's body, the knife creating a new thin line as it pressed into his skin. Cody watched in horror as fresh blood dripped down Trev's side. He didn't know what to do, and his eyes darted around for a way to get Alejandro to move into position.

"Did you really think you could take over my area?" He pointed that bloody knife in his direction and took a threatening step forward. "I will cut you, like I…." Alejandro stopped talking, and it took a moment for Cody's brain to catch up to the fact that he had a hole in the middle of his forehead. Alejandro's body dropped with a resounding thump. There was so much blood already on the floor it was hard to tell Alejandro's from Trev's. Putting away the gun, he darted around the already forgotten ass wipe. His only regret was not putting the bullet in the fucker himself.

He didn't know where to touch or hold that wouldn't cause more pain. "Trev, look at me. We're going to get you out of here. You're going to be okay." He held Trev's battered face in his hands, and eyes opened slightly between the purplish swollen skin. Those blue eyes that stole the air from his chest stared out through thin slits to look at him.

"Cody?" Trev's voice sounded terrible like he'd been screaming for days at a concert.

"Don't try to talk." He laid a hand on his bloody cheeks swiping gently with his thumb. "Arek, we need to get him out of here," he yelled.

Cody's head was on a swivel as he searched for the release of the heavy chains holding Trev. Arek came storming into the room a moment later and ran straight to his brother, as Cody finding what he searched for, ran to the loops on the wall. Hand over hand, he lowered the chains slowly to the ground. Arek guided Trev's body to lay gently on the floor and then unzipped a small pouch pulling out an assortment of bandages.

Cody pulled the vest off over his head and quickly peeled off his t-shirt. "Here, use this too." He tossed it to Arek and put the heavy vest back on.

Cody knelt down beside Trev and didn't know how to help. He suddenly wished he'd gone to school to be a doctor or some other helpful shit like that. Something cool touched his hand, and he looked down to see Trev's hand lying on top of his. He quickly grabbed the man's hand and brought it up to his lips. He didn't care if Arek or anyone saw.

"I'm…ss…sorr…y," Trev managed to say.

"Shh, you're going to be fine." He squeezed Trev's hand.

"Okay, that's the best I can do right now. We need to get him to a doctor." Arek slid his arms under his brother and picked him up like he weighed nothing. "No evidence of Trev being here can remain."

Cody stood with them, not wanting to let go of the hand he held.

"I want to go with you."

"No, do as I fucking say," Arek barked out as he walked away. "Get rid of the evidence. I'll look after my brother."

The muscle in Cody's jaw twitched as teeth ground together. He wanted to argue, he wanted to throw a fit and say that he should go, but the truth was he barely knew Trev, and Arek was his twin.

"I'll burn it all down. Nothing of what happened here will remain," Cody called out. A shiver ran through his body as Arek paused at the door to look back at him.

Arek nodded. "Good, and I'll call you when I get him to safety so you can join."

Cody watched the two brothers disappear into the corridor he'd emerged from, and his heart constricted in his chest. Trev had to pull through. He had to live. He stared down at Alejandro and felt cheated that he didn't get to kill him. Pointing the gun at Alejandro, he pulled the trigger until the clip clicked empty.

Fucker.

Chapter 19

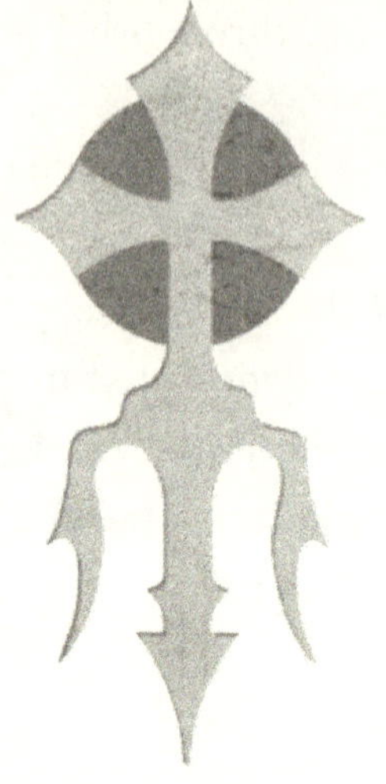

Arek raced along the darkened street, the shitty lights flickering as he flew past rattling the polls. He needed to avoid the police like a thief in the night, and he trusted Delilah to show him the best route.

"In fifty meters, turn right."

He slammed on the breaks and skidded around the designated corner, the scent of burning rubber strong as smoke rose behind him. The Hummer revved loudly as he punched his foot to the floor. He kept his eyes on the road, he didn't dare to look back at his brother, or he was going to lose his shit, and he needed to keep it together.

The sound of ringing resounded as the line he was dialing connected, one ring, two rings, three rings.

"For fuck's sake, pick the fuck up," he yelled, slamming his hand off the steering wheel. As it began to ring once more, it cut off a groggy voice answering. "Hello?"

"I'm calling in a special order," Arek swallowed hard. He'd never met this contact, but The Righteous had given him the number in case of an emergency, and this constituted as a mother-fucking emergency in his book.

"What would you like to order?" the man asked.

"Codeword bagpiper. I need a number three with hot sauce."

"Very well, you will find what you need at 555 Parkside Drive." The line went dead.

"Sweet Delilah, plot fastest route to 555 Parkside Drive." The windshield flashed, and the place he was heading to glowed as a green dot. It looked like a farmhouse just outside of the city limits. It took only a few seconds for the computer to take in all the stoplights, cameras, police, and anything else that could be a potential issue before plotting the course across the windshield.

Shit, twenty minutes. He prayed that Trev could hang on that long. He should never have backed off from the missions. Trev had been out of this part of the game for too long. Arek smacked his hand against the steering wheel until his hand was numb, the fear bubbling into an acidic taste in his mouth. This was all his fault.

Trev made a whimpering moan from the back seat. Arek looked back at his brother and knew he was in the throes of a dream. In their case, it was more like a nightmare. The whimpers became louder, and Trev's body jerked on the bench seat.

"Hang in there, Trev. I've got you, brother."

The black beast flew down the highway, and soon, he was pulling off past a rundown motel, its red glowing light unsurprisingly flashing vacancy. There were no other buildings that could be seen for miles, which suited him just fine.

"Destination one mile ahead on the right-hand side."

Arek had to force his foot off the gas to be able to make the turn onto the unmarked driveway—it was lined with thick trees and shrubs, creating a dense wall of foliage. There was a fresh set of tracks in the dry dirt, and he traced their entry until the old farmhouse came into view.

He parked the Hummer and jumped out to be greeted by an older white-haired man with glasses coming out of the house. "Bring him in this way," the man called out and then disappeared back inside.

"We're here. You're going to be alright," he said as he gingerly pulled Trev from the vehicle. Trev's forehead was sweaty, his skin clammy as he shivered and mumbled in his passed-out state. Some of the blood on his chest had wiped off, and Arek could clearly see the electrical burns, bruises, and other cuts marring his skin.

One thing was certain, if Trev died, his soul would go with him.

By the time he pulled the last of the dead bodies into the main portion of the warehouse, Cody's muscles shook. He wasn't taking any chances, and it was a good thing he made another sweep as he found a very intoxicated and passed-out member that had tried to stumble in another door and ended up snoring half in and half out the doorway.

After shooting the annoying fucker, he dragged him in as well and dropped him on the growing pile. He stood back and stared at the mountain of bodies and couldn't help but think back. Tyson had him do this anytime he decided to dispose of a large group. It was sad that this was a normal occurrence for him.

He wandered away in search of anything useful and found an office that didn't have a lot, but he took what it had and loaded it in his car that he'd pulled up. Once he was certain he was ready, he walked back inside. After soaking the pile of flesh in gasoline, he walked a line to the back door. Dropping the can, Cody pulled a lighter out of his pocket—flicking on the little wheel, he stared at the dancing flame. For the first time, he didn't feel any guilt for the deaths that happened here tonight.

The scent of gasoline was strong in his nose, and he smiled as he tossed the lighter toward the line he made on the floor. It ignited in a rush that had him covering his eyes, and then it stormed away down the hall and around the corner. Dashing out the door, he jumped in his car and was just pulling out of the parking lot when the building exploded and rocked the car as flames blew out the high windows. Glass rained down on his vehicle, the little pieces making a tinkling sound on the roof of his car.

He stared in the rearview mirror as the car streaked away from the scene and then smiled at his own reflection. He wasn't like Tyson, but some of the same darkness had certainly crawled inside his soul.

Chapter 20

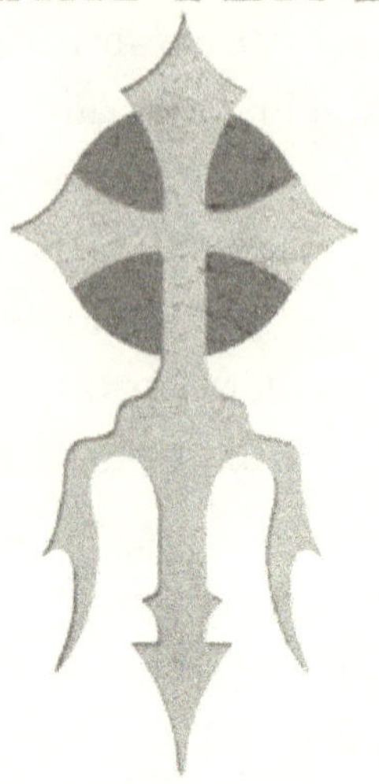

Trev held the reins of his pony, giving him a pat on his dappled coat. He'd learned to ride almost before he learned to walk. This was his second pony. The first one got too old and had to be retired when he was six. Now, at the age of eight, he had a larger pony, Doc's Dancing Devil, who was as fast as lightning.

"Are you scared," he asked Melissa. Her blonde braids whipped back and forth as she shook her head no.

"I'm not afraid of anything. When I grow up, I'm going to be a professional cowgirl and win all the buckles," she said and fixed the pretty pink Stetson on her head. "Help me up, and I'll show you."

Trev smiled at his best friend. "Alright, give me your leg, and I'll toss you up."

Mel bent her left leg, and he gripped her knee, giving her a boost into the saddle. Before he could give any further instruction, she pulled the reins out of his hands with a jerk and gave the pony a hard kick. "Hee yeah."

Doc leaped forward, with a wicked burst of speed, almost knocking him over. Mel and his pony raced right for the open fields. He could hear Mel's cheers of excitement from the barn as he stomped inside to get a ride for himself.

The barn melted away, and he found himself on his bike instead. He leaned forward on the handlebars as he watched Mel roll in the dark brown pig shit with his brother. He couldn't stop the tears from falling as he laughed so hard he couldn't see. He'd never laughed so much, and his stomach hurt, but he couldn't stop. Arek tried to run out of the slop, the pigs scattering and making a racket as Mel yelled like a wildling and jumped on his brother again. Her once pretty Sunday dress was black and brown with layers of caked on muck.

"Trev, get her off of me," Arek yelled, his hand reaching out for him from the slop.

He fell off his bike, consumed with the hysterical bouts of laughter. Arek was arrogant and had this coming. He'd been relentless in his teasing of Mel, poking fun of her at church, but Trev knew his brother was in for it when he stole one of the blue ribbons from her braid. He absolutely refused to give it back, and when she threatened to hurt him on their walk home if Arek didn't, he'd made the mistake of asking what she could do—she was just a girl.

"Trev, she's gonna kill me. Help me."

Pushing himself to his feet, he dusted off the dirt from his Sunday best and sauntered toward the two human piglets.

"Mel, let him up before you suffocate him in the pig shit," Trev said.

"But he deserves it. Fitting end for a male pig." She made snorting noises at the back of his brother's head.

Trev leaned on the split rail and bit his lip to stop from laughing again as he watched the show. Mel was now sitting on Arek as he tried to get up and proceeded to kick his legs out like he was a bronco.

"Please, for me?"

"Fine." Mel stood and gave Arek one final push. "You owe me a new set of ribbons." She marched through the pig shit like it was the most normal thing in the world. She gave him a wink before replacing the amused look with a scowl and looked back at Arek once more. "And a new outfit, this was my best dress."

The scene before him shifted, and he looked around the dark gym with the glittering streamers, flashing lights, and terrible music playing. Trev hated school dances, they were a waste of time, but Mel had insisted the three of them go. Trev sipped his pop and looked around for his brother and best friend, who had seemingly disappeared. He spotted Arek first. He was on the dance floor holding Betty-Ann closer than her parents would approve. At seventeen, his brother was a horn dog, full-on messing around with any of the girls that would have him. He'd caught him making out with Emma before classes started, and now here he was feeling up Betty-Ann.

"Did you miss me?" Mel bumped his arm as she seemingly appeared from nowhere.

Pop went up and out his nose as his next sip was sloshed all over his face. Mel grabbed some napkins from the table he'd been propped up against while laughing. He sputtered and gasped as the pop left a trail of burning wetness.

"Thanks," he said, shooting Mel a glare.

"Don't be like that. In fact, come on. I want to show you something." He barely got the pop sat down before she jerked his arm as she practically dragged him out the gymnasium doors.

"Where are we going?"

"It's a surprise, you'll see." Her soft green eyes reminded him of a cat, full of mischief. She came to a halt and peered around the corner into the next hallway before looking back at him with a finger over her lips.

"You're going to get us kicked out of school," he whispered.

"They'd never kick us out. We have the highest gpa in the entire school. Besides, when have you ever gotten into trouble for anything?" Mel rolled her eyes at him. "A slap on the wrist at worst." She peered around the corner and, this time, took his hand before pulling him along.

Why did he always go along with her craziness?

A teacher monitoring the halls just turned the corner at the far end of the hall, his shadow slowly getting further away. She pushed open a door he'd never been through and immediately pulled her to a halt. "The roof?"

"Come on, Trev." She pulled on his hand and smiled.

Groaning, he climbed the steps with Mel, and as she pushed open the roof door, he took a deep breath of the cool evening air.

"Isn't it stunning?" Mel pointed to the sky that was cloudless and sparkled with millions of stars.

"Yeah, it is," he admitted, staring up at the dark sky just as a falling star zoomed past.

"Quick, make a wish." Mel closed her eyes, and he found himself staring at her instead. They'd been friends since they were in diapers, but he would have to be blind not to notice how beautiful she'd become. His eyes were glued to her lush lips, and he loved how she bit the one side when she thought. Would she taste as good as she smelt? There was always the lingering scent of orchids that followed her around.

"Are you going to kiss me or just continue to stare?"

Trev flushed hotly, as his eyes flicked up to Mel's. She'd caught him staring. He was going to deny it, make up some stupid excuse, but she didn't give him the opportunity and instead raised up on her toes. His breath caught a moment before her lips touched his.

Her lips were warm and soft, not at all like he'd been expecting as they pressed together. He hated to admit that this was his first kiss. It felt a little awkward—he had no idea what he was supposed to do next. A spark of emotion he couldn't explain formed in his chest.

Mel lowered herself down breaking the kiss, her cheeks a bright pink. "I've wanted to do that for a while," she admitted quietly.

He hadn't wanted it to end so soon. Trev smiled. "Really?"

She rolled her eyes at him. "Of course, stupid, didn't you notice me flirting with you?"

He rubbed the back of his neck and tried to look at anything other than Mel. "Not really."

"Boys," she huffed out.

"So, what does this make us?" he asked, not sure what this meant for their friendship. She lifted her shoulders and fluffed out her wavy hair.

"Let's not label it. Everyone that labels their relationships breaks-up. I don't

want us to end up breaking up like that. We can just be friends that like one another a little more. You can still see other people, and so can I."

"Do I get to kiss you again?" Trev asked.

"Unbelievable," Mel said and then grabbed him, pulling him in for another kiss. He smiled against her lips. This felt right.

Cody's ass had gone numb hours ago as he sat in the chair beside Trev's bed. He'd just finished another prayer, hoping this one would be heard. He had no idea if God listened to his begging. He certainly hadn't warranted God's love in a long time. He unclasped his hands, letting the small gold cross drop, but he had to try whatever he could.

The soft beeping of the monitors and the subtle rise and fall of the sheets covering Trev's body were the only indications that Trev was indeed still alive. The surgery had been touch and go. The doctor had looked so sullen when he exited the makeshift operation room that Cody thought Trev had already died, and his heart had slammed right through the floor.

Cody realized at that moment that his feelings had grown over their months of client-lawyer relationship into more than even he'd expected. The subtle brushes of their skin as Trev would point out something in the law books he'd drag along always sent a shock through his system. Yet, it was the way he always looked at him like he was a human, a flawed and screwed up human, but not a monster that sealed the deal.

The doctor made it clear that his vitals were stable, but he wasn't out of the woods. Trev's wounds had been serious, and the loss of blood had taken a heavy toll.

He glanced up at Trev's swollen and bruised face and couldn't stand staring at the garish abuse. It was too much of a reminder of the things Tyson had done, but worse was the fact that it was a reminder of the things he had done. No one got to sit at the bedside of those he'd beaten, and no one even knew where their bodies were.

The wind rattled the window, and he stared at the branch gently smacking against the dirty glass. His soul was much like this house, battered and forgotten.

"How's he doing?" Arek asked, startling Cody as he walked into the room.

"No change." Cody leaned back but kept his hand on Trev's arm. He ran his thumb back and forth across Trev's skin, not wanting him to feel alone. Maybe it was crazy to show this much affection after Trev ordered him to move out and not touch him, but he couldn't leave when Trev needed him.

"This is my fault." Arek rubbed his face as he leaned against the wall, the faded and torn wallpaper a perfect representation of how Arek looked. His usually perfect hair was standing in all directions, his tanned skin looked pale, dark shadows under his eyes. And, the guy was fidgety as all fuck. He hadn't sat still a moment since Cody arrived. His inability to park it had forced Cody to order him out of the room once already. The energy he'd been giving off was all too nerve-wracking, and he didn't think that was what Trev needed around him right about now.

"What do you mean this is your fault?"

"You know what we do, right?"

"Sort of, I know what the rumors say you do, and the little you've mentioned," Cody said as Arek pushed off the wall to pace once more across the floor.

"The Righteous' mission is simple, clean up the shit plaguing our streets." He stopped and held his hands out to the side as if to emphasize the statement. "We're free to choose who we want to go after most of the time, but in some cases, we are given a target that is a higher level asset for one reason or another. I'm sure it is the same for all those that took the oath to be part of the group, but we do tend to get tougher targets with regularity."

"Okay, but what does that have to do with tonight? Was Alejandro your target?"

"Yes and no. We would've had to go through him at some point or used him in some fashion to get to the Golden Dragons. Just as Tyson and the Crimson Vipers were pawns in a larger picture, so were the Streetlores. I don't really know the specifics of what Trev was up to because I took a step back, and Trev wouldn't involve me. That's why this is my fault."

Cody tracked Arek as he resumed his walking and then looked back to Trev. "So you decided to take a step back from going out in the field, from taking out targets?"

"Yes, I just said that," he sighed and ran a hand through his hair. "Sorry, I didn't mean to be an ass. I'm just worried, and when I worry, I tend to asshole-out."

"It's fine. Trev is your brother. I'm sure I'd be the same if Renee was laying here."

Arek shivered and hit him with a hard glare. "Don't ever say shit like that again, not even as an example."

"Back to tonight," Cody prompted.

"With your sister pregnant, I just wanted some normal for a short time, and I didn't want to put Renee or the baby under any stress. I told Trev I wanted to back away until the baby was born."

Arek grabbed the plastic water bottle off the small table in the corner and stared at the clear liquid. Cody took the opportunity to study him closer. Arek had a wildness that coursed under his skin. He could almost see the animal-like quality that existed in his soul. He never wanted to be on the wrong side of that particular side of fucked up.

"He said he understood." Arek looked over at him, his eyes a strange kind of haunted laying bare in his blue depths. "He said he'd take care of everything, but I should never have asked." Arek's chest was rising and falling like he'd been running, not standing perfectly statue-like. From across the dimly lit room, it was easy to see the shimmer of unshed tears in the man's eyes.

"Trev hasn't done active duty on his own since we landed back on American soil. He finished his bar exam and has been the cover boy for our operation ever since." Arek turned and, with a resounding bang, smashed his fist into the wall. The force created a fist-sized hole, and the old home rattled with the impact. "Fuck. My brother has always looked out for me, had my back, and I didn't have his."

"I don't think Trev would see it that way. I mean, the guy is pretty good at speaking his mind."

"You don't understand. He always puts me and my needs first. I was the troublemaker, the shit disturber, the one flirting with getting arrested and screwing with all the women. Trev has saved my ass more times than I can count. Shit, our last deployment. . . if it weren't for him, I'd be face down in dirt begging to be shot just to end the pain." Arek's eyes were fixated on Trev's still form.

"I thought I'd grown up and was past being self-centred, but the moment I was given the excuse to step back and let my brother take the reins, I didn't hesitate in asking him." Agony etched into every feature on Arek's face.

"It didn't even cross my mind that something terrible could happen." Arek finally looked at him, and his eyes were like staring at a ghost. "How stupid is that?"

"I want to be angry with you and have someone other than that warehouse of dead men to be pissed at," Cody said. Arek looked away, crossing his arms over his chest. "The thing is, if Trev didn't want you to take time away or thought he needed your help, he would've asked."

The pacing started up again. This time, he shook his head and was mumbling to himself. The soft thump of his boots was as rhythmic as a grandfather clock.

"You don't get it. You just don't get it."

Rubbing at his eyes, Cody wanted to stand up and punch Arek until he sat his fucking ass down, but he needed to remain cool. Taking a deep breath, he tried again. "Arek, you may be right that this was a bad time to back away, but you have to stop beating yourself up. Trev would've filled you in if he needed to."

"No, he wouldn't. Trev is a number one—an alpha, a wolf. He protects his pack, and he doesn't expect it to protect him. I need some air, call me if anything changes."

"I'll yell for you."

Arek stormed out of the room, his normally stealthy boots banging loudly down the hallway. The front screen door banged signaling that he had indeed left the farmhouse. Almost instantly, the atmosphere changed. The buzz surrounding Arek followed him like a swarm of bees. He had no idea how his sister could stand being around that nervous energy all the time—then again, maybe it was her that calmed the wild.

His eyes fell on Trev. His form was way too still. The bright white bandages wrapping him were much like that of a mummy in one of those Egyptian coffin-things. Just the thought of a coffin sent a shiver racing down his spine.

"Come on, Trev. You need to fight." He glanced at the door to make sure Arek hadn't pulled his silent cat thing. "I don't think your brother will do well if you die. I mean, I want you to pull through as well, even if it's to order me out of your house again." Cody smirked as he picked up Trev's hand, linking their fingers together.

He stared at their laced fingers. Arek's assessment of Trev did provide insight into Trev's psyche and his icy disposition. He understood the concept of placing the welfare of someone you love above your own happiness and wellbeing, fuck, he'd done that for his own sister. Hadn't he? It placed weight and responsibility on you that turned into a single-mindedness forcing you to do things you normally wouldn't. He'd pushed everyone around him away, didn't dare make any real connections or friends.

The little monitor unexpectedly began to beep faster as soft moans and incoherent words slipped from swollen lips.

A soft sheen had broken out on Trev's brow. Standing, he felt Trev's forehead with the back of his hand. "Trev, it's okay, you're okay. Arek and I are here."

"Mel," was the only coherent word Trev said before the monitor settled and Trev fell motionless once more.

It begged the question, who the hell was Mel?

Chapter 21

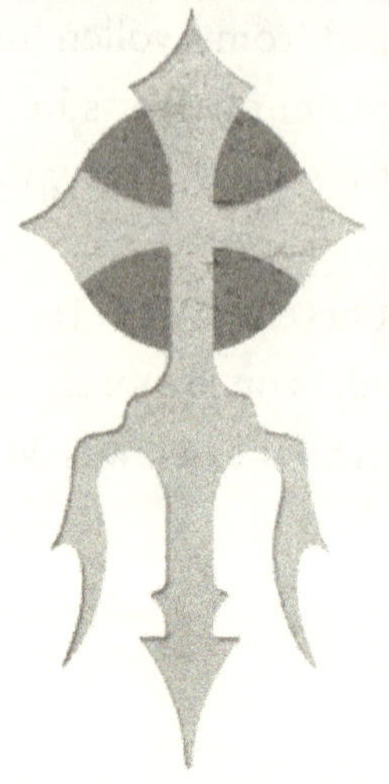

Trev stood on the edge of a high cliff, and he stared out over the lush green trees and sparkling blue water below. The sun was warm on his skin. He looked up and closed his eyes, soaking in the golden light and the beauty and perfection of this place. He always wanted to live near the mountains, to retire and move to a place that had land to farm and a view like this one.

"Hey there, stranger." Arms wrapped around his waist, and he smiled and turned in the hold to look down into the prettiest pair of green eyes he'd ever known. He'd missed these eyes. He missed that smile.

"Hey, yourself." Trev didn't hesitate, he cupped Mel's cheeks and kissed the lips he knew so well. She smelt like sweet honey and sunshine. She smelt like home. He breathed her in and relaxed into the softness of her embrace. Reluctantly he drew back from the kiss and laid his forehead against hers, savoring the feel of her. "I've missed you."

"I've missed you more," Mel said.

"You always did have to win." Trev kissed the tip of her nose.

Mel smiled before she stepped back but entwined their fingers. "Of course, someone had to keep you in line."

For the first time in a very long time, he felt relaxed. A warm sensation of peace flowed over his skin. "Am I dead? Is this heaven? If so, I don't know how I got here, and I certainly do not deserve it after everything I've done."

"No, you're not dead, well at least not yet—you always were a stubborn one."

Trev laughed at the teasing poke. Mel had always seen through him. "So you're saying that I could still end up visiting the hot and roasty?"

"Oh please, we both know you'd end up negotiating your way out of that one. You were born with the silver tongue of the devil himself."

He wrapped his arm around Mel's shoulder as they laughed—just like old times. It was unbelievably peaceful here, wherever here was. The birds sang noisily in the trees as they wandered along the wide well-groomed trail that led toward the water's edge.

"So, if I'm not dead..."

"Then why are you here?" Mel completed for him. "Because you need to let what happened to me go."

His body stiffened at the mention of her death. "I can't do that. I was the commanding officer that day. No matter what, I would have guilt, but you died because of me. I wouldn't listen to you, and I should have. I shouldn't have been so selfish. I should've let you go before..."

Mel pulled on his waist, bringing him to a stop. "Hold up there, soldier boy. I've always made my own choices. You and me being together had nothing to do with my death. That's a pretty vain way of looking at things if you ask me."

"Vain? Mel, you think I didn't hear what Miller said to you? You think I didn't hear how with me in charge of the mission, your unit was tormenting you about being a lesser leader? You even told me yourself that you had concerns about them not respecting you as long as we stayed together and I didn't listen." Trev looked at the glittering waters edge in the distance and the pain from that day came roaring back. "I was naive to think that they would see the great soldier you were, that..."

"Trev." Mel gave him a little shake. "Come off it. That conversation happened over a year before I died. Miller had always been a problem. No matter whose command he was under, you were like the only one he listened to, and no one knew why. Hell, you saw his records, talent up the wazoo, but he didn't handle authority well."

"Mel."

"No, let me finish. When you asked me to pick one person to come on the mission from my unit, I chose Miller. I chose him because at the end of the day, I knew he was the best person for the job, and I didn't care that he was trying to get under my skin."

"I don't believe you." Trev crossed his arms over his chest, and Mel immediately placed her hands on her hips as they stared one another down. If it wasn't for the painful memories and emotions he couldn't escape when staring into her beautiful face, he might have laughed.

"Trev, I thought I could reform Miller. Shit, I thought he'd listen to me because my style of authority was so different than what he'd had. I don't know, maybe I saw him as a challenge, but let's be clear, it was my choice to keep him on my team and my choice to take him on that mission. Just like it was also my choice to confront him that morning and have the argument I'd been avoiding. Me being distracted had nothing to do with you."

Trev looked away from Mel as tears threatened to make an appearance. "I saw you walk away from him, angry. I saw you head for the shoulder of the road." Trev stopped to gulp air as his chest rose and fell quickly. He could feel the beginnings of the same attack as in the bedroom starting. Mel reached out, grabbing both his hands into her own, forcing him to cup her face. "Look at me, Trev, and breathe."

He did as she asked and stared into her calm eyes as tears that he hadn't shed since her death flowed from his eyes.

"I really need you to listen to me, soldier. I wasn't upset that I was going to have to take leave. I was not distracted because we were pregnant." A soft sob escaped him as the tears fell harder—he tried to look away, but she wouldn't let him and caught his eye once more. "My death, our child's death was tragic, but

it was an accident that I own alone. You need to let our deaths go. You need to let us go." He stared down at her stomach and reached out, placing his hand on her belly. Dropping to his knees, he wrapped his arms around her waist as he laid his ear against the imaginary bump.

He let it all out. So many tears, so much pain, so many days and nights that he blamed himself for their deaths. Mel didn't say anything as he sobbed. She ran her hands through his hair and let him do what he needed to.

"You were my one shot at happiness in this shit world, Mel. You were my best friend, my love, my future, and I lost you. I lost us. I lost everything." He turned his head to look up at her. She was the spitting image of health and serenity. Golden light bathed her, making her look like she was shimmering. "I couldn't wait to get back and have our family, to..."

"I know. Trev, I know what you lost. I lost it all too. I lost you. I have missed this argumentative, arrogant, and yet so fucking sexy face so much." Trev couldn't help but smile a little. Mel always had a way with words. She reminded him of Arek and his total bluntness.

Mel stepped back, pulling him to his feet. "I will agree that you've lost a lot, but you're full of shit if you think I was your one shot at happiness."

"It feels that way, I have been so..."

"Closed off."

"Yes, I can't move on. I don't deserve to move on."

"Trevor Alexander Anderson, you stop that right this minute."

He bit his lip and then laughed as he looked into her stern expression. Other than his mother, she was the only one that would dare speak to him like that. "I mean it, I'm not going to let you blame yourself anymore for my choices, and neither are you. You can't control everything. You can't protect everyone. This burden is exhausting, and you are ruining your current chance at happiness."

"I don't know what you mean."

She cocked an eyebrow at him, and he wanted to kiss the sass right off her face. From the time they were able to walk, she could stare him down with that look. "Why are you holding back from Cody? Shit, if a dead person can see the attraction you two have, then come on, man, get with the damn program."

Trev laughed and pulled Mel into a hug. It was good to have someone call him on his shit that wasn't his brother. "He is quite hot. I will give him that."

"Pfft, boy, if I were alive, I would arm wrestle you for a chance at that. Hell, I'd suggest we take him together. That would have some serious possibilities." He couldn't help the stupid grin from spreading across his face. The guilt that had been constricting his heart and dragging his soul down eased as he stared into Mel's smiling face.

"You really aren't angry with me? You really don't blame me?"

"Trev, you are highly intelligent, so don't be stupid. You know as well as I do that I was happy to be a mother. I would've had ten kids with you. Being your wife and a mom was my ultimate dream come true since we were like eight." She lifted a shoulder and sighed. "We were not meant to be, and fate had other ideas. Just know you were not the reason I was distracted. You were not the reason I missed that IED that day." Her face grew serious. "I truly am at peace, and I know we will see one another again, but this is not it. It's not your destiny to join me yet."

This time Mel initiated the kiss. It was perfect and sweet, just like the woman herself. "But, it is time for you to go. You have a whole world out there waiting for you. You never know, you just might find that fairy tale ending you think you're so unworthy of. And for the love of all that is sexy in this world, take that boy up on his offer—you know I would." Mel smiled and placed another soft kiss on his lips.

"You really are the best, Mel. I was spoiled having you in my life for as long as I had you," Trev said as he traced his thumb down her cheek. He knew this was the goodbye he'd never gotten. Her skin was so soft, her eyes brighter than he remembered, but it was her heart he missed the most, her purity and honesty that kept him grounded.

"I know."

Pulling her close, he had to take what he could get in this moment, so he captured her lips. The kiss spoke of all the lost 'I love you's', all the laughs they no longer got to share, and all the passion he wished he'd shown more often.

They were both breathing hard when he stopped ravaging her lips. "I don't want to let you go again."

"I know, neither do I, but you must." Wrapping her arms around his waist, Mel laid her head over his heart. He couldn't remember how many times they'd stood like this, but this one felt different. It felt final.

He reluctantly let her step back as she broke the hug. Reaching up, she wiped the tears from his cheeks. "Don't cry, soldier boy. I hate to see you so sad."

He gave her a meek smile as he reined in the sadness. "It's easier said than done."

"Do me a favor and tell that brother of yours I'm happy for him. He got a good one. Renee will keep him in line." Trev laughed. There was no truer statement. Mel's face grew serious, and she gave his hand a squeeze. "Also, keep your eyes open. One of our own is going to need you soon."

"Who?" he asked, standing a little straighter.

"Just remember what I said and trust your gut." A breeze picked up and blew her hair around her face. She turned her head and closed her eyes, giving him the most stunning picture to remember forever. He knew before she opened her mouth again what she was going to say. It was time, and she needed to go.

"I have to go now, but I'll be seeing you again, soldier boy."

"You know I hate it when you call me that."

"Oh, I know." Mel gave his hand a final squeeze, and as she walked away, he held on, wanting their fingers to touch for as long as possible. His arm fell by his side as she pulled free, and he wanted to chase after her, tell her he didn't care, he wanted to remain here forever, but she'd told him it wasn't his time. Mel stopped and looked over her shoulder. "Trev, I'm always looking out for you. I'm always with you, no matter what, and so is your son." She smiled and resumed her walk once more. This time, she did not look back.

Emotion so raw it clogged his throat as he stared at her back until she was nothing more than a tiny speck in the distance. Taking in deep, ragged breaths he stared at the pebbled path they'd traveled. Not wasting another moment, he took his first step.

Chapter 22

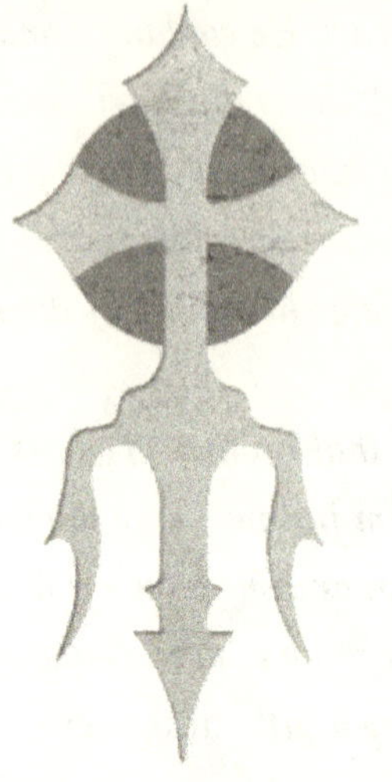

The first thing Trev was aware of was that he fucking hurt everywhere. There was not a single part of his body that felt normal or didn't scream as he tried to move. It took a number of attempts, but he managed to peel his heavy lids open. He stared at the ceiling and then flicked his eyes around the room. He was in his own bed but had no recollection of how he got here. The last thing he remembered was being electrocuted, and he thought he saw Arek and Cody, but then it was all a dark void of nothingness. He should be dead, that much he did know. The other thing he was acutely aware of was how badly he needed to use the washroom.

A soft snore reached his ears, and he lifted his head slightly to see Cody asleep on the small loveseat by the fireplace. His long body was stretched out comically, legs, arms, and head all hanging off the small space that was so not designed to be slept on unless you were a child.

Trev licked his lips. His mouth and throat felt dry, like an animal had decided to shred up his throat. Removing a comforter had never been so difficult. He struggled with the material, his arms weak, and hands not wanting to work properly. With a final yank, he managed to free himself, but had to close his eyes and catch his breath. He stared down his body at the bandages that stretched from under his armpits to almost his crotch and then a separate one on his leg. Only a pair of black boxers divided the two pieces of stark white wrapping.

He felt around the bandage, and all the points he knew should hurt most certainly did, but the pain told him he was most certainly alive. He winced as he swung one leg at a time over the side of the bed, his heart rate accelerating from the small excursion. His stomach and sides throbbed from the sharp pain. He wrapped his arm around his waist and closed his eyes to settle his stomach which was threatening to turn inside out.

How long had he been out? Every limb felt like lead as he refocused on his task and pushed himself to his feet. Trev took a couple of very unsteady steps and sucked in a sharp breath, a small groan slipping from his mouth as his shoulder hit the wall, and he grabbed the dresser to stay upright.

Cody's eyes snapped open and he leaped off the couch in an act of amazing agility. Zero to sixty in less than a second, Cody was by his side and wrapping Trev's arm around his shoulders. He groaned again with the stretch, but it did feel better to alleviate some of the weight. He expected the small voice in his head that always screamed to push Cody far away to start up, but this time it remained silent.

"How long have you been awake?" Cody asked.

"Not long. Can you get me to the washroom?"

"Of course." Their steps were slow, but they made it, and he stared at the toilet like it was Mount Kilimanjaro.

"Did you want me to stay?"

"No, just can you wait outside the door?" Cody nodded and slipped outside but kept the door open a crack. He was going to argue, but that would've taken more energy than he had. Once finished, the door opened as he was washing his hands and Cody gripped him again to help him back out. "Thanks. I will have to assume this is what it feels like to be hit by a truck or maybe a train."

He closed his eyes and bit back the pain as he lowered himself down onto the loveseat.

"I have to go get Arek." Cody turned to leave, but Trev grabbed his hand. As silver met blue, they stared at one another for a number of long breaths.

"Sit for a moment, please. I can't deal with my brother just yet—I can imagine what state he was in and need a moment to gather my wits." Cody sat, and once more, it was obvious the couch was too small as their legs touched. "I thought I told you to move out."

Cody's body stiffened as he looked away from his eyes.

"I'm happy you didn't listen." He laid his hand on Cody's. He didn't know how to express what he wanted to say.

The corner of Cody's mouth pulled up, showing off a sexy dimple, but his eyes were guarded. Trev couldn't blame him after how he'd treated Cody. He owed him an explanation.

Changing tactics for now, he decided to ask something else. "How did Arek get to me in time?"

"That AI tech you two have is pretty fierce. It went all 911 as soon as you were shot." Cody raised his shoulder and let it drop. "Arek said it wouldn't normally react that early, but he'd recently made some alterations." Cody paused. "I was with Arek at the time the alert came through. Your brother took me with him."

"He what? Son of a..."

"Don't be mad with him. I demanded he take me, and honestly, even if he hadn't, I would've followed."

Trev rolled his eyes at Cody. "Yes, you do seem to have a knack for not doing what you're told. You and my brother have that in common."

"We weren't that far away, which was lucky. Good thing too, if we'd been any later, you'd be dead, and I don't think Arek would've handled that well." Cody didn't say why, but Trev could guess.

Trev aborted the argument he was about to make. His eyes dropped to their now interlaced fingers and thought how comfortable it felt familiar and yet, so different than Mel. There was a spark traveling up his arm, his pulse quickened, and even with the fierce amounts of pain, he wanted a much more intimate moment between them.

"I'm not very good at this," Trev said. He looked back up into Cody's eyes, admiring the view as he took in the body under the tight shirt. He swallowed hard.

"Not very good at what?"

"This...whatever this is between us. I haven't been with anyone in a long time, and I'm afraid I've lost the art of flirting or acting human," Trev joked.

Cody smirked, his body relaxing into the love seat as he rested his head on his hand. "I think you are doing pretty well. The snarky remarks could be toned down, though."

A flush spread across Trev's body. "I guess I need to apologize to you again. It seems to be a bad habit that I'm making where you are concerned. I do have my reasons, I just..."

"It's okay. You don't need to tell me right now. I really do have to go get Arek before he finds you upright, and I end up diced sushi." Cody leaned in a little, lowering his voice. "Your brother is fucking scary." He made to stand, but Trev gripped his hand harder.

Confusion crossed Cody's features. Trev cupped the side of Cody's face and drew him in before he lost his nerve. There was no resistance, and as those soft lips touched his own, the last of the baggage that had been chained around his soul faded away.

He moaned into the soft contact and deepened the kiss until their tongues battled for dominance. The passion and connection between them was electric and burned with a white-hot desire. Trev's cock stood at attention inside the thin material he was sporting and was so ready to take this to the next level regardless of what the rest of his body said. He traced the dips of Cody's body, his finger exploring the plains of the man he'd wanted to touch from the first moment they met. There was the ripple of muscle on his washboard abs that made him moan into Cody's mouth before his hand found the large bulge inside his jeans.

Gripping the length, he gave it a squeeze and earned a strangled groan from Cody's lips. Cody's body shuddered as he broke the kiss and pulled away to stand. They were both breathing hard, and Cody's eyes were trained on the undeniable erection that was tenting out Trev's boxers. Trev stared up at Cody and wondered if he lost his chance to see if they could become something more.

"Oh, you are testing my resolve, but you're in no shape for what I would do to you if we go any further right now. Besides, if I don't get Arek, he will cut mine off, and then I wouldn't get to enjoy you at all."

Trev smirked as Cody marched across the floor and disappeared out the door.

He stared down at the tent in his boxers. *Might as well do something else useful then.* He focused his eyes on his dresser and slowly heaved himself to his feet.

By the time he emerged from the bathroom, dressed, and cleaned up, Arek and Cody were back. There was a stark contrast between the two. Cody looked cool as a cucumber while Arek paced at high speed like a fucking annoying fly. Arek spied him first, and he tensed for what he knew was coming as Arek sprinted the short distance and wrapped him in a hug.

He sucked in a sharp breath as his body screamed with the assault. "Oh shit, I'm sorry," Arek said but refused to break contact. "I can't let you go. Don't you ever fucking scare me like that again, you mother fucker, it almost killed me," Arek said. Trev laughed and wrapped his brother in his own embrace. "It's just so good to see you awake."

"I love you too, Arek," Trev said softly, and his brother's body shuddered and finally relaxed. "How long was I out?" He asked, finally getting Arek to break his iron grip.

"Long enough to scare the fucking shit out of me, make me drink a case of Pepto-Bismol, and for Renee to order me to sleep on the couch because I was driving her insane."

Trev laughed, he could picture all of that. "Come on, help a guy out. I need to sit down again." For a moment, he thought Arek was going to pick him up, but with a glare, he wrapped an arm around his waist instead.

"What the hell were you thinking doing that job alone?" Arek started the moment his ass found the seat. "I mean, really? There were over twenty men in that place, plus the lunatic himself. You'd never let me try a move that stupid. Do you even care that I almost had a fucking heart attack when I saw you hanging from those chains?" Trev just let his brother rant. No point in interrupting his roll. It would only drag the shit train out longer. "I thought you were dead, and it would've been my fault, you fucking prick. I could not have lived with that, the guilt that I killed my best friend, my only damn brother. No, no, not again. If I have to put some tracking shit in your skin like a sci-fi flick, I will do it." Arek pointed the mother finger at him, and he looked so much like their mother in that moment, he burst out laughing and then grabbed at his sore side.

Shit, that hurt.

"Don't you laugh at me, you cocksucker. No matter how much I love your ass, I will kick it to tomorrow and back again if you don't tell me what the hell you were trying to accomplish with that suicidal mission."

"If you'd let your motor mouth take a break, I'd be happy to tell you." Trev pointed to the chair, and Arek collapsed into it like his body had finally given out from the stress. "You know that I got the offer to feed intel to Alejandro, but I couldn't find any. I questioned every lead we had, and the night that Cody followed me, I managed to steal a great number of things, but there wasn't a single piece of information on who runs the Golden Dragons or how to find a contact."

"So what? You were planning on taking out Alejandro instead?"

"Yes, but not because of that. Shit, where is Sally?" He asked as panic bloomed in his chest.

"She's in the kitchen with Renee. Why?"

"Did you not notice her living here?" Trev lifted his eyebrow in question.

"I was a little preoccupied, so forgive me for not noticing a person that is always here anyway." Arek crossed his arms over his chest, his face a classic pout.

Trev shook his head at his brother in amazement. "Sally came to me at the courthouse. She was frazzled and told me that one of Alejandro's men had paid her a visit and threatened her at home. They even left a dead cat on her doorstep when she ignored his threat. She found the file. You know, the file?"

Arek sat up straight. "Sally knows...like everything?"

"Yes, and instead of handing it over, she came to me and gave me the stick with all the info on it and a detailed description of what the guy looked like. She was mortified she'd even downloaded it. I took her home to get clothes, and once we arrived here, I got ready and left again. And before you ask, no one was here when I arrived."

"We were already at the races," Arek said to Cody. Trev didn't know what that meant, but that was a question for another time.

"Anyway, I figured I could kill two birds with one stone since he is one of the largest purchasers and distributors of Golden Dragons' drugs. I'd extract my information, torture the guy that dared to threaten a sweet old lady, and with Alejandro out of the picture, the gang would fold." Trev pushed himself up a little straighter. "The Dragons would either have to put several new boots on the ground to sell for them, or they would be looking for a new big fish to take Alejandro's place." Trev winced as he reached for the glass of water on the table, but Cody was faster and grabbed it for him. He offered him a smile as thanks before taking a long gulp of the cool liquid.

"Here, take this. The doc prescribed it to help with the pain." Cody held out a couple of white pills. Trev took the offering and tossed the pills back. He wasn't normally one for any form of drug, but this pain required an exception.

"Please tell me you searched the office?" Trev asked.

"Color me a little too concerned with keeping you alive to worry about that."

"So the building?"

"Burnt to the ground," Cody finished for Arek.

A pounding started behind his eyes, and Trev rubbed his eyes. "I went through all that for nothing."

"No, not for nothing." Cody looked between Trev and Arek. "First, let me get this straight. All you want is a way to get access to the Golden Dragons?" Cody asked.

"Yeah, we've been trying for months," Trev answered, and Cody's lip curled up.

"Not only did I clean out the office, but you guys just don't know where to look. You didn't have to go through all that to find them. All you had to do was ask me."

Trev's face fell. "You know them?"

"Not where they are, but I know their second-in-command. Arek you remember Spike down at the Underground?"

"Yeah," Arek answered as he clenched his fists.

"He's the Golden Dragons' number two. They run all their pickups and drop-offs through the street races, and if you want an in, you're looking at him."

A trickle of fear gripped Trev. "Oh no, we are not doing that."

"Why not? I race there all the time. The guys know me and…" Cody held up a finger as Trev opened his mouth. "Alejandro already thought that I'd killed off Tyson for some reason. I could definitely play it off that I wanted their territories. Ice Man was ruthless. They would buy that I had my own ambitions. Besides, the two of you would stand out like sore thumbs down there, and they are skittish with new people. It took me years to build a relationship strong enough to buy their product."

"Cody has a point," Arek said.

Trev managed to stand and made his way to the window to stare outside. He'd already lost Mel, did he want to risk Cody's life on a mission as well?

"I don't know if I can allow this." Trev squeezed his eyes shut as the headache thumped a little harder.

"Trev, I know you want to protect me. I even understand that you lashing out at me when I followed you was because you didn't want me to get hurt, but I have lived this life since I was twelve and living full time with Tyson since nineteen. I know these people, how they think, how they operate, all of it. I am your best shot at getting close to the Dragons." Trev sighed as Cody's hands touched his shoulders. "I can protect myself, and we have time to plan. We don't have to rush into this tonight. To be honest, even with the three of us, it's going to be tough. At last count, Tyson figured they had to have over a hundred boots on the ground that I know of."

"You are simultaneously making a point to allow you to go and to tell you to sit your ass the fuck down." Trev glanced at Cody in the window and then resumed his staring at the backyard.

Cody laughed, the deep sound racing over his skin like an intimate caress. He slowly raised his gaze to look the man in the eyes. Could he let go of his fears? "Arek, can you give us a few minutes to talk?"

"Take as much time as you like. Now that I'm not a pacing mess, I'm going to go fuck the shit out of my beautiful fiancé and then pass out for like a week."

"So didn't need to hear that about my baby sister." Cody shot daggers at Arek.

"Dude, trust me, that girl is no baby. Not with the dirty things she'll do with that tongue." Arek smiled as Cody clenched his fists and a growl-like sound rippled from his throat. "Fucking with you for the rest of your life is going to be so much fun," could be heard as the door closed behind him.

"I may have to kill your brother yet."

"Get in line." The two of them smiled at one another. The moment felt like the first natural and easy moment between them.

"Cody, I don't want to lose you to a war that Arek and I agreed to fight. You should not be so willing to jump into the fray."

"I've spent my whole life fighting. Fighting for a meal, fighting for an education, fighting for my sister. Fighting is what I know. It may not be what I wanted to do with my life, but it is what it is. At least fighting with you and Arek to keep drugs off the street is a worthy cause." Cody wandered away, and Trev watched the emotions play over Cody's face. "I sold that shit to kids, man. To kids that were not even teens yet because I was ordered to do so and was too fucking weak to kill Tyson myself. I was no better than those in the Streetlores or the GD's. This is a chance to do a little good, turn some of that shit around."

"You really want to do this? To put your neck on the line for an organization you know very little about and for the two of us who you barely know?"

Cody stepped in so close that the delicious scent of his skin made Trev's head light. *Or was it the painkillers?* He didn't care, his body warmed with Cody's nearness. "What I know is that you saved me from spending the rest of my life behind bars for things that I've never been proud of—risking it all for a good cause and..." Cody drew the back of his knuckles down Trev's cheek. "I would do that a thousand times over." Cody's lips hovered just above his, he could almost taste the minty freshness of his breath, and his whole body shivered with the potentness of their connection. "Can I ask you something?"

"What do you want to know?"

"On one of your visits to the prison you said you understood why I did what I did. That you knew that feeling, was that true?"

"It is true. Different reasons, different circumstances, but that soul sucking feeling, that's the exact same."

Cody gave him a lopsided grin as he ran his hand through his hair. "I never did understand why you came to see me all the time. I didn't deserve your friendship or your dedication to my case."

The room spun a little and Trev grabbed Cody's shoulder to steady himself.

"That's enough talking for now, you better lay down. You need to rest." Trev let Cody help him to the bed and got comfortable once more. The drugs now fully flowing throughout his system had his eyes drooping heavily. Trev grabbed Cody's hand before he could drift too far. "Will you lay with me?"

Cody smiled wide, producing a second amazingly sexy dimple for a matching pair. Trev held open the covers for Cody and sighed as he scooted under and pressed his body up against his own. "Go to sleep. I'll be here when you wake up."

"Cody?"

"Yeah?"

"You have more to offer someone than you realize." Cody's body shuddered against his own, as those strong arms gripped him a little tighter.

Trev relaxed into Cody's hold and breathed deeply the scent of a man he could distinguish anywhere. What his future held, he could not even begin to guess, but he was certain that whatever it was, this man would be part of it.

Chapter 23

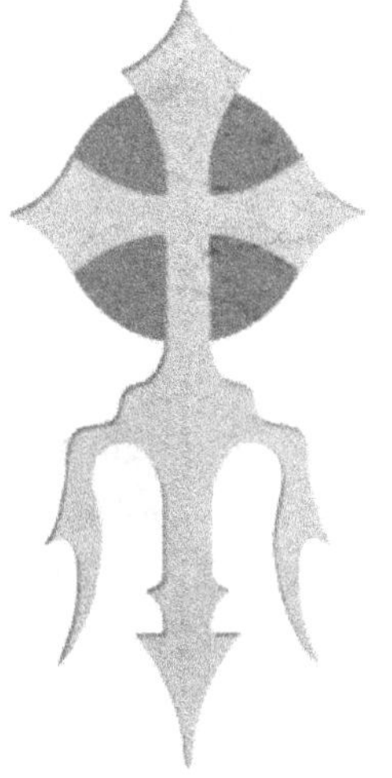

Cody woke up with a start, his heart hammering, and adrenaline spiking, and not for a good reason. His head swung to the door and the loud commotion that was going on. It was dark outside, and he was disoriented. The loud sound of yelling and gunfire kicked his instincts and brain into high alert. Trev was trying to sit up just as the door to the bedroom burst open, and Arek ran in, herding Sally, Renee, and J.J. like cattle.

A small red dot lit up the far wall through the window right near Arek's head. "Get down," Cody yelled and yanked the cover over his head as he pushed Trev flat against the bed. Rolling over Trev's body, he held himself up but acted like a human shield as the window exploded a moment later. Glass rained down on his back, with little thuds as the sound of gunfire and splintering wood was loud in his ears.

"Get in the washroom now," Arek ordered. Cody dared to peek over his shoulder to see the other three crawling toward the open washroom door. Arek, on the other hand, ran for the side of the window. He pulled up the gun he was carrying like this was just another normal day in the neighborhood and looked through the scope. "Come out, come out wherever you are," Arek whispered.

"This was not how I envisioned the first time you were on top of me," Trev said, as his fingertips ran teasingly down Cody's back. If this had been any other time, he would have ravaged that cocky mouth, but instead, his brain squealed to a halt.

"How can you joke around at a time like this?"

Trev smiled back, his whole face lighting up as if he'd just asked the stupidest question ever. "I've seen worse, and Arek has a gun. We're good unless they have grenades. That could get messy."

"I think those pain meds have gone to your head."

Arek opened fire out the shattered window. "Got you, you fucker. Stupid whack-a-moles. Come on, let's move." Arek grabbed the comforter, whipping it off Cody's back, and proceeded to lay it out on the floor. "For the glass." Arek pointed to the ground and the crunching under his boots.

They moved as quickly as Trev was able to, the entire time he wanted to pick him up and run for the bathroom, but figured Trev would beat his ass if he tried.

"These guys want to play? Oh, I can fucking play," Arek mumbled as he stormed across the bedroom and pulled on a random book. Cody whistled as the bookshelf moved out of the way, producing a selection of guns and other toys that would put anything Tyson had to shame.

Cody helped Trev get into the shower with the other three and was worried as he stared at the thin line of pink on the bandage on his leg.

"You're bleeding."

"I'll be fine. Just get me a gun," Trev said.

J.J. ripped away from Renee's arms. "J.J., get back here."

"No, I want to stay with Uncle Trev." J.J. curled up under Trev's arm, his small arms wrapping around his stomach.

"J.J., Uncle Trev is injured," Cody tried to reason. The kid only buried his head.

Trev held up his hand to stop him as Cody stood to grab J.J. "He's fine. We'll all be fine as long as Arek doesn't blow us all up as he exterminates whoever that is. Just get me a gun and go make sure he doesn't shoot the house down."

Arek picked that moment to march into the bathroom, and it was Renee that swore first. His sister's expression said it all as she took in her fiancé. Arek looked like he just stepped out of the Terminator movie. His face was painted in black stripes while an assortment of guns and knives hung off his body, his eyes wild. "Here." Arek held out a gun to Trev.

"Where are they?"

"Your office for now. Delilah had the police dispatched to the other side of town to buy us time." They shared a brotherly moment to which only they seemed to be privy.

"We'll be fine. I have a lot of enemies as an attorney. We can spin this if they show up. Just maybe don't greet them looking like that." Arek smirked at the jab. "Don't die out there."

"Keep them safe."

"With my life."

Arek turned that death glare on Cody. "Let's get you ready. I plan on making sure no one walks out of here alive." He stomped back out of the room.

Trev grabbed his arm before he could stand. "Stay safe."

He nodded, and Trev let go. Jumping up, he closed the bathroom door and made his way over to Arek who was holding out equipment for him to put on.

"Is this a normal Friday for you guys?"

"Only since I met your family," Arek shot back, a glimmer of excitement in his eyes.

"You worry me, Arek."

"I know, I like it that way. Now put this on." He held out a bulletproof vest and a sleek-looking band with the same eyepiece as on the helmets. As soon as he was suited up, Arek handed him enough weapons to take out the whole block. "Alright, let's party."

"We need to work on your definition of party." Cody shook his head as he followed Arek out the bedroom door. The closer they drew to the stairs, the easier it was to hear them talking. "What are they looking for?" Cody asked as something crashed that sounded a lot like a desk being flipped over.

"Not sure. Delilah, give me a visual of the office."

The screen flashed, and suddenly, Cody was staring at the office in real-time from a camera that was obviously hidden. He had to wonder just how many other cameras were hidden in this place. The morning in the gym flashed through his mind.

"Those are more of Alejandro's men." Arek looked back at him. "Did you miss one?"

"Don't look at me. I made sure every last one of the Streetlores in the warehouse was dead," Cody whispered. "Wait, that guy, the one that just walked into the room. That looks like the guy Trev said was the one harassing Sally."

"He's after the money and drugs to take over the number one spot. Fucking hydras. Delilah, how many are around the house?"

"There are four hostiles outside and six on the lower level," the AI responded.

"No need for stealth. Shoot first, ask questions later." He opened his mouth to ask what exactly that meant when Arek sprinted down the stairs, guns blazing.

I guess that answers that question.

Cody gave chase and reached the bottom stairs, having to step over a body just as the house plummeted into darkness. The lense turned to night vision without him asking, and once more, he marveled over the tech. A man came bursting through the splintered and off the hinges front door, white shirt under his fancy suit practically glowing. Cody fired as the guy reached out for the railing to the stairs, and the front of the shirt was suddenly not so white.

"Shit." He dove behind the hallway wall as a bullet smacked a little too close for comfort beside him. Drywall dust and bits of wood coated him as more bullets flew in the front door.

"Delilah?" he whispered tentatively.

"Yes, Master Cody?"

Master? He could get used to that. "Can you show me the hostiles outside the house?"

The screen began to flip through images when a loud crash and a body sailed into the hallway. A second later Arek followed like the deadly predator he was. The guy was groaning and trying the crawl away. Smashing through a door will do that. Arek stepped on the guy's back, halting his movement before he shot him in the head without even looking. In an eerie almost robotic movement Arek turned his attention to the office and marched on.

The image stopped when the camera picked up movement in the backyard. The three left outside were sneaking toward the back door. Cody changed course, letting Arek deal with the ones in the house, and ran for the kitchen. He got low, watching the shadows as they passed the window nearing the sliding glass door. The guys hastily shot at the door to break it.

Guess they weren't worried about a quiet entry.

Cody slid back into the shadows of the corner and waited like a snake ready to strike.

The small party of three was far too focused on the sounds going on in the office to notice their real threat. In all his years with Tyson, he'd never experienced this level of shit-storm before, and he'd seen some crazy shit. Raising his gun, he fired two quick shots hitting the two that were directly in front of him. The third guy spun as he fired and ended up using the fridge as a shield. Cody rolled out of the way as the guy's gun rounded the fridge to shoot at him blindly.

This house was going to need some serious repairs. He could only imagine the look on Trev's face when he saw the mess.

"If you leave now, I won't kill you," Cody called out from his own hiding spot.

"Je ne suis pas né d'hier."

"Dude, I have no idea what you just said."

"Would you like me to translate?" Delilah came through his earpiece, and he rolled his eyes.

"No, I don't want you to translate," Cody said.

"Qui Moi?" The guy asked, and Cody wanted to smack himself in the forehead. That's it, forget this. Rolling out from behind his hiding spot, he fired, catching the guy in the leg. The man screamed as he crumpled to the ground. The face that stared back at him was young, nineteen maybe. His hand wavered as he pointed the gun at the scared young face.

Taking him by surprise, the guy's face twisted in rage, his gun raising to point at him, and then he fell silent. Eyes wide, the body went limp as blood seeped across the marble floor. Cody looked up at Arek, his face hidden in the shadows.

"Even children know how to use guns, never falter, or you will end up dead. I thought you'd know that by now." Turning, Arek walked out, and he was left staring at the face that could easily have been him not long ago. Not sure why he was drawn to the young man, he crawled across the floor and wiped the hair away from his face, and closing his eyes.

"Why couldn't you have just left?" Peeling himself off the floor, he walked out of the kitchen to search out his family, but there was a new scar etched on his soul.

Chapter 24

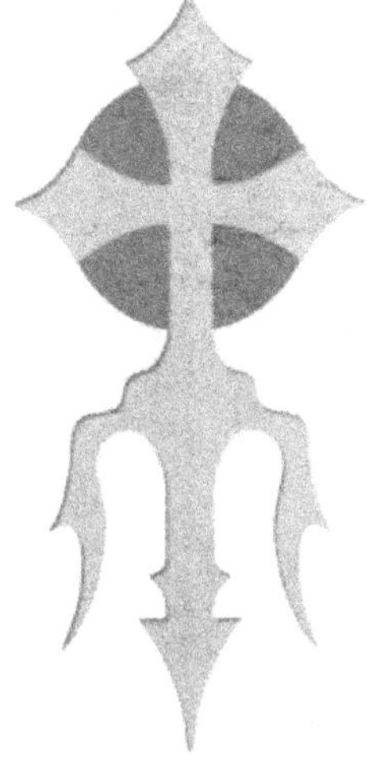

Trev felt like he was propped up in the corner of the basement's torture room, like a rag doll. The stark white and easily washable walls were hurting his eyes to stare at. He'd never had to use this room and hoped it would remain that way when he had it built, but apparently it would be tainted with red along with his and Arek's soul.

Arek yelled with barely contained rage as his fist collided with the man handcuffed to the chair. The loud yell coupled with his brother's incessant rave music thumping was making his head pound harder. All they needed were some fucking glow sticks. Arek had cuffed the man with his ankles and hands each attached to one of the four legs of the chair. The metal cuffs that were securing his wrists behind his back rattled against the metal chair as he jerked from the blow.

He just really wanted this to be over so he could lay back down for a few hours before he would be required to arrange the clean up. Arek waved his bottle of whiskey back and forth as he wiggled his ass to the new song. He was starting to wonder if the reason he was so successful at torture was because people just wanted the fucking music and dancing to stop—he sure as hell did.

Trev glanced at his phone, checking up on the latest regarding the police who were supposed to be trying to find the house. So far, there were three cars driving in circles as Delilah scrambled their equipment. The hope was that they would give up and run along home. So far, it worked out, and Cody and Sally were out cleaning up the debris. He hated the idea of moving the family from this house, but it seemed it was something they would have to do, at least until renovations were complete.

Something metal clanking on the table had him glancing up as the music was lowered to a reasonable decibel.

"Why did you come here, Lorena?" Arek asked the man in front of him.

"Stop calling me that," the man said and spit blood out on the floor.

"Why, it suits you." Arek smiled wide.

The man Arek nicknamed Lorena had blood dripping from his broken nose and a cut at the corner of his mouth. If looks could kill, Arek would've been dead.

"Lorena, why do you make your life so difficult, does it look like you're going anywhere, anytime soon?" Arek held out his hands to show off the room with it's assortment of weapons hanging from the walls and the chains that could hold a bear. "Just answer the question, why did you come here?" Arek rolled out his shoulders and cracked his knuckles as he slowly made his way over to Lorena again.

"Fuck you."

Arek's fist made an audible noise as it connected with the man's face. Trev had to concede he was pretty impressed that his brother had showed enough restraint to keep this one alive.

Once more, silence greeted them. This guy was tough. So far, he had taken all that Arek had thrown at him and done so with a smile. Well, a bloody smile now, with fewer teeth, but it was a smile nonetheless.

Lorena, or better known as Alejandro's second looked over at him and smirked. "I'm surprised to see you alive. Last I heard you were strung up like a dead cow."

"Yes, how the tables have turned." Trev pushed himself up and fought off the budding migraine.

"I liked you better hanging from your wrists. You won't see me scream like you did." His face contorted with an arrogant grin.

Trev wouldn't take that bet, he'd seen his brother work his magic on too many occasions. "The difference is, my chances of walking out of here are far better than yours. So smile all you want."

The sour scent of sweat and fear was strong even though the guy was putting on a good front. Arek would break him—the twinkle of excitement that danced in his brother's eye was enough to terrify those that understood his urges.

Still ignoring Arek, Lorena spoke again. "I told Alejandro not to trust you. You can never trust a lawyer, they are born liars and thieves. I knew you would betray us." The guy spat more blood on the floor. "You should be skinned alive and fed to a pack of hyenas."

"Keep talking. I really like your ideas," Arek's eyes were murderous.

"I just didn't realize there were two of you." He shook his head, the look of disgust written all over his face. "So what is this? Are you the brains, and this one is the brawn?"

"Correction, Trev is the nice one." Arek jumped like a wild man, the guy letting out a yelp as he landed, straddling his lap. "I'm the psycho." Grabbing Lorena by the neck, Arek kissed his forehead, his tongue drawing little circles. The man was swearing a blue streak that was a mix of Spanish and Portuguese as he tried to jerk away.

Laughing, Arek stood and pulled the t-shirt off over his head. He let the guy take in the sandman tattoo on his peck before slowly turning to purposely show off his back. Arek wandered toward the bottle he was nursing and Trev watched Lorena's eyes follow Arek. Shock was written on every feature of his face.

"No, that's not possible," the guy said, his eyes wide as they stared at Arek's back. "El Fantasma, you are a ghost. You don't exist."

"I assure you we are very real," Arek said and took another swig of the alcohol. He stroked the tattoo on his chest. "You see this? I'm the Sandman. Trev over there is Crosshairs. Together we make Father Time. You may have heard of us."

"Arek that is in the past," Trev rubbed his eyes. He needed to lay down and Arek's antics were drawing out the inevitable.

"What made us will never be in the past." They shared a moment between them, and Trev simply nodded.

"Alejandro tortured the wrong person and you Lorena—." Arek paused to make sure he had the man's full attention. "Are going to pay the price for his sins," he said as he spun and walked out of the room.

Trev watched their captive closely, the look on his face giving away just how fast the hamsters in his brain were running on their wheels. A droplet of sweat ran down the side of his face and dripped off his chin.

"I see the lights going on in your head. If I may offer a piece of advice, it would be wise to answer my brother's questions when he comes back. He has a flair for the dramatic in a way that most cannot stomach."

Lorena ran his tongue along the cut in his bottom lip. "Where has he gone?"

"I don't know, but knowing him, it can't mean anything very good for you considering this room has so many painful toys. The best you can hope for at this point is mercy."

"Fuck you."

Why did those being tortured always make it so hard on themselves? He was no better. He wouldn't have given up any information no matter what Alejandro had done. He respected this man for that, but he just didn't understand it considering the piece of garbage in question.

Trev reached out to the small table near him and cracked open a bottle of water.

"I'm not sure why you are being loyal to a man that is already dead. Was Alejandro a family member?" Trev took a sip of his water. Lorena shifted uncomfortably as the water slid down Trev's throat. "Thirsty?" Trev held out the bottle as an offering, but the guy looked away, his chin lifting in defiance. "Alright then."

"We were all family. You killed my family." Lorena pulled on the heavy bindings for a second time with no success. The muscles in his neck and forearm flexed with the strain. The burst of energy was short-lived, and he flopped back into the metal chair, the chains holding him jingling.

"Maybe that's true, and maybe I was protecting what's mine. I have it on good authority that you were the one that threatened a woman old enough to be your grandmother." With a heave that hurt every part of his body, he managed to pull himself to his feet. Using a cane for support, Trev limped a little closer. He was still having trouble seeing out of his one swollen eye, but he could see well enough to know that the guy was no longer confident. His jaw twitched, the tendon fluttering under his skin as he looked away from Trevor's eyes. "Ah, see you now understand. The lights have finally turned on. Like Alejandro, I covet loyalty above all else."

"I hadn't planned on hurting her unless Alejandro ordered it. I just wanted to scare her a little."

"Well, you did that, and now here we are." Trev could hear Arek return, and by the sadistic whistle he had going on, Trev wasn't sure he wanted to know what Arek planned. He grimaced as he saw what Arek had in his hands and decided he better sit back down. Arek closed the door and locked it, a smirk playing on his lips with the sound of the click.

"What the fuck do you plan on doing with that?" The guy asked as Arek walked toward him. You could feel the energy in the room shift—

Arek's excitement and the tension mixed with terror created a potent combination.

Trev got re-seated and really wished it hadn't come to this. Arek pet the industrial blender like a child, his eyes falling on the piece of kitchen equipment with love.

"Well, I thought I'd start with your fingers. You won't die if we remove those, and then we will have to see." Arek tapped his chin as he thought. "There are just so many possibilities, and there's a lot of things this baby can do. Her dicing skills are out of this world." Arek started around the guy in the chair and then stopped. "That is, unless, of course, you've changed your mind and want to tell us what you know about us, what you were looking for, and how many people you told. You get the idea."

The arrogant mask was once more in place. Trev wasn't sure if this guy thought Arek was joking, but it only took a glance at the feral look on his brother's face to know that he was dead serious—but worse was that, internally, Arek was hoping the guy would continue to refuse.

Arek shrugged and resumed his whistling. The man's eyes tracked Arek, and yet he was doing his best to act nonchalant. It was an interesting dance between the men from where Trev sat. Arek laid out the extension cord and then plugged in the vicious blender with more than enough power to do what his brother had threatened. Grabbing a few other tools off the table, Arek smiled wide as he wandered back over to the man.

Where had the little boy who rolled around in pig shit with girls gone? Arek may be worried about him, but Trev was more worried about Arek.

The loud whirr of the blender fired up, and the guy flinched but refused to look behind him. Trev had to give the guy credit. He'd figured the man would have shat himself by now.

"Don't fucking touch me," The man yanked hard on the restraints, his hands curling into fists.

"This is your very last warning," Arek yelled above the noise of the music and whipping blades.

"Do your worst."

Arek leaned around so the man could see his face. "Fuck don't say things like that to me. You'll get my cock hard."

Giving the man a wink, Arek sat the blender aside and picked up the hammer. With a few hard and quick strikes, the man's fists loosened. Using the pliers next, the man hollered as, one by one, Arek twisted and mercilessly broke the fingers with a resounding snap.

Trev refused to look away. He didn't care for torture and certainly didn't get off on it like the demons that lived in Arek's mind, but he'd chosen this path willingly, and that meant he wasn't allowed to not be okay or hide from the brutal truth of their tasks.

The tools were cast aside for the still revving blender with its small yet undeniably sharp blades. The man's angry shouts of pain turned to howls of true panic as his now useless hand was shoved into the blender. Higher and higher-pitched wails, his voice reached, his large body once more straining to try and escape as he thrashed against the heavy bindings.

The maniacal laugh that came from Arek could be heard above everything else. Trev shivered at the sound. There was a good chance he was going to have to talk Arek down off the ledge of insanity after this. He'd worked hard to leash the dark demons that haunted Arek, but this man had come into their home and threatened their family. There was no coming back from that for Lorena—no matter what he said or how much he begged, Arek was going to kill him, and Trev could only play the safety net on the other side.

No preparation readies one for the sound of flesh and bone being crushed and ripped apart. It was a noise you never wanted to hear. The man's wails turned to ear piercing howls that made him wince as he was sure even the walls would have run away if they could have. The man became violent as he jerked back and forth in the bindings. His neck and arms were bulging as his back arched off the chair like he was possessed. His face was twisted and contorted with the extreme pain, his eyes attempting to roll back into his head. The little motor tried to stall out and then revved louder as it cut into more of the man's flesh, the screaming reaching a whole new crescendo.

Blood flowed into the blender at a steady pace, giving it the look of something more in line with a summer punch than blood, with bits of flesh floating around in the spinning liquid. The blender clicked off, and Arek stood. Rolling his shoulders, he closed his eyes, and Trev knew he was letting the sound of the man's screams bathe him with their terror. He casually stepped around the banshee-ing man who was attempting to scream the house down. A red line dripped onto the grey concrete of the unfinished space and ran in a thin river toward the drain under the precisely placed chair.

Arek held up the glass container in front of Lorena's face, and surprisingly the yells grew impossibly louder as his bulging eyes tracked a finger slowly swirling around the red liquid substance with flecks of pinkish flesh.

"Would you like to tell me what you know now? Or would you prefer I find something else to blend off?"

Snot ran in long bubbling streams down Lorena's chin as tears poured from his eyes. He gasped for air, his mouth opening and closing as he tried to push words out that didn't want to form properly.

"This is a limited-time offer. If you are wise, you will speak up now. There are a great many things that can be cut off of the human body before you die." Arek leaned in close to the man, the disgusting red concoction sloshing a little onto its original owner. The man whimpered and pulled as far away as he was able. His eyes avoiding the slushy liquid that fell in his lap. The stench of ammonia was strong as a yellow stream slid down the pant leg and joined the blood. "And I know them all," he said close to the man's ear.

"Give him a moment, brother. He's still in shock. It's not every day you have a body part blended off."

Arek glanced his way and huffed loudly as he stood straight and crossed his arms like he was four and pouting over no dessert. The man gasped a little, a soft sob coming from his mouth. "I did warn him. What did he think I was going to do, give him the blender as a birthday gift?"

Trev lifted an eyebrow at his brother and received an eye roll for his efforts, but Arek sat the container on the floor and proceeded to sit down like he was getting ready for storytime. Trev had to stop himself from conveying any emotion, but the image of Arek sitting like that was way too reminiscent of their time as children. It was a time when Arek was carefree and wasn't shrouded in a cloak of death. A time he wished he could go back and change so many things. Maybe more souls would have died, maybe more would have lived, that he couldn't say for sure, but one thing was certain—Arek would not be this harbinger of death, and his own soul might have been salvageable. Now…

"This is the part where you start talking," Arek prompted a little too happily. "Or I can continue, of course."

"I-I came for revenge. For the money," Lorena sucked in a deep breath before continuing. "And for the drugs he stole." The man dared a peek at Trev before focusing on Arek once more.

"That's all well and good, but why else were you here, and of course, how did you find out about Sally or where we live in the first place? We don't exactly have a listed address."

The man gulped as he stared into Arek's passive face. "Alejandro got a tip that you weren't who you said you were. I don't know who from, but the guy said we would find the answers at your house. He gave me the address for Sally, and I followed her here."

"Who is this guy?" Arek asked the million-dollar question. As far as Trev knew, no one outside of those that lived here knew where they lived or what they did, for that matter.

"I don't know. I really don't—Alejandro didn't believe the guy at first because the man hung up before he could ask any questions." His face was paling, and Trev knew he was on the verge of passing out.

Arek jumped up and grabbed some smelling salts from his little workbench of fun and brought it back for the man to sniff. His eyes shot open as if he'd just gotten a shot of adrenaline.

"So basically, what you are saying is that you can't offer me any useful information? This is disappointing and yet is so much more entertaining news." Arek bent and picked up the glass container and shrugged. "I guess that means I better get back to work."

"No, no, please…I may—I may know one helpful thing."

Arek paused, and Trev knew he was playing a cat and mouse game with this man's desperation. He'd become something of a pro at mind-fucking a person just as thoroughly as he destroyed their body.

"Alright, I will hear you out."

The guy sagged against the chair, but his victory would be short-lived. There would not be any leaving this room, not for him anyway, and the one-time mercy option had expired.

"He-he spoke as if he knew you, and… he, mentioned something about the Golden Dragon's."

Arek sighed loudly. "Fine, I guess I can work with that. Now, who all did you tell about us and that you were coming here tonight?"

There was an inner turmoil in the man's eyes. Trev had seen this enough to know that he was carefully weighing his options. If Trev was tied to the chair he'd be thinking that on the one hand, if he admitted no one else knew, he admitted that he didn't have any backup looking for him, making him an easy mark. On the other hand, if he lied, he would eventually get caught in the lie, and where would that get him? He was pretty sure by the way his eyes flicked around the room that he was weighing these exact options.

"The family scattered when Alejandro died, but I wanted to keep the group going. Those here were all that I had left." Lorena whimpered, his head falling in defeat. Trev almost felt sorry for him.

"Hence the drugs, money, and possibly blackmail information, yes?" Arek prompted.

He nodded. "Yes."

Trev held his breath and braced against the pain as he stood once more. Arek didn't pay him any attention. He was too caught up in the act he had created. Arek sat the blood-filled container on the counter and picked up one of the knives spinning it in his hand. Each step was agonizing, and yet he knew that whatever Arek had planned for this man would be far worse.

"Why are you holding a knife? I thought you'd let me go if I talked?" Like a wild animal, the man fought as Arek took his time stalking closer.

"I never said that. Did I say that?" Arek laid his hand on his chest and looked to Trev as he shuffled closer to the door.

Trev shook his head no. "I don't recall you saying that, brother."

"I didn't think so. I mean, why did you think I called you Lorena?"

The man whimpered as Arek leaned on the arms of the chair. "I don't know who that is."

Arek's grin would have stopped Satan in his tracks. "The famous Lorena cut her husband's dick off. She is a girl after my own heart." Arek spun the sharp blade in his open palm, the metal glinting and reflecting off the walls.

Lorena's lower lip trembled. "Please don't do this. I talked—I gave you everything I know."

"Here is the thing. We." Arek tapped his chest and then pointed at Trev. "We were content to let the survivors of the Streetlores scurry into whatever hole was fitting, and we wouldn't have bothered with any of you. Instead, you led your men into my home and shot it up like it was fucking Independence Day. Then your men proceeded to fire upon my son and pregnant fiancé, as well as a woman that is also like family to me. Not to mention at my injured brother and his prospective boyfriend. You know, the Ice Man?" Arek lifted a brow at Lorena. "No one puts what's mine at risk." Arek practically growled. "No one."

"Please, I'm sorry. I'm so sorry. I didn't know, please. I'll scurry as you put it, I'll go wherever you want, you'll never see me again."

"Oh, I know you're sorry, and you're about to be a lot more so." Arek cut Lorena's belt, and the man yelped and tried to jerk away as that sharp knife cut through the material of his pants like butter. "I'm going to grip your pathetic excuse of a cock in my hand and pull it so hard that you are going to cry as it feels like it may just rip right off your body." The man's hips bucked around as Arek cut the boxers that lay beneath, exposing the flaccid and shriveled up cock that had been hiding behind the fabric. Trev was sure that if the man could, he would've sucked his dick and balls up into his body. "Then, I'm going to take this blade right here and ever so slowly, press it through the base of that cock. I'm going to let you sit like that, staring at the knife impaling your cock for however long I choose." Arek ran the tip of the knife down Lorena's stomach, another whimper leaving his lips. "A day maybe, or a week… how about a month? It should be good and festered with infection by then. I'm sure you'll be begging me to cut it off just to end the pain if you haven't already died. Then once I'm good and ready, I'll slice that knife with agonizingly slow precision, through your useless cock until that fucker turns into two hotdogs for roasting or maybe the bun, but you get the idea."

It was a single word, but he put as much authority into it as possible. "Arek." His brother's head snapped in his direction. "Come here." Arek's face twisted as he looked back and forth between prey and where he stood. Relinquishing, he straightened and cursed under his breath as he marched the few strides.

Trev grabbed Arek's chin as soon as he was close enough and forced him to look into his eyes. "I don't care what you do to him, but under no circumstance do you go back to your bedroom in this mental state."

"I wouldn't hurt Renee." Arek's eyes went wide.

"It doesn't matter if you would or wouldn't, don't go to her like this. Go for a run, a swim in the pool, I don't fucking care what you do, but you cool off and wash away this darkness before you head to that bedroom."

"Trev," Arek started, but Trev squeezed his brother's chin harder.

"That's an order." He left no room for interpretation.

Arek slowly nodded, straightening his back at the command. "Yes, Sir."

He released Arek and looked at the man in the chair. They were going to need some cleaners for this one. As Trev unlocked the door, Lorena began begging again in earnest. The annoying rave music was cranked up, spiking the throbbing in his head. Just before the click of the door, Trev heard the beginnings of the screams resume.

Maybe it's not my soul you should have been looking out for, Mel.

Chapter 25

Nope, Cody couldn't sleep, not after spending a few hours in Trev's bed, and especially after that attack on the house. He'd heard Trev make his way past his door over an hour ago, and he wondered if he would be asleep by now.

Did he sleep naked?

"Shit." He swung his legs over the side of the bed. Looking at the bathroom door, he contemplated going and rubbing one out in the shower. The issue was he'd already done that, and it hadn't helped.

Dropping to the floor, he lowered himself to the ground and then jumped up, trying to think about anything other than Trev in bed, alone. Proceeding to do some burpees, Cody felt his heart rate spiking from the physical exertion. He turned his attention to what Trev and Arek had been up to downstairs. A private torture room, you don't see that in too many blueprints. Cody had to wonder if the builder knew what he was building or if the guy just didn't give a fuck as long as he got paid. He'd opted for clean-up duty instead. He'd spent way too much time cutting people up and making them scream and never developed a taste for it.

"This isn't working," he mumbled as he jumped to his feet and paced from the bathroom to the bed. Stopping, he turned to stare at the closed door and couldn't take it anymore. Feeling like a teenager, he poked his head out of the bedroom and listened to see if anyone was awake. The house had two wings divided at the top of the stairs, and each side held multiple bedrooms. He'd chosen a room in the same half of the hallway as Trev, while Sally, J.J., Arek, and Renee were in the other half.

Not hearing anyone moving around, he padded his way along the cool floor toward the room Trev was currently occupying. The master suite was in desperate need of repair. Most obviously, it needed a new window since his had been smashed and was currently boarded-up, so Trev was staying in another room. Was it really safe to sneak into his room while he was sleeping? In Trev's current state, he figured he was as safe as he was going to get.

Was he really going to do this?

His hand paused on the door handle. Not a lick of guilt surfaced. Yup, he was doing this.

The door opened silently to the much smaller room. He stood in the doorway and watched the slow rise and fall of Trev's bare chest. The moonlight filtered through the gap in the thick drapes and showed off the angles of that handsome face and perfectly cut jaw. The dips and curves of his chest and, of course, the toned arm currently draped across his face made him look like a playgirl pin-up calendar model or maybe the cover for a romance book. Cody slipped his hand into his silk boxers and gave his cock a few strokes, bringing it to full attention with his touch. He'd never seen a sexier sight than this man at this moment.

Giving his length a squeeze, he forced himself to let go before he came like a fucking Peeping Tom in the doorway. A soft mumble came from Trev, the small sound sending a ripple of excitement traveling through his body and raising the hair on his arms. Fuck, this man was hot. He had more assets than any one person should be figuratively and legally allowed to have.

As stealthy as a ninja, he closed the door and glanced at Trev to make sure he was still asleep before he slunk his way over to the bed. He intended to simply lift the covers and slip in beside him, holding him while he slept, but instead, he found himself rounding the side of the bed. Trev was breathing deeply. Cody's eyes traveled the form under the gunmetal grey sheet. It was like staring at rich eye candy.

Every muscle flexed as his eyes fell on the lump under the sheets where his cock would be. He couldn't look away. He stood transfixed to the spot staring at what was definitively Trev's substantial length laying on his stomach. He licked his lips, remembering all too well how good Trev had felt in his mouth, and he was salivating at the thought of finally tasting all of him. The image of Trev letting go and coming in his mouth had his own cock kicking in his boxers with a building ache that was both painful and delicious.

Slipping his hand into his boxers, he stroked his shaft and wanted to come all over that way too sexy face and mark him as his own. The image was insane. He wasn't a fucking animal, and yet, the urge was strong to act like one.

Like a movie playing out, he watched his hand reach out for the thin piece of material that was blocking his view. The anticipation was almost unbearable and was causing his hand to shake. It was so wrong to do this while Trev was incapacitated and asleep, but he had to see it. Even just a glimpse of that thick cock with its smooth, silky head.

His pulse was loud in his ears as the blood pounded through his body like a fucking storm brewing. Just a little closer, his fingertips brushed the edge of the fabric when Trev's hand shot out and grabbed his wrist hard like a fucking viper snatching its prey. He almost yelled out at the sudden and fierce movement. Cody's eyes were wide as he stood frozen in place. He gulped, locking eyes with Trev and those sky blues of his hard, unwavering stare.

"Well, well, what have we here? Don't you know it is unwise to try and sneak up on a sleeping ex-SEAL?"

"Did you hear me come in?" Cody's tone was quiet.

"I've been awake long enough."

"Are you going to kick me out?"

"That depends."

"On?" Cody was very aware that Trev hadn't let go of his wrist. Trev's strong fingers pressed into his skin and was sending his pulse racing.

"What were you planning on doing once you pulled the sheet down? I'm assuming that this is what you were after." Trev's mouth twitched, one side lifting ever so slightly, as his hand pushed the sheet a little lower.

Cody licked his lips, his eyes focused on Trev's hand as he teasingly ran his fingers over his own cock. Trev ran two fingers along the side of his length, the sheet forming to the shape of the prize it was hiding. His heart pounded like a drum in his ears.

"Speak up Cody, is this what you wanted?"

It felt like he was in the middle of the fucking hottest interrogation scene of his life. He licked his lips—his eyes not missing the fact that the cock under the sheet was a great deal longer than it had been a minute ago.

"I was planning on finishing what I started in the gym."

"You were going to suck off an unconscious man?" Trev's brow creased, making Cody's body flush hot all over. He could feel a trickle of nervous sweat trailing down his back.

He lifted his shoulder and let it drop. "You going to say you didn't want me to?" Cody bent over until his lips brushed against Trev's. "I'd have to call you a liar."

"I wouldn't challenge me, Cody."

Standing straight once more, Cody opened his mouth to answer, but no sound would come out. His brain was misfiring. Nothing made sense. It was like his thoughts had turned to a pile of mush as he stared into those all-consuming eyes. Trev grabbed the sheet and tossed it aside, revealing the fact he was indeed sleeping naked.

Cody groaned, his body responding in the most carnal way. He had to clench his fist and remind himself that the bandages that practically glowed bright white in the darkened room were on Trev for a reason.

"Is this what you wanted?" Trev slid his hand down his body until his hand gripped the hard length in his hand. Cody groaned as Trev's hand slowly stroked his cock.

Cody licked his lips, his eyes drawn to the shiny drops of precome coating the tip of the sexiest fucking cock he'd ever laid eyes on—still unable to find his voice, he nodded slowly, his eyes singularly focused on what he desired.

"Then what are you waiting for? Get to work," Trev said, his voice husky.

Cody peeked back up at Trev's eyes, eyes that with a single look would have him on his knees begging to be fucked. "Are you serious?"

"Get to work or get out, Cody." Trev released his wrist.

He loved this side of Trev. Normally, the Dom thing would turn him off, but Trev was different. He had this nonchalant air that dared him to walk out, which of course, made him want the fucker all the more.

He hesitated a moment too long, his brain catching up to the words Trev said, so Trev spoke again. "Do I need to make my order more clear? Suck my cock, Cody, since it's your fault that it's hard, or use the door and get out."

He couldn't move fast enough to get around the bed and crawl up onto the other side. He had this urge to say, 'Yes, Sir.' He'd always been the one in charge of his sexual experiences, but it turned him on more than he ever thought it would to be ordered around by this man.

Kneeling on the bed, he allowed his eyes to take in the sensual man laid out before him. His eyes couldn't decide what to look at. The long muscular legs, the tight abs that could still be seen under the bandages, the shoulders that made his mouth water, or the cock that stood hard before him. The man was like an all you could eat buffet. Tongue tingling, he leaned down and licked Trev's hip bone, drawing a wet line across the warm skin to just below his belly button, the tip of the beautiful cock hitting his cheek as he did so. He so badly wanted to kiss every part of Trev's body, but the bandages halted his assault every way he went to move and limited his options.

Hand trembling, he reached out and ran his fingers down the muscular leg that flexed under his touch. As his fingers drew up that perfectly toned leg, he kept going until he could cup the heavy sac in his hand. Even drawn up tight, it was a solid handful, and he marveled over the feeling as he gently rolled those jewels around in his hand. Cody turned his head and resumed licking the rim of Trev's cock.

"Enough with the teasing," Trev said, his tone stern.

Cody lifted his head and gave Trev a hard stare. Under any other circumstances, he would have lavished up the opportunity to wrestle for the top. Tonight though, he wanted this.

Wrapping his hand around the thick shaft, he shuddered as it surged in his hand. His lips parted, and he slid his mouth over the slick head.

Cody closed his eyes, savoring the clean taste of his skin and the tantalizing salty flavor. He'd perfected his deep-throating skills over the years, but even so, it took a great deal of concentration not to gag on the long shaft. Trev gripped his hair, and he knew what was coming as Trev's hand tightened. Hips flexing up and hand pushing down, Trev forced himself the rest of the way down Cody's throat. His nostrils flared as he struggled to breathe as his nose settled against Trev's stomach.

He fought the urge to panic and moaned as his body relaxed into the sensation of his throat being stretched. There was nothing like that quiet moment before you started to suck.

Trev groaned as Cody swallowed, the movement constricting around the cock lodged in his throat. He drew his mouth up in what he knew would be a torturous pace, savoring every little flinch and moan that spoke of the pleasure he was giving. There was nothing about Trev he didn't like—he was drowning in the waves of need to please this man, to win more than just his body. Everything about him, including the heated cock in his mouth, was sexy and driving him wild.

Trev groaned as he picked up the pace. "Take your boxers off. I want to see you."

Releasing Trev, he whipped the boxers off in earnest and had to fight with the material as they hooked on his foot. Annoyed, he tossed them across the room, and as luck would have it, they landed on a family portrait hanging on the wall. He stared at the face of who he could only assume was Trev's mother, one eye staring between the folds of material, and swallowed hard. Trev made a throaty sound, and Cody didn't miss the smirk on Trev's face. He flushed and cleared his throat.

"Don't worry. I won't tell her," Trev said, unable to contain his amusement.

"You better not." He smiled back.

He grabbed their two cocks at once and dropped his mouth to the one in front of him, desperate to feast on Trev. His hand worked as feverishly as his mouth and added in a subtle twist of his wrist that he knew would only heighten the sensations.

Cody wanted Trev to let go, to scream, and to yell his fucking name. He yanked on his own cock furiously, like he was mad at it while he worshiped Trev's. It unbelievably swelled even more in size, and Cody's ass flexed at the thought of this monster inside of him.

Pushing Trev's un-injured leg further away, he swirled his tongue around the sensitive underside and sucked each of the sacs into his mouth, earning himself another strangled groan.

"You like that," Cody asked in between licks.

"Yes."

Dropping his head, he resumed his sucking of the soft skin that was drawn up tight to Trev's body. He made sure to take time drawing each one of those delicate sacs into his mouth and give them the attention they deserved.

Taking a chance, Cody slid his hand under Trev's body and tentatively slipped one finger closer to his intended destination. Trev flexed his cheeks together, forcing him to stop his movement. Cody lifted his head, the crown jewels falling from his mouth with an audible pop to meet Trev's stare.

"I thought you said you trust me?"

"I do." Trev laid his head back down.

"Then trust me," Cody whispered. He wiggled his fingers under Trev's body and waited for him to relax. As soon as those muscled cheeks softened under his touch, he continued the journey until his finger made contact with the pink star and was rewarded with a guttural sigh.

He pressed on the delicate button that he planned on getting inside one night—his finger rubbing small circles along the rim of the puckered skin. It was his turn to smirk as Trev's hand reached out and gripped his ass, a throaty sound of pure pleasure escaping his lips.

Trev's hand gripped Cody's and halted the furious jerking of his aching dick. All he could think was, please, if there is a god, do not stop this now.

Trev had lifted his head, his intense stare now shrouded by the shadows, but he could still feel the weight of them. He held perfectly still like an animal in a trap, and he didn't know what to do.

"Let go right now. If you're going to come, then it's because I made you. Do you understand?"

Relief and another surge of heat that would have singed anyone that touched him raced through his system. A single drop of the precome made an appearance and dropped to the bed as he let go of himself and let Trev takeover.

"Oh fuck," Cody groaned as Trev wrapped his fingers around his shaft. Cody had to remove his hand from under Trev to brace himself on his arms as Trev's hand expertly stroked him from base to tip. There was no fast or hard jerking like he'd been doing to himself. No, this was sensual and made him want to dive into this feeling forever.

He rose up on his knees and sat back on his heels letting Trev have full access to his body in any way he wanted.

The man was good, too good. He flinched and arched his back as he managed to apply the exact amount of pressure he liked. Cody bit his lip determined not to let go until he made Trev lose control.

"Come here." Trev let go and winced a little but got himself moved to the center of the bed. "Get on top of me."

"But what if I hurt you?"

"You won't. I trust you." That one statement meant more to Cody than any physical interaction they could share.

Nodding, he swung his leg over Trev's chest like he was mounting a motorcycle and then shifted back until his cock was in line with Trev's mouth.

He'd wanted to try this so many times, but his fucks were more about getting off quickly. There was no getting to know them or spending quality time, and there sure as hell hadn't been this level of intimacy.

Leaning forward, he settled himself into position to not hurt Trev and sucked in a sharp breath as Trev's hot tongue licked at his cock.

"I should warn you. I don't have a gag reflex." Cody didn't have time to process the words before he shamelessly cried out. Trev seamlessly took his cock all the way down his throat in a single highly impressive maneuver. He was no slouch in the dick department, and no one had taken him all the way down their throat before, not once.

"Fuck me. Is there anything you can't do well?" he growled out. Arms shaking, he dipped lower and resumed his sucking, the flavor like candy on his tongue.

They worked at first in time, with one another, a teasing and yet sinful dance of bobbing heads and hands exploring the intimate parts of their bodies. Trev slid his hands up his back and around to his chest and stomach. The caress of his touch was just as arousing as the sucking.

He had been lulled into thinking he was in control, but he should have expected Trev to pull out a trick or two. He'd been utterly unprepared for the intense sucking and gentle twist to his balls. A distinct sucking sound filled the room as Trev worked him over and blanked his mind to anything else other than the feel of his mouth on his cock.

"Son of a bitch." Cody came hard and in a rush. He couldn't have stopped it if he wanted to. The powerful orgasm had him yelling and clenching the sheets as he tried not to drop onto Trev. He could feel the waves of his orgasm rack his body as the man drank him down like a cold beer on a hot summer day.

His hand was still wrapped around Trev's cock, but he couldn't focus on his task as his body continued to quake. Trev's tongue did something that he couldn't even explain, but he had to brace himself as the second wave of pleasure bubbled up and gripped him.

"Fuck, fuck, fuck…Trev." Cody collapsed onto a forearm, barely managing to keep his weight off the man beneath him. His head swam in a sea of euphoria. Everything felt light and heavy at the same time. He was panting hard as sweat rolled down his shoulders. Cody gave himself a heave and landed on his back. "What did you do to me?"

A soft chuckle filled the room. "I win." Cody managed to push himself up enough to see the smug look on Trev's face. "This is not my first rodeo."

Why the thought of Trev with someone else bothered him, he had no idea, but he didn't like it. In fact, there was a good chance he'd bury someone if anyone else tried to touch him. Trev was his.

"You think so, do you? I'm not finished with you," Cody growled out as a surge of energy coursed through his body. Cody shifted his body off of Trev's as gingerly as his shaking legs would allow and gripped the man's chin in his hand. There was a depth to the connection as Cody lowered his head to claim Trev's mouth. There was no tentative exploring this time. He hungrily feasted on the soft lips and welcomed the battle of tongues as they kissed. His hands roamed over the shoulders that he'd craved to hang onto as he was fucked good and hard.

On a gasp, he broke the kiss and loved to see Trev's lips were as swollen and well serviced as his felt.

Cody brought Trev's hand to his mouth and craved to see more of the spark of earnestness in Trev's eyes as he drew his middle finger into his mouth. Cody's tongue swirled around the digit, mimicking what he was about to continue with the still very hard cock.

"I'm not leaving this room until you've screamed my name. That's a promise."

Trev's eyes flared with heat, challenge, or desire. Cody wasn't sure, but the quick flick of his tongue on his bottom lip had him releasing Trev's hand to get into position to finish what he started.

Chapter 26

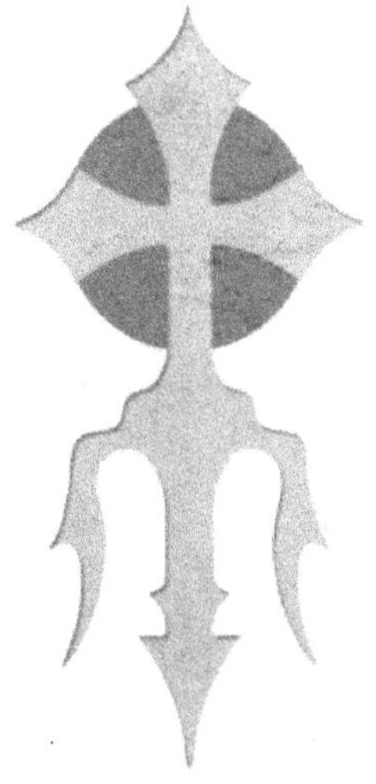

Trev's eyes were heavy, and yet his heart felt lighter than it had since Mel passed. He wished she could've been a part of this. She would have loved Cody.

They'd shared a few lovers over their time, but this was different. She'd told him as much in his dream. Was it a dream, or had he really been that close to death? He knew it was the latter, even though it seemed like a crazy fucking thought. There was comfort in knowing he'd see her again one day and his unborn son.

He slowly ran his fingers up and down Cody's arm as he soaked up the warmth from his body. Cody's head rested on his shoulder, and he could just make out his closed eyes and the relaxed features of his satisfied expression. "Mmm, I like that." Cody was quiet for a long time before he spoke again. "Can I ask you something personal?"

"You may ask."

Cody laughed, his body rumbling with the sound. "Don't think I didn't notice how you didn't say if you'd answer."

His lip pulled up in a lopsided smile. "A lawyer never promises to answer the question."

Cody's eyes fluttered open, and he shifted so that they could look at one another. "Okay, fine." Cody looked away from his eyes. A nervousness was surrounding him and changing the mood of the room.

Not wanting them to go back to the way things had been before, he broached the subject again. "Ask what you want to ask. I will answer as much as I'm comfortable with."

Cody bit his lip, his thick lashes shrouding his silver eyes as he spoke. "Who is Mel?"

Trev sucked in a deep breath, totally unprepared for that question. It was like a gut punch, and he looked away from Cody to stare out the gap in the drapery at the deep golden hues of the sun just beginning to rise. Of all the questions Cody could've asked, that was the only one he didn't know how to answer.

"Did Arek tell you about her?" he asked tightly, still not looking over at Cody. The muscle in his jaw twitched as his teeth ground together at the thought of Arek betraying his trust.

"No, you kept saying her name when you were out of it. In fact, it was the only thing you said after you passed out."

"Oh." He rubbed his eyes and then slowly turned his head to stare into Cody's liquid silver depths. Why was telling this part of his past so hard? Even as fucked up as Arek was, he was still able to share his pain easier. "I don't know how to answer the question."

Trev could read the insecurity in Cody's eyes, and he wanted to set his mind at ease that there was nothing to worry about, and yet he couldn't help feeling like telling him all about Mel wasn't going to help.

"Just tell me the truth."

Trev pushed himself up, his stomach muscles screaming with the movement. Okay, getting stabbed sucked ass. It was up there on his list of unfavorite injuries, especially when it was performed with a knife the size of a fucking machete.

He waited until Cody got comfortable, laying on his side staring at him. "Mel was my everything." He noticed the subtle flinch that Cody did, but to his credit, he didn't interrupt. "I'd known Mel my whole life. Our parents were friends, and Arek, myself, and Mel all grew up together. Riding the bus together, helping do farm chores together, I mean, we might as well have all been born of the same parents. We were that close. Other than Arek, she was my best friend and sometimes my only friend."

Cody laughed. "Why do I find that hard to believe?"

"Seriously, Arek has always been the social butterfly—the popular football star and the woman magnet. I was a geek that preferred my books and a good conversation. At sixteen, that was not exactly popular."

"Alright, I'll give you that, but I'm sure it's not as dramatic as she was your only friend," Cody said, a twinkle of a tease playing across his face.

"Believe what you will, but it is the truth. Mel was like the west winds, wild and free-spirited, and yet so grounded in her beliefs. She'd run you headlong into a fire and save you all at the same time." He stared at the far wall and pictured her amazing smile as she'd run through the wheat, her hair blowing around her face. No matter what, she'd always own a part of his heart and soul.

"She sounds amazing."

"She really was. We started dating in high school, her idea, of course. I wanted to ask her out, but I never would have. She knew it and took the initiative. She was also the one who said we should experiment with other lovers and each other at the same time. It was also her that realized before even I did that I was not just into girls. I mean, I realized it but didn't want to face it. She was having none of that. She talked me into our first threesome at eighteen with another guy that I didn't know. Hell, I didn't even know his name.

Man, she was...I don't have the words." Trev paused to take a steadying breath. "She helped me explore myself. If it wasn't for her, I don't know if I would've been that brave. She helped me find my brave." He looked to Cody. The truth of how he really saw himself felt good to get off his chest.

"I don't know anyone else that would've been so open or free spirited, especially from the small town we were from. It was all, you get a job, get married, have babies, and it better be in that order," he mocked his father's voice and laughed hard, and Cody smiled along with him. "She was unconventional and did what she wanted when she wanted and always called you out on your shit. You either learned to accept that or you couldn't be friends."

"I have a hard time picturing someone like that and Arek getting along," Cody grinned and it made Trev laugh.

"Oh they had some epic fights, words, fists, you name it they would endlessly pick at one another."

"Anyway, you should've seen the look on my father's face when one dinner she randomly decided it was time my parents knew that I was bisexual. I told her I was too scared to open up to them, so she took the proverbial bull by the horns. I was mortified. I wanted to run from the room like I was born as this huge sin and I was sure that they were going to have me flogged in church the next Sunday in front of the whole town." Trev looked at his hands as the memories flooded back like it just happened yesterday. "She told me that I shouldn't be ashamed of who I was and ordered—yes, ordered—my parents to be understanding." He rubbed his face and looked over at Cody. "Was it her place to do so? No, but I'll be honest I can't say when or if I ever would've told them if it wasn't for her."

"I can't picture you that shy or insecure, you're so...you."

Trev let out a laugh. "You'd think so but trust me I wasn't always this man you see now. The man that can take control and be in charge or save a life. I could barely save myself from myself."

Cody stared at him, his face passive. "So what happened?"

Trev lifted his shoulders and sighed. "Have you ever met someone that can sell ice to you in the middle of a blizzard when it's negative twenty out?"

"I know the type."

"Well, that was kind of how the conversation went. She found a way to answer their questions and by the end I think my parents thought it was entirely their idea for me to be bi-sexual to begin with. Arek and I sat there dumbfounded, it felt a little Twilight Zone like. But, I can't deny that I felt free, like this weight around my neck had been lifted."

Cody's voice was soft and sincere. "That is some friendship."

"Yeah, it really was. I told her everything, we had no secrets, and we always had one another's back. She was the only person that Arek has ever been jealous of."

"I can't picture Arek being jealous over anyone for anything." Cody smirked.

"Right? I do think it is because they were too much alike. I think he knew no matter how hard he tried, he'd never match her natural wild streak or feared I'd choose her over him if forced to make the choice. Arek doesn't share his toys well if you haven't noticed."

Cody rolled onto his back laughing hard. "I can see that. Arek is simply a little like flying too close to the sun, and she sounds like she was all wings and the sun at the same time."

"That's a very accurate description of both Arek and Mel. After high school, Mel said she wanted to enlist in the Navy. That she wanted to see some of the world and do some good for God and country before she settled down, she asked me if I wanted to join and Arek followed. I think he did it because he liked the idea of looking like a hero, I just wanted to be near Mel."

"You didn't have the same drive to serve your country?"

"Not like her. My dream had always been to become a lawyer, but I would've followed her to hell and back even if she hadn't asked. Arek, on the other hand, loved the opportunity to play with big bad toys." He stopped talking and pulled the sheet up higher on his waist.

"What happened to her?"

"She was so tough, far stronger than I'd ever been. The three of us ended up as SEALs. I think she scared just about everyone she met. We both worked our way up the ranks until we each led our own units. Then one night, Arek and I were approached to take on this impossible task. We were so arrogant. I knew we could die, but we were good, no, we were fucking great, and I felt invincible like we could take on anything and always come out on top." He crossed his arms over his chest and chewed on his lower lip as he pictured the meeting that night. "We were asked to pick the best twelve members for the mission, and it had to stay covert. If we were discovered, we would be left behind, command's hands washed of us."

"What the fuck? Who asks you to do the impossible and then says we will leave you if you can't complete it?" Cody sat up, wrapping his arms around his knees.

"Who do you think?" Trev lifted an eyebrow at Cody, and he rolled his eyes in response. "Anyway, we spent a week deciding and picking a team from the best of the best. I scowered through records. It didn't matter from what organization. I only had one prerequisite—you needed to be deadly and the best at what you did. My mistake was instantly picking Mel to come and then asking her to pick a member from her unit."

"I don't understand. Why was that an issue? Was she not qualified?"

Trev laughed and then grabbed at his stomach as a sharp pain lanced his innards. "Oh no, she was more than qualified. Mel had come to me almost a year or so before that mission and said we needed to stop seeing one another, that she was not being seen as an equal. I didn't believe her. I mean, I did, but I didn't see it the way she did. I saw it as the guys razing her, but that they still respected her. I fucked up. I should've agreed, but I selfishly never wanted to let her go, not after all we'd been through. I planned on marrying her." Trev clutched the sheet hard as anger burned in his gut.

"The two of you were engaged?"

"Yes and no. Not officially, but we'd talked about it—I had secretly purchased a ring to give her, I just hadn't found the right time. Anyway, she chose this one guy from her unit, highly skilled but had a huge chip on his shoulder. The type of person that saw every personal shortcoming as everyone else's fault and not his own."

"I've met the type. Bad combo on a tough mission."

Trev snorted and looked up to the ceiling as he tried to rein in the tears that wanted to fall. He hadn't talked about Mel to anyone since her death. Not even Arek knew the whole story. "The day before we left for the mission, Mel pulled me aside. She was visibly upset and…." Trev stopped again, his throat clogging as he forced the words out. "She realized she was pregnant, and I was going to be a dad."

"Oh fuck, Trev. I'm sorry." Cody grabbed his hand, and he held on tight.

"I asked her not to go, I even tried ordering her to stay behind, but she wouldn't hear of it. The mission was difficult, but she said she'd make it her last and then go on leave. We talked and argued right into the next morning when we were to ship out. I never wanted to hinder her ambition, but I just had this awful feeling I couldn't shake." Trev had to stop talking. He stared at the stream of sunlight that was looking like it was glittering on the bedspread.

Come on, Soldier Boy. You can do it.

He could hear her in his head, and he smirked.

"It was a four-day journey to our destination by truck to get to the *secret* jump plane and on the morning of the third day, she ended up in an argument with the guy she'd chosen to join the mission. I could hear him tell her that the only reason she was still in charge was that she had tits and gave a good blowjob. It was fashionable to have her in charge, but she didn't really deserve it. The argument got loud and ignorant enough that I wanted to pummel his face in, but one searing look from her had me frozen in place. I thought he was going to hit her, and if he had there wouldn't have been any holding me back."

"She needed to fix it."

"Yes, I got it, but she was…well, you know." Trev took a shaky breath, his hand squeezing the life out of Cody's for support. "The look she gave me, I thought for sure she regretted us staying together, that she was going to have to go on leave because of us. I felt terrible as she stormed away to get some air, and…." He couldn't hold back the tears as the pain he'd let out in his dream decided to make an appearance while he was awake.

"Hey, it's okay." Cody gripped him in a hug, and he clung to him as he wrestled with the overwhelming drowning sensation. "You don't have to say anymore."

"I need to say this." Trev took a moment to compose himself. "We were in this area, we didn't travel much and didn't know the roads well. I yelled for her to stop as she made her way around the truck. She looked back at me as her foot stepped on a land mine. One minute she was there, the next…her, my child, my best friend, my everything was gone. She was just gone. The explosion threw me back between the trucks. I clawed at the ground, trying to get to her, but Arek wouldn't let me. He wrestled me to the ground as I screamed like my physical heart was being ripped from my chest. I've blamed myself every single day since for her death." He pulled away from Cody's hold to sit up. "I should've ordered to stay behind, I should've listened to my gut."

"She would've hated you for it," Cody said quietly.

"Maybe, but she would still be alive even if she never wanted to see me again." Trev groaned as she forced himself to stand.

Cody jumped up to help him, but he shook his head no. He limped his way to the dresser and stared down at the dog tags he always wore—one of his and one of hers, and the diamond ring that was nestled between—picking up the tags, he tossed the chain at Cody.

Catching them, he stared at the damaged and charred metal and the shiny ring. "This one was hers," Cody said as he rubbed at the blackened surface.

"Arek refused to move on until he found her tags for me. He only ever found the one. I was… I shouldn't have continued to lead, we should've aborted, but there were lives at risk and we were their one shot at being rescued. It was a bad omen from that moment on, and the mission went completely off the rails, but I did what I was trained to do, complete the mission." He pulled himself up straight, ignoring the pain that was a sharp stabbing in his sides. "We lost six of our own, spent a month in the worst hell you can imagine, but we saved some very important people only to get home to be dishonorably discharged. We were a disgrace until The Righteous gave us the opportunity to continue helping save the world in a different way. They paid for me to finish school and got us set up here in Cali."

Cody looked at the tags in his hand, and, taking Trev by surprise, he stepped forward and placed the chain over his head, the weight feeling natural against his skin. He leaned into the hand that cupped his face and felt something inside of him shift as soft lips found his. There was no desperate heat behind the kiss. Instead, Cody managed to pour warmth and comfort into the gentle touch. The understanding he was showing for someone that had meant so much to him had a new stream of tears dripping down his cheeks—the wet, salty flavor mingling with their joined lips.

Breaking the kiss, they stood with their foreheads touching, the quiet moment yelled their feelings louder than any words.

"Coffee?" Cody said quietly.

"Cappuccino."

Trev wasn't sure he would ever feel the same way for Cody as he had for Mel, and maybe he wasn't supposed to. Maybe it was unique and different all on its own and was meant to be kept locked up in a special place of his heart. But, as Cody made his way to the closet and walked out with two housecoats, new possibilities presented themselves, a different path forming in his mind and one that struck him as integrally special to his heart.

He smiled at Cody as he helped him into the plush material.

He looked up to the ceiling and smiled.

One step at a time, Mel. One step at a time.

Chapter 27

Arek groaned as he stumbled toward the kitchen. Last night had been invigorating. There was nothing quite like good old-fashioned torture. He really should have worked for the likes of Al Capone or something. He would've been good at that job.

He yawned, his path veering. "Shit," he muttered as he walked into the decorative table in the hallway, all the pictures and the decorative antiques rattling. Arek grabbed the little frilly egg thing that Trev insisted on buying and righted it in the holder. He rubbed at the spot that was sure to bruise before continuing on his way.

The problem was his brain was still muddled. Yes, he enjoyed himself last night, but the moment he'd stepped into the bedroom and stared at his sleeping soon-to-be fiancé, guilt washed over him. Not because the guy didn't deserve it, he certainly did, but because he was tying Renee, an unbelievably beautiful soul, to him in a few short months.

Trev, as usual, had been right to order him to cool off. He'd have gone to the bedroom all macho man and pumped up, ready to take on the world in the worst way possible, and she didn't need to see that. Neither did their child or J.J. or hell, really anyone other than those that deserved his brand of fun. Not that the fucker downstairs thought it was a good time. The darkness of his demons scared him at times, yet they turned into fuzzy kittens around Renee. When he finally went to bed he stood for a long time staring down at Renee's sleeping form. He reached out and tucked back a stray strand of hair that was making her nose wiggle as it tickled her cheek. He had no desire to return to the basement and continue what he'd been doing since that moment. He called in the cleaners to finish the job quietly and take the body away.

Arek stepped into the kitchen and rubbed his eyes but could feel he was not alone. He glanced over at the table, expecting to see Trev or Cody, but what he hadn't been expecting was to see both of them together and wearing matching fucking outfits. His eyes scanned over the fluffy black housecoats and matching slippers. This was so not happening.

"It is way too fucking early to look at this shit. Did you forget where your closet was, or did you decide you want to be like J.J. and copy Trev too?" Arek poured a coffee and turned to look at the two men that hadn't moved or said a word since he entered the kitchen. He quickly pushed away the rest of the morning fog and wandered toward them, stopping when he reached the end of the island to stare at the two. There was something different about his brother this morning. He seemed lighter, a little shimmery, as fucked up as that thought was.

His eyes flicked between the two men, the glance as accusatory as he meant it to be. Trev was an iron mask and completely unreadable, but the happiness in Cody's eyes gave away the story. "Did you two?" He waggled his finger between them. "You did, didn't you?" Trev blushed, and Cody looked away—Arek had his answer. "Yes. I knew you two would eventually. You can almost feel the chemistry between you guys."

Laughing, he grabbed Trev's shoulder. "You dirty dog, you finally got back on the horse. I know you and Mel were close, but it was about fucking time."

Cody glared up at him, but he ignored the look, if he wanted to be jealous he could do it on his own time.

"Arek, I've repeatedly asked you not to mention her, why do you insist on saying her name to me?"

"Fuck man, lay off it, already. We were all friends, and I miss her too, just as I miss Scooter. But you went and put your entire life on hold for like forever since she died. I'm happy to see you dust off the old stick is all."

Cody jumped from the stool and pushed him back from the table.

Arek took in the hard glare and clenched fists by Cody's side—his own fists clenching in response. "What the fuck is your problem?"

"Don't be a dick man," Cody practically growled, taking a step toward him.

His eyebrows lifted in confusion, not sure where the hell all this hostility was coming from, but he would've snarled if he could. "Are you for real?" He got up in Cody's face, their noses a breath away from touching. "He's my fucking brother. I can congratulate him if I want to."

"Enough, you two. I don't need nor want a fight in the middle of the kitchen, especially over me."

"He started it. I was just trying to congratulate you, say I was fucking happy for the two of you," Arek fumed, looking around Cody to his brother.

"It's your attitude. How can you act so nonchalant over Mel dying when you were going to be an Uncle? Do you have no respect for your brother's feelings? That's not exactly something you simply get back on a horse after, for fuck's sake."

Arek's mouth fell open, his heart-stopping in his chest as the words set off every form of bell and flag that could ring and wave.

Trev stood from the table, a deep sigh loud in the sudden quiet. "Arek didn't know."

Cody's eyes widened, shock registering as he spun to stare at Trev with almost the same dumbfounded expression. Arek was confident it was painted all over his own face.

"Oh shit, I just assumed. Fuck, Trev, I'm sorry," Cody said, the horror of his mistake visible in his eyes. He looked so mortified and his mouth opened and closed at an obvious loss of words.

Arek's brain and heart kicked back into gear. "Why the hell did you never say anything to me? Why did you keep this hidden for so long?" He rubbed at the pain in his chest, at the thought of his brother dealing with the loss on his own. He'd never guessed, never even contemplated that it was a possibility. I mean, he knew they started sleeping together in high school and had continued when they deployed, but pregnant?

Trev opened his mouth, but thundering feet sounded, and a moment later, J.J. stormed into the kitchen, closely followed by Renee.

"Uncle Trev." The small body slammed into Trev with all the force of a little car, but he didn't let it show if he was in pain. That said it all. Arek watched as his brother slowly kneeled to J.J.'s height and talked to him even though it would've hurt like a fucker to do so, and he had his answer. He never burdened someone, even when it wasn't burdening—but Arek knew that Trev would feel like it was and would choose to deal with it alone. Even knowing that didn't stop the horrible feeling of not being trusted enough to hold onto this life-altering information. He was his brother, his twin, his person, whatever the fuck that means. How many times had they shared a drink in silence? How many times had Trev forced him to talk about the shit doing the backstroke like a fucking Olympic swimmer in the back of his head? And instead, Trev chose to share the information with Cody?

Renee's arm slid around his waist, and he couldn't stop from leaning into her as his knees shook.

"Did we come in at a bad time?" Renee asked.

"No, but we do need to have an adult meeting as soon as breakfast is complete. If the three of you could meet me in my office in say an hour?"

Trev stood from the crouched position, his movement slow. Cody flinched, ready to assist, but Trev stood tall on his own. J.J. proceeded to hang onto his leg for dear life, his small face pressed so hard that it was mushing his cheek.

"Can I come too?" J.J. asked, his bottom lip jutted out.

"Normally, I'd say yes, but this meeting has to be for just the grown-ups," Trev answered.

J.J. stepped back and crossed his arms over his chest, a dramatic sigh leaving his lips that had them all smiling. "I know that this is about the men that broke in. I'm not dumb, you know."

"Okay, you've been hanging out with Uncle Trev a bit too much. Come on, let's get you your toast and juice, little man," Renee intervened, steering the still pouting J.J. away from the three of them.

"Brother." Trev held up his hand.

"Not now, not here. We will discuss this later." Discussion closed, Trev limped out of the kitchen, leaving himself and Cody to stare after him.

"I'm sorry, man. I really thought you knew," Cody whispered.

"You'd think so, wouldn't you?"

Chapter 28

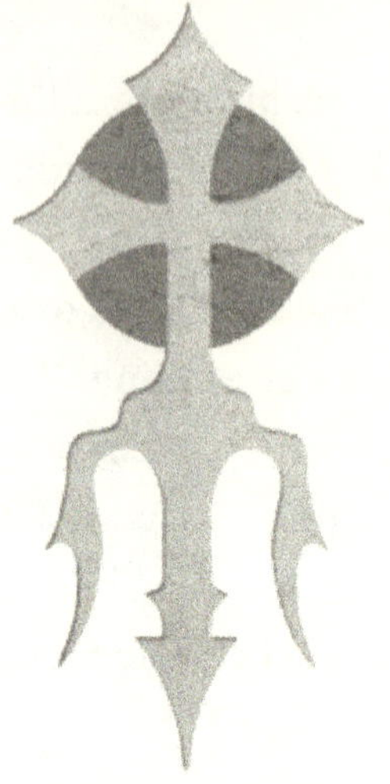

Trev sat at his desk and stared around at the destruction and oddly didn't feel much. The normal rage he'd feel over the damage to his precious possessions didn't make an appearance. Cody, Sally, and Renee, along with a few of The Righteous cleaners, had gotten rid of all the debris, including the collector pieces and antiques that had once adorned the room. Unfortunately, nothing could mask the holes in the walls, the blood-stained floor, or the cracks of the partially smashed window behind him.

Trev's hands shook as they sat on the desk. He stared at his fingers as they trembled and took a deep breath. It had taken more strength than he'd been expecting to shower and dress, his side was aching with a vengeance once more, and the only thing he could think about was crawling back into bed. He hated this useless feeling, and he wanted to get back to normal. He had court in a few days and hadn't even looked over the paperwork Sally had prepared. His face looked like one of his clients had pummeled the shit out of him. Oh, that's right—one of them had.

He heard the group before he saw them, and as they walked in Renee's eyes filled up with tears the moment she looked at him. He wanted to groan in annoyance. This was why he didn't share.

"Don't mind me, I'm really sorry, it's just the hormones. I can't stop the crying. I cried because I spilt milk at breakfast and then all over Sally when she asked if I was okay." She waved at her face. If she was lying, he couldn't tell, but it was not worth calling her out over. If she knew, then she knew and he hoped this was the last time it was discussed.

"Let's get down to the matter at hand, shall we? It has become clear this house is no longer safe. So, until the house can be repaired and upgraded, I recommend that we relocate to the penthouse downtown."

"I hate that penthouse," Arek groaned. "There is so little privacy, and there is no place to park Delilah."

"I know it's not ideal, but it will be safer until we figure out who knows where we are and remove them from the equation. I am working on a solution for Delilah."

"I didn't know you guys had a penthouse," Renee said.

"We don't use it often. That was where Trev was hiding out when he was ignoring us," Arek said. His tone left no room for interpretation. He was pissed.

"I don't care where we are, as long as we are safe." Cody shrugged.

"You would say that," Arek mumbled.

"What the hell is that supposed to mean?" Cody snapped back.

"Enough. The two of you, cut it out. I don't have the energy for this shit. I'm pulling rank, and we are moving to the penthouse. Get your shit packed up and be ready to go by lunch—the second piece of business, this mysterious person that knows us. I'm going to have Delilah start to compile a list of potential people. As soon as the list is compiled, I'll let you know."

"Do you think it's going to be someone you defended?" Cody asked.

"I honestly don't have a clue. Arek has always been good at making sure there are no witnesses. I was a little less efficient of late, but based on what the guy from last night said, the person seemed to know more than anyone should."

"That brings us to our next piece of business, the Golden Dragons. Are we still pursuing the car racing avenue?"

Cody smiled wide. "I'm down for it, and I know that I can get Spike to give up the goods or at least create a drop somewhere other than the races if given a bit of time to work him. We get along better than the rest of those that pick up, and he will believe that I got sick of Tyson's bullying. They all figured I'd go postal on his ass one day."

"I don't like this. I don't want you getting involved with another gang. You just got out, just got your freedom restored." Renee crossed her arms over her chest. "And you promised to stay out of all of this while I was pregnant, Arek, and here you are, ready to dive back into all this danger. I mean, look at Trev. That could've happened to you. He could've died."

"Renee, I know you're hoping that I will give this all up one day, but that's not happening for a while, and like you said, Trev is in no shape to continue with the mission."

"As for me, sis, you don't get a vote. This is my life, I'm a grown-ass adult, and I want to do this for the right reasons for a change. I've spent years on the wrong side of the fight because I was forced to be, and this is an opportunity to make a difference."

Renee pointed her finger at Cody, already looking very mother-like as she gave him her best glare. "You can also make a difference by going back to school. You could finish your degree and not put yourself in the middle of all this."

"Do you really hate what we do that much, Renee?" Trev asked, the room going quiet as she turned to face him.

"Do I love the idea of Arek killing people even if they are assholes? No, not really, but that isn't what really bothers me. The good Lord knows I've watched people die in the streets for far less." She took a moment to look around the room. "Don't you get it? It's all of your safety that I have an issue with, and don't tell me you have a better chance of getting run over by a car than getting killed on one of your so-called missions." She waved her hands in the air. "I'm sorry if I want my soon-to-be husband and family to be safe."

"Please don't say it like that. These so-called missions help a lot of people. We stop the worst that is out there, everyone that joins does. Rapists, serial killers, drug and human traffickers." Arek listed off all the offences that were on The Righteous hit list. "Renee there are those of us that hunt down people that steal and hurt children, can you tell me that you want them to stop?"

Renee bit her lip and sucked in a breath as her hands covered her belly. "No, but it doesn't mean I'm not scared every time you walk out that door."

"I don't know how to make you feel better about that. We are no different than those that still serve and if anything, we are safer. But, this organization, it gave me my life back, Renee. You wouldn't even recognize the person that came back from overseas if it wasn't for The Righteous and Trev. You certainly wouldn't have wanted to marry that person, let alone have a child with him."

"Besides, sis, I still plan on finishing my education, but not right this moment," Cody added. "I need to save money, and Trev mentioned that if I'm a good asset, they will pay for school. I can't turn that down."

"I don't know," Renee mumbled. "I just love all of you, and I feel useless and..." The tears flowed again and she scrubbed at her face like she was mad with her own reaction. "This is really not the best time to be asking me these questions. All I can picture is you all dead somewhere and my mothering over protectiveness is going haywire right now."

Trev's eyes flicked between the three people as they continued to debate their points. He grabbed his head as the back and forth continued and the dull ache in his head increased to a roar. Not that he didn't love everyone in this room, but fuck, it was easier to make decisions when it was just him and Arek.

"Are you okay?" Cody asked, the room falling silent.

He lifted his head from his hands, taking in their concerned expressions, before leaning back in his chair. "I need to speak to my brother alone, please."

Renee and Cody shared a look, and he thought they might argue, but after a nod, they made their way out of the office, closing him and Arek in together. "Would you like a drink?" He offered when the room remained silent.

"No."

"What happened to the guy that said it's five o'clock somewhere?" Trev tried to decipher the expression on his brother's face, but he refused to look at him directly.

"I guess he fucked off to the same place as my brother who shared everything with me, or so I thought."

"I intended to tell you Arek," Trev said.

Arek turned his glare that could make a new recruit cry on him. He grabbed the back of the chair across from the desk, the leather complaining with the hard grip.

"Oh, really, and when were you planning on doing that? When we are old and grey? When we can barely remember our names, and our dicks don't work anymore?"

"Don't be ridiculous." Trev closed his eyes, praying for patience.

"I'm not. It's been years Trev, fucking years since her death and you never thought that mentioning you were going to be a father was important enough to share with me? That I'd want to know you suffered through that pain?"

"I couldn't share, Arek." Trev aimed for calm, but his nerves were fraying at a rapid pace.

"All you had to do was open your mouth and speak the words, like all the times you made me share the feelings and memories I didn't want to share. How many times did you make me go through the details of Scooter's death?" Arek pushed the chair, and it slammed into the desk as he fumed.

Trev stared into his brother's eyes and couldn't hold it back anymore. Standing faster than he should've, he slammed his hands down on the desk, and everything on it leaped into the air.

"I had to get you to open up Arek, you needed to understand it wasn't your fault. You were slipping into this black hole, the night terrors and the P.T.S.D. episodes were claiming you."

"So what you're saying is that you haven't changed? That what happened didn't affect you? Because I call bullshit. You are not the man that enlisted either brother."

"Arek I couldn't have told you," Trev yelled. It was something he rarely did and Arek took a step back from the desk. "I love you, brother, but you have never been there for me, not the way I was for you. I didn't feel I could come to you and honestly it was my pain to share or not share."

Arek's eyes grew wide. "That's not true, I've always had your back."

"Yes, it is. Can you tell me anything about our time before joining the Navy or The Righteous that bothered me? Like when my pony died of colic, what did you say to me? To stop crying there were tons of other ponies. Or how about the time I fell off the hay wagon and broke my arm which ruined my chances of playing football junior year." You took my spot as quarterback." Trev stood up straight even though the pain in his side started screaming, but he ignored it. "Or how about you tell me what you said to me when it came out that I was bi-sexual. You can't can you? That's because you didn't say anything, you didn't ask me once if I was okay. Not once."

Arek's mouth opened and then closed, only to open again, like a fish, but no words formed. "I have been there for you for every hurt, every set back, every victory you have accomplished, and I have been there for everyone. If you needed encouraging words or a shoulder to lean on it was me you ran to, and who was there every single time you decided to do something stupid and reckless? It was me that risked jail time for you when you and your buddies decided to steal a cruiser to go joy riding? The only time you've had my back was once we enlisted."

"That's not fair, Trev. I've never been great with words. I thought I was being comforting with the pony by telling you it wouldn't be your last. I was only acting as a place holder as quarterback until you got back, but you decided not to re-join once you were healed. And as far as the bi-sexual, I didn't know what to say. I didn't care that you were, I figured if you wanted to talk about it you would. That doesn't mean I'm a bad brother." Arek paused and crossed his arms over his chest. "Besides you were always sharing everything with Mel." Arek looked away from his eyes. "I always had to fight her for your attention."

Trev laughed, the sound not at all joyous. "I didn't have to tell Mel anything. That's the point. She paid attention. Mel actually noticed me. I've had my doubts that until we got into the Navy if you even liked me, let alone loved me, brother," the last word sour on his tongue.

"Are you kidding me? I idolized you. Why do you think I tried so hard to step into your shoes and seem cool? You were naturally more gifted at everything." He held up his fingers as he began his list. "All the teachers loved you and your straight-A's that came so easy to you. Our parents thought of you as the golden child, and Mel worshiped the ground you walked on." Arek pointed at him. "Just once, I wanted to know what it felt like to be so perfect at everything."

"Bullshit! Arek, I would have sat at a lunch table on my own if it wasn't for Mel. Our lockers were side by side, and even when we were at them together, you wouldn't acknowledge me unless you were alone."

"You're making that shit up." Arek crossed his arms over his chest. "I loved your ass and was always jealous of you and how good you had it."

"Oh, for fuck's sake, we are so off track." Trev fumed. "When was I going to share this news with you, Arek? When Mel first died, and we were still on mission? I had to pull my head out of all that grief, compartmentalize it so we could go on and all the while I could barely breathe. Or how about when we got back, and you were a wreck because of all the shit you had going on? Would that have been a good time to dump all my emotional baggage on you?" Trev ran his hand through his hair. "Have you taken a moment to consider the thought that I couldn't share because I knew it would turn into this."

"This what?" Arek barked out. Trev sighed and looked away from Arek. "Say it, Trev, you know you want to. This what?"

"I didn't want my hurt somehow becoming all about you, which it has."

"Take that back." Arek stomped around the desk.

"No, you are fucking selfish and always have been, and you know it. I didn't tell you because I needed to take care of me and you, like I always have," Trev yelled.

As soon as the words left his mouth he regretted them. They had their differences, but Arek was right about one thing, they processed differently and the issues they had as children and teens were nothing to what they faced overseas. He never once felt that he wasn't safe with Arek at his six, and that meant more than all the other issues combined. The pained look in Arek's eyes had him regretting his loose tongue.

"If that's how you really feel, then maybe you'd be better off without me around." Arek turned and marched for the door.

"Arek." Trev took a step to follow his brother when the world spun. He reached for the desk as his knees gave out. His arm slammed off the side of the desk as he continued to fall for the floor, the world going dark.

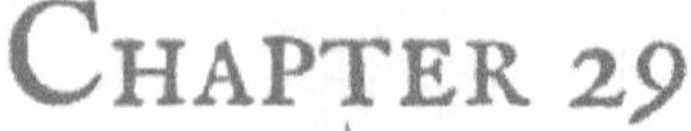

Chapter 29

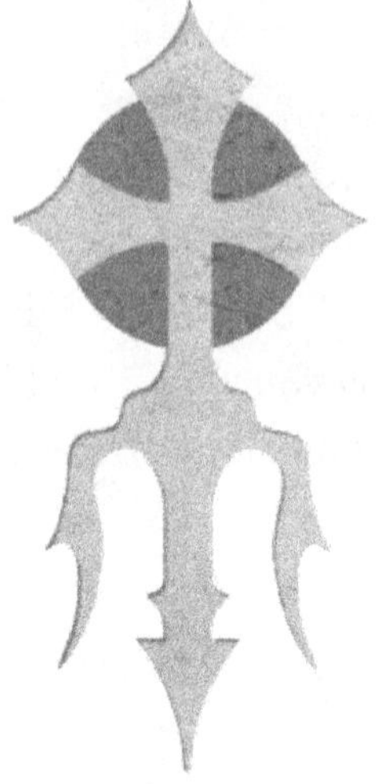

Arek yelled Trev's name as the thud and crash had him looking to see Trev laying face down on the ground. He ran for his brother, forgetting in a blink what they'd even been arguing over. "Cody," he yelled as he fumbled around in his jeans, trying to grab his cell.

He slowly flipped Trev over, and he was still breathing, but his skin was clammy. He carefully lifted Trev's head into his lap and brushed the hair away from his forehead. "Cody, for fuck's sake, get in here," he bellowed the house down.

"Come on, come on," he muttered as Cody burst into the office.

"What the hell did you do to him?" Cody skidded in on his knees as he came to a halt beside Trev's still body.

He shot Cody a glare. "I didn't do anything. He just collapsed. Come on, pick up." The phone connected, and the same gruff voice as the night he'd first called answered. "The special order has gone sour. I need to order another."

"Meet me…"

"No, you meet me this time. I'm not picking up the order and taking it anywhere," Arek growled into the phone, his hand squeezing it a little too tight. He was met with deep breathing and silence.

"Fine, text the address." The line went dead.

He quickly sent their address and then turned his attention to Cody. "The doctor is on his way. Help me get him moved to his bedroom." As he and Cody lifted Trev's body, he was once more faced with some harsh realities. His brother was right. He couldn't remember a single time he'd ever asked anything about Trev or what was going on in his life. How was that possible? The harder he tried, the less he could remember, and finally, he stopped trying for now.

"Come on, Trev. I'd trade places with you right now if I could. I'm so sorry you felt like you couldn't come to me," he said as they laid Trev out on the bed. He looked up to Cody. "Keep an eye out for the doctor to arrive. I'm staying with my brother."

Cody's eyes ran over Trev's still form. "Okay."

"Oh, and Cody," he called out just as Cody was about to walk out the door. The other man stared back at him, hand on the door. "I'm happy he felt comfortable enough to open up to you." He looked away before Cody could see the tears forming in his eyes.

"Don't you dare die on me, brother. You're right. I need you—I've always needed you, and I'm sorry I can be such a prick." He squeezed Trev's hand in his own.

Cody stood just inside the door to the same room that the torture had taken place not long ago. A makeshift surgery area was now in place, plastic hanging from the ceiling, a silver slab table in the middle of the floor, the scent of antiseptic strong in his nose. He tried his best to be a fly on the wall as the doctor spoke to Arek. The two men blurred behind the plastic but were easily distinguishable. He couldn't help the guilt as the doctor mentioned Trev had been pushing himself too fast and was overexerting himself. Some of the internal stitching had come undone. The doctor had to go back in and fix what Trev had torn, and Cody pictured all that had happened since Trev had first woken. It would be too much for anyone, even if they were a superhero.

"He should be fine now, but he has to rest in bed for at least a week, preferably two, he shouldn't be up other than to eat and use the bathroom. I don't care what you have to do to keep him quiet, tie him down if you have to, but it's a must, or he's going to do even more damage. We were lucky this time," the doctor said, pushing the plastic wall aside to step out—the clear rattling material reminded him of the show Dexter. The older man pulled off his mask and ripped off the gloves he'd been wearing. Arek was right on his heels, doing the same thing. The doc wandered over to the large case he'd brought with him and dug around in one of the front compartments. "Here, he is going to need to take two of these, twice a day." He handed over a small labelless bottle. On the streets, he wouldn't have dared to take anything that he didn't know the exact contents of, but Arek took the bottle from the doc and shoved it in his pocket, no questions asked.

"Can we move him upstairs?" Arek asked as he slipped out of the matching blue booties and gowns they were all wearing.

"If you think you are going to have any more incidents here, then no. Move him somewhere quiet and safe. I brought a collapsible stretcher you can use to move him around. It's out in the truck."

"Can you stay with him?" Arek asked Cody as he followed the doc.

"You don't even have to ask." Cody wandered over to the plastic, his heart hammering in his chest as he reached for the clear wall. Like a veil to another world, he pushed the screen aside and swallowed as he stared at the man on the table. He looked dead. The heart monitor showed he was indeed alive, but his normally tanned skin was pale, and his chest barely moved.

He perched his ass on the edge of the table, unable to take his eyes off of Trev's face. He wondered if he was dreaming again and who it would be of this time. He felt shitty for even thinking it but really hoped that at some point, he'd enter his subconscious. Picking up Trev's cool hand, he held it between his own and closed his eyes.

"Dear God, I promised I wouldn't ask any more favors, but honestly, I didn't think I'd be in this position again. Please look out for Trev, help him heal, and let him live. I don't need to tell you this, but he has been through a lot, and he loves his family and takes care of others. I—just please help him. If you need to take me in return, then do it, but don't take Trev away yet. He has too much left to do. Amen."

The plastic rattled, and he looked over at Arek, they didn't say anything, but Cody knew he'd heard every word.

"Come on. We're going to take him to the penthouse. I've arranged to take him up the back way." Arek held out the stretcher he was carrying for Cody to take. "For what it's worth, I hope that God is listening and if not him, then Mel, because if anyone can make God listen, it would be that woman." Arek gave him a small smile.

Cody may not be able to help Trev right now, but there was something he could do.

Chapter 30

Cody jogged up the concrete steps of the rundown apartment building. The small group of guys crowded out front parted like the red sea when they caught sight of him. He ignored them. If they believed he was still the Ice Man, that worked in his favor. The Ice Man wouldn't bother giving them a second glance. The stench of garbage permeated the air as he pulled open the glass door that might as well be metal with the grating on either side. He jumped back as a cat hissed at him and darted out the door. Even the strays don't want to stay here. That didn't say much for the hospitality.

It wasn't a huge building, only six floors, but of course, Ray's apartment was on the top. He said it was less likely that a stray bullet accidentally killed his sister up here. Sadly, he had a point. Cody didn't bother trying the elevator. It hadn't worked since some jackass started a fire in it two years ago. He sprinted up the stairs, the stale air doing nothing good for the mold and piss smell—if he weren't used to worse, it would've made him gag.

Cody could clearly hear the television blaring inside the apartment as he closed the distance and raised his hand to knock.

"Who the fuck is there?" Came the barking reply.

"Is that any way to talk to your best friend?"

The heavy lock clicked, and the chain was next as Ray opened the door. Ray's greeting was beaten to the punch when his little sister ran straight to Cody.

"Cody," Little Spice shrieked and ran at him. She wrapped her arms around his waist and squeezed tight. She grinned ridiculously up at him, pink braces, which were a new addition, flashing as she did. Her hair was in her usual pigtails, but they now had this little bun with bobbles that was all the rage.

"Hey, Little Spice." He hugged her back and then held her at arms' length and pretended to look her over like he hadn't seen her a few months ago. "When did you get so big and so darn pretty?" Her cheeks flushed at the compliment, her eyes batting up at him.

"Alright, that's enough flirting with my sister. Get your ass in here."

"Actually, this is a convo we need to have in private. Can you spare a minute?" Cody asked.

Ray crossed his arms giving her his best brotherly stare, and she rolled her eyes and walked away. "Yeah, yeah, I'm always on a need-to-know basis," she sassed.

Ray stepped out into the hall, the door closing behind him. "I fear for the man that marries her. So what's up?" They looked up and down the hall to make sure there were no unwanted ears.

"I have a job and an opportunity to make a lot of money and to get us both out of this neighborhood, but to do it, I need to gather the remaining Crimson Vipers together."

"I thought you were staying out of the game?" Ray leaned against the wall as he gave him a pointed look.

"I'm not really getting back into the game, I'm just pretending to, but I need it to look convincing. Can you help me?" Cody held out his hand with the small wad of cash in it.

Ray took the cash, his eyes going wide as he counted out the money. "This is enough to pay for a month of meds, man. Where did you get this?"

"It's my money. I didn't steal it. I've been setting money aside for the right reasons, and helping Little Spice is on that list."

"This is a lot of money. I can't take this." He held the wad back out, and Cody crossed his arms over his chest.

"I'm not taking it back. Besides, I need your help, and that is fair compensation for what I'm asking."

Ray stuffed the money into his pocket. "Alright, tell me. Who are you trying to pull one over on?" Ray asked.

Cody lowered his voice, stepping in a little closer to Ray. "Spike."

Ray let out a low whistle. "That is one big fish you are going after. Do I want to know why?"

"It's better if you don't right now, but I will fill you in when the time is right. Can you get the group gathered, spread the word that I'm taking control of this entire area as well as the Streelores' old territory?"

"Do you know what happened to Alejandro?" Ray asked, and Cody just looked away from his friend.

"Dude, you really are the Ice Man, and I'm mother fucking happy you like me," Ray said, making them both smirk. "I'll see what I can do. What're your new digits?"

Cody relayed the number and gave his friend a fist pump before heading back out of the apartment building. Step one of laying ground-work was done. Now he just needed to wait for word to get out. He had no doubts that Ray would be able to pull off what he wanted, no doubt at all.

Trev blinked a few times before he was able to get his eyes fully open. His side felt just as sore as the first day he'd woken up from the operation. He went to feel his side, but his hands jerked to a halt. He turned his head to look at his wrists, and they were both strapped down with thick leather cuffs.

What the fuck? Did I die and wake up in a BDSM fantasy? If so, I could've done without the pain in my side.

"They won't give. I made sure of that." Arek stepped into view.

"Do I want to know?" Trev asked, giving the restraints a tug just to make sure Arek was telling the truth.

"The doc said you have to lay low for two weeks, and if I had to, I should tie you to the bed to do so. I took him at his word." Arek inspected his nails, and all Trev could picture was punching his brother in the face.

"I really don't think he meant for you to tie me down literally, Arek. Besides, I need to pee."

"I have a bucket. I'll just put it under your dick." Arek held up a small metal bucket, and Trev thought his brother was joking until he started to lift the sheet.

"If you put that bucket under my fucking dick, we are no longer brothers. I swear on Mel's grave, I will disown you." He glared at his irritating brother, freezing him mid-sheet lift.

"You promise to get right back into bed once you've gone to the washroom?"

Trev sighed. He was too tired for this. "Yes, I promise. Now can you please untie me?" The metal bucket clanged as Arek tossed it on the ground.

"Oh, I could get into this look." Cody paused as he walked into the room, his eyes traveling over Trev's restrained body. Trev flushed hot, his body responding to the undeniably heated expression on Cody's face. "If you like to be tied, I'm all in."

"Hey, get kinky when I'm not in the room. I don't need to have that visual in my head. Besides, Trev, you aren't getting any until you're all better, so that mast you're sporting can lower the sail until I say you can play again."

"I can honestly say this is not how I pictured waking up…ever." Trev laid his head on the pillow and stared at the ceiling as Arek released his wrists. He gave them a rub and then sucked in a sharp breath as he sat up, even with Arek's help. "What happened anyway?"

"You passed out. The doc said you've been overdoing it, and you pulled some of the internal stitching. He had to cut you open again," Arek said as he helped him stand.

"Well, that explains why I feel like I was just stabbed again." He took a few steps while Arek was holding onto his hips from behind. Trev looked over his shoulder. "You can let me go."

Arek sighed but released him so he could go to the washroom on his own. Nothing gave you a better glimpse into what you would be like at eighty than when your brother offered to hold your pecker to pee. He had visions of them hanging onto one another over a toilet as they each tried to hit the still target. He shook his head as he leaned against the counter and washed his hands. Trev's eyes found his own in the mirror and stared at himself. He looked like a bag of rat shit that had been run over by a transport truck, and he didn't feel much better.

Trev slowly ventured out into the bedroom, and Arek jumped to attention, holding out his favorite housecoat and slippers. He looked like a trained monkey.

"What are you doing?" He asked.

"I just thought you'd like to put this on." Arek smiled wide, and Trev crossed his arms over his chest.

"I think I'm going to leave you two alone for a few minutes. I have someone I want you to meet when you're done—we'll be in the living room." Cody pushed away from where he'd been leaning against the door frame and disappeared down the hall.

"Here, let me help you." Arek dashed over and held out the housecoat for Trev.

Sighing, he let his brother help, and then, before he could do anything else, he grabbed Arek by the shoulders. "Stop it."

"I don't understand. I'm just trying to be nice and considerate. Isn't that what you want?"

"I appreciate that, but I have always loved you the way you were. I don't need you to become my dancing monkey for me to love you."

"That's not what I'm doing." Arek's face darkened as he looked away. "Fine, I might be a little. . .you scared me again. Twice now, you have given me a heart attack. I feel like this is karma for all the shit I've put you through."

"I can't say anything about karma, that bitch and I have our own issues." He gave a chuckle, but Arek's face didn't lighten. "I'm sorry I didn't tell you." Trev dropped his hands from his brother's shoulders.

"I just wish I'd been the type of brother you could come to—you have no idea how it tears me up inside that you didn't feel like you could talk to me. I was supposed to be the one person you could confide in and...." Trev stared into his brother's eyes, which held just as many scars as his own. "I failed."

"Our sorrows and wounds are healed when we touch them with compassion," Trev said, holding out his hand to his brother.

"Did you just quote Buddha to me?" Arek lifted a brow at him.

"This is the most honest conversation we've ever had. I love you but turning into someone else is not what I want. Unless you're offering to stop putting your foot in it?"

Arek's face lit up as he held his hands out to the side. "It's all part of the Arek experience, but for you... I would do anything."

"Don't make me cry. I'll fucking punch you in the face." Trev pulled on Arek's arm until he stepped in for a hug. "Brothers, we stand together," Trev said.

"Apart we fall," Arek finished as they gripped one another tight. Trev stepped back, breaking the embrace, but the lighter mood remained. Arek smiled. "Come on, we better go see what stray Cody has dragged in."

Trev glanced at his brother as they ventured down the hall. It was like seeing him for the first time. There was no bitterness, no walls and he didn't see the boy who he'd been, but the man he is now.

Chapter 31

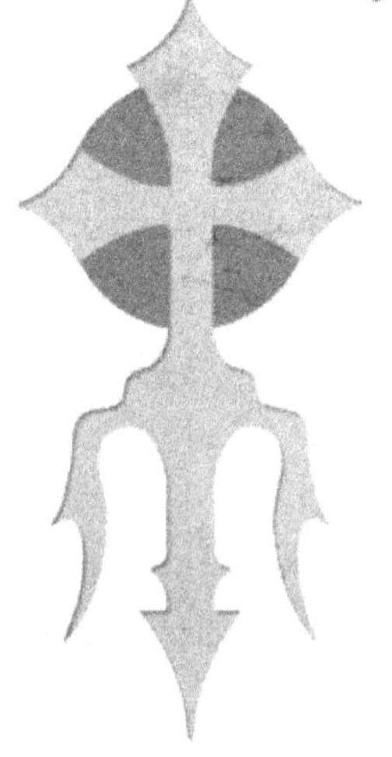

Cody couldn't help worrying about what was going on between Trev and Arek—Trev didn't need another setback. Two operations so close together, and his stubborn ass didn't want to accept any help. Arek should've left him tied to the bed.

Renee laughed, and he looked into the smoky reflection to see her smiling as Ray told another one of his famous dad jokes. That was what Little Spice called them. J.J. was sitting up straight in a large leather chair that most likely belonged to Trev and stared at Ray like he was about to bust out the Spanish Inquisition. There was a slight glare on his face, and his lips pressed together as he openly analyzed this newcomer. The kid was smart, much smarter than he'd been at that age. He'd been more interested in fart sounds. It hurt to think J.J. had to grow up so fast —how he wished he could turn back time.

"Just use the bloody cane. It looks dignified," Arek complained.

Cody smirked as he heard Arek and Trev heading their way, the distinct sound of bickering echoing along the hallway.

"I'll dignify you if you don't stop treating me like I'm dying," Trev growled back.

"You did almost die, so take the cane, or I'm beating you with it," Arek snarled back, and everyone, including himself, couldn't help but laugh.

"Are you sure you want me to have a weapon?" Trev said, but there was now a distinct thump sound as the cane hit the floor.

"I can walk faster than your turtle pace, I think I'll be okay."

"Jerk."

"Stubborn."

A moment later, the pair came into view, and as usual, his stomach flipped with the wild butterflies at the sight of Trev—he was intoxicating to his system.

"Sit here, Uncle Trev." J.J. bounced out of the chair, patting it with his small hand like he was inviting a dog to jump up.

"Thank you, J.J. Are you going to sit with me?" Trev's movements were slow as he walked over and lowered himself into the chair.

"Can I?" J.J. grinned.

"May I," Trev corrected but smiled back.

"May I?"

"Of course, but I can't lift you right now."

J.J. cocked a hip and placed his small fist against it just like Renee would. "I'm a big boy. I don't need you to lift me."

Cody glanced at Ray, who'd been quiet, and held back the laugh that wanted to burst out. His mouth was hanging open as he watched the exchange. J.J. loved Arek, but he had an undeniable bond with Trev. He was slowly turning into his mini-me, and Cody figured that by the time he went back to school, he'd show up in a tailor-made suit with a small briefcase.

Instead of sitting on the seat with Trev or in his lap, J.J. made his way up the wide armrest until he could sit with his back against the cushion and his feet stretched out. He crossed his ankles and his arms over his chest like a pint-sized bouncer as he resumed his glare at Ray.

Cody cleared his throat to cover the chuckle. "Ray, this is Arek and Trev." He held out his arm to indicate who was who. "Guys, this is my best friend, Ray."

Arek held out his knuckles for Ray to hit. "Nice to meet you, man."

"Likewise."

"So why is Ray here?" Trev asked, getting straight to the point. His eyes never left Ray's face, but Cody knew the question was directed at him.

"Ray is helping me reassemble what is left of the CV's and a few of the stragglers from the SK's to be my..." Cody's eyes flicked to J.J. "Team." All eyes turned his way, and Cody swallowed hard. "Fake team, I just need things to seem real when we talk to Spike."

"Ah, I see." Arek nodded cluing into the coded conversation.

"And how do we know we can trust what Ray is telling us about the teams?" Again, the question was directed at himself, but Trev had already turned his head to watch Ray's reaction. His friend looked very uncomfortable under the intense stare as he wiped his hands on his jeans and fidgeted on the fancy leather couch.

"The people in this room are the only people in the world that I trust." Cody returned to the assembled group and waited for Trev to meet his gaze before continuing. "I know you don't have any reason to believe Ray, but believe me when I tell you that he will not stab us in the back."

Trev's eyes broke their connection to give Ray his scrutiny. Those cool blue depths could make anyone shiver and Ray wiggled in his seat under the fierce look. "He better not." Trev didn't elaborate, but he didn't have to. It was clear that if Ray did anything to jeopardize anyone here, he would pay with his life. "Tell me then, why are you here, Ray? This information could have been given over a phone call."

"I invited him." Cody once more found his throat dry as Trev looked his way. "I also told him about the larger team and how you are like a captain, and I made him swear not to say a word." It was subtle, but the slight narrowing of Trev's eyes and lift of his brow was as loud as being screamed at by him. "Ray can be a real asset, and...I was hoping we could make it a regular gig."

"Do you want to become part of–the team?" Trev asked Ray, and the room was so quiet Cody could hear him swallow. Cody opened his mouth to jump in for his friend, but Trev held up his hand, freezing the words in his throat. "Do you, Ray?"

"Cody told me a little of what you do, and yeah, I think I can help," Ray said.

"Are you sure you're up for that kind of commitment? We are a dedicated and very loyal group." Trev relaxed into the seat, his arms resting on the arm rest.

"Yeah, I can do this, I'm like a worm I hear all the dirt. Plus, I have a very sick sister that I need to make bank for, and Cody said this could pay better than my nine to five and the few runs I have to do currently. Bonus is I've never been inside the pen, so no record."

"You do understand this is a secret team? You can't go telling people what you do when they start to ask how you suddenly have more money?"

"Yeah I get it, and I promise. Listen, I'm sorry if Cody jumped the gun, said more than he should. We've been friends since almost diapers, I'd always have his back."

"Yes, well, it has become a theme of late around this house, and although you are not the first, I will make sure you are the last."

"Coffee is made," Sally said, walking in and breaking the building tension like a pin to a balloon. "I also made fresh muffins."

"Muffins," J.J. jumped off the arm of Trev's chair and bounced around as Sally placed the tray of cups and coffee on the low table. "I'll be right back with the muffins. Come on J.J., you can help me, and I'll let you pick the biggest one out of the pile first."

"Yes! Sally did you hear? We're making a team! I hope it's basketball, I like basketball."

Cody smacked his forehead and shook his head even though he couldn't stop grinning.

Once J.J. was out of ear shot, Trev continued. "Next time make sure he is out of the room before we discuss business." Trev said, flicking a glance his way. "Ray, I cannot put your name forward to work directly for The Righteous. You must have been part of some branch of the military or able to go for training for that. With your sister's illness, I will assume that is not a possibility." Ray's face fell, his shoulders sagging slightly. "But what I can do is have you work for me. We can sort out your job title and responsibilities later, but in the meantime, you will move your family in here with us. This is non-negotiable. Those that work for me, from now on, will remain safe under my roof, is that understood?"

"Are you serious?" Ray piped up, looking around the enormous penthouse.

"I'm not much of a kidder, Ray. So yes, I am serious. Also, all of your sisters' medical bills will be handed over immediately. No more odd jobs where you can be arrested. We cannot have you in the system if you are going to work for me, is that understood?"

"Yes, Sir."

"Call me Trev. Cody, tell me about what you plan for the meeting with Spike?"

Cody could barely contain his growing excitement as he laid out the idea for everyone. The group lapped into lighter discussion and stuffed themselves with the array of goodies Sally had made. Cody couldn't help gazing at Trev or stop the ideas of how he was going to thank him once alone.

He shook his head in wonder, it had only taken one chance meeting between Renee and Arek to turn his whole life around.

Chapter 32

Cody backed his car into a spot at the end of the row. The races were well underway by this time of night.

"You see those two over there?" He nodded toward the car a little further up and across the street. On the surface, it didn't look like anything out of the ordinary. The hood and trunk were open, showing off what the vehicle had to offer. The two people heading toward the car were chatting, and the guy was grabbing a girl's ass as she pointed at the car. Little M proceeded to push that cute little pink-haired girl up against the car as they played tonsil hockey.

"Yeah, I see them," Arek said, staring at their ghostly reflection in the windshield.

"That is Little M, and his girl. He works for L.L."

"Whose L.L.?"

Cody smirked. "Lickable Lilith."

"I shouldn't have asked."

"It's a nickname she gave herself. She has a thing for tongues, and she wears a gold replica of her tongue as a necklace. Has a thing for collecting them from the people that don't pay her on time."

Arek lifted a brow. "And people call me weird," he muttered, making Cody laugh.

"Anyway, the bag he's holding that looks like a race giveaway with the emblem on it, that has the drugs in it L.L. has purchased."

"You're shitting me?" Arek watched as Little M put the bag in the trunk and closed it, all the while acting as if it was a normal date. They slipped into the car and a moment later pulled out and headed back the way they arrived.

"Nope. We never see anyone from the GD other than Spike. If they are here, they blend in and don't announce themselves. You get a random text once a week with a question mark. You send in your order by texting back a number that always stands for grams and a letter that designates what you want. E100 would be one-hundred grams of Ecstasy. You are then texted a time for your pickup and nothing else. You arrive, do a few races or hang around as a spectator until your time, and then you make your way over to Spike. You always say the same thing, it's a nice night for a race, and he will respond, 'Yes, it is. What time would you like?'"

"And you give him the time of your pickup," Arek finished for him.

"Correct. If you want to race, you say, I'm feeling lucky instead."

"Simple and yet very efficient," Arek said as he stared at the fairly large group of people. "I guess I could pick off each one of these purchasers. It would be like fish in a barrel."

Cody couldn't tell if he was joking, but he had the feeling Arek wasn't as his eyes scanned the crowd. He could almost see Arek calculating if he could kill everyone here tonight.

"The cops never show up?" Arek asked.

"Nope, not once in all the time I've been doing this. Only two reasons for that—they're either scared, or the GD have ties to the police and a little green is exchanging hands."

"Very interesting." Arek rubbed his hand aimlessly on his jeans, but Cody knew what that meant. Trev had already given him a run down on Arek's unusual quirks.

"We are not killing anyone tonight," he gave Arek a hard glare.

"I wouldn't dream of it." The smile Arek gave him was far from comforting. "I promise I'll be on my very best behavior."

Cody gave his face a rub. This was not seeming like a good idea at the moment. "So just remember, let me do the talking."

"Mmhmm," Arek said, pushing open his door and getting out.

Cody followed suit and glanced at Arek over the roof of the car. He said a little prayer that Arek didn't decide to go all Matrix on him. Avoiding a spray of bullets was not his idea of a good time. He cracked his neck as he looked for his target. Two cars finishing a race roared past, the breeze they created billowing the bottom of his shirt. He took a deep breath loving the smell of the rubber and fumes, the vibration of the engines making the hair stand on the back of his neck. Oh, fuck yeah, he got off on this shit. An image of bending Trev face down over the hood of his car had his body heating up and his cock twitching. Cody quickly pushed the tantalizing fantasy aside. He needed to be on point tonight.

Arek fell into step beside him, his face a hard mask that screamed killer—well, it certainly wasn't an I'm happy to be here look, but at least he didn't seem out of place. A cheer rose as two more cars squealed from the starting line, smoke rising in pillars. The scantily clad girl that had given the go bent over, wiggling her ass at the spectators. More cheers went up for a different reason, along with a few offers that shouldn't have been yelled in public. Then again, this was a different type of crowd. They liked all things rough and rowdy and the more illegal, the better.

Cody grabbed Arek's arm, drawing him to a halt. "You didn't bring a weapon, right?" he whispered.

An evil glint lit up Arek's face. "I plead the fifth."

"If you're caught..."

"Then it's on like Donkey Kong." Arek winked at him, and he swallowed the unsettled feeling swimming around his gut.

Fuck.

Releasing Arek's arm, he continued on his way toward Spike, where he stood in the bed of the truck. The raised pickup truck was like the black pearl of the sea and glittered with its custom paint job. He nodded to Spike as he looked his way.

"Ice Man."

"Spike."

"What brings you to the races?" he asked, the tip of his cigarette glowing and casting a shadow on his face.

"I need a few new races."

Spike pulled the smoke from his mouth and tossed it on the sidewalk. "I don't have any races for you," he finally said.

"Not right now, but maybe there will be a matchup for me next week?" Cody asked. Spike's eyes flicked to Arek, who was playing the part of a statue well. "I have a new number, and maybe you can let me know if you can fit me in?" He held up the sleek new phone he'd purchased.

"Hey, Spike. Who won?" The guy who was running the finish line called out.

"Blue Bonnet," he answered, not looking the man's way but instead keeping his eyes fixed on Arek.

"Who is he?" Spike leaned on the edge of his truck bed, the large silver rings he wore standing out against the dark vehicle.

"This is my new navigator—it was time for a new co-pilot. He is..." Cody looked to Arek, whose eyes were locked with Spike's, in some sort of silent pissing match. "Extremely good at what he does, I needed his skill set for the more challenging races that are to come."

Spike turned his head, the multi-colored mohawk flopping slightly with the twist of his head. "Are you going to try and take over my races, Ice Man? I've heard you've been on quite the journey lately. A few of my better racing participants have had some unfortunate crashes, and the mangled wrecks have been reformed. Planning on cutting my brake lines?"

Cody gave a small laugh. "Word gets around. I have taken in some strays, but even I don't have ambitions that high. I can't say I'm crying over the unfortunate wreck that Tyson and Alejandro were in—you race that fast on a hairpin turn long enough, your luck is going to run out."

Spike gave a snort but pulled out his cell phone. "I'll let you know if there is room for you next week. What're your new digits?"

Cody relayed his cell number before stuffing it back in his jeans. Spike stood, now towering over them from the truck bed, he gave Arek another once over before resuming his leaning position against the roof of his truck. They'd been dismissed. Either the ploy worked, and he'd get a text. Or they were fucked.

They watched a few races, but Arek never said a word. His eyes didn't even flick in the direction of the woman hanging out of the winning car, shaking her naked tits for the crowd.

He leaned in and whispered. "How many could you kill if we had to?" he asked out of curiosity.

There was a slow intake of breath that spoke all of its own the distance Arek had run to become this harbinger of death. The Sandman and all his jagged scars were laid bare in Arek's face as he turned in his direction.

"There are some questions in this world you shouldn't ask." Cody swallowed hard as the breeze of another set of cars ruffled Arek's hair. "And there are some things you don't want to know the answer to." Cody searched his face for any sign he was kidding. The locked jaw and flat dead stare made his blood run cold. Arek always had jokes, but he was quickly learning there was this complicated layer of truth to everything he said. Arek looked away once more. Arek gripped his bicep and leaned in close, the whispered words as potent as a viper bite. "Sometimes, I don't want to know the answer."

Well shit.

Chapter 33

A knock sounded at his office door. Trev lifted his head from the paperwork he was reading over. "Come in."

Sally opened the door and came in carrying a tray of assorted finger foods. "Sally, you know you don't have to keep making my lunch?"

Her weathered face lit up like a Christmas tree. "I know, but I genuinely love being here and doing this. It's been so long since there was anyone around other than my own company to cook for—besides, I wouldn't have a family again without you." She blinked back the coming tears and cleared her throat. "Enjoy. Oh, and Arek and Cody just arrived back. They are currently bickering in the hallway." A sly smirk lifted the corner of her mouth.

"What else is new with those two? It has become a sport. Thank you, Sally. You can leave the door open. They will just fling it open anyway."

He could hear his brother and…what was Cody? He was certainly more than a friend, but boyfriend seemed too formal for what they had.

He could be his lover, but that seemed inaccurate since they'd only had one sexual experience in the last three weeks. Cody refused to do anything more than cuddle him at night or exchange a few kisses while he healed. No matter how many times he tried to convince Cody that his setback had nothing to do with what they'd done, he wouldn't budge. It was causing a serious case of discomfort at night when all he could feel was Cody's body pressed up against his own. His body wash strong in his nose as his arm draped over his body. Cody had a cute snore, he didn't think he'd ever use those two words in the same sentence, but the rhythmical soft rumble had become comforting. He was a blanket hog though and on more than one occasion he had to wrestle the blankets back as if he was trying to steal from a hibernating bear.

His fanciful reverie was burst with a jolt as the two stormed into the office, their yelling loud in the small room.

"You didn't have to kill the guy," Cody growled as he and Arek stomped into the room, coming to a stop in the middle of the much smaller office. He was fine with the penthouse situation, but he did miss his larger office, especially at times like this.

He watched the exchange, and what was once annoyance had turned into amusement. It was his daily dose of soap opera. They gave him a laugh at least once a day with their grumpy old men re-enactment.

"The guy couldn't be trusted. He was going to try something shady. I saw him eyeing up the merch. Trust me. He was up to no good." Arek crossed his arms, puffing out his chest.

"And your answer is to put a gun in his mouth and make everyone else watch as you blow his head off?"

"It was for dramatic effect. Dead is dead." Arek looked at his nails, picking something out. "Now, no one is going to try anything unless they want the same fate or worse."

"For fuck's sake. Your brother is impossible," Cody fumed.

"Oh, I know," Trev said quietly. Arek opened his mouth to say something and instead fixed him with a glare as the words registered.

"Don't you start too," Arek pouted.

"I'm just speaking the truth, and…" Trev held up his finger as his cell began to ring, showing a scrambled number that spelled Righteous out in a code. Figuring it was a standard recorded message, he grabbed a notepad and pen before he picked up. "Crosshairs - Alpha, Zulu, Charlie, Kilo, Foxtrot, six, six, six," he relayed his signature authentication.

A machine distorted voice came from the other end. "There is someone you should represent at the LAPD nearest to you."

"Who is this?" Trev asked as he pressed speaker on his phone and then hit the call trace.

"Who I am is of no consequence. Her name is Maeve. She is innocent, and that is all you need to know."

The phone showed that the trace was bouncing all over the place. "I don't do random, charity cases. Are you paying for this client?"

There was a deep chuckle. "No, but you will find what she has to say to be very interesting."

Trev flicked his gaze to Arek, who shrugged in response to the silent question. "How do you know where I am?"

"I know everything. Just like I know you're trying to triangulate this call, but it will do no good. Go see the girl."

"Does this person have anything to do with…" Before he finished the question, the line went dead. The trace beeped, showing it couldn't locate the caller.

"What do you think that is about?" Arek asked, his face a mirror of concern.

"I don't know, but to know my number and have it call in the same way as our mission calls, means it has to be someone from The Righteous. The question becomes, why don't they want us to know who they are?"

"Only one way to find out," Arek said as he shrugged.

"I guess a road trip is in order."

. . .

Trev pulled the Bentley into a newly vacated spot outside the station. This was the second Department he'd visited, annoyed that he had to search for this mystery person. Arek was not far away in case this was some sort of trap.

Slipping out of the vehicle, he grabbed his briefcase and made sure his suit jacket was smooth before heading for the front door. An officer on his way out held the door open, and Trev nodded to the man before marching forward.

The front counter was directly in front of him, and the girl, Kim, working the front desk, who'd seen him arrive at least a hundred times, waved and fixed her pencil skirt as she headed over.

"Mr. Anderson, I didn't know we'd be seeing you today. Isn't it a little late for a client meeting," she asked as she gave him a flirty smile.

"Good evening, Kim. It was a last-minute case, or I would've called ahead," he lied and offered a small smile in return. "I'm here to see Maeve," he said, and the girl's face fell.

"I don't know how you defend people like her." She looked around and leaned forward. "She's a cop killer. I don't know if this is one you want to get involved in."

"I am fair to all those that need my assistance. Now, if you could have one of the officers set up the interview room?"

Kim straightened. "Yes, of course, I'm sorry. I'll be right back."

He stared at the poster on the far wall. The drab eighties image was faded and badly needed to be changed out. Then again, he didn't think that they'd painted since then either—the bland grey paint was chipping and peeling while large rectangles of unfaded squares from posters and items that had been hanging and removed created an abstract patchwork.

The metal door off to his left clicked, and an officer stepped out.

"Mr. Anderson, please follow me," the officer said as he held the door open for Trev to walk through.

Trev subtly passed the officer he knew, a small stack of cash. "Make sure that we are not disturbed for any reason other than the place is collapsing around us, and make sure no one accidentally turns on the cameras."

"Yes, sir." The young officer stuffed the money in his pocket before pushing open the door.

Trev wasn't sure what he'd been expecting to find, but the woman sitting at the table was certainly not it. Her soft amber eyes followed him as he made his way to the other side of the table. She didn't say anything until the door was closed.

"Who are you?" Maeve asked. They'd taken all of her jewelry when she was locked up, but Trev noted the holes lining her ear and the one in her nose. Her bright purple hair hung in what he would consider a sassy cut that showed off the tattoo of a hummingbird on her neck.

Trev seated himself and opened his briefcase before answering. "I am here to see about representing you."

"I didn't call a lawyer."

"I'm well aware of that, Maeve. In fact, I find it intriguing that you haven't called anyone since you arrived," he said, and she sat back as much as she could on the metal chair which was bolted to the floor. She laced her fingers together, the cuffs rattling

"You know my name, but I don't know yours. I hardly think this is a good way to start a dance card."

"Is that what this is? A dance?" Trev pulled out a small silver recorder and held it up to show her what he had before pressing record and laying it down on the table.

"Look Mister, I don't know what you want or who called you, but I'm not buying what you're selling, so you can pack your shit up and go. For all I know, you're working for the fucker that put me in here."

"I don't have any idea what that is supposed to mean. So, let me get this straight, you are telling me that you don't need the best defense attorney in the State, maybe the country to represent you when you are charged with killing a detective?"

She narrowed her eyes at him. "Like I told that bunch of deaf douchebaggery out there, I didn't kill that cop. I have no idea how they pinned this shit on me, but I'm no killer." Maeve shrugged. "At least not unless I have to be," she mumbled.

"Alright, convince me. I am a captive audience and on your side. Start from the beginning."

Her keen eyes gave him a hard stare. "How do I know you're not one of them?"

"Who exactly is one of them," Trev asked.

"Whoever it is that is setting me up?" She looked around the room and rubbed at her arms. "I feel like they're always watching me. Every person in this place is giving me cut eye."

"Cut eye?"

"Yeah, you know, like yo bitch I'm gonna cut you up. Cut eye." Maeve shook out her vibrant colored hair.

Trev lifted an eyebrow and gave a nod to the camera that had remained, as he asked, off. "You see that camera?" Once Maeve looked up at the camera, Trev continued. "I made sure that whatever happens in here stays in here but, I have no way to make you believe that I am not one of your alleged enemies. I will tell you that my name is Trevor Anderson, and I really am a defense attorney."

Maeve's eyes grew wide, and she looked around the room, her eyes looking to the camera.

"It's off," Trev said, answering the question.

Maeve leaned in as close as she could and lowered her voice. "Hold your wild horses just a minute. You said your name is Trevor Anderson?"

Trev lifted an eyebrow at her. "I'm pretty sure I just stated that I am."

She shook her head no. "I mean, the Trevor, aka Trev, you know..." she lowered her voice further. "Crosshairs."

It was Trev's turn to sit back and give this girl a hard look. Reaching out he hit stop on the recording device. Whatever was said next he didn't want any record of.

She didn't seem like she'd been military, but only someone from The Righteous or his old unit, which was mostly dead would know that name. "How do you know that name?"

"It's true, isn't it?" She was barely containing the excitement coming off of her. "Oh my god, I can't believe it's really you. I've heard all about you."

Maeve bounced around in her seat like she was suddenly on her way to the carnival.

"I'll make you a deal. You tell me how you know that name, and I'll tell you if you are correct?"

Maeve bit her lip, the wheels in her mind very obviously spinning. "Okay, deal. I'm one of Morry's girls."

Trev sat back in his chair as a wave of shock flowed through him. That was a name he hadn't heard since he'd returned, but he knew Morry well, and he knew that she had her own unique brand of cleaning up trash.

"She sent you didn't she, that's how you knew. I love her so much. Okay what do you want to know, lets get started."

This just got a lot more interesting.

Chapter 34

Trev opened the penthouse door, and he was greeted by silence. The surprise caused his senses to go on high alert.

"Delilah, are there any hostiles in the penthouse?" He whispered into his phone.

"There is only one heat signature registering," the AI reported.

"Who does the heat signature belong to?"

"Master Cody." Trev's body relaxed, and he closed the door, placing his finger over the security panel to re-lock him inside.

Where the heck was everyone?

Trev followed the delicious aroma, the unmistakable scent of grilling meat strong in his nose. He made his way to the kitchen and stood in the doorway to appreciate the view. Cody had his headphones on, his body swaying to the unknown music—he was busy pouring something into smaller bowls before he bent over and placed them in the oven. The corner of Trev's mouth pulled up as he watched the tantalizing show.

Cody didn't know it yet, but Trev was plotting to get him naked once and for all. Cody turned to flip the grilled meat and jumped back as his eyes landed on him. "Jesus Christ, you gave me a heart attack—I thought this place always alerted you when someone walked in?"

Trev sat down his coat and briefcase. "That's only if you're not me." He gave Cody a cheeky smile.

"Well, a little warning would've been nice, I'm supposed to be this badass gangster, and I almost squealed louder than J.J. over a spider."

Trev laughed and noticed that his side only mildly twinged. "Where is everyone? It's normally a zoo in here."

"They are all at the house checking out the new repairs and upgrades, and they thought they would stay away for the night." Cody lifted his eyes and locked his stare with him. There was a devious glint in his eye as he grinned. A surge of heat rushed down his body and straight to his cock. "I decided to try making dinner. Sally has been showing me the basics. I may have shot a little too high with the souffle for dessert."

"That's fine. I have always been more of a salty over sweet kind of guy." Cody licked his lips as they stared at one another. Trev didn't elaborate, but the implication hung in the air between them. The temperature in the room rose with each second that passed. Trev pulled on the knot of his tie and flicked open the top couple buttons of the grey dress shirt. He loved the way Cody's breathing visibly quickened and pupils dilated with his every move.

"Ouch." Cody jumped back from the stove, shaking his finger, before putting it in his mouth. Trev's cock hardened as he watched that finger slip between his lips. "That will teach me not to get distracted while cooking."

"I think it's best if I go get changed before I distract you any further, and trust me, I'm tempted." He grabbed his discarded items and marched the long hall toward the bedroom, not waiting for a reply.

By the time he stepped foot into the kitchen again, the table was set, including a bottle of wine as Cody filled the plates. "Thank you for doing this."

Cody sat the plates down and slid into the seat across from him. "Don't mention it. So how was your meeting with Maeve?"

"There is a lot to unpack there, so why don't we wait until Arek is present? Besides, I don't want to waste this rare moment of alone time on work talk."

"What would you like to discuss then?" Cody cut into his steak, and Trev smirked as Cody cut it into perfectly even strips. The simple act speaking to the personality that lay under the once Ice Man exterior. Each day they spent together he recognized subtle changes in Cody, like he was poking his head out of a cocoon and re-inventing himself. Everything Cody did from the way he poured the wine to the fact he held his knife and fork so prim and proper completely fascinated him.

"Have you decided if you're going to meet your father? You do know that Renee is never going to stop pestering you until you do."

Cody sighed and ate another mouthful, giving him time to dig into his own plate of delicious food. "I don't know. It's like the fact he left has been wiped away for her, and I don't understand why."

"Not to be facetious, but maybe if you talked to him, you'd find out the answer."

"I'm not going to like arguing with a lawyer all the time, am I?" Cody raised an eyebrow, but his lip followed with the light humor.

"Only if you want to be wrong all the time." Trev smiled, and they both broke out in laughter.

By the time dinner was finished, Trev was more determined than ever to get Cody naked and lay him out on the table like he was the dessert and the souffle be damned. His cock hadn't deflated once during the meal, and every time Cody stood, the thing would throb all the more as he bent over and showed off his firm ass. He wanted another taste of this all too sexy man. He wanted to feel the corded muscles of his back flex under his touch and hear Cody call out his name as he made him come.

Trev stood and helped remove the dishes and made sure to brush by Cody, enjoying the sharp intake of breath.

"Are you okay," he asked, placing a hand on Cody's shoulder, knowing full well the reason why Cody had reacted.

"I'm fine." Cody glanced over his shoulder and froze as their eyes met.

Leaning in close he laid a feather light kiss on Cody's neck and his body trembled under his touch. "Are you sure you're fine?"

Trev was tempted to pick Cody up and sit him on the counter, rip off the snug jeans that had been tempting him all night.

"Answer me Cody, are you sure you're fine?" The heat radiating off Cody's body was soaking into his own and stirred a dark need that had the dominant side of his personality roaring to life.

"I…I…" Cody's eyes flutter closed as he gave the sensitive skin on his neck another kiss, his tongue tracing a thin wet line up to the glittering diamond of his earlobe.

"You don't seem alright," Trev whispered, giving that delectable piece of skin a gentle nibble with his teeth. Cody groaned, his hands splaying flat against the counter.

Trev leaned one hand on the counter, partially trapping Cody as his body pressed into him. Another sharp intake of air and a low guttural moan escaped Cody's lips.

"I think you need to come with me." Trev whispered in his ear. Sliding his hand around the front of Cody's jeans and giving the hard length inside a squeeze. "Right now," he ordered, then walked out of the room.

Trev could feel Cody's presence stalking him. He looked over his shoulder and admired the hungry look in Cody's eyes as he watched his ass move. The tension between them was a physical creature and filled the hallway toward his destination. Pushing open the door, warm air and the distinct scent of chlorine washed over him.

He turned to face Cody as the door closed to the indoor pool. "Get undressed."

"I'm not normally a fan of being ordered around," Cody said as he pulled his t-shirt off over his head.

"You will be tonight." Trev stepped in close to the man that had stirred his heart back to life. His hand ran over the hard pad of Cody's peck and admired the way it flexed under his touch. "Tonight, you're mine, and I'm going to do what I want—and by the time I'm through, you're going to scream my name and beg me to stop because you simply can't take any more."

Cody's eyes flared as they stood toe to toe, their bodies almost touching. "What do you want me to do next?" Cody finally said.

Trev's mind was already picturing taking Cody from behind, he wanted him bent over his bed and yelling his name as he slammed his cock home. He'd get there. First, he needed to make him beg.

Cody couldn't stop his hands from shaking as Trev smirked and stepped away. Those blue eyes stared at him like they alone could rip off his clothes. He'd never seen Trev this feral. He'd always sensed that underneath the calm exterior lay an entirely other kind of animal. A man, that with a single touch or glance could make him do whatever he wanted. God help him, he wanted whatever Trev had planned. His hands fumbled on the button of his jeans, his fingers clumsy on the small metal piece.

His legs forgot how to work, freezing in place, the air in his lungs ceasing to move altogether as Trev tossed his shirt on one of the poolside chairs. In a graceful movement that would put anyone else to shame, Trev's jeans slipped over his hard-ass, and fuck him. The man was commando. His eyes traced every line of his athletic body. He was addictive, like a fucking drug. He needed this hit. This was the first time he'd seen Trev unhindered by clothes and he was like sweet candy to his eyes, and a shot of adrenaline to his veins. Only two vertical bandages remained that miraculously blended with his skin.

"I thought I told you to get undressed?" Trev asked. His voice was rough, and his heart missed a few beats as it went haywire. Trev turned toward him, and Cody's knees shook at the sight of him in all his glory. "Get undressed, or I'm going to my room, alone."

The threat was clear, and there was no doubt in his mind that Trev would follow through. He wasn't the type of man to make idle threats. Jumping into action, he yanked on the stupid ends of his jeans and cursed over buying a button-down fly. Finally getting them to release from their little holes, he pushed them down and, in his haste, almost ended up falling face-first on the hard tile.

He was burning these fucking jeans the first chance he got. Kicking his leg out like a wild man, he was finally free of the jeans and sent them flying. A splashing sound in the meantime announced Trev was in the water. He turned to watch the man under the glistening blue ripples. Trev was like a torpedo streaking toward him. His mouth ran dry as Trev stood like some fucking Armani commercial, his mouth partially open as he pushed the wet hair away from his eyes. The water glistened a liquid silver color as it travelled down his body and reflected the moonbeams shining through the large window.

"Instead of staring, hurry up and join me." Trev's face changed ever so subtly. If you didn't know him, you wouldn't have seen it, but there was a fire of desire that burned in those blue depths. His tongue ran across his lower lip and Cody couldn't stop the moan that escaped his lips. Stripping out of the boxers he'd been wearing, he stepped toward the water and rolled his shoulders in anticipation of what was to come. His eyes stayed locked with the man in the pool, like two lions entering the same arena, but he already knew he would submit to Trev. He wanted to, the man's presence alone commanded it, and at some point he would get his chance to return the favor, but not tonight.

He was sure Trev could hear his heart pounding the closer he got, and he shivered, his body reaching heights of need that he'd never experienced. The perfectly temperate water did very little to quell the rising heat in his body that was threatening to burn him up.

"How do you always look so calm," Cody asked breathlessly.

The muscles in Trev's jaw twitched, his eyes glinting with humor. "Years of practice I guess."

Stepping up to Trev, they simply stared at one another, and he was determined not to make the first move. This was Trev's show tonight. The sound of the whirlpool was all that could be heard as the tension climbed higher until Cody thought he might choke on it or cave and dive for the man.

As he drew in his next breath Trev cupped his face and crashed their lips together. Even standing naked in the pool together, he hadn't been expecting the sudden assault and gasped at the ferocity of the kiss. Trev licked at his lower lip, and his body finally caught up to the act as Cody opened his mouth to allow access. Their tongues met and danced and a terrifying realization spread throughout his body. This was the first time he'd had a genuinely passionate kiss that meant more than fucking. The all-consuming sensation of not only their lips moving in sync but how his emotions were trying to burst free was overwhelming.

Cody deepened the kiss, unable to get enough and yet not able to get any closer. "Oh, Fuck," he mumbled into Trev's mouth as their bodies rubbed up against one another. Their equally hard cocks fought as their tongues had. The water felt wonderful as it pressed between their bodies, their skin sliding and adding delicious moments of friction.

As if they'd been thinking the same thing, their hands moved almost in sync. Cody gripped Trev's hard shoulders before sliding down the planes of his back that flexed under his touch. His cock surged hard between their bodies, already screaming for release. Reaching down, he took hold of the ass he'd be dreaming about getting his hands on and pulled Trev as close as he could. No space was left. The flushness of their bodies had pressed even the water away and that still didn't feel like enough.

Was it natural to feel like he wanted to be consumed? That he wanted to consume this man, to somehow meld into one?

Trev groaned as their bodies rubbed harder together, their cocks delightfully trapped between their bodies and still managing to touch. His groan was the sexiest sound in the world, it was now his favorite sound, and he wanted to hear Trev do it again. Trev broke the kiss first, and Cody didn't realize until that moment just how swollen his cock had become. He wasn't given time to have a rational thought before Trev lowered his head and drew his tongue up the side of his neck.

"You taste better than any dessert," Trev whispered just before he latched onto his neck and began to suck. He hadn't had a hickey since high school, didn't like the idea of being marked, but holy fuck, his body bucked under the sensation of those lips latched onto his neck. His eyes fluttered closed, and his already unsteady legs began to buckle. He gripped the back of Trev's head, his fingers running through his damp hair as he pulled him closer, urging him on to continue to make him, his.

Trev pulled his legs around his waist, and with the help of the water buoyancy, Trev walked them toward the wall. Cody tried not to squeeze Trev's side, all too aware of the wounds that were still apparent on his sides and yet he didn't seem to notice at all.

Cody sucked in a sharp breath as his back came into contact with the cool tile, and still, Trev didn't release his neck. The sensation of his tongue swirling in a circle over the sensitive skin had him flexing his ass, rubbing his cock up the front of Trev's six-pack. He felt like a rowdy teen humping on a crush's leg—he was slowly coming undone at the seams.

Trev released his neck, but only long enough for him to claim a nipple, his tongue flicking over the silver barbell.

"Fuck." His head fell back, and he arched his chest into Trev's hungry mouth—his tongue expertly massaged and licked and had him swearing like a trucker as it flicked over the sensitive little nub. He didn't even feel Trev's hand sliding between their bodies until his hand grabbed hold of his cock.

"Fuck me," Cody yelled as he stroked him fast and hard in time with his tongue lapping at his nipple. He was so close, he didn't want to come yet, but his body was battling his restraint. He tried to form words to stop Trev before he blew his load, but no words would form in his mouth.

Cody was just about to be thrown over the edge of no return when Trev stopped and stepped back, releasing him altogether. Cody's feet drifted down, his foggy brain screaming that it wanted the release as bad as his body did. His eyes snapped up to Trev, and he shuddered with the intensity in that stare. Here was the man that was also a killer, an apex predator, and staring into those wild eyes, he'd never been more fucking turned on in his life.

If he died right now in this moment, he would die a happy man. To have tasted this kind of connection, this kind of raw passion, was rare and he'd cherish it til his last breath.

"Get on the ledge," Trev ordered.

"What?"

"The ledge, sit that fucking hot ass on the ledge now." Trev pointed to the side of the pool.

Arms shaking, he braced himself and jumped up out of the water, his ass finding the side of the pool with a thud. Hands slid up his legs as Trev stepped between them—Trev's eyes were focused on the cock standing between his legs, and that heated look was as effective as any touch. He jerked like an electric shock had raced through his system as Trev's hands gripped the upper part of his quads—those thumbs pressing in on the sensitive indents between his legs. His cock flexed hard and smacked him in the stomach as a clear fluid slid over the head.

"Oh fuck, oh fuck, fuck, fuck," Cody swore as Trev's hot tongue drew lines up his shaft, licking away the droplets of water and other things.

His eyes fluttered closed as Trev serviced his taught and drawn-up balls one at a time, his tongue like magic. Unable to help himself, he ran his hands through the short messy hair, mentally willing Trev to stop teasing him. As amazing as this was, his cock felt like it was going to burst with the throbbing ache if he didn't find relief soon.

He was practically panting, his breathing rapid as that hot, wet tongue flicked over his highly sensitive cock head. Trev blessedly lowered his mouth down over his aching shaft, and even though he knew the man could do it, it still didn't stop his shock at feeling the gulp and then him sliding all the way into Trev's hot mouth. Trev didn't stop until his nose hit his stomach. Cody's hands gripped Trev's hair hard, his lungs unable to draw in breath with the immense pleasure as Trev swallowed, the muscles constricting like a vice around his shaft.

"I'm…I…oh, shit, Trev," he stammered.

Like a man possessed, Trev bobbed his head, his hands twisting in a playful manner with each movement up and down, giving his balls a rub accentuating every little sensation. He couldn't hold back the load and screamed Trev's name as he came harder than he ever thought possible. The force of the climax arching his back and lifted his ass off the tile as every muscle flexed and screamed with the immense pleasure coursing through his system.

Cody stared at the ceiling, not even sure when he laid all the way back. His head was still foggy, his body heavy with limbs that had forgotten how to move.

Trev appeared above him. The sight of his still perfectly erect cock and glittering eyes had his heart pounding triple-time once more.

He held out a fluffy black towel, the corner of his mouth pulling up. "Come on. We are not done yet," Trev said.

Cody turned his head and watched Trev's bare feet pad along the grey tile as his naked ass flexed with each stride. He wasn't even sure he could handle round two. He pulled himself from the pool, and he managed to wrap the towel around his waist without looking as unsteady as he felt.

Trev had his towel neatly in place, their clothes under his arm as he held out his other hand for Cody to take. He bit his lip as his hand reached for Trev's, and as contact was made, he had to hold back the strangling emotion that gripped his chest. He'd never held hands with anyone. Cody looked down at their fingers entwined and never wanted this to disappear. As his eyes found Trev's conviction gripped his heart, he would lay down his life for this man, and he would find a way to make him his forever.

Trev pulled Cody inside the bedroom and slammed the door closed as he pushed him back against the wood door. It had been so long since he felt this way. Since he felt alive and filled with the warmth of hope.

Cody moaned into his mouth as he claimed those lips once more.

"I need you now," he panted as he broke the kiss.

"Take me however you want me." The liquid silver depths of Cody's eyes smiled at him, the side of his eyes crinkling just slightly with the heated stare. After all the trauma that Cody had seen and been through, the fact that he'd hand himself over like this meant the world to Trev. Cupping Cody's face, he laid a chaste kiss on his lips, never taking his eyes off the other man.

"Get on the bed, on your hands and knees."

"Yes, Sir," Cody said, making him chuckle.

Trev stepped back, allowing Cody to move away from the door, and was rewarded with a show as he stripped off the towel and dropped it to the floor on the way to the bed. His cock raged inside behind his own towel. He slipped his hand between the fold to give himself a few slow strokes as he watched the show. Cody gave him a teasing glance over his shoulder as his hands and knees found the bed in a standard doggy-style pose. His heavy cock waited between his legs, offering the fantastic view of a lifetime. Cody gently swayed his ass back and forth as if daring him to take what he wanted. And take what he wanted, he would.

Trev ran his hand down Cody's back, his body arching with the trailing touch that ended with him cupping his ass. The way his muscles flexed and skin heated captivated him.

Dropping to his knees, his hands gripped Cody's cheeks and spread them wide. Trev took a moment to appreciate the view before he moved in and twirled his tongue along the delectable sac between his legs.

"Oh, bloody hell," Cody groaned, the muscles beneath his fingers flexing hard as he gradually increased his sucking. Cody's labored breaths spurring him on. He released the sweet spot and drew lines from one sensitive area to another, until he reached his final goal.

A throaty groan that was close to a growl reached Trev's ears as his tongue swirled little circles along the rose bud's rim. Taking his time he worked Cody over, earning moans and shaking limbs until he was satisfied that the walls he planned on stretching were ready for the next step.

He grabbed the lube he'd set out earlier and slathered a large glob onto his fingers as well as the sexy ass that was presented to him.

"Are you sure about this?" he asked as he tossed the tube on the bed. He held up his fingers as Cody smiled wide in return.

"Fuck me, Trev, and stop worrying. I wouldn't be on all fours if I didn't want to be." He swayed that ass back and forth again. "And don't hold back."

Trev's muscles shook as the temperature rose along with the raging desire in his body. He smeared the thick, greasy substance on his cock and groaned. He'd been hard for so long that he was near his breaking point and knew he wasn't going to last long.

Using the remaining lube, he slowly worked first one and then a second finger into Cody's tight ass. Stretching him open further to accommodate his size.

"Relax for me Cody," Trev said softly, but followed the gentle command with a smack to the round flesh.

"Fuck me, Trev," Cody groaned.

Trev pressed down with his fingers finding the pleasure button and, Cody immediately swore. Trev's body was shaking as Cody neared another orgasm.

"Fuck, you're too good. You keep doing that, and I'm going to be done for the night too soon."

"Well, we can't have that." Satisfied that Cody was indeed prepped, he stepped up behind him, and what felt like heaven and hell, he slowly entered the clenching hole. His breathing was heavy, as he stopped just a couple inches in to give Cody time to adjust.

"Holy fuck, you're big," Cody groaned and dropped his head toward the bed. Trev rubbed circles on Cody's ass, and lower back as he waited for the clenching muscles to relax.

"Too much?" Trev asked and yet and silently prayed he said no. Now that he had Cody laid out like his fantasies, he never wanted to have to stop.

"No, keep going. You feel fucking awesome."

It was a slow progress of inches and retreat as he rocked into the tight hole. Trev not only wanted Cody to relax but tease him into the pleasure, the initial pain wiped away. The sexy sound of Cody begging to be fucked hard was what he was waiting for.

He was breathing hard, beads of sweat dripping down his body by the time he was fully sheathed inside Cody. The passage was more than tight. It felt like a hot, throbbing, vice around his sensitive and ready-to-explode cock. He took a steadying breath, trying to rein himself in to make this last longer. Ever so slowly, he backed out until just the end remained sheathed, but Cody wasn't having any of Trev's tightly controlled personality and slammed his ass back into him.

"Oh fuck," Trev yelled as the sensation shot through his body.

"Naughty." Trev gave Cody's backside a sharp smack and pulled away until just the tip of his cock remained once more.

"Trev, please."

Trev smiled at Cody's begging, but he wanted more. "Don't do that again, you move when I tell you, you can."

Cody groaned which ended in a whimper as he conceded to the command and made his cock jump inside Cody's body. Closing his eyes he pressed back into that magical hole and pleasure raced throughout his body. Once he was as far as he could go he slowly caressed his hips in a circle and earned more muffled swearing from the man beneath him.

Leaning forward he gripped Cody's shoulders and took a moment to savor the feel of their bodies pressed tightly together. Their skin hot and breaths short with desire.

"I'm going to fuck you now," he whispered. Cody's body shuddered beneath him. Rearing back he pulled almost out and gripped Cody's ass hard. Trev rammed himself home again, his balls slapping into Cody's backside with every stroke.

"You can move now," Trev gritted out, his teeth tightly clenched as was the rest of his body.

Cody's body rocked back, meeting his own in a mad rush. "Yes, fuck, yes. I'm going to come again, shit," Cody yelled. His weight slightly shifting as he jerked furiously on his own cock that had once more grown hard and ready.

Like a volcano, Trev could feel his own climax rising from the depths of his body. His speed quickening to the point he could no longer hear anything other than his own pulse-pounding and the slap of skin meeting skin as they both feverishly met over and over again.

With one final stroke, he thrust himself forward, his fingers digging into the soft flesh of Cody's ass as his cock exploded. He yelled, the scream a feral sound. He repeated the action, his muscles flexing hard as another stream shot out. He couldn't say how many times he came, but by the time he was finally empty, the copious amount of come was seeping out around his still surprisingly engorged cock.

Cody had fallen forward, his face laying on the mattress, breathing hard. "I don't think I can move," Trev admitted as he leaned his weight against Cody. Every part of his body felt weak and rubbery. Just the thought of pulling out of his ass seemed like too much work.

"Then don't. I don't want you to leave me yet."

There was something in the phrasing that caught Trev's attention. He slowly retreated and bit his lip hard to keep from yelling. He was so sensitive. Once free, he knelt on the bed and forced Cody to sit up. Like himself, he was slow with his movements and groaned as he repositioned himself.

Gripping Cody's chin in his hand, he forced him to stare him in the eyes. "I'm not going to leave you." Cody's eye flicked away, and he squeezed his chin a little firmer until Cody looked back into his eyes. "Do you hear me? I'm not leaving you. I want us. I want you."

A lone tear slowly slid down Cody's cheek, his eyes saying more than any words could portray.

"Come on, let's go get cleaned up." Trev kissed Cody's lips softly, offering the small piece of comfort he could at this moment. Standing, he held out his hand to Cody.

Dark scars etched their souls, and yet as Cody's eyes found his own, the realization hit him—the darkness was no longer his soul's only companion.

Chapter 35

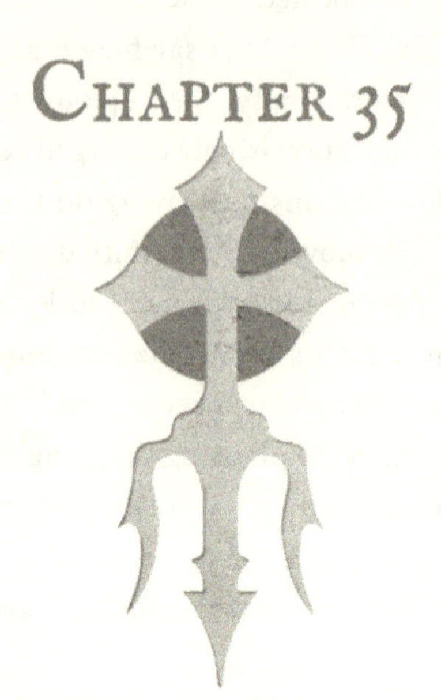

Trev's eyes snapped open with the sound of his door banging against the wall. He'd normally grab for his concealed gun, but he recognized the high-pitched wail of excitement as J.J. ran across the room. Cody sat up just as J.J. made his superman leap and landed on the bed with a bounce.

"J.J.," Arek called out from the hall. His feet could be heard as Arek pursued the pint-sized intruder.

With some effort Trev pushed himself up into a sitting position and let J.J. take in the scenario—his inquisitive eyes looked first at Cody and then to himself. He could see the wheels turning in his head as he tried to process the situation. He wouldn't lie to him. He wouldn't make up some story that was unhealthy, and if he and Cody remained together, J.J. would see them as any other couple.

Panting Arek burst through the door and took in the odd moment.

"J.J., you can't go running into Uncle Trev's room like that without knocking."

Pulling himself up into a cross-legged position, J.J. looked over at Arek. "Why?"

Arek's mouth dropped open, closed, and then opened again, his face going red as he genuinely seemed at a loss for an explanation. Trev loved seeing his brother off-balance, but today he would come to his rescue.

"Because sometimes J.J., I am doing things that are private and for adults only." He crossed his hands, laying them on his stomach. Cody seemed frozen in place, Trev glanced to the side, and the man hadn't so much as blinked except for his eyes bouncing between his little brother and back to Trev.

"You mean like having sleepovers?" J.J. finally asked.

"Yes."

"Like Nae Nae and Arek?"

"Yes, sometimes just like that."

His cute chubby finger pointed to Cody and then to him. "So you two were having a sleepover?"

"Yes, as a matter of fact, we were."

"Oh." J.J. grabbed at the soft comforter, running his finger over the pattern. His big brown eyes found his, and he smiled. "Are you going to marry my brother like Arek is marrying Nae Nae?"

Trev looked over at Cody and couldn't hold back the laugh at the slack jawed, wide-eyed expression. "I don't know yet J.J., but we certainly like one another. Would Cody and I being together be alright with you?"

His small shoulders lifted and dropped. "What would I call you?" Trev twisted his head as he pondered that question, not sure what he meant. "Would you be my brole or my uncler?"

Trev looked around the room and couldn't stop the hysterical laughter that bubbled to the surface. Of all the things he thought would be J.J.'s concern, this was not it.

"Did he just sort of ship us?" Cody panted out between the bouts of laughter.

"I think he did." Trev reached down and grabbed the adorable child under the arms. J.J. squealed as he lifted him above his head like a small airplane. There was a slight twinge of pain, but to see the smile on J.J.'s face made the pain worth it.

Placing him down between himself and Cody, he tickled his sides until he was gasping for breath through the giggles. "J.J., you can call Cody or me whatever you like. The point is we are family. That's all that matters. Do you understand?"

"Yeah. I can't wait to tell my teacher that my brother and uncle are getting married." J.J. crawled off the bed and bounded away past Arek.

"Well, that should be an interesting conversation for his teacher," Trev smirked at Arek. "Good luck explaining that one." He smiled at his own joke as he waved Arek back out the door. "Make sure he stays out a little longer. I have some…" Trev looked over at Cody's smiling face. "Unfinished morning business to attend to."

"That kid is going to give me grey hairs," Arek muttered as he closed the door.

"You're really okay with him thinking we might get married?" Cody asked. "I mean, after everything with Mel…"

He placed a hand on Cody's to stop him from finishing the thought. "Why don't you come here, and I'll show you how okay I am with the idea of placing a ring on your finger."

By the time he and Cody emerged from the bed, it was close to lunch. He'd made a point to treat Cody's sore back and hips with a little TLC and smirked at the amazing thank you he received in return.

Trev hadn't stayed in bed past six a.m., other than while he was injured, in forever. He felt refreshed and rejuvenated as he slipped the suit jacket into place.

"Fuck, you really are the sexiest man I've ever laid eyes on," Cody remarked. He was leaning against the open-door frame waiting for him to finish up. "I could watch you dress all day."

"And here I thought it was me getting undressed that intrigued you," Trev said teasingly.

"Oh, don't worry, I fucking love that too."

"As much as I'd like for us to simply close the door, there is some work we need to address."

Cody rubbed at his hair. "Yeah, reality sucks."

Trev stopped as he reached Cody and laid a hand on his chest. "Not this reality, and not the family waiting for us out there. The rest is just noise to be controlled at different decibels. Come on, I'm famished, and I can smell Sally's cooking."

Linking their fingers, he gave Cody a tug to follow. He was surprised to learn that Cody had never been in a real relationship before. It made sense after learning even more about the gruesome inner workings of Tyson—no one you cared for would be safe. The most disturbing thing was that Cody didn't think he'd live past twenty-five, so why get attached to someone? Many of the details of his time with the Vipers, Cody didn't want to share. Trev understood that, but what he did learn had his blood boiling. As they lay together talking, he traced the jagged scar on Cody's face that could easily have taken his eye and learned it was from a particularly harsh beating he took at the hands of Tyson. It hurt to see how casual Cody was about being abused. If he could pull Tyson from the grave and kill him again, he would've. He no longer thought that Arek's actions had been excessive. If anything, they hadn't been near painful enough.

Everyone stopped talking as they walked into the kitchen, their eyes instinctively being drawn to their clasped hands. Renee looked ready to cry. Everyone else, other than Ray's daughter Simone, a.k.a Little Spice, was smiling and seemed ready to burst at the seams. Simone was only eight, but she had a huge crush on Cody, and it was evident as she crossed her arms and scowled that she was not impressed with the new situation.

"You can all stop staring now," Trev said, and like a switch was flipped, the room erupted in noise once more. Giving Cody a wink, he let go of his hand to go and speak to Arek.

"After breakfast, we need to have a meeting," he whispered to Arek and stole a piece of bacon off the massive platter.

"About your new client?"

"That and I have a favor to ask."

Arek nodded and gave Sally's shoulder a squeeze as he passed. Some things just couldn't be purchased with money.

"So what's the scoop with this Maeve person?" Arek asked an hour later as he flopped down into a chair. If you didn't know the man, you might say he'd just run a marathon with his melodramatic show.

Cody stood by the door looking like a guard with his arms crossed while Ray quietly sat beside Arek. He was playing the part of a statue well.

"For starters, I do believe she is being framed. Whoever this caller was, they either saw it happen or had prior knowledge. Why is she being framed? That I haven't pieced together, but it is a top-level job, one that costs large sums of money to pull off."

Trev slid the image of Maeve across the table for them to see the picture. "She looks like she should be the leader of a punk rock band, not behind bars," Arek commented and passed the picture on. "Could she even hurt a fly?"

"She is deadlier than she appears. She is one of Morry's girls."

Arek's eyes grew wide. "No shit. Did she say how Morry is, or why she is here on her behalf?"

"Wait, who is Morry?" Cody asked, walking forward to lay the picture on the desk.

"The mission I told you about, our last one." Trev pointed to Arek. "Morry is one of us, and she is as tough as they come." Trev leaned back in his chair.

"Morry is one of The Righteous?" Ray asked.

"Yes, she is. She runs a unique rehab facility for drug addicts at the heart of a desert in Arizona and also runs quite a large biker gang. They deal guns and jewels mostly, but never drugs—for obvious reasons. There is more that she is involved in, but the point is when Maeve says she is one of Morry's girls, it means she arrived there broken and was reborn or would die."

"She kills those that don't make it out of rehab?" Cody asked, his eyes wide.

"She has her own brand of cleaning up, just like we do, and yes, as far as I know, you either get right or die trying."

"Damn, that is harsh," Ray mumbled. "You all don't mess around."

"The thing is, the evidence is saying Maeve killed a police detective, but she swears she's never seen the guy and wouldn't do that unless he was a dirty mark."

"So, the cop wasn't on her list," Arek asked.

"No, so he was either on someone's list, and she is the fallout, or she was convenient collateral damage. I personally believe it was the first."

"What evidence do they have?" Arek asked.

Trev sighed as he thought over the long list. "For starters, she can't remember the whole night." They all lifted an eyebrow, and he held up his hand to stop them before they asked the same question he had. "She can't recall because she was partying it up at a bar on her night off and woke up in an alley covered in blood miles away. But, she has no defensive wounds."

Trev held up a finger to count off the holes in the case. "Was on the other side of town." A second finger was lifted. "She had zero motive to kill the father of two kids, who from what I can tell was squeaky clean." He lifted the third finger. "And she had enough alcohol in her system to knock over an elephant. They, unfortunately, didn't bother to test her for drugs when they dragged her into the station."

"You think she was roofied?" Ray asked.

"I do, and with enough of something to wipe her memory of being at the detective's murder."

"So, you think she was there?" Arek chimed in.

"I'm not one hundred percent sure, but it would be the easiest way to ensure all the DNA lines up. She conveniently had the murder weapon still on her when they found her passed out a couple of alliey's over. Based on the photos it was clenched in her hand like a total amateur and she is no amateur with a knife. According to her. I could be sceptical but it is all a little too convenient. The problem is I cannot say who she works for or how I know she wouldn't do this. If she did do this, why would she be this sloppy?"

Cody snorted a laugh. "What you can't work with—well, jury members, you see, I know my client didn't do it because she is not that sloppy of a murderer. In fact, she works for a secret organization that stalks and murders low life criminals for a living, as you can clearly see this case against my client simply makes no sense."

Trev smirked back. "I do not think it would have the outcome we desire, no."

"If she didn't do it, then why frame her? Seems like an odd target unless you knew…shit," Arek froze, his eyes going wide as it registered what Trev was already thinking. "It had to be someone that knew what she does for Morry. That's fucked up," Arek said. He stood and began to pace as he thought. "And if they knew what she does for Morry, then they most likely know who Morry really is, and if that's the case, then we could all be at risk and worse they have to have money…I don't like this. Whoever is doing this needs to die."

"Agreed, the problem is, they are way ahead of us. They obviously know who we are and what we did overseas, but we don't know who they are. I've been going over so many strange issues that have cropped up of late, including Alejandro being tipped off that I was not acting in his best interest and how they found our home."

"Son of a bitch. Whoever this person is, is going to die." Arek cracked his knuckles, his eyes hard with the darkness that danced in their depths.

"Should we continue to pursue the Spike angle? Arek, Ray, and I have that meeting off-site with him tonight. Are we still going?"

Trev sighed and then slowly stood to lean his hands against the desk. "Yes, go, but be careful. If someone knows who we are, there is no telling what they have planned next. Everything and everyone is an option and a threat, except for those under this roof."

Cody nodded. "Okay, I'll go get ready."

"Same. I will go get changed," Ray stood and made his way toward Cody.

"Arek, can you remain behind a moment?" He called out as Arek marched across the floor. Trev scribbled a name and address down on a piece of paper and handed it to his brother.

Arek glanced at the paper. "Who's this?"

"He is a man I had planned on eliminating, but I'm not field-ready yet." He rubbed at his side where the physical exercise of last night had taken its toll. "Eliminate him anyway you like, and as quickly as you can make it happen."

A wicked smile lifted the corner of his mouth. "I'm getting free reign?"

"He is a teen rapist that just made his final payment to society in my bank account. Now I think it's time he paid the rest of his debt with your unique brand of justice."

"Have I told you lately how much I fucking love you," Arek asked, making them laugh.

"Get out of here. I have work to do—oh and Arek," he called out as Arek reached the door, his twin's eyes locking with his own.

Arek smiled wide. "Don't worry. He will scream like no one before him ever has." With that, the office door clicked into place.

Chapter 36

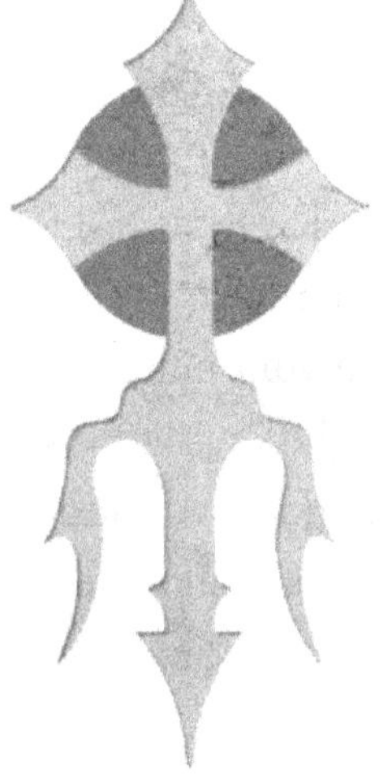

Cody rolled his shoulders, the leather jacket creaking as he stepped out of his car. He scanned the empty lot, the deserted building, and overflowing garbage bins, not doing anything to settle the uneasiness in his mind. Ray closed his door, and the sound practically echoed, sending a shiver down Cody's spine as he stuffed his gun into the belt of his jeans.

The Mustang he'd won was certainly coming in handy as it rumbled up beside him, and Arek parked the sexy car. "Any of this seeming right to you?" Cody called out as Arek got out.

Cody's eyes scanned the only lit building on the entire street, the windows glowing a muted orange through the thick dirt coating.

"No, and I suddenly wish I'd brought Delilah instead. Actually though, she may still be able to help us." Arek walked away, talking on his phone.

"If you're not solid with this, you can stay in the car," Cody said to Ray. "You have a lot to lose."

"We all have a lot to lose. Besides, I can't have you going back and telling Little Spice that I was a chicken, and you get all the glory." Ray gave him a smile.

"I think I'll be on her hated list for awhile, she was pretty pissed with me at breakfast."

"She'll get over it, you're her hero."

Cody didn't want to be anyone's hero or have any glory. If he could, he'd walk away from all this shit and live a simple life. He'd even prefer a private island for them all to go to and hide away from death and darkness. Now that he'd gotten the taste of a real home and happiness, he was terrified that at any moment, the carpet was going to be yanked out from underneath his feet. Not to mention the mental image of Trev walking out of a lagoon looking like fucking model had certain parts of him hard and revved to go. The corner of his mouth lifted at the thought.

Three more cars pulled up that were members from the old Crimson Vipers. The eight guys got out and walked over. "Boss, sorry we're late," they said almost as one. He lifted an eyebrow at them.

Arek caught his attention as he jogged out of the shadows. "We'll talk about it later," he said to the group before he walked over to where the man was holding up his phone. "The back of the building is vacant. There are no cars parked there, and Delilah can't see inside the building since there are no cameras in or around it. A mile down the road, a number of trucks came and went from this direction, but it's been quiet since."

"What do you want to do?" Cody asked.

"Let's go inside. If Spike is holed up in here, he will be pissed that we didn't show, and if he's not, then we need to keep our eyes open for a trap."

Cody nodded and turned to his group. "Alright, let's go, but be ready for anything and what Arek says is law," he called out to the small group.

Arek led the party to the front door, he gave the old glass door a tug, and it opened, a small bell chiming, the sound loud in the otherwise quiet space. He stuck his head inside the lit front foyer and then waved them inside. The old reception area was not very large, and the door off to the side was hanging off its hinges. Giving it a push, Arek moved the broken door out of the way and pointed to his eyes the message loud and clear.

Not that Cody had any intention of letting his guard down. He stepped into the warehouse, and the shitty fluorescent lights hanging from the ceiling swayed gently and flickered slightly, casting eerie shadows along the walls. There was no noise but for the sound of their own breathing and their boots on the concrete floor. More lights automatically flicked on as they walked, the motion sensors revealing a number of long rows of high metal racking. They appeared to stop about halfway toward the back of the building, which opened up into what looked to be a vacant space, but from this far away, it was hard to tell for sure.

Arek used hand signals to divide the group up and spread them out to travel down the rows, leaving the three of them together once more. Arek's eyes shot around the space and up to the ceiling as he took in everything. Cody tried to see this place through his eyes, what he might be looking for.

Cody could just make out his men on either side as they moved, guns out and moving just as cautiously. There was a soft click sound and Arek held up his fist, the two of them stopped mid-stride. Something caught Cody's attention, and he stared at the small baggie on the floor. Bending over, he grabbed the small piece of plastic, that was half under the shelving unit and flipped it over in his palm.

His eyes grew wide as he stared at the logo and opened his mouth to call to Arek when Arek yelled to get down. Like they'd been in the calm before the storm all hell broke loose. Bullets flew in every direction and pinged off the metal racking, sending them off in erratic directions. Arek dropped to his knee and fired two shots to his left and then one to the right.

"Get out," Arek looked at him. "Now."

He grabbed Ray's arm, who seemed paralyzed to the spot, and ran back the way they'd just come. More shots were fired, and he ducked and covered his head with his free arm as he ran, practically dragging Ray behind him with his long strides. They burst through the door outside as police cars, lights and sirens streaked up the street toward them. He faltered in his step, unsure if they should still head to the car or try to hide.

"Get to the car and follow me," Arek yelled, running past them.

"What about the cops?" he said as the first car screeched to a stop.

"They're going to be preoccupied," Arek said, jumping in the Mustang and revving the engine.

"Turn off the car and get out with your hands up." A loudspeaker blared.

"I hope you know what you're doing," Cody mumbled just as the group of Vipers came running out the front door, their guns firing. He started his car, and the wheels squealed, smoke rising into the air as the car fishtailed and took off after Arek.

He hit answer as his phone rang. "We're not out of the woods yet, there are more lights ahead, and you see that light up ahead." Cody leaned forward, looking up at the light Arek mentioned, and swore as he spotted the helicopter.

"What the fuck is going on?"

"It was a setup, and if we didn't die inside, it was designed to take us out one way or another. Our saving grace is the guys in there are fucking idiots and I spotted the plan before we were trapped. Stay on my ass like sticky fly paper. I'm going to call Trev." Arek hung up just as the car was bathed in bright white light.

"Cody?" Ray said.

"What?"

"I...I think I was shot."

Cody's head whipped to the right, and Ray held up his hand that was covered in blood.

"I, I didn't feel it."

"Shit," Cody swore, trying to keep up with Arek weaving through traffic at breakneck speeds. He leaned forwards, trying to slip out of his leather jacket.

"Fuck," he swore as he fought with his one sleeve. Finally freeing himself, he handed the jacket to Ray. "Look at me, don't panic, you're going to be fine. Just apply pressure with this to the wound."

He swerved to the right to avoid rear-ending a car in front of him and drove up the shoulder until he could cut back across the traffic. Cody hit the call button on his steering wheel.

"Call Arek." The car didn't respond, and he smacked his hand on the steering wheel. He fumbled with his phone, his hands shaking as he tried to get it unlocked. "Come on, come on."

"Watch out," Ray said.

He looked up just in time to veer around a transport truck, it blasted the air horn as they zoomed by, and then back again to not have a head-on collision. He was losing ground on Arek. He got to his latest call list and hit the last call to come in.

It rang once before Arek picked up. "What's wrong? Why are you slowing down?"

"Ray's been hit, and he's losing a lot of blood." He looked over at his best friend, and the man's head lolled to the side, his hands slipping from the jacket. "He's passing out. Fuck, Arek, I need to help him." Cody reached out and grabbed the jacket pressing it against his friend's side. Panic was setting in as Ray barely responded to the hard touch.

"Follow me to where we took Trev."

"He needs a hospital."

"Cody, pull your shit together. We can't go to a hospital, and you know it. Now follow me. We are not far, and the chopper will be gone soon." The line disconnected before Cody could argue anymore.

"Cody."

"Hey, we are almost there, just hang on. Okay, buddy?" he glanced over at Ray. His eyes were half-open, his breathing fast, but it was his skin turning a strange greyish color that had him freaking out inside.

"Promise me." He wet his lips. "You'll look after Simone."

"Shit, don't talk like that man, you're going to be fine."

Ray's hand found his on the jacket and gave it a squeeze. "Promise me, she has no one else. Please."

"It's not even a question you need to ask. Of course, I will look out for her, but I'm not going to fucking need to—don't you dare die on me, you asshole. I promised you a better life." Ray's hand slipped away from his own. "No."

The helicopter veered off, turning back the way they'd just come. He didn't know what Arek did and didn't care as they flew down the highway toward the farmhouse that was seeing too much of them lately.

"Stay with me, Ray. Please." His body shook, tears streaming down his face. He was too scared to look over and just kept his eyes on the road as he prayed once more for a miracle and yet feared he'd already filled his quota.

Trev topped the flashing button that Arek was calling and then hit the speaker button on his phone. Might as well do two things at once. He signed his name to the letter in front of him. "How did it go?"

"We need you and Delilah." Trev grabbed his phone, jumped from his seat, and ran for the office door in one swift movement.

"What happened?"

"It was a set-up, and we have a fucking helicopter and at least four cruisers that I can see further back chasing us down."

"I'm on my way." He ran past the kitchen and yelled for Sally to stay here just as Renee stepped into the living room doorway.

"Are they okay?" she called out.

"I don't know," he shouted back before the door closed behind him. "Shit." The elevator ride down had never seemed so slow in his life. He sprinted down the street the short distance to the private parking space he'd purchased and, as fast as he could without drawing any more attention, unlocked the door.

"Sweet Delilah, get fired up," he said as he neared the vehicle. The door unlocked, and the engine roared to life in his presence. "I need you to trace Arek's phone and set an interception route."

He pulled the Hummer out onto the street, the garage door sliding down behind them. Luckily, it was late, and the traffic was sparse. He had to agree with Arek that they needed the house back. This was inconvenient.

"Interception trajectory established."

The map and dots appeared on the glass. "Shit, that's going to take too much time." He drummed his fingers on the steering wheel as he brainstormed, an idea coming to him. "Delilah set off all of the alarms."

"Would you like car alarms or building alarms to sound?"

"All of them. Anything and everything within a mile radius of this location, especially the banks, I need them all to sound. Send a text to Renee to ignore the alarm in the building and stay in the condo."

Trev pressed his foot down on the gas, the Hummer flying along the street. Headlights and horns flashed and sounded, even from driving cars whose passengers looked stunned by the sudden chaos. People were coming out of buildings and staring up at them as fire alarms from all around them began to go off. The noise was loud enough to be heard over the roar of the engine. The light outside the National Bank was flashing, and he smirked. That would draw everyone back this way, or at least he hoped.

"Status update on emergency vehicles pursuing Arek."

"Vehicles are turning back this way, would you like to stop the sirens?"

"No, keep them going until the police are safely within the city limits."

It took longer than he would've liked, but finally, Trev turned off the highway onto the out-of-the-way location where Arek's phone stopped moving. As the lights of the Hummer rounded the gentle knoll toward the farmhouse, his heart sank.

Arek was sitting on his ass, head in his hands with his back to the Mustang. Yet, it was Cody sitting beside the passenger side of his car as he held Ray in his arms, that gripped his heart in a stranglehold.

He jogged over to Arek, and his brother looked up at him. "You, okay?"

"Physically," was the only thing he said before burying his head in his hands once again. "I'll be fine," he mumbled. "Fucking shit show."

Knowing there was nothing he could do to help Arek right then, he slowly stepped toward Cody. He could hear the soft sobs before he saw Cody's tears dripping onto his friend's face. He knelt down beside Cody and gripped his shoulder. His pain-filled eyes found his, and his heart sank through the floor. There was such anger in them, such hatred.

"I'm sorry," Trev said. For the first time in a very long time he was at a loss as to what to do.

Cody clutched at Ray, gripping his body with closed fists, as if holding him tighter would make a difference.

Ray had been his only friend in a hell that no one could fully comprehend, and like a toxic plague Cody managed to destroy his friend's future in his wake.

"This is my fault. I shouldn't have let him get wrapped up in my shit. I invited him into this life like he would be better off," Cody's sentences ran together. "I promised him a way out that didn't end up with him dead or arrested. Does this look better off?" Cody asked, his body shaking as he cradled his friend's head. "He was a good person, and he didn't deserve this…I…I."

Waves of nausea and grief so strong ripped through his body and took his breath away. He gasped for air as the reality set in.

"It should've been me. Why did I live, and he die? I was shot twice and I fucking lived. It's not fair." Tears streamed down his face until he was no longer able to see, his sobs nearing hysterical, he leaned into Trev. Cody buried his head against his chest and let Trev wrap him up in his arms.

"I deserved to die, I hurt so many people, did so many terrible things." Cody lifted his head and stared into Trev's calm eyes. "I raped people, did you know that? I'm a real sweetheart. You picked a winner to hook your wagon to." Cody waited to see disgust in Trev's face, but he showed no change in the concerned stare. "That piece of shit, Tyson ordered me to do it, but I did. It was my hands that hurt those people, that did his devil's work. Ray never hurt anyone." He lost control again and pulled Ray's body up until he could lay his head where his heart once beat.

"It should've been me."

"Don't say that Cody, please," Trev said, his voice quiet as he gave his shoulder a squeeze.

"Then why, Trev? Then tell me why did God take him? Take this good soul and not my blackened one." Cody mumbled as another wave of grief gripped him in it's grasp. Cody roared a scream into the night, like that might expel some of this torment.

He collapsed into Trev's arms as his body grew weak. "I don't have an answer to that Cody," Trev said and kissed the top of his head.

The pain was a living creature inside his chest as it tried to rip his heart out and he wished it would. Anything to stop this ache, to stop the guilt, to bring back a good man. There was nothing that Trev could say to make this better.

His best friend was dead and he had to live with that on his conscious for the rest of his life. Trev gripped him harder like he knew he was ready to dive off the cliff into the sea of sorrow.

"I promise you, Cody, whoever did this will pay," Trev whispered into his ear. "I'll make sure they pay for Ray's death."

Cody nodded, but it was a lie to think that the death of another would change anything. That it would make any of this okay. Cody looked down into the sightless eyes of his best friend.

"I'm so sorry," he whispered, as he gently closed Ray's eyes for the last time.

Chapter 37

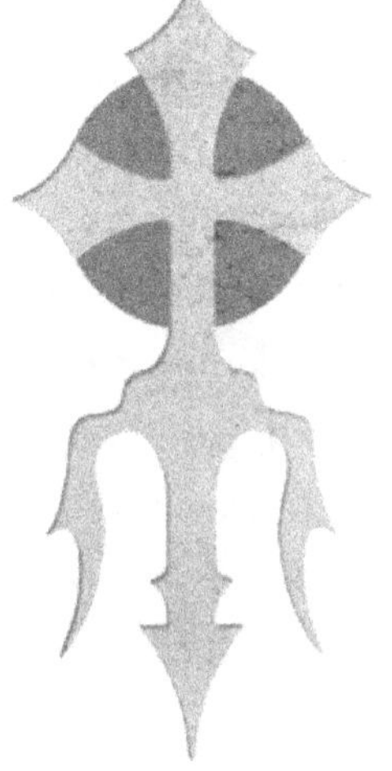

Trev stood quietly by the gravesite. His eyes fixed on another tombstone in a long line he'd paid his respects to—his black wraparounds hiding the dark circles from lack of sleep. The funeral took longer than he expected to get arranged, but he had made sure it was beautiful. The short time he'd known Ray, it was easy to see that he, much like his name, had a sunny personality that was easy to like.

Stunning teal and yellow flowers lined the lid of the glittering black casket as the minister spoke. It was fitting that it was drizzling. It felt like the only tears left to shed was that of God himself.

Trev looked over at Simone as Cody stood with his arm wrapped around the young girl's shoulders. Arek mirrored his position with Renee tucked under his arm, as Sally held J.J.'s hand, and of course, J.J. held the small stuffed tiger Arek had given him. Trev sucked in a deep breath as he folded his hands over the long black coat he was wearing.

Simone hadn't spoken to anyone since the night her brother and last living relative had died. She'd screamed for Cody to get out of her room and slammed the door in his face. The look on Cody's face had been pure agony as he sagged against the door and wouldn't leave.

It was the first time in a very long time that Trev didn't know what to do to solve the problem. There was no one for him to immediately kill, no amount of money would make this better, and he wasn't great with warm and sentimental expressions of comfort.

Cody pulled away from his touch more than once since that night. He was barely eating and had taken to sleeping in a spare bedroom. No matter how many times he tried, Cody pushed him away and even now refused to make eye contact. It was easy to see Cody blamed not only himself but also him for Ray's death. The shiny perfect world had slipped through his fingers and felt like an illusion, something that had been but a glimmer of happiness to dangle before his eyes like a carrot, and then just as quickly, it was stripped away.

The limo ride to the house was quiet. He watched the cemetery disappear into the distance and contemplated his next move. Whatever it was, he would end this. It was on him to at the very least settle the score.

Everyone slowly shuffled into the kitchen, but he made his way to the office and closed the door. Pouring himself a scotch, he wandered over to the window and view that at one time seemed so peaceful. Now, as he looked out over the lush green with the ocean in the distance, he felt more isolated than he ever had before he'd met Cody.

Trev put his hand in his pocket and pulled out the small empty baggy he'd been carrying around with him since he found it on Cody the night Ray died. He stared at the symbol on the front and cursed himself for not checking into this spider symbol sooner. He'd seen it before. Arek had sent him a picture of this, but it seemed inconsequential at the time of the arcade shooting. Something to be analyzed at a later date, now guilt gnawed at the back of his gut.

Would knowing who this belongs to have saved Ray? Would it have made a difference in anything they'd done? He didn't have the answer to that, but he was determined to find out.

"Come in," he called out as a knock sounded at his door. He stuffed the baggie back into his pants as Cody and Arek walked in and closed the door.

"What's the plan?" Arek asked.

"There is no plan." Trev turned to face the two men.

"What do you mean there is no plan? You always have a plan." Arek opened his arms, disbelief evident on his face.

Placing the glass to his lips, he swallowed back the rest of his drink before wandering over to his desk. "Correction, there is no plan that includes the two of you. You can show yourselves out." Trev dismissed them, but they remained standing in the middle of his office like fucking annoying garden gnomes.

"What?" he asked, his anger simmering just a hair.

"What exactly does that mean?" Cody piped up and crossed his arms over his chest.

"It means exactly what it means. The two of you will no longer be involved in any plans going forward. Now please see yourselves out. I have work to do."

Arek, as was his nature, did the complete opposite and walked closer, parking himself in the chair across from Trev.

"See, that is the part I don't get. Why are we not involved? If anyone should be involved, it is us." Arek pointed to himself and then pointed his thumb over his shoulder to indicate Cody.

Trev ran his hand through his hair and sat back in his chair to glance between the two men he cared most for in this world. "Because this makes the most sense."

"Can you stop being a lawyer for a moment and just straight up tell us what the hell is going on?" Cody snapped.

Trev's heated glare found Cody. "What's going on is that we just left the gravesite of a man that was the last living relative for a young girl living under this roof. That means you will effectively be taking over a parenting role—one that cannot afford you dying."

He turned his hard stare on Arek. "You are about to be a father and already have an adorable four-year-old out there that looks up to you as a father. Hence neither of you are in a position that can afford you to be hurt or worse. I, on the other hand, do not have any such ties to anyone. I will finish this so life can go on, and you can both do as you please, here or elsewhere. As soon as this mission is finished, I will be letting The Righteous know we will no longer be taking any jobs," he said, and Arek's mouth fell open. "Now, both of you, please see yourselves out."

"Trev, you can't be serious?" Arek's jaw was twitching as his quick temper poked its head from the sand.

"Arek, I'm not arguing with you about this. The decision has been made." Arek shot up out of the chair like his ass had a spring under it.

"You can't do this," Arek growled. "I won't let you."

Cody grabbed Arek's shoulder and whispered in his ear. Arek swore a streak that would make a trucker blush but stomped out the door, slamming it in his wake, the paintings all hopping and twisting sideways.

Great something else to fix.

"Why are you doing this," Cody asked, his voice much softer than a moment ago.

Trev grabbed the scotch to pour himself another glass. "I thought I just explained my reasons?"

Cody wandered around the desk and knelt down beside him, placing his hand on his arm. "No, why are you putting these walls up again? Why are you freezing Arek out, but more importantly, why are you freezing me out?"

"I'm not. You already did that on your own." Trev pushed his chair back and stood to put space between them. "You've made it clear where we stand."

"Are you talking about me staying in the spare room? I had to do that. I was a wreck, and I didn't want you seeing me like that. Having to console me constantly, I…I just needed some space, to pull myself together." Cody slowly stood and stepped toward him.

"That hurt, yes, but what I'm talking about is the look in your eyes. The anger and hate I see in them." He looked away from Cody as emotions bubbled to the surface.

Why couldn't he have just left the fucking room?

"I'm sorry Ray got killed, I really am, and I will do what I can to at least bring him justice, but I can't have anyone else look at me like that. I've shouldered the blame for too many deaths.—I'm at my limit. Please just go." Trev made his way to the center of the room, unable to look at Cody.

"I don't blame you. Is that really what you think?"

"Fine, if you won't leave, I will." Trev marched for his door, but Cody leaped over the desk and darted in front of him, his back pressed to the door. "Get out of my way."

"No."

He threatened. "Get out of my way, Cody. Don't make me remove you."

"I'm not moving until you hear me out," Cody said stubbornly.

"Why are you doing this to me? Can't you see this is hard enough? Do you hate me that much?" Trev clenched his fists, his anger and pain breaking free of its cage.

Taking him by surprise, Cody pushed off the door and grabbed his face—his silver eyes fierce with emotion. "I don't hate you. I'm fucking in love with you," he said a moment before their lips crashed together.

Trev's entire being felt scrambled and thrown into a blender as his body responded, lighting up with the feel of Cody touching him. Meanwhile, his brain raced to keep up with this sudden change of events. Cody's words were slowly seeping into the deep recesses of his conscious. Breaking the kiss, Cody pulled him tight against his body as he laid soft kisses along his neck.

"Did you hear me?" Cody whispered in his ear.

He had to push the fog in his brain aside to try and think straight. "I don't understand."

"I was blaming myself. I needed time to process my role in Ray's death."

"Then why push me away when I tried to reach out to you?"

"I'm sorry. I'm not used to having someone in my life to lean on, to count on, to share anything with, especially my emotions."

Trev closed his eyes and pulled Cody into him. The crushing weight that had been hanging around his neck lifting. He'd been so certain that Cody blamed him. "But why—." Cody laid a finger on his lips, stopping the question.

"Later, I will try to explain everything later, but right now, I'm going to walk over to the door and lock it. Then you're going to get out of these clothes so I can fuck you over your desk the way I've been dreaming of since I first saw you sitting there."

"You think so, do you?"

"I know so, and you know what else I know?"

"What's that?" Trev asked.

"You're going to submit to me, and you're going to do so willingly." Cody grabbed his ass and gave it a squeeze, his finger rubbing up and down the crack. "This ass is mine," Cody bit out possessively. Trev shuddered with Cody's words, heat spreading throughout his body. "Please, I need this. I'm sorry I locked myself away. I shouldn't have done it, but I need you more than I ever thought possible. I felt lost without you."

Trev's eyes locked with Cody's earnest gaze, and he knew before he opened his mouth that he wouldn't deny him. He never wanted to deny him anything.

"Then what are you waiting for?" He smiled before their lips met again.

Chapter 38

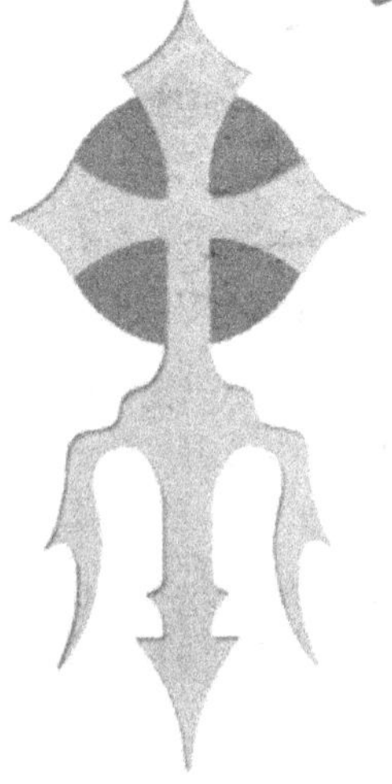

Cody hadn't been joking about bending Trev over his desk. It had been a fantasy the moment he laid eyes on the large table and the man that sat behind it.

He couldn't get to the door fast enough to lock it. His heart was speeding so quickly. He thought he might pass out before he got to see Trev naked. He'd never meant to hurt Trev, and as Cody turned and stared at the man, he methodically took off his cufflinks. Trev was an island in the storm, the calm and steady that everyone instinctively gathered around. Cody's eyes traced Trev's precise movements and smirked —he now understood the cool quirk that was only one layer to the complex man.

Maybe it was wrong to want to have sex after just burying his best friend. The thing was, he'd spent days mourning his friend alone, and in doing so, he had jeopardized the one thing that made him feel sane and whole.

Was he over Ray's death? No, he might never be able to forgive himself for what happened, and as soon as he left this office, there was a huge responsibility waiting for him. But right now, he needed to mend things with Trev. He craved this connection between them as much as Trev's physical touch. Ray would've been the first to say go for it, and that was exactly what he planned to do.

He licked his lips as Trev pulled his dress shirt out of his pants and one at a time popped the little white buttons to reveal the perfectly sculpted body beneath. His eyes traced the white line of the scars that may never fade. It was his reminder that he almost lost Trev twice—once due to his own actions.

His tie was undone and hanging around his neck. Cody wanted to take a photograph of this moment and save it as his screensaver so he would never forget it.

"Do you have lube in here?"

A single eyebrow lifted as Trev shot him a quick glance. "Are you suggesting I sit behind my desk and jack off when I'm alone in my office?" The dark glint in Trev's eye had him groaning with the thought of the man doing just that. His own cock surged inside his pants, and he reached down to rub off some of the tension. He loved the fact that Trev's eyes followed the movement. It gave him some very distinct ideas for another time.

"Let's just say I wouldn't complain if you said you did."

A warm chuckle filled the room as Trev turned his way. "I do have lube in here, but sadly it has never been used, and neither has my virgin desk."

Cody flushed so hot that he thought he might melt on the spot. "Where is it?"

"Bottom drawer of the desk. Left-hand side."

Cody was already on the move before Trev finished speaking. Bending over, he yanked open the drawer and gripped the small tube but froze as he stood up. His eyes were locked on the photo on Trev's desk—how many times had he been in here and never paid attention to the photo of Trev's unit. Reaching out, he picked up the photograph, and his eyes immediately found the stunning blonde that Trev had his arm wrapped around. Trev hadn't been lying, Mel was beautiful, but more than that, they looked genuinely happy. The emotion in his eyes captured their feelings. It was a moment made for fairy tales and movies.

"Are you okay?" He glanced up to see Trev staring at him from the other side of the room.

He found his throat choked up with emotion as he tried to speak. Cody coughed as he cleared the tightness away and sat the photo back on the desk. "You were so happy, Mel is—."

"My past," Trev said, quietly.

"I'm still sorry for what you lost."

Trev cocked his head, and Cody felt like he was being inspected. He couldn't have moved if he wanted to with the intense stare. He was rooted to the spot as Trev approached him. "You worry too much about what I have lost and don't seem to see what I have gained. Yes, Mel will always be in my heart, and what we had was unique." Trev grabbed his hand and laid it over his heart. He could feel the rhythmical thump under his warm skin. "But, that does not mean I don't have room for you or that we can't find our own special story, our unique."

A vortex of emotion swirled inside of him—it was as if he was being tossed around in a windstorm, unable to get his bearings. There was no fear as they stared into each other's eyes—he was beginning to wonder if Trev was capable of that emotion.

"I want to hurt you in the best way possible." His voice was as rough as sandpaper as he spoke.

He traced the square jaw before he ran the pad of his thumb over Trev's full bottom lip. He sucked in a sharp breath, and Trev sucked his thumb into his mouth. The hot, rough sensation had a direct line to the hard shaft still trapped in his pants. A shiver raced down his spine, and he groaned, the need ticking another notch higher. "I don't deserve you, but I plan on keeping you all the same. Now give me your tie."

Trev pulled on the one end of the black silk material—Cody's eyes followed it as it snaked around Trev's neck to pool like a whip in his hands. "Am I going to need a safe word, Cody?"

"Oh, fuck," he groaned. "You might."

Trev held out the tie and smiled. "Alright then, I choose Un-Ass."

He couldn't help but laugh as he took the tie. "That's definitely direct."

"Military term, I'm sure the meaning is clear enough." Trev smirked as his pants pooled to the floor.

"Definitely..." The rest of the sentence flew out the window as Trev pulled the boxers he was wearing down. "Turn around, and give me your hands," he managed to croak out.

Trev smirked at him, challenge evident in his eyes, but he didn't resist and did as he was told. It was at that moment Cody understood, no matter what he did, he was never in control. Like a lion at a circus, this predator allowed him to feel in control, but there was no longer any doubt in his mind that if Trev decided to turn on him, he would be no match. Not physically nor otherwise, the control had always remained in Trev's hands. Why the thought of being that much out of control had his cock standing at attention with more carnal lust than he'd ever experienced, he had no idea.

Trev stood perfectly still as he slipped the soft black material around the crossed wrists, looping the ends together in a firm knot. His hands shook as he worked, the adrenaline and excitement making it hard to concentrate. Stepping close to Trev's body, he nipped at the side of his neck, the distinct and addictive cologne he always wore seeping into his senses.

He was starved for this man. His hands slid across wide shoulders, the muscles flexing under his touch. Free to do what he wanted, he ran his fingertips across Trev's ribs while his tongue traveled up the side of

Trev's neck to grip his earlobe in his teeth. Finding Trev's hard little nipples, he tweaked them hard enough to draw a gasp as he bit down harder on the sensitive piece of flesh.

Trev groaned and pushed back ever so slightly into him, making him smile. "You like that?" He repeated the same action and was rewarded as Trev arched his back, pressing his chest into his hands. "Answer me."

"Yes, I like it."

"And how about this?" Cody swirled his fingers lower until he was able to grip the hard cock. Stroking the hard length, he made sure to pay special attention to the spot that made him shiver at the base of his cock. It didn't take long for his hand to be coated in the slippery pre-cum that was seeping from the tip. He closed his eyes as Trev laid his head back on his shoulder, his breathing faster with each gentle tug. He paused when he reached the base of the long shaft and massaged the tight sac in his hand. The reaction was instant as Trev's ass pressed firmer into his own groin, the tied hands taking advantage of their position, groped at him through the dress pants.

"When I ask you a question, I expect you to answer," he whispered into Trev's ear.

"Yes, I like that."

"You just like it?"

"No, it feels fucking incredible."

He smiled wide. Giving Trev one final stroke, he forced himself to let go of Trev's tempting cock. "Turn around." Cody shuddered as Trev did as he asked, and those polarizing eyes locked with his. His heart tripled in time and pounded so fast it felt like a rabbit in his chest. "On your knees."

"Are you planning on executing me?" Trev smirked as he smoothly lowered himself to his knees.

Cody smiled wide. "Only if I'm doing it with my cock in your mouth."

"I think I've proven I can take it." Trev's eyebrow lifted cockily, almost in challenge.

"That you have," Cody said. He started to lower the zipper on his pants and stopped. "You undo them. Use your teeth." He'd wiped that cocky smile off his face one way or another.

He should've known that the man would find a way to make it look easy. His tongue teasingly swirled around the little metal piece before he took hold of it with his teeth and pulled at the perfect angle to slide down. Using his teeth once more, he gripped the open flap of material and gave it a tug until the pants fell to the floor.

"I will find something you are not perfect at."

"You will be searching for a long time."

Cody believed every word of that statement. "You know what to do next, don't make me ask."

"Yes, Sir," Trev bit out cheekily. He wasn't sure if he wanted to smack the cheeky, defiant look off his face or melt on the spot because those two words sounded so fucking hot coming out of his mouth.

A soft growl left his lips, and Trev nuzzled his face into his crotch as his tongue and teeth worked their magic. It took mere seconds for him to be standing naked before Trev, and he glanced toward the window, groaning as he watched their reflection in the glass. The view of his cock slipping into the hot awaiting mouth was almost too much, and he bit down hard on his lip to keep from blowing his load prematurely.

Gripping Trev's hair in his fist, he was not gentle as he rocked his hips back and forth, forcing the long length down Trev's throat.

"Fuck, you feel good," he groaned as Trev swallowed around his shaft. He couldn't decide which was better, the view from above or the one in the window, and found himself flicking his eyes back and forth. His movements became jerky, and he knew he was playing with fire. Trev was too good—he was already close but couldn't seem to stop the sounds of slurping growing louder.

"Ahh," he bit out as he fought his body's urges to let go and come.

Forcing himself to stop, he pulled back, freeing himself of that hot mouth. There was no way he was wasting this opportunity to get into this man's ass. Trev's puffy lips and hooded stare were too much to resist, and leaned down and cupped his face, crashing their lips together. The kiss turned desperate, as if they were trying to communicate a deeper meaning through the act.

Trev never broke the kiss but managed to stand. Their bodies pressed into one another—their inflated shafts trapped between them in a glorious duo as they moved. His hands instinctively shifted down to cup the hard ass cheeks that he'd dreamt about for months drawing them closer together.

Cody gasped as he broke the heady kiss. "Bend over your desk."

Trev looked to the desk and then back into his eyes. "Please move the large notes calendar. I don't think Sally would appreciate writing on it with come stains all over it."

He shook his head in amazement that Trev could even think about something like that at a time like this. He might have been insulted if it wasn't for the fact it was so delightfully Trev to think about everyone, twenty steps out.

"I'm not going to be gentle," Cody said as he grabbed the large paper and leather thing off Trev's desk and laid it aside.

"I know."

Cody licked his lips. "Okay then, bend over."

The corner of Trev's lips pulled up a defiant glint in his eyes. "Make me."

A flush of heat raced through Cody's body with those two little words. He didn't think it was possible to be any more turned on, but Trev managed to make the impossible possible.

Trev got right up in his face, their noses almost touching—those sky-blue eyes fierce with their intensity. "Just remember I know where you sleep, and payback will most certainly find you."

Cody swallowed hard, his pulse pounding hard. "I guess I'll have to take my chances," he said, surprised that his voice came out at all, let alone sounded confident.

The image of waking up to Trev pinning him to the bed as he fucked him hard was dancing firmly in his mind—more than ever, he wanted to push that button. Taking Trev by the shoulders, he turned him to face the desk, and with pressure on Trev's back, he pointed to the desk. "Bend over, now." There was resistance, but Trev finally submitted and leaned over until his cheek and chest touched the desk. He sucked in a sharp breath, his restrained hands clenching into fists as he came into contact with the cool wooden surface.

"Spread 'em." Cody tapped his foot against the insides of Trev's feet and groaned as that delicious ass opened enough for him to see his prize. Hands shaking, he grabbed the small tube of lube and coated his cock before squeezing more onto his destination and fingers.

As much as he wanted to slam home, he was tempted to teach Trev a fun lesson. He couldn't bring himself to hurt him purposely. Besides, it was going to be more fun to make him beg for his release than it was to make him scream in pain. He slowly slipped a finger into the tight hole and made sure to press firmly down as he did. He knew the moment he hit Trev's prostate and smiled as Trev groaned and closed his eyes.

"Oh fuck," Trev said and squirmed on the desk. Like a cat with a ball, Cody watched Trev's ass wriggle back and forth as he deliberately teased that special spot. Trev's ass cheeks flexed, his hips thrusting forward as his panting increased.

Sensing he was getting a little too close, Cody pulled his finger back and worked at making the entrance pliable for his girth.

"Fuck, you're a tease," Trev mumbled.

"Is this what you want?" He ran a couple of fingers over the sweet spot once more and gave it a few quick rubs drawing a few choice words from Trev's slack jaw when he stopped once more.

He teased the rim of his clenching hole as he leaned over Trev's body to get close to his ear.

"Tell me what you want." He dipped his fingers in, but not far enough to give Trev any relief. "Say the words, or I leave you on your desk like this…wanting…needing and unable to satisfy the craving," Cody whispered. Goosebumps rose on Trev's body with his words, and he loved the reaction. "Say it, that's an order."

Trev licked his lips, his eyes turning to look at him. The raw need Cody saw in their depths was almost enough to give the man what they both craved, but he'd drawn his line, and he intended to stay on his side.

"Fuck me," Trev finally said.

He continued to tease him, sinking his fingers deep and then withdrawing them. "How?"

"Hard and fast. Please."

It was the please that did it, it was most likely one of the only times he would ever get this man to beg for anything, and he wasn't going to squander it. Stepping up behind him, he gave himself a few firm strokes before lining up with the now well-prepared hole. Cody gripped Trev's hips hard and had to take a few moments of teasing to get his ass to relax. Every swear word known to man tumbled from Trev's lips as Cody found a steady rhythm and sank a little deeper with each thrust. He'd never been in such a tight hole, and he was sweating from the extreme effort of finally sinking all the way in.

They were panting in time with one another as he held still to catch his breath. Trev flexed his muscles and firmly locked him inside of his ass.

Trev moaned, the sound almost a whimper of pleasure as Cody eased back out to repeat the movement. Every little grunt and pant that tumbled from Trev's mouth was sweet bliss to his ears.

The emotional build up had him dangling by a thread, but the sensation thrumming though his body with each flex of Trev's ass was pushing him headlong towards his orgasm.

"Holy fuck, I can't…I just can't," was all Cody could get out before the control he'd been hanging on so hard to crashed around him.

Grabbing onto the tie and locking hands with Trev, he pulled out and rammed into him like a man possessed. The level of carnal need was overpowering and driving him on. Flesh met flesh, the sound of their mutual groaning and swearing intensified the moment.

Sweat coated his chest as he neared the peak of his release, and he didn't know how much longer he could hold out. He was just about to give in and order Trev to come when his body quaked beneath him. Wrapping his hand around Trev's throat, he pulled up and buried his face into the crook of his neck. Reaching around, he grabbed hold of Trev's cock and somehow managed to keep his own rhythm.

"Fuck," Trev yelled, his body going rigid as the first stream of his release found the desk. Cody's internal chokehold he had on his orgasm dissolved, and he came harder than he ever had before. The release was violent and wracked his body. His orgasm bordered on painful—it was that strong.

As the last spurt left his body, his knees gave way, and he fell to the floor, taking Trev with him. They landed in a pile of limbs wrapped around one another. Laying there, panting hard, his cock still buried in Trev's ass, neither seemed to have an interest in leaving the comforting wet warmth anytime soon. Cody fumbled slowly with the tie, but the simple knot gave way, and Trev groaned as he rolled his shoulders forward.

"I don't want to move," Cody mumbled into the side of Trev's neck.

"Then don't." Trev pulled Cody's arm more firmly around his body. Comfortable ease washed over him until Trev spoke again. "Oh, and Cody?"

"Mmhmm," he mumbled.

"If you ever push me away again, we're through."

Cody swallowed hard. "I understand."

Chapter 39

Trev took a deep breath of the breeze, ruffling his almost too long hair. He turned in a slow circle and spotted Mel sitting on a log tossing pebbles into the crystal-clear water.

He started to walk and looked down as sand squished between his toes.

"Don't be a stick in the mud. Come join me." Mel waved him over.

He stuffed his hands in his pant pockets and strolled his way across the beach to stare down at her. "Am I dying again? Was I shot in my sleep or bleeding out, and no one knows?"

Mel rolled her eyes at him. "Who says they don't know? Maybe they're the ones that shot you. The Lord knows I thought about it a time or two." She smiled wickedly and then laughed. "Always so dramatic, and you say Arek is the dramatic one. He can't hold a candle to you."

"Oh, please, do not compare me to my brother." Trev crossed his arms over his chest. "I love him, but he is—nevermind."

She held out her hand, and he instinctively reached for her. She felt warm and soft as he slipped his hand into hers. "Just sit with me for a minute," Mel said.

Trev lowered himself down to the large log, and they sat in silence except for the soft rippling of the water and the chirping of birds. Unable to take it any longer, he turned to stare at Mel's profile.

"If I'm not dying, then why am I here? Why am I seeing you now after all this time? I mean, where were you when I really needed to see you? Where were you when I was drinking too much and closed myself off from the world as I buried myself in work?"

"That's a lot of why's to unpack." She gave him her teasing smirk. Reaching out, she lifted the chain around his neck and held their mutual tag and the ring he bought for her in her hand. "I would've said yes, you know? I didn't need a grand gesture or some fairy tale moment. We were the fairy tale moment." Her eyes locked with his. "Trev, I'm here because you're still holding on to me, but you have no more reason too."

"Of course, I'm going to hang on to our memories, my feelings. I can't just sweep that away. You can't expect that of me."

"I wouldn't ask you to do that, and I will be honest. Selfishly, I don't want you to." Mel laid the dog tags on his chest and linked their fingers together.

"Then what do you mean," Trev asked, his frustration and pain churning in his gut. Seeing her again to say goodbye had been one thing, but now this was an evil tease. To touch her and smell her and talk to her, but knowing it was fleeting was a horrible trick on his system.

"Why didn't you say I love you?"

"What do you mean? I told you I loved you every day. Usually more than that." Mel cocked her eyebrow at him. Her patented don't be stupid look crossing her face. "You mean Cody." Trev looked away from her intense stare to take in the serene water.

"He told you he loves you, and you side-stepped it. Why?" She squeezed his hand, and he looked away as she tried to catch his stare.

"Because I don't know if I do yet, why are you pushing this so hard?" Trev

released Mel's hand and stood, going to the water's edge. The cool water slipped over his feet and backed out again in a perfect rhythmical fashion.

"Trevor Alexander Anderson, don't you dare try to pull that shit on me. I know you love him. I can see it in your eyes. I know better than anyone what that warm puppy look means."

"I don't have a puppy look," Trev mumbled.

Mel closed the distance and took his hands in hers once more. "Stop holding back. You asked why I am here now? I'm here because you weren't ready to move on before, but you are now, and yet you are clinging to what was. You may say you have left the past behind, but it's time to prove it."

He took a deep breath. "I hate that you know me so well."

She gave him a smile, but it didn't reach her eyes this time. "What we had was a gift, but so is this new life you've built. Grasp it and hang on with all you have." Mel laid her hand on his cheek and ran her thumb across his skin. It felt warm and familiar. It was a gesture she'd done a million times over their years together.

"He pushed me away. I can't play those games—I won't play those games. You know, if I'm in, I'm all in. If I say those words—" Trev ran a hand through his hair as he pictured what it was like knowing Cody was down the hall but had locked him out. The pain of being physically, emotionally, and mentally pushed away—he never wanted to do that again.

"I know, but don't you think you're being a bit hard on him? He's never been in a relationship before, never had a stable home. You're the first real relationship untainted by scars. He's going to need a moment to catch up to the great and wonderful Trevor Anderson." She raised her voice and lifted her hand in the air like she was announcing him into a boxing match.

"Really, you went there." He tried for annoyance but knew she would see right through it.

"Someone has to give you a slap upside the head. The two of you are going to have growing pains, but he is right for you."

"It's hard for me to hear you say this, Mel." He shook his head and sucked in a shuddering breath. "I thought that about you." He couldn't help feeling small

as he looked down to the ground. Like he was a kid begging to have his toy back after his parents had taken it away.

Taking his chin in her hand, she forced him to look at her. "I want you to be happy and to step into this new life you've built. Tell him how you really feel, Trev. I mean it. Don't hold back because of me, not anymore."

"You always did know how to get your way." He tucked a piece of her hair behind her ear. "Okay, if this is what you really want, then I will."

"No, no more if it is what I want. The point is for you to start doing what you want." The breeze picked up a little more, the scent of jasmine and honeysuckle strong in the air. Mel looked over her shoulder and then back up at him.

"You have to go," Trev asked as she sighed.

"No, you do. Time to wake up, Trev." Raising up on her toes, she placed a chaste kiss on his lips. "I won't be back. This is your final push off the ledge to a second chance. Don't waste it." She walked behind him, running her hand across his shoulders. "I'll see you in another life, soldier boy."

Trev turned to call out to her, but she was already gone. He stared up and down the beach, but he was once more alone.

Trev sucked in a deep breath and sat up straight in bed with a start. He rubbed at his eyes as the images of bright colors and the scent of jasmine still filled his nose.

"Are you okay?" Cody placed a hand on his shoulder just as his phone rattled on the nightstand.

"I will be. Give me a second," Trev said as he grabbed the annoying device. Who the hell calls someone at three in the morning? "Mr. Anderson here. . .What? Why? That is no reason . . . Yes, I understand. When is she being moved?" He sighed as the information sank in. "Very well, I will be there shortly." Trev hung up the phone and wanted to flop back down in bed, curl up with Cody and go back to sleep, but that was not going to happen.

"Who was that?"

He turned to stare into the inquisitive silver eyes. "They are moving Maeve to a maximum-security prison later today."

"Holy shit, she hasn't even had her trial yet, and they are sending her to max?" Cody sat up straight as Trev slipped his legs over the side to find his slippers.

"I know. Whoever is pulling the strings on this has deep pockets and a lot of pull. Neither is a good thing." He made his way across the floor but stopped just before he stepped into the washroom. "Did you want to join me in the shower?"

A smile spread across Cody's face as he jumped up and walked toward him. "Do fish live in water?"

"Is this a trick question?"

Cody laughed as he met him at the door. "No, it's not a trick question. The answer is yes. The answer is always yes.

Chapter 40

The stupid smile wouldn't leave Cody's face. He found himself more than once frozen with a spoonful of Lucky Charms halfway to his mouth as he thought about Trev.

"You do know it's like seven at night, right?" Arek poked his head in the kitchen, startling him out of another revere.

"Yeah, just needed a snack. Did Trev say anything to you about when he'd be back?"

"Nope, and I don't fucking care," Arek grumbled and disappeared into the hall.

Cody sat the half-eaten bowl on the counter and jogged out to catch up to Arek. "Where are you going?"

"To see what I can find out at the races. That fucker Spike set us up. It's time I paid him a visit." Arek swung a black leather jacket on, the thing barely covering the knives and guns he had strapped to his body.

"Ok, first, Trev told us not to make a move without him saying so. Second, you can't go with all those weapons."

"First, I don't give a fuck what my brother says—I'm keeping the jobs going, and I will do it without him if I have to. Second, I don't give a flying fuck about the no-weapons policy. Every single one of them will end up with a new hole in their head until I find the answers I'm after."

Cody groaned and rubbed his eyes. This was not going to win any points with Trev, but he couldn't let Arek go alone. "Count me in. I need to know who got Ray killed."

Arek studied his face and nodded. "Alright, go put more than that shit on. I don't need any helicopter cock shows." He nodded toward the grey sweatpants he was wearing, raising an eyebrow at the look.

"Five minutes." Cody sprinted down the hall and managed to get changed and strapped in less than the allotted time. Good thing too, Arek was pacing the front hall looking ready to bolt faster than a groom with cold feet.

"Took you long enough," Arek mumbled and then yanked open the door and stuck his head out to look around.

"What are you doing?"

"Making sure Trev didn't pull in."

"Are we fucking twelve now?" Cody crossed his arms over his chest as Arek turned to glare at him.

"Alright, hotshot, you call him and tell him where we are going and why."

The smugness seeped away at the thought of that conversation. In fact, he was having second thoughts about going at all. He chewed on his lower lip as he contemplated the repercussions of this move.

"You can't do it either. You're just as big of a chicken shit." Arek grabbed the Porsche keys off the decorative hook. "Here's the thing, if we can get proof that Spike set us up and find out why, the mission will be looked at as a success, and Trev will put all this nonsense of leaving The Righteous behind."

"Is that really a good thing? I mean, Renee would be happier if you quit, and it would definitely be safer all around if there were no more missions."

Cody stared at Arek's hand as he suddenly leaned onto his shoulders and gave them a squeeze. Eyes deathly intense stared into his own. "I know you don't know me that well, but let's just say the missions and the guys that find justice help keep my head from swimming in dangerous waters." Cody swallowed hard as he took in the glint in Arek's eyes. He was a man that could cut your balls off like it was a third-grade art class project while singing a song and eating a sandwich at the same time.

"Fine, if we're going to go, we better get out of here. I expected Trev home already. We had fun plans if you know what I mean."

Arek nodded and started out the door, and Cody almost collided with him as he stopped and spun around, holding a finger up in front of his face. "Since you brought it up. Next time you plan on having a daytime bump and grind in Trev's office, could you make sure J.J. is not home. I had to tell him that you two were watching the Discovery channel, and the fucking kid told me he knew every episode, and those noises didn't come from any animal. Too fucking smart," Arek mumbled as he turned and marched down the steps.

Well, that was awkward.

Cody shook his head and locked up as he rushed to catch up to Arek and skidded to a halt as he took in the garage and the missing vehicles.

"Ah, where is my car and the mustang?" Cody blinked a few times like that might put them back in their rightful places.

"Oh, I burned them. Now get in."

"You what?" Cody's mouth dropped open as fast as his heart fell through the floor. "That car was my baby, I…."

"It was also used in a chase from the police who are most likely still looking for it. It had to go." Arek lifted a shoulder like this all made sense.

"Have you ever heard of a fucking paint job?" Cody clenched his fists as he thought of his baby going up in flames like some random piece of trash.

"Huh, yeah, I guess I could've done." Arek tapped his chin then laid his hands on the top of the Porsche as if he might leap over the roof. "Then again, no amount of scrubbing was going to get rid of the bloodstains, smartass. Now stop blubbering and get in the fucking car or stay here."

Arek's door slammed as he got behind the wheel. The words Arek had said finally sunk in, and Cody's hands shook for a different reason. Taking a deep breath, he slipped into the passenger seat and barely got the door closed when Arek stomped his foot to the floor, making the car leap forward out of the open garage door.

"Jesus H, man. My leg was still half out the door." Cody glared at Arek as he snapped the seatbelt in place.

"Be faster next time." Cody envisioned what it would be like to mess up that pretty face. "I see you staring at me like that, and I wouldn't think about it unless you want to end up under the car."

"You really are…."

"Don't say the word crazy." Arek glanced over at him. "I really have an aversion to that word."

Just when he thought they could be friends, Arek went sideways. "I have to know, would you really kill me? Take me out and burn me like the cars?" Cody gripped the holy shit handle as they screeched around the corner at a red light, causing drivers to blow their horns as they scared the shit out of them.

"No, but only because Trev is in love with you and you're J.J. and Renee's brother. You will forever get a free pass around the Arek-opoly board unless you hurt Trev." Those eyes that could cut you down where you stood bore a hole right through him. "If you break my brother's heart, no one will ever find your body, and I'll enjoy every second of it."

"Well, wasn't this a fun conversation?"

"Please, I'm a fuzzy little pussy cat in comparison to the crazy fuck you used to room with."

The worst part of that statement was that it was true. Cody opted to simply watch the city fly by as they streaked for their destination. He could picture Ray in the backseat cracking a joke, and he had to stop himself from falling down that dark hole.

Cody rubbed his face as he switched gears in his brain. Arek said that Trev loved him, but Trev hadn't said it back. How could Arek be so certain? Did Trev say something to his brother? That seemed unlikely. It was probably a guess, one that he could only hope was true.

The industrial section was quiet for race night. They should normally have seen a couple of dozen cars either coming or going by now.

"Park here, don't pull up where we normally go especially driving this. If Spike is here, he is going to spot this out-of-place car and have his men scoop us up before we get close," Cody said and pointed to a tucked-away spot, and Arek seamlessly backed the car into the small space.

"Arek, please don't go in there like it's the fucking wild west. I really don't feel like dying tonight."

Arek smiled, the corner of his mouth pulling up just enough to show off his incisor like he was a dog growling at him. "I got you. You have nothing to worry about." Arek punched him in the arm just as the interior light went out.

This was a bad fucking idea in a long list of bad fucking ideas.

They strolled down the quiet street toward the loud noises of engines revving. Both of them slipped around the corner, trying to blend with the others who were loitering about along the sidewalk. It wasn't quite dark yet. The sun was a ball of fiery orange in the sky casting a stunning glow on everything.

"Do you see Spike?" Arek stopped moving, his eyes flicking back and forth. "If he wasn't standing in the bed of his truck, where would he be?"

Cody stared at the empty truck bed and began doing the same scan of the crowd. "He seems to be over there." Cody pointed to the back of a mohawk. Arek led the way, his eyes never leaving their target, even when a woman bumped into him. It was as if she never existed.

"Hold up." Arek held out his arm, catching Cody in the gut. He let out a groan with the sudden impact. Before he could ask what the fuck was going on, Arek grabbed him by the arm and pulled him behind a nearby parked truck.

"What the hell are you doing?" Cody looked through the dark window trying to make out Spike or who he was talking to.

"The guy that Spike is talking to, I know him. Well, know him is too strong a word. I've seen him before," Arek whispered.

Cody stared at the man as Spike stepped off to the side and handed off a white envelope. "He looks like a random guy. I've never seen him before here, but that looked like money Spike handed over." The truck owner looked over at them, and Cody nodded to the truck owner and smiled. "Sick truck, best vehicle here," he called out, lying through his teeth.

The guy nodded and turned back to his discussion. "That fucker." Arek's voice dropped the words gravelly as he continued to swear.

"Who is he?"

"Let's just say I saw him at an arcade." Arek pulled the hood up on his sweater despite the warm weather. "I need to follow him."

"What about Spike?"

"I'll deal with him another time. I don't believe in coincidences, and this is too big of one to pass up."

"Alright, let's go," Cody said as the random man walked away from Spike. The guy hunched his shoulders down like he was trying to make himself small as he made his way along the opposite sidewalk. He was heading the way they'd arrived, and Arek waited until he was a good distance ahead before they followed. They reached the intersection they'd emerged from, but the man continued to walk toward a green suped-up Civic further down the road.

Arek burst into a jog for the Porsche, but before Cody made it to the parking space, Arek turned and caught him off guard with the hardest right hook he'd ever felt. Unable to stop his momentum, he slammed hard into the fist which connected with his jaw like a sledgehammer. He was thrown back and knocked on his ass like a cartoon character. He saw stars and little birds as he crumbled to the ground in a heap.

"Sorry, man, but I can't take you. If you die, both your sister and Trev will be devastated. Can't have that shit on my conscience."

Cody shook his head, trying to clear it of the ringing, and managed to get himself half-upright, leaning against the brick wall when the Porsche sped out of the lot past him.

"Son of a bitch."

This was definitely a bad idea.

Chapter 41

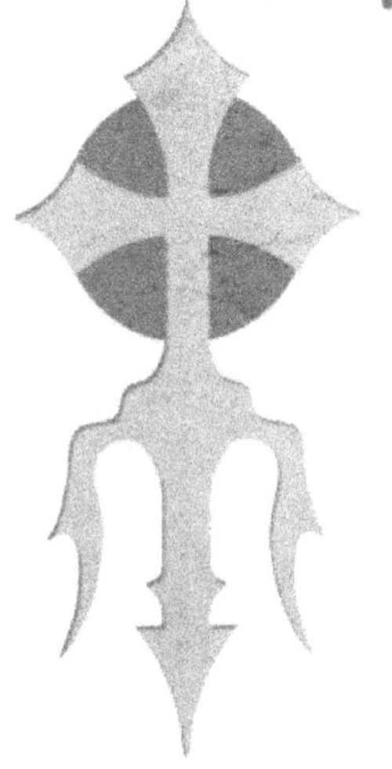

Trev tapped the steering wheel, his fingers in time to the classic Mozart concerto playing. It wasn't doing much to soothe the tension tightening his shoulders and making his head pound.

His mind kept going around and around as he thought about all he'd learned. It had become very clear that someone was setting Maeve up, but the question that was circling the drain in his brain was why. From what he'd learned, Maeve was a recruiter—she found those that needed and wanted a second chance at life and offered them an opportunity to turn their shit around.

Did she take out targets? Maeve was one of Morry's girls. That screamed loud and clear if she needed to protect herself, she would do what she had to. The thing was, she couldn't think of a single target that would piss off someone with political or financial backing. It had to be one or the other, possibly both, to be able to pull off this manufactured illusion. Was she a random target? Someone fit the bill for this murder, and whoever was covering this up had more to do with the dead detective than they did her. That still didn't explain the mysterious call on his phone.

"I need a drink," Trev mumbled as he made the final turn toward the house. The motion detectors and garage door opened as he pulled into the driveway and effortlessly slid the Bentley into its spot. He was happy to be back at the house, and the added security features were a bonus.

It didn't look like Arek was home, which was good. He had other ideas about releasing this pent-up frustration, and all of those ideas were tied around one particular silver-eyed man.

He placed his hand on the security panel just as his phone rang. Speak of the devil. "Hey there, I just got home. I'll see you in a minute."

"I'm not home. Fuck, my head hurts. Your brother is an asshole," Cody groaned.

Trev froze in place, his instincts for disaster spiking. "Well, that is something that I already knew, but where are you two?"

"Okay, don't kill me." The phone went silent, but he could still hear Cody breathing. "Arek wanted to come down to the races and see if he could figure out who ratted us out and got Ray killed," Cody said, the words tumbling out quickly. "He doesn't want you to stop taking missions from The Righteous and thought if he could find the rat, you would give up the idea."

"I don't like where this is going."

"Shit, Trev, I should've tried to stop him, got him to talk to you first. I shouldn't have gone with him, but fuck," Cody paused, his breathing loud. "I needed to find out who killed Ray. I hope you understand."

"Tell me what happened."

Cody relayed the story all while Trev opened the hidden panel of weapons and chose his favorite gun. He loaded it and grabbed an extra clip as he stomped toward Delilah. "I don't know where he went, but Trev, I'm really, really, fucking sorry."

"I'll find him. Do you need a ride?"

"Nah, I'm good."

Trev paused his mouth open as the words, I love you, stuck in his throat. "Be safe." Trev hit end on the call. "Shit, shit, shit. Arek I may kill you myself. Delilah, track Arek's phone."

Arek pulled the Porsche into a shadowed parking spot down the road from the crappy old home. This neighborhood would've once been an aspiring must-move-to location but had been ravaged by those that sought to destroy pretty things. A lone garbage bag rolled down the street, and that was all you needed to know about the area. He didn't even want to leave his baby unattended in a place like this, but as he watched Mr. Arcade walk up to his front steps and disappear inside, he had to know who he was.

Arek remembered the strange man's face who had praised him after he had killed the man with a gun to his head. His over-enthusiastic proclamation that Arek should be branded a hero was seared into his brain. He pulled on his leather gloves and waited until the lights flicked on upstairs before making his move. He slipped out of the car, making a dash across the quiet street to the backyard.

A lone dog barked from a yard further down the row of dilapidated homes while a cat yowled as it looked for a mate to satisfy its needs. The back door was unsurprisingly locked, but the window that would be too high for most people to get in was open a crack. Arek looked around for any signs of movement from the neighboring homes. When nothing moved, he leaped for the ledge of the open window.

Pulling himself up, he looked inside, the window peered into the kitchen, but there was no movement. He braced his feet on the wall and pushed up on the window until it was open enough that he could slip through. Hands on the counter, he rolled the rest of the way and landed softly in a crouch position. Every fiber of his being stood at attention as he tried to pick up on any potential threat. This guy didn't seem like the sort to have any sophisticated tech, but Arek wasn't taking any chances and searched for any form of detection alarm as he moved through the kitchen toward the hallway.

A pipe rattled nearby as water rushed past in a nearby wall. The telltale signs of a toilet being flushed was the only sound in the moldy-smelling home. He made his way up the stairs, testing each one for signs that would give him away before reaching his target. The lights were glowing brightly in the hallway, and he laid flat against the darkened stairwell as the distinct sound of feet drew closer. The man turned before reaching the stairs, and the door closed with a squeak and a click a moment before the sound of a shower reached Arek's ears.

He waited for a few more breaths to make sure that whoever this guy was, wasn't going to re-emerge before continuing to the top landing. The place was relatively small, a three-bedroom, one-bath on the upper-level type of spot. He poked his head into one bedroom, but the room was bare of any furniture, only blotchy paint from a leak in the roof. He turned his attention to the next room, and it was set up like an office. There was a lone desk with a lamp and a chair, not exactly exciting. This guy didn't even have a single plant to cheer the shithole up.

Arek made his way to the desk, but other than a couple of pens, it didn't have anything of interest. He walked around to check the drawers and froze as his eyes caught the wall opposite the desk.

"What the fuck?" He breathed out quietly as he made his way toward the wall that had been turned into a stalker's delight. Pictures of both himself, Trev, Sally, Cody, and Renee lined the walls. Pictures of him with J.J. and Renee at the park. Sally was heading into their home for work. Cody was standing with Tyson at some warehouse, and even them running from the building where they were to meet Spike.

Pictures of their cars and dates and times of schedule, it was all thoroughly mapped out.

Arek's blood was like lava in his veins as he stared at all the proof he needed that this man was somehow involved in sabotaging them. But what made his blood run like ice water was the centerpiece of the wall. A blown-up picture of Trev standing outside of the courthouse with a red bullseye painted around his head. The words, must die, were scribbled across his face.

He took in the disturbing wall and then read the words splashed across the top like a title, *Die Rechtschaffenen wird gefallen.* His German was rusty, but he was pretty sure that it said the Righteous would fall.

The water in the shower shut off, and he made his way across the hall to wait for the man that was going to find himself on the wrong side of his gun.

Arek sized up the room and smirked as he opened the closet door and stepped inside the dark space, blending in with the clothes. The television sitting on a stand in the corner of the room was turned on to one of the news channels. The sound of bare feet moved around the room. Arek tracked his movements in his mind, easily picturing where the piece of shit was with each footfall which sent small vibrations across the wooden surface. There was a distinct pause and a squeak of the bed. Then the bed moved again as the man-made his way toward the closet with now muffled strides.

As soon as the door began to open, Arek raised his gun. The asshole didn't even notice him until the barrel hit him in the forehead. Wide, surprised eyes met his, and he stared back, knowing that he would look like the Reaper that nightmares were made of.

The guy was as naked except for a pair of tighty-whities and fluffy socks. It was a good look for Tom Cruise, but it did nothing for this man.

"Hands up, and back away slowly," Arek ordered and was prepared for the fucker to try and bolt. He was mildly disappointed when instead, the man did as he was asked to do. "Sit on the bed." The man backed up until his knees touched the bed and lowered himself to the noisy seat.

He made to put his hands down, and Arek shook his head no. "Keep them up."

Arek kept the gun trained on the unknown man but made his way over to a chair in the corner, the only piece of decent furniture in the room. He sat down and stared, taking in the features of the man and trying to decipher why he'd hate him and his brother.

"I know who you are now. You're the man that saved me from the guys at the arcade," the man tried, his face smoothly shifting into a mask of mock excitement, but it didn't reach his eyes.

"Save it. I saw your fan room." Arek let his eyes roam over the bare chest that was still wet with water. Scars and tattoos covered half the right side of his body and arm, but none of them stood out except one. One of the Navy, but it had been tattooed over with a fancy pirate like X.

"Who are you really? And can you spare me the bullshit answer?" Arek growled.

"Can I put my arms down, Arek?" The man sneered, drawing out his name like it tasted bad. The man lowered his hands before he said it was alright, giving him a wide grin as he proceeded to lean back on his hands. The stupid look disappeared, his eyes hardening into a glare like he didn't have a gun trained on him. "You know I'm happy this is all out in the open now."

"Who the fuck are you?" Arek took in the shaggy hair and dark beard and tried to place him on one of his missions and just couldn't.

"Oh, no, is the scary Sandman going to shoot me? Who will ever save me?" The man mocked, and Arek wanted to growl at his stupid face. "You really don't recognize me, do you? I guess you wouldn't have left me to die, trapped like a rat under rubble. What kind of person does that?"

Arek's arm slowly lowered. The voice was so familiar, and yet the face… "You're not Scooter. What kind of game are you playing at?"

The man laughed and smacked his hand on the bed. "You don't recognize your old friend?"

"Shut the fuck up. You're not Scooter." Imagines of that night he lost his friend flashed through his mind.

"I had to claw my way out of that rubble alone and desperate. I spent months searching for my friend that left me all alone to die."

"Knock it off," Arek growled, his hand shaking as more flashes lit up behind his eyes.

"I saved your life, and you left me to die—to never see my wife or my little girl again? What kind of a friend does that?"

Arek's reality shifted, and he was suddenly staring down into Scooter's face, staring into his eyes as he pulled the trigger. "Ah," Arek grabbed at his head as ringing erupted in his head, each image more painful than the next.

"'Don't leave me here,' I called out to you," the man said.

Arek knew the guy was moving, he was able to see him through the flashes of his past, but he was powerless to stop him, or to stop the images that plagued his mind. Overtaken with the split reality, he gasped and tried to push the memories away.

A shadow cast over him, the cool feel of metal being pressed to his forehead. "You always thought you were such a big shot, you and your brother. The infallible and perfect twins of death. What a load of shit." The metal bit into his skin as the gun was pressed harder. Another flash exploded like the building behind his eyes. He clenched his eyes shut trying to force his brain to behave, to fucking pull itself out of the muddy depths of hell. His body shook violently and then, as quick as they came, the images disappeared. Opening his eyes Arek stared up at the man that had so easily gotten the upper hand. He took a deep steadying breath, the cool metal, helping him refocus. "The Righteous is nothing. It's a figment of your imagination, nothing more than something for you to cling your pathetic existence to."

The man's face was contorted in rage as he stood over Arek, but his hand didn't shake.

"You're not Scooter," Arek said, his voice strained as he fought his rage to not make the move the man wanted him too. Swallowing he could hear Trev in his head, *stay calm soldier and regain the upper hand*. He flicked his eyes up to lock with the gaze of the man, trying to make him think he was insane.

The images of his friend's head leaking all over the floor was vivid in his mind. He didn't dream all of that—he didn't leave his friend to suffocate in his blood as he was slowly crushed to death. Scooter's soft blue eyes had stared at him with earnest and tears streaking down his cheeks as his tattooed left forearm with his daughter's name gripped his hand. Those two things alone told him that this man was a liar.

The man sneered, a sick laugh coming from his mouth.

"No, no. I'm not, but your mental scars are so fun and easy to pick at —one by one, the little scabs can be lifted to make you bleed all over again. Do you think I haven't noticed your twitches, your triggers? You were always so weak. That's why you needed your brother to take care of you."

"Shut up. You don't know what you're talking about." He tried to stand, but the gun was pressed harder into his forehead.

"I wouldn't do that, Arek. It's not a good idea. You were always running around half-cocked, and Trevor was always swooping in and saving you. Do you even know how much we all despised you? How much we all laughed at you behind your back?"

"If it's me you hate so much, why is it Trev that you have the shrine around?"

"Because Trev is my ultimate trophy. The one that caused me months in hell while I was tortured within an inch of my life. He was the one that left me behind. You, well, you are one of the best ways to get to your brother. I have to admit. I was fairly annoyed that Alejandro almost ruined my plans. I thought you would do what you'd always do when your brother gave you orders and would track down Alejandro yourself. I never considered Trevor to be the one to go in alone."

The man backed off enough that the gun no longer touched Arek's skin. His finger rubbed at the trigger of his gun, but he didn't think he could mask his movement enough to get a shot off. His mind raced as he continued to try and figure out who this man was.

"It was me you wanted to be tortured, not Trev."

"Very good. The whole twin thing does have its downside. I was hoping he'd kill you and display your body in one of his favorite horrific fashions. Piece by piece, take everything away from the golden boy until he had nothing left."

There was a maniacal tone to the guy's voice. A giddy vibration that Arek understood better than most. How many times had he made that same sound when he killed those he hunted? The one difference was the unstable factor. The way his eye flinched at the corner, and his jaw clenched in his cheek. It spoke volumes and told him all he needed not to know about his chances of survival. Whatever make-believe story this man had cooked up in his brain about himself and Trev, he believed it.

"And the arcade? Was that a fluke, or did you set that up as well?"

The man looked like the fucking Joker as he smiled and cocked his head to the side. There was something about the way he moved that clicked familiar in Arek's mind, a memory that was just out of reach.

"That was what you call God smiling down on me."

"Yeah, I'm pretty sure he wasn't smiling down on your fucking crazy ass." The knee caught him in the chin, slamming his jaw closed and his head back. "Fuck," he groaned as he fell back onto the chair. Arek rubbed at his jaw and glared up at the freak in front of him.

"Such a smartass, always with the jokes. You never knew when to fucking shut up. I think that's what I hated most about you besides your arrogance of course. Maybe I'll start with cutting out your tongue, send the infallible Crosshairs one rotting piece of his Sandman at a time. I'd pay money to see the look on his face as each box arrived. The knowledge that his precious twin was dead and each found memento a new level of torture." The man shuddered and smiled through the thick beard. "It was a mistake to leave me behind, a big fucking mistake."

"Wait a minute. Trev didn't order anyone to be left behind on any mission."

"Is that what you think? Your brother is not as perfect as he lets everyone believe. He left me for dead, and I have been planning my payback ever since." The guy twisted his neck, his neck cracking as he did so. "I should be thanking the two of you. It was because of you that I found my true calling. The Righteous has fallen, and you will be next. Now get on your knees, hands behind your head."

Arek didn't move until the man yelled, his hand shaking as he did. He was out of options, and for once, he couldn't calculate or muscle his way out of this.

"You don't have to do this. Whatever wrong you think was done, we can make it right. I have a kid on the way, man. Don't make my child grow up without a father."

"Your kid will be better off without you in their life." The guy's finger slowly pressed on the trigger, and Arek prepared for his only shot to make it out of this. Once he was on his knees, he was done. "I've been looking forward to this for so long I just want to savor the look on your face a little longer," The man snorted a giddy sort of sound. "Okay, I'm good now."

The man sighed like he'd taken a sip of a cool drink on a hot day, his eyes eerily relaxed. "Get on your fucking knees, Arek, at least die like a man."

Arek clenched the arms of the chair, his muscles twitching to dive off to the side. If he was going to die, he was going to die fighting, not on his knees.

Chapter 42

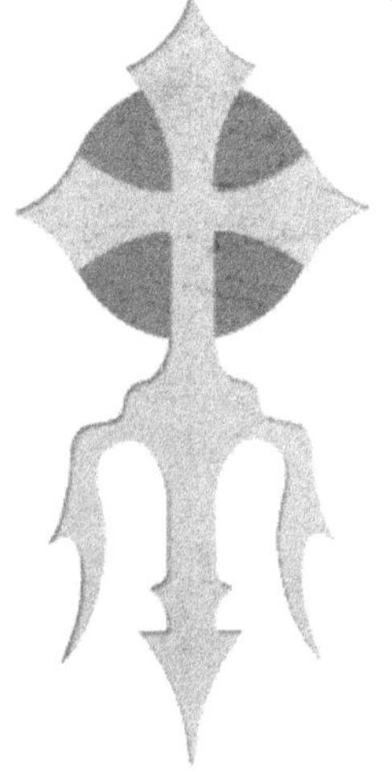

It took a few minutes, but Trev found Arek's signal in a house and broke the lock on the backdoor. The door handle made a soft click as the mechanics snapped inside the old door. As soon as he stuck his head inside, he could hear talking and paused in the dark kitchen to get his bearings. He looked up at the ceiling as the floor squeaked. Pulling his gun, he moved like a ghost through the space. With an agonizingly slow pace, he made his way up the stairs.

He was one with the dark as he moved. Trev paused in the shadows outside the bedroom door to take in the situation. He knew who this was, the look on Arek's face said he didn't have a clue, but then again, this man didn't cause the most amazing person in Arek's life to die. Those voices, those faces never left you—like apparitions, they were always there in the peripheral of your vision as they taunted you.

He hadn't paid attention to the interview, not the way he should've been, distractions were fatal, and his blasé cost Ray his life. It was a mistake he wouldn't make again.

He had believed this man was dead. He hadn't celebrated his demise, but he would've been lying if he said that he'd shed a tear. Never did he think he would be faced with this particular demon again.

"I've been looking forward to this for so long. I just want to savor the look on your face a little longer," Miller snorted a giddy sort of sound. "Okay, I'm good now."

Miller sighed like he'd taken a sip of a cool drink on a hot day, his eyes eerily relaxed.

"Get on your fucking knees, Arek, at least die like a man," Miller said. The thin thread between sanity and insanity was getting ready to break.

"Hello, Miller."

Arek and Miller looked his way, shock registering on both their faces a moment before Trev pulled the trigger. Miller yelled and stumbled back as the shot took him in the shoulder. The next one was a stomach wound, and Miller's gun clattered to the floor as he gripped at the wound.

"Trevor…I…you…."

"You really should've stayed dead, Miller," Trev said and finished the job, a hole forming where his eye had been a moment earlier. The man collapsed into a heap on the dirty wooden floor, his arm smacking the television knocking it to the floor with a crash. Trev's long coat brushed the floor softly, the swooshing the only loud sound in the otherwise quiet room.

He stared down at the man that had tortured Mel. Her kindness and fairness had no effect on him. Trev had seen the pleasure Miller got from emotionally beating her beautiful soul down. No, he would never feel guilty for this death. She was stolen from this world too soon, and her death was now paid for with Miller's blood.

He took a shuddering breath as he watched the pool of blood grow larger. There was no peace. This kill was just finishing what he'd already thought was done.

"How long have you been here?" Arek stood from the chair and stared down at the body, mimicking his position.

"Long enough."

"You were almost too late."

Trev glared at his brother. "And whose fault is that?"

Arek shrugged, not answering the question before looking down at Miller. "I didn't recognize him at all. He looks—so different." Arek lifted his head, and Trev could feel the stare like it was a touch.

"I didn't leave him behind the way he believes. I did think he was dead, though." He looked at his twin and shrugged. "We were arguing about Mel's death, about what he'd said to her just before...." Trev looked away from Arek's eyes. "Before that happened, when the building we were in took the first of the RPGs that claimed Scooter. I'd come running out to join the rest of you in the fight, and in all the confusion and rubble, I didn't see him. The room we'd been in was gone under a mountain of debris. The smoke and dust were thick with the crumbling building and fire. I assumed he'd either run off or suffered the same fate as Scooter. Never did I think that I'd left him there alive."

His eyes took in the lifeless body.

"No matter how much I hated him, I couldn't have done that. He was still a soldier under my command. I would've brought him home whether he deserved it or not."

Arek gripped his shoulder but didn't say anything for quite some time. "What do you think he meant about The Righteous," Arek finally asked, breaking the silence.

"I don't know, not yet anyway."

"Maybe we should've kept him alive long enough to find out," Arek commented as he wandered away to search the room.

"Really? Is that what you think is best? Torture a man who was so obviously damaged by whatever happened to him in the sandbox after leaving him there to fend for himself. Does your brand of justice seem fair for that?"

Arek pulled a small black book from the dresser drawer and thumbed through the pages before holding it up like a prize. "Fair, maybe not, but it would've been nice to know how he found us in the first place. Then again, if he was tortured for months, I don't know if even I could get him to talk, not without it getting really messy." He lifted a shoulder and let it drop before he stuffed the book in his back pocket.

"There are lines that even I wouldn't ask you to cross, Arek. Lines even you shouldn't be willing to, do you hear me?"

Arek bit his lip and stared at Miller's body, his face shifting to that of the man that could and would kill anything that breathed.

"He sent men to our house and shot at my pregnant fiancée, Trev. No amount of brotherhood can allow me to forget the look of fear in Renee's eyes as those men burst through the door. He's better off dead because what I would've done would've been far worse, lines be damned."

They stared at one another for a minute. The dark that you could almost see swirling around Arek drifted away, and he smiled wide. "You really need to see the shrine to us in the other room. If he hadn't been a creepy stalker set on killing us, I'd actually be rather flattered. At least we have the answer as to who was setting us up and got Ray killed."

Trev nodded but didn't voice that he was concerned this went deeper than one pissed-off and emotionally damaged soldier. Arek was already too deep mentally into this. He needed to throw him a lifeline, not push his head under deeper.

"Do you want me to get rid of the body, or do you want to grab the stuff in the other room and just go?"

"Show me the room, and dig out the bullets. We leave nothing behind. Then we will burn it all down."

Twenty minutes later, Trev stood alone. He stared up at the house as orange flames flickered in the windows. The fire hadn't fully engulfed the house yet, but it wouldn't be long now. Sirens wailed in the distance as fire trucks made their way to the scene.

Trev opened his palm. The metal of Miller's tags cool against his skin as the reflection of the flames danced in the metal.

Squeezing the tags tight, the metal bent in half the edge, digging into his palm. There was a sweet bite of pain as a single drop dripped to the ground.

Trev climbed in behind the wheel of the Hummer and closed the door to a part of his past he never wanted to think about again.

The Hummer revved to life. "Delilah, play Beethoven's, Fur Elise." The music filled the space as he passed the flashing lights of the emergency vehicles.

He had questions that needed to be answered, and he was determined to get them, one way or another.

Epilogue

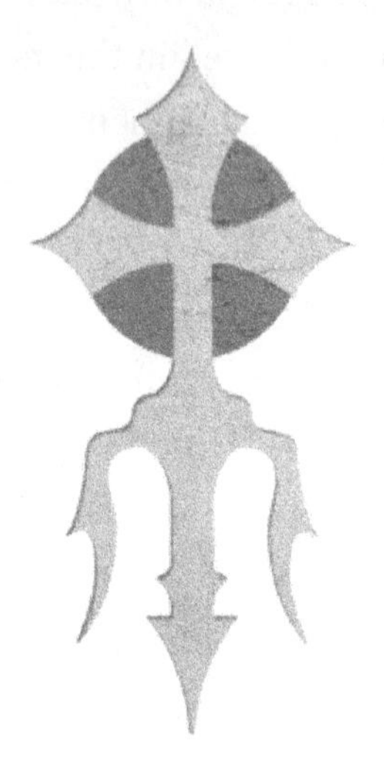

Trev slipped the Bentley into his reserved spot at the courthouse. It was a big day, today was the closing arguments in Maeve's murder trial, and things had not been looking good. He'd only lost one case since he'd become a lawyer, but he had a feeling that this was going to be his second. He saw the writing on the wall. The jury members lapped up the lies that the prosecution had spoon-fed them. He recognized the final nail in the coffin of his case being hammered in when the pregnant widow of the deceased detective got up on the stand.

As for the rest of the question marks in his life, Spike had mysteriously disappeared. The races became no more, and they were back to square one with the Golden Dragons and who was running them. Maybe Arek had been right, and he should've kept Miller alive long enough to get some answers, but no matter how many times he went over that night in his mind, he couldn't picture torturing him.

"You know what I'm going to get the moment I graduate law school,"

Cody asked, pulling Trev out of his thoughts. He glanced over at Cody, who looked amazing in the dark blue suit. He was smoothing out the front and double-checking that his tie was straight.

"Should I be afraid to ask?" He smiled as Cody gave him his patented don't be a jerk look. "What do you want to get?"

"A Lamborghini. I always wanted one, and besides, I better look the part if I'm going to be working alongside you."

Cody gave him a heated smirk over the roof of the car as they removed their briefcases. "I must admit *Anderson and Walters* does have a nice ring to it."

They walked side by side, their strides in time with one another, when a sound caught Trev's ears. He halted, and Cody took an extra stride before turning to stare at him.

"What is it?" Cody looked around for a sign of a threat.

The sharp and distinct call of a kestrel reached his ears, and he turned in the direction. A man shrouded in a tattered coat, the hood of a hoodie was up and hiding his face, but Trev knew who it was. He made his way toward the man, and as he did, the guy turned and wandered into the alley beside the courthouse.

"Where are you going? Do you know that guy," Cody asked, his voice low with concern.

"It's alright."

The guy was leaning up against the wall about halfway along the alley. His arms crossed over his chest. His position appeared more annoyed than relaxed.

He came to a halt a few feet away, and slowly the man looked up at him from under the grey hood. "Kestrel, you are a hard man to find."

"Ever think I didn't want to be found, Sir?"

"Call me Trev. I'm not your sir anymore." Kes had always been a difficult personality to gauge, but after their last mission and what happened, he'd retreated in on himself. He pulled away from everything and everyone. "Can I ask why you are dressed like you're homeless?"

Trev took in the boots coming apart at the seams and the gloves with the fingers cut out, not to mention the distinct scent of old moldy clothes surrounding Kes.

"Maybe because I am one," Kes said. His voice was laced with irritation. "You asked me to meet you, and here I am. What do you want, Sir?"

Trev bit his lip and decided to let it go. Kes was never going to change, and if the man wanted to live on the streets, that was his choice. "I need your help."

"You know I don't take special jobs, we've been through this, and the answer is and always will be no." Kes pushed off the wall and began walking away.

Trev called out at Kes's back. "It's for Morry." Kes froze, his back rigid as he slowly turned around.

"What about her?"

"One of Morry's girls, one of her good friends, is in trouble, and she needs our help. To pull this off, I'm going to need your help."

Kes nodded toward Cody. "Who's he?"

Trev looked up at Cody, his face that of the stone-cold killer of the Ice Man he could be. "My fiancé."

Kes's eyebrows shot up. "What?"

"Do you have a problem with me being in love with him?" Trev folded his hands in front of his crisp suit, his shoulders straightening as he waited for a response.

"No…I…" Kes cleared his throat. "I just didn't think I'd ever see you, you know…shit." Kes rubbed at his eyes and then tried again. "Sir, you and Mel were…fuck don't make me say it." He folded his arms over his chest, looking away from Trev's stare.

Trev nodded, acknowledging the awkward mention of Mel and what had happened. "We all need to grow and move on Kes, maybe one day you will too."

"Only the devil dances on my doorstep."

Trev sighed, he wasn't going to change Kes's mind, and it wasn't his place to help him if he didn't want help. His hand had already been smacked more than once for thinking that it was his responsibility to fix Kes.

"So, what do you say, Kes, are you in?"

"For Morry, I'm always in. What do you need me to do?"

BROOKLYN

If you like it dark and edgy then look no further. Brooklyn Cross has always had a deep passion for writing that stemmed from a wild imagination. When she is not busy typing away about the next character you will fall in love with, you can find her walking with her dogs on the farm and sipping a hot cup of coffee.

In addition to getting her degree in business she was highly competitive in the equestrian sport of dressage, with aspirations of an Olympic dream. She is an entrepreneur at heart and has coached and trained many of a riding enthusiast or their wonderful mounts, but always found herself drawn to writing full-time.

"Writing is what I love. I just want to be authentic with my characters. To tell a story that others can immerse themselves in and enjoy, but also relate too. If I can make you smile, laugh, cry, or your heart pound then I have done my job. To drop people into my worlds and for a short time have you live alongside my characters, is what I have always wanted."

CROSS

Thank You

for reading Sleeping with the Dark
If you enjoyed this book please consider leaving a review. Reviews are the best way to show your love and are always appreciated.
If you would like to be among the first to know about new releases in The Righteous Series then join my Facebook Group Crossfire - A Brooklyn Cross Reader Group
Look for more books in The Righteous Series

STALK ME LINKS

Brooklyn Cross (Author of Dark Side of the Cloth) | Goodreads

(20+) Brooklyn Cross | Facebook

(20+) Crossfire - A Brooklyn Cross Reader Group | Facebook

Brooklyn Cross (@author_brooklyncross) • Instagram photos and videos

Find 'authorbrooklyncross' on TikTok | TikTok Search

HIDING IN THE DARK

CHAPTER 1

Ashley stared at the circular glowing buttons of the elevator as she made her slow descent to the ground floor of the medical building. Her heart beating faster with each passing second.

"Ashley, you must understand that you will only ever get worse. We can do our best to keep the symptoms from progressing any further, but there is no cure."

"So, what you're saying is that there is a chance I won't get any worse?"

Thump, thump, thump. She placed her hand over her heart and felt her heart pound.

"It is a very slim possibility, but theoretically, it is possible with the right medication and if you follow the steps I've laid out for you...."

The continuous loop of words running through her head like a broken record was adding to the pressure building behind her eyes. She rubbed her eyelids in hopes of relieving the sensation.

The elevator dinged at the wrong floor, and too many people made their way through the silver doors. She was tempted to get out and run the rest of the way down the staircase but squished herself into the corner. The man in front of her stepped on her foot, and she jerked her foot out from under his, but he still didn't apologize.

Rude.

Didn't he know she'd just received life-altering news? Did any of these people give a shit about what she was going through? No, of course not. The woman across the way was too busy on the phone discussing what she was going to cook for dinner while the guy in the middle was annoyingly humming some stupid song.

Her heart fluttered with the wild burst of emotion that shifted between annoyance and desperation. She sucked in a deep breath and gripped the silver railing to hold the semblance of her emotional state together.

As soon as the doors opened, she pushed her way out through the throng of people ignoring the angry yells and speed-walked toward the exit. Bursting outside, she lifted her hand to block the bright glare of the setting sun. She had to get out of here. Her breathing was fast and shallow, her head light with what she knew were symptoms of shock. She had no intention of passing out here on the sidewalk.

Waving her hand like a wild woman, she flagged down a passing taxi and yanked open the door, slamming it behind her.

"Where to?" the driver asked.

Ashley just stared at him in the rear-view mirror, unsure what to say. She didn't want to go back to her apartment and sit there alone.

"Lady, I'm sorry, but you need to pick a location, or I have to take the next customer."

"Salvation Place, take me there, please." The driver gave her a once over, and normally she would feel compelled to explain that she wasn't going there for a free meal or a place to stay, but she didn't have the energy. People seemed to want to believe the worst in others. Just because she was going to a shelter meant she was scamming the system.

It was windy this evening. The palm trees' leaves billowed out like bright green flags as the tops of the trees swayed. The sun's reflection rippled like bright orange and pink waves off of the glass buildings. Ashley dug around in the small green backpack she carried and pulled out her phone. The problem was she didn't know who to call.

She stared at the dark screen, her own image staring back at her on the shiny surface. Her mother and father would mean well, but she could already hear that conversation, and it was not one she wanted to have right now. Her parents were hippies to their core. They would say it would be all about positive thinking and for her to keep her chin up. That she should've started meditation sooner and that she needed to move back home so they could help take care of her.

She didn't need to be taken care of, she didn't need to be more positive, and she sure as heck didn't need to have her feelings dusted aside with a simple, keep your chin up when she was entitled to her feelings. Giving up on the idea of calling someone, she put the phone back in the bag and pulled out her wallet as they neared her destination.

"Thanks," she said as the car came to a halt, and she handed over more money than she needed to give him. She just wanted to get out of the car, keep moving and not think too much right now. Thinking led to feeling, and feeling was going to lead to a breakdown.

"Hey lady, this is way too much!"

She slammed the door ignoring the driver, and jogged toward the big old church that had been converted a few years earlier.

"Hey Charlie," she called out, waving to the elderly man that had worked here as a caretaker longer than it had been a shelter.

"You're early." Charlie leaned against the mop he was using to clean the floor. His weather face with the distinct smile lines around his eyes crinkled as he gave her a scrutinizing look.

"Yeah, I got off work early. Is Dennis in yet?" She continued toward the door to the back, not wanting to get into a heart-to-heart. Right about now, she wished she would have learned not to wear her heart on her sleeve. It was like a neon sign for other people to ask her what was wrong.

"He's in his office. Ashley?" She paused, hand on the wooden door, and plastered a smile on her face as she looked over her shoulder at Charlie. "Are you okay, girl? I don't mean to pry, but you seem off."

She waved her hand in the air and made a goofy face, sure that Charlie saw right through her ploy. "Oh yeah, I'm fine. Just work stuff, family stuff, you know how it is."

"Mmhmm." Charlie lifted a brow at her but started whistling as he continued to mop the floor.

Sighing, she pushed through the door and nodded to the few people that were already here for the night, or maybe they hadn't left. Beds were hard to come by at the shelter. Some who stayed here regularly rarely left the small space and bed given to them to use for sleep.

The open space looked like it was being set up for an office building because Dennis, who managed this place, wanted to give people some privacy. He had found old cubicle partitions that were being tossed away by a large corporation. The cubical setup didn't allow for as many beds, but she had to admit that she'd want a small space to call her own if she were living here.

Ashley passed the dining hall and waved to those that were already setting up the long table for serving food, but she continued down the hall to the lone office in the back. Dennis's door was closed, and she paused, going over the lie she planned on telling for as long as she could get away with it.

Stupid or not, Ashley couldn't face her new reality and couldn't even think the words in her head yet, let alone say them aloud. Pulling the happy, carefree mask in place, she knocked on the office door.

"It's open," Dennis called back.

She opened the door to find him pacing the room on the phone—he held up a finger. "What do you want me to do? We are a not-for-profit organization. We rely on donations to keep our doors open to those that need it most. What? That's completely unreasonable. How are we supposed to raise that much money that fast?"

There was a long pause as Dennis listened to whoever was on the other end, his face growing redder by the second. Ashley worried he was going to have a stroke.

"Oh yeah? Happy fucking Thanksgiving to you too." He went to slam his phone down and then realized it was a cell and hit the end button like that would have the same effect.

"The building owner again," she asked, closing the door behind her.

"That man doesn't have a heart. He has millions. This place is nothing more than a tax write-off for him, but now he wants to sell it to a developer unless we can come up with the back rent that's due by the end of next month." Dennis flopped down into the rollie desk chair that complained about the added weight.

"That would mean he's going to kick us out before the new year. Merry fucking Christmas." Dennis sighed. Tossing the phone on the desk and stared up at her. "It is a problem for another day and not one you should have to worry about, but if you have some magic fairy dust, I will sell my soul for some right about now."

"Sorry, no magic fairy dust, but I was coming to say that I can volunteer whole days for the next couple weeks."

"What about your work?"

Ashley swallowed hard and stuck with her lie as much as she hated to lie to Dennis. "I have some vacation time coming to me, and this is how I would like to use it."

"You do know most people actually take time off from work, right? Go somewhere tropical or kick their feet up and read a book. How about you spend time with your friends or go visit your family?"

She crossed her arms over her chest. "Do you not want me here volunteering, Dennis?"

"No, it's just—" He waved his hands like he was swatting away a fly and closed his eyes. "You know we can always use the extra help. If this is the place you want to spend your vacation, who am I to tell you otherwise."

The weight that was pressing on her lifted as he agreed to let her come here. Sitting alone in her apartment with her thoughts for the next couple of weeks was not going to be healthy for her sanity.

"Thanks Dennis, I will head out and help with dinner prep. Other than fairy dust, if you need anything else, let me know." Ashley turned and opened the door but paused as Dennis called her name, and she looked over her shoulder at Dennis.

"Thank you, I do appreciate the extra set of hands, and you know you are welcome here."

A small genuine smile lifted the corners of her mouth as she nodded and saw herself out. One battle was done, the rest of her life—well, that would have to wait for now.

CPSIA information can be obtained
at www.ICGtesting.com
Printed in the USA
BVHW081118100323
660172BV00007B/223